Chinook

Chinook

Roc Roth

VANTAGE PRESS
New York

This is a work of fiction. Any similarity between the
names and characters in this book and any real persons,
living or dead, is purely coincidental.

Cover design by Susan Thomas

FIRST EDITION

Copyright © 2007 by Roc Roth

Published by Vantage Press, Inc.
419 Park Ave. South, New York, NY 10016

Manufactured in the United States of America
ISBN: 978-0-533-15625-2

Library of Congress Catalog Card No.: 2006908312

0 9 8 7 6 5 4 3 2 1

To all the people I have known in my life
and to Thomas Hardy,
English novelist and poet (born 1840, died 1926)

Chinook

Book One

1

Chinook:

I am the Spirit of the great western wind; they call me CHINOOK. I
start out in the Pacific Ocean on the Japanese Current. Egged on by the
lows off the coast I blow toward the land picking up moisture and
warmth as I rush eastward. Soon I sweep on to the shore, causing the
waves to pound the coasts of Northern California, Oregon and Washington. I plunge over the coastal mountains bringing warmth and rain
to the valleys. My fingers then find the opening in the Cascade Mountains carved out by the powerful western river, the Columbia. Through
this gorge I blow filling the deserts with warmth, melting feet of snow
in hours. On over the vast Inland Empire where men grow apples and
wheat. Over the Blue and Wallowa mountain ranges, and into Idaho.
Feeling my way I follow the Snake River into potato country. Piling up
against the Rocky Mountains I push around the Teton Range and into
Wyoming, blowing over the oilmen, the cowboys and their cattle herds.
Before my warmth, temperatures rise thirty, forty degrees in hours,
causing men to change. Some men go crazy, and beat their wives. Some
men go to the bars, to hide themselves. Some men saddle their horses
and ride into the wilderness to lose themselves, and some men grab
their rifles and head for the mountains.

The man of the West considers himself superior to the men of the
East. The Eastern man needs his Unions, his clubs, his society, to
shield him from the world; from his bosses, and their companies. He
thinks these seek to exploit his industry, and strip him of his dignity.
When he looks out the window of his home he sees crowded streets, ten-
ements and the dirt of industrial society. When the men of the West
look out their windows they see deserts that stretch to snow capped
mountains. From the mountains, streams flow into lakes filled with
trout, to rivers filled with salmon, then to the Pacific. They look out on
hills covered with pine, firs, cedars and spruce, valleys filled with orchards, vegetables and grains. Western man doesn't need society to
shield him from exploitation. What he needs is his rifle, fishing pole

3

and his knife; these will feed and protect his family from whatever hungers or dangers life serves up.

I, Chinook the Spirit will lead you through our story, and show you through the eyes of the people herein how the West has changed.

Chinook:
The Douglas House, enlisted men's club and hotel, Lancaster Gate, London, England, December 23, 1962.

Airman 1st class Jimmy Dale Burns, U.S. Air Force, stood on the columned front porch of the Douglas House and looked at the pea souper fog that hung over London like a thick wet sheet. He couldn't see across the courtyard, let alone to the Bayswater Road just beyond the wrought iron fence that enclosed the circular drive to the club. It was almost eleven o'clock at night, and he knew the last tube from Lancaster Gate station had left at 10:30. He needed to get to the Piccadilly Line to go to the base at South Ruislip, where he was stationed. He remembered he once caught a train at Hyde Park Corner station; it was at midnight, he thought. That meant crossing Hyde Park at night during a thick fog, but he actually liked the fogs—they seem mysterious, like an old Sherlock Holmes movie. He got across Bayswater Road at the zebra crossing, and entered the park at the Victoria Gate. Once in the park the fog settled around him like a shroud; it was dark. To catch his breath, he wrapped his scarf around his face. Well, just like a real Londoner, they all did that during the real pea soupers. He took the Ring path to the Serpentine path, which would take him to the station. The lampposts on the paths gave out a faint muted light, but he could follow them. The fog was so thick he could hear people walking toward him but not see them until they brushed past. Twice he ran into someone who with a mumbled "pardon," hurried on. He didn't see her standing beside the lamppost, she was wrapped up in a big old black woolen coat.

"Hello, Laddie," she said in a soft Scottish burr, right into his ear.

He almost jumped out of his skin, spun his head around and looked into her eyes. Her eyes were all he could see of her in the dim light.

"Wood'e like to spend a warm night out'o this chill?"

He was stunned. "I, I, I," was all he could say.

Trying to get his heart to stop pounding and his brain in gear, he blurted, "Only have five pounds."

4

"Well tis a bit less than I get normally you know, but as it is latish and a bitter night, t'will do. Wood'e like to follow to me flat?"

Chinook:

This was a big decision for Jimmy. He was a virgin. Oh, he and his old girlfriend in high school had gotten naked a few times, but it was just for play, there was no consummation. It's not that they didn't want to, it was just that they were scared of pregnancy. They had seen friends do it and at seventeen or eighteen, had to get married, their plans for their young lives ruined. Becky and he had planned to get married after he got out of basic training, and tech school, and got his first stripe.

After about two months he got the letter most lonely G.I.s dread.

"Dear Jim," it said, not the normal "Darling Jimmy." "I am afraid I have fallen in love with Ralph Skinner and we must break up. I had hoped to wait until you came home to tell you, but we are to be married before the date you return. I know that soon you will meet a nice girl who will make you happy. Your Friend Becky."

For one week Jimmy was sick at heart, but usually these things pass quickly.

When he received his assignment to England they told him the English girls were fast and easy. Well he found the English girls about the same as the American girls; you could only go so far, then the door slammed closed. He had one bit of revenge though. After he had been in Europe for a couple of months, a letter arrived from Miss Becky Anderson. MISS?

He had seen Becky only once, when he was home on leave, before being shipped overseas. He was driving through town and she was walking down the street. He had wanted to stop and talk to her, but because of the hurt and embarrassment drove on past. All their old friends had said that though they weren't married, the wedding was set, and they were hot and heavy. Still when he saw her his heart gave a big thump; he still wasn't over her.

He went back to his room after mail call and opened the letter.

"Jimmy Darling, I know I haven't the right to get in touch with you, but I'm in a fix. I'm pregnant and when Ralph heard he left the state. I have tried to get in touch with him, but his mother won't tell me where he is. Someone said he went to Seattle to get a job at Boeing, where his brother works. I still love you and if you could find it in your heart to marry me, I would be the most grateful and best wife any man

5

ever had. PLEASE, PLEASE, let me know as soon as you can. I think about you all the time now, and know I was a fool to let you go, because I would be your wife now. I'm waiting for your reply darling. Your Becky."

Jimmy couldn't repress a smirk. He had always hated Ralph Skinner's guts, and when Becky said she loved him, it had been even harder to take her leaving him.

His reply: "Dear Becky. I am sorry to hear about you and Ralph. I am afraid that I am in love with an English girl now, her name is Mavis, she is very beautiful and sweet, I could never leave her. You were right when you said in your letter that I would find a nice girl to love. I am sure Ralph will be back soon and your problems will end. Your Friend Jimmy."

{Of course Mavis was a complete lie. He did have a date with a girl named Mavis once, but she drank up all his money and left with the bartender.}

Jimmy looked into her eyes. This could be the chance he'd been waiting for since he had been in England. Finally when the other guys talked about their conquests, he could brag about his conquest too without lying.

"Yes," he heard himself say, "but I will have to stay the night because all the trains stop running at midnight."

"Och weel, that weel be fine, dearie, come w'me."

They walked up Park Lane, over Bayswater Road, then up the Edgware Road, turning right into a warren of streets with older buildings. Finally she walked up some steps in a worn looking red brick building, opening the door with her key. Up another flight of stairs to the second floor and opened the door to her room. From the cold of the hall the room felt warm, stuffy and smelled of urine. He could see a small coal fire burning in the fireplace. She turned on a small lamp and removed her coat and scarf, and her hair fell down. Jimmy could see, even in the dim light, it was the most startling shade of red orange.

She came to him. "Take off your coat, Laddie," she said. He complied. She smiled at him. "Would you like to take off me frock, or shall I?"

"I guess I could do it," he said. His hands shook as he tried to unbutton the front of her dress. She helped him, and when he had finished, she pulled the top of the dress off her shoulders and quickly reached up behind her back and unhooked her bra. She let Jimmy pull off her bra; she let her dress fall to the floor, and because she had no panties on stood before him naked. How different she was than Becky, who had small pointed breasts with dark nipples, and was petite. The top of Becky's head only came to his chin, and she had dark hair. These tits were big and hung down with large red nipples; she was a woman of considerable heft, as tall as him. She had very white skin, and her body hair was red like her head.

"Come on, Laddie, let's get your clothes off." She sat him down on the bed, took off his shoes, and helped him undress. It was a good thing she did, as Jimmy was in no condition to do it himself. She lay down on the bed, and pulled Jimmy onto her.

Chinook:

Ah Jimmy you have, at the age of twenty-two, become a man. This was the reason you are on this earth, to procreate. Man was told by god to go forth and multiply, to cover the earth with his kind. He has been doing that to the best of his ability since the time he, with his mate, left the Garden of Eden.

It was over very quickly. Jimmy lay on her with his eyes closed, panting like he had just ran a mile. Slowly he opened them and looked down at her.

"Och weel, that was a bit quick, Laddie. Still I suppose you'll be wantin' more in a wee bitty. Off with you, Laddie," she said.

Jimmy didn't want to get off, he wanted to lie there feeling her body under him. She gave him a small shove. "Come on, here is a dressing gown. Doon the hall on your left is the loo. Be quiet now, don't be disturbin' the neighbors. I'm not wanted here as it is."

The dressing gown was of high quality, and was for a man much bigger than him. The cold of the hall felt good after the stuffy room. He washed himself and got a chill, burr, damn it was cold in that bathroom. When he was returning to the room, he thought he heard a baby cry. Sure enough, when he opened the door there was the woman bending over a squirming infant changing its diaper, and singing a small tune.

She looked up at him as he entered. "Dirty nappy, needed changing, and it time my wee bonnie bairn had a bit o'grub." She lay down on the bed with the baby beside her. She waved him over, and they lay with the baby between them. With her fingers she pulled her nipple tight and placed it in the crying baby's mouth; it started sucking instantly. She gave a little gasp, and settled down, the sucking sounding very like a little pump.

7

"Weel, Laddie, I know you're an American," she said. "Tell me a wee bit about yourself."

"Yes, my name is Jimmy Burns and I'm from a small farming town, er, village named Low Sky in the state of Oregon."

"Oh," she said, "I've heard of this Oregon, I think, in school and in the pictures, cowboys and wagon trains being attacked by Red Indians on the Oregon Trail." She gave him a big smile.

"Yes, that's the one ," he said.

"Tell me about this Oregon."

"Well, it is a western state just north of California. It is on the Pacific Ocean. It has tall snow capped mountains with lots of big trees and in the valleys, farms."

"Och weel sounds a wee bit like me Scotland. I would like to see your Oregon someday."

There was an audible "POP" and her nipple came out of the baby's mouth. It started to cry instantly. With a deft movement she reinserted it and the baby started to suck contentedly again.

"Does it hurt?" he asked.

"Ay, when I first started, it hurt something awful, but now it's fine, fine. Makes me feel all mutherly, you know."

They lay there with the baby between them and didn't talk. He ran his hand gently over her naked body from her shoulder to her hip and wondered how she came to be here.

Chinook:

Kathleen Mary Ross was born in the village of Lockmaddy, on the island of North Uist in Scotland's Western Isles. Her mother was a blue-eyed blonde from Larne, Ireland. Her father was a deck hand on the ferrys that ran between Larne and Stranraer, in Scotland when they met. After they were married, he was hired by P&O lines, and moved to Lockmaddy, where in a year he was made Master of the Deck. When Kathleen was fifteen, he was promoted to Captain and they moved to Stornoway, Isle of Harris.

At the age of eighteen Kathleen fell in love with a man ten years her senior, named John Mackenzie. John was a fisherman with his own boat, and considered a man of substance. Kathleen was a big girl, at 5'11", not beautiful, but with startling red hair, fair skin and blue eyes; she would catch your eye. She was flattered that a man of John Mackenzie's stature would love her; all her friends were jealous. When she found that she was pregnant she was very frightened, especially of her father who was a hard man and raised his only daughter very strictly. John said not to worry, he loved her, and they would marry. They set the date, but one week before the day John went out fishing and never returned. They found his wrecked boat the next day, but he was lost. The night she heard he was dead she was so frightened that she prayed that god would take the baby away. Her prayer was answered and the next morning her mother found her in a pool of blood in her bed. The doctor told her mother she had a miscarriage. Seeing her daughter so confused and scared, her mother took pity, and with the doctor made a pact that this problem would never leave the room. Thus her father never found out about the baby, but Kathleen could never get over the guilt of that late night prayer.

Over her father's wishes she left for London at the age of twenty-one. She enrolled at the London Secretarial School, and after graduation was hired at the Belgium Embassy as a clerk/typist. There after two years she met a tall black man from the Republic of Congo. Leopold Nyangwe was the grandson of a great Chief of the Kikongo tribe, and the son of an important civil servant in the provincial government of the Belgium Congo. Because of that, he was educated in a Catholic mission school in Leopoldville. He was an extraordinarily good scholar. He was sent to Louvain University in Belgium, and then finally to Cambridge University in England. He was a man of the world; he spoke Kikongo, Tshiluba and Lingala, the three main dialects of the Congo, Latin, French, and the clipped parlance of the English upper classes. He was forty-five, she was twenty-three. He was a leader of his country, and was a confidant of President Kasavubu. He knew the King Baudouin of Belgium, and Dag Hammarskjold, the Secretary-General of the United Nations before his fatal air crash.

He was suave, sophisticated and had a wife and eight daughters in Brazzaville. He asked her out to dinner; she accepted. By the end of dinner she was totally helplessly in love. John, her father and all the other men she had known, seemed crude and ignorant beside this man. When he undressed her later that night he admired her; he had never seen a woman the color of her before. She had her first orgasm that night, and was his mistress from that moment on.

He divided his time between London and The Congo. This went on for two years. In the autumn of 1961 he returned home for a year not knowing Kathleen was pregnant. This time she wasn't frightened; she wanted to have this baby, hoping it would purge that prayer that she uttered that horrible night in Stornoway. Finally the guilt would be appeased.

She had worked until the seventh month of her pregnancy; because she was a big girl she hid the changes in her body better than a smaller woman could. Finally it could not be explained any longer as a mere weight gain. She was called into the office by her supervisor: "Sorry, we can't employ you any more, no proper facilities in the office for a woman in this condition etc, etc." She had savings, moved to a cheaper room, registered for the dole and was doing fine until the baby was born in July. Her money went fast then, and the allotment she received from the dole didn't quite cover all her expenses. The butcher who owned the shop in the next street asked her about her large bill and when she would pay. She begged him for time, and told him her problem. They worked out a payment; he would come see her after closing on half-day Thursday, and the bill would be paid in sex. He was a jolly chap with a wife and two children, but this would scratch an itch he had had for some time. After the butcher it was easy to make extra money. He suggested he send around some of his mates, they were for the most part respectable married men, they were grateful, and paid her well.

Kathleen became a prostitute. She was making enough off these lads to live well, but with Christmas coming they stopped, except for the butcher. She thought it was guilt because of the holiday season, and would pick up where they left off after the New Year. On a Friday night the second week of December, there was a knock on her door. She opened it and there stood Leopold; he was just back from Africa that morning. She was in her old dressing gown, and had not bathed for two days, but he took her in his arms and they made love. All the time they had spent apart slipped away and she was in love again. He was stunned to find he had a son, the only son he ever fathered. He held him, and looked at him and couldn't get enough of him. He stayed until Monday, saying he would return the next weekend, but she never saw him again. The night she met Jimmy was the first night she had ever walked the streets. She wasn't as confident as she seemed but she needed money for food.

After the baby was fed, she put on her old nightgown and went to the loo. In ten minutes she was back shivering from the cold. "Tis a bitter cold night."

She jumped into bed with Jimmy and snuggled in his arms. "Tell me, Laddie, are you in the American forces?"

"Yes," he replied, "the U.S. Airforce."

"Och weel, me muther warned me all me life about sailors, but nerr' once did she say anthin' about airmen, so I guess you are alright then."

She thought that was funny and giggled. He tickled her, kissed her, and this time she didn't have to help him when he made love to her. After they were finished they curled up in each other's arms and fell asleep.

Consciousness came slowly to Jimmy. His head pounded with pain and his mouth tasted like a dirty old shoe. It was daylight and the curtains were drawn back from the window. A muted white light strained by the fog filled the room. Kathleen was bent over her baby wrapping him in a blanket. He whimpered like a small puppy.

She heard Jimmy groan. "Well, Laddie, looks like you are still with the liven', I was beginnin' to wonder.

"Me bairn is feeling poor'ly. I'm wondering could you go to the shops for me and get food?"

"Ok," he said.

Jimmy dressed, went to the bathroom and took the shopping list she had made for him. She gave him directions, "out the door, left then left again and you'll be at the shops." She looked at him, a frown on her brow. "I cannot take me sick bairn out in this fog, Laddie, I'm dependen' on you now!"

When Jimmy went out the door of the building the fog was worse, if that was possible, than the night before. The buildings across the street were barely visible—just dark hulks in the fog. He could smell the coal smoke and diesel fumes that were trapped in this heavy blanket that was covering the city. Old London Town was in for it, this one would last two weeks and be a killer.

Left and left again and there were the shops. Every shop specialized; he got bacon at the butcher, bread at the bakery, milk, butter and eggs at the dairy, and tomatoes at the green grocer. The baskets she had given him were soon full and back to the room he went. When he walked into the room Kathleen's face lit up in a smile.

"Thank you, Laddie, I was pra'in you'd come back."

Chinook:

The thought of not coming back never crossed Jimmy's mind. He wasn't that kind of man, he was brought up to do the right thing, and he had a kind heart. Also Jimmy was in love, in love with a prostitute that was true, but still in love. A different kind of love than he ever had for Becky; a consummated love that all men have for that first woman that makes them a man. There would always be a place in his heart for

11

Kathleen, and he would never forget the woman who gave him her body. So many women take men's money or love, and give them nothing in return but hurt, or humiliation.

Kathleen took the shopping and in a few minutes the room was filled with the smells of cooking. Jimmy was famished; he wolfed down the bacon and eggs, fried bread and tomatoes she made. Jimmy had lied to Kathleen in the park the night before. He had had eleven pounds in his pocket, and when he was leaving that morning he gave her six pounds, just leaving himself enough to get a tube and bus ticket back to Base.

She took the money. "You needn't give me this, Laddie. You bought the food and that was all I needed."

He pressed the money into her hand and said, "Can I come back again? It won't be for two weeks as I am on duty through the holidays."

"O' course, Laddie, you can come when it suits you." She gave him a kiss on the cheek and pressed her ample breasts into his chest.

Jimmy liked that. He held her closely; she looked at him. "Let's wait for that until next time, Laddie." She smiled at him. "I am afraid I am cum'en down with the same as me bairn." Her skin did feel hot on his arms, so he put on his coat and went out into the fog. He memorized the street names back to the Edgware Road so as to find his way back in two weeks time. One street name would stay with him forever, "Crawford Street."

2

Jimmy caught the Piccadilly Line train at Hyde Park Corner station and in twenty minutes was at Eastcoat station where he caught a bus to South Ruislip base. He noted how much whiter the fog was out in the suburbs. The pollution levels were much lower out here than in the city.

The Christmas week went fast.

He called home on New Years Eve at midnight; the time was eight hours difference from England to the West Coast so at four P.M. the phone rang in the farmhouse. His mom and dad were so glad to hear from him. They hadn't seen him for three years and could hardly wait until February when he would be home. Home for good he told them, because they were letting him out early, rather than assign him a stateside base for the five months he had left on his enlistment.

He thought about Kathleen all the time. Now that he was no longer a virgin his need was greater than it had been before. Now he knew what he was missing.

He shared a room on base with another Airman, Steve Moore. Steve was from Cutbank, Montana, "where men were men and the sheep were nervous." Anyway, that was the way Steve always explained it when anyone would ask. Their room had two bunk beds {Jimmy's on top}, two lockers and one sink. It had a window that looked out over a small garden/court yard. This had been his home for three years since he had been in England.

If he could only hold her, just for a few minutes, life would be sweet. He lay in bed every night and tried to feel her, he wanted her so badly. On the day after New Year's, he felt like he was coming down with a case of the flu. That night he took three aspirins and went to bed early.

Steve liked to hang out in the local pub every night, playing darts and drinking beer. He had developed a taste for the heavy, dark, warm, English beverage. He got in late that night and overslept the next morning. He woke up just before eight A.M., looked at the clock, hauled on his fatigues, shook Jimmy. "Come on, buddy, it's late," and ran to his duty station.

At nine-thirty Sergeant Hopkins said to him, "You bunk with airman Burns. You know where he is?"

Steve said, "He was in bed this morning, I shook him before coming to work."

"Well he ain't here. Go get him up. If you get him back here before ten I won't report him AWOL."

Steve ran to the room. Damn, he had left his keys in his locker. He banged on the door. "Jimmy, get up, man, you are in a pile of shit." He heard a moan from the room, but that was all. After a few minutes he ran back to the Sergeant.

"Sarge, I can't wake him up, but I can hear him in there."

"Fuck, you assholes are going to lose me a stripe. Airman Cano, go report Airman Burns to sick bay. Come on, Moore, let's roust him out."

"Thanks, Sarge, I'm kind of worried about him."

They went to the room. "You got your keys, Moore?"

"No, Sarge, I left the damn things in my locker this morning."

"Shit, Burns, this is Sergeant Hopkins, get your ass up." No answer. "Beat on the damn door, Moore." Just a low moan.

"Well, let's go down to the Air Police shack. Maybe they got a master key to these fuckin' rooms."

"Sorry guys," said the A.P. Sergeant on duty. "I'll tell you though we can get in by breaking a window, if you have a window?"

"Sure, Sarge, we got one," said Moore.

"I tell you, Moore, if Burns is drunk and not sick I'll bust him back to fuckin' Basic. He better be sick," said Hopkins.

The A.P. Sergeant broke the window with his nightstick and Sergeant Hopkins climbed in. He went to the bed and grabbed the blankets pulling them back.

"Holy fuckin' hell. Moore, call an ambulance, this guy is sick."

Jimmy was bathed in sweat, his skin was red and hot and he'd had lost control of his bladder and bowels. The smell made Sergeant Hopkins jerk his head back and wince.

Jimmy had felt the shake Steve had given him in the morning. He had heard the pounding on the door and the calling of his name, but it was all caught up in his dream.

He was with Kathleen in a place, maybe in her room, because he could smell the coal and the urine. She was with him; they were surrounded with a gray fog. He could touch her, feel her, taste her.

He heard the door slam on the ambulance, the siren rang in his

14

head, but she held his hand to comfort him and told him it would be all right.

*   *   *

Doctor John Heuwit, Major U.S. Air Force, sat in the little office off the room, where Jimmy was in quarantine. Jimmy had been in a coma for five days but his vital signs were picking up. John thought he would wake up anytime now.

John had been on duty the day they brought Jimmy in. The symptoms displayed by the patient were very extraordinary; swollen face, hot skin, no control over body functions, and finally, enlarged testicles. Even in a coma he moaned when they were touched. John knew he had a new problem here.

He had the nurse call Doctor Red Smith, Colonel and commander of the South Ruislip hospital. "Sir, sorry to bother you at home but I got a problem here I need help with." After Colonel Red, as all his troops called him behind his back, finished his examination, he ordered Jimmy put in quarantine, and called USAFE head quarters in Brussels. He ordered Sergeant Hopkins, Airman Moore, the A.P. Sergeant and everyone in the ambulance into quarantine also. He isolated Jimmy to the room he was in now; Major Heuwit volunteered to be isolated with him.

The word came back from USAFE to keep a steady I.V. drip of penicillin going into Jimmy's veins.

The next day Colonel Smith got a call from a Doctor Linus Williams, chief of staff of The Royal Tropical Diseases Hospital in London. In a very clipped English accent he said, "Doctor Smith, I am Doctor Williams of HM government, a specialist in tropical infections. I would very much like to examine the young chap that you have there, I have spoken to your Embassy and to General Jones and I must stress this is of some urgency."

"Of course, Doctor, everyone whom has ever worked in infectious diseases has heard your name. I would be honored to work with you."

Exactly one hour later a large black Rolls Royce pulled up to the main gate of the base. The Air Police Airman at the gate, having been warned of this august arrival, snapped to attention and waved the car with its distinguished guests on to the base.

An Air Police jeep, with an officer in it, guided the car to the front door of the base hospital where Colonel Smith and his staff awaited.

Doctor Williams introduced himself and his assistant Doctor Luewellan. They both along with Doctor Smith, examined Jimmy.

"Tell me, Doctor Heuwit," Doctor Williams said to John, "when the young chap arrived had he lost the control of his bladder and bowels?"

"Yes," said John, "also his testicles were very swollen."

"Ah, what a lucky young man we have here. Generally by that stage of the infection death is close on. Come, gentlemen, to this office and I will give you an update of what we know at this point."

When they were all seated in the small office Doctor Williams continued. "In the Republic of Congo there is an region called The Kasai which is named after the river that drains that area. About one year ago a rather good deposit of lead was discovered there and the government along with a French company opened a mine.

"This was in virgin jungle, you understand, never saw any development until this time. About two months ago the first signs of the infection this young chap here has, reared its ugly head. Within a few weeks, many of the native workers had come down with it. The incubation period of the infection seems to be from one to two weeks. Death usually occurred the second or third day of the onset of the symptoms.

"Well, it seems that one Leopold Nyangwe, who is the charge d'affaire at the Belgium embassy, representing the Republic of Congo, visited there. Leaving for London directly, after having spent ten days at the mine site. When he arrived at Heathrow, he went to his mistress's flat, a prostitute who had born him a son. That was a Friday. On Monday, he went to his flat telling his concierge that he was coming down with the flu.

"Unfortunately, the concierge was the last person to see him alive. Two days later they opened his room, after not getting a response, and he was dead. Two weeks later his paramour, and her son were also dead.

"She infected the owner of a butcher shop round the corner. He died. The butcher chap infected his wife but at the moment she is out of danger and will live. His children are in quarantine, but seem unaffected.

"It is possible that disease has less tendency to kill somewhere round the third person infected, strictly conjecture of course. When we heard of your chap, we were worried that it had gotten into your troops. When our chaps interviewed the people at the building, where the young prostitute lived, one lady there said she had seen a young man, possibly an American, coming and going on Christmas Eve day. So we took for granted this was the young American.

"It is wise to keep all the people he had contact with in quarantine for at lease two weeks. The death count seems to be about 170 or 180 citizens of the Congo, two French citizens, a young engineer on leave home who also infected his wife, and three British subjects. Hopefully your chap will pull through and that will be the end of it. Any questions?"

"Yes, Doctor Williams," said Colonel Red. "Does anyone know what caused this. Was it a microbe?"

"I'm sorry, we don't know exactly what it is, we are still testing tissue samples of the deceased but we haven't gotten, what would you Americans say, a handle on it. Penicillin seems to stop it so it must be a virus of some sort."

After the meeting the British doctors left. Heuwit looked at Colonel Red. "Damn, sir, do you think we just escaped a worldwide epidemic? This stuff sounds a lot like the Bubonic Plague."

"Yes," replied Colonel Red, "or maybe a Spanish Flu. It may still be a global disaster. I got the feeling Doctor Williams wasn't ready to put it to bed yet."

"Funny," Colonel Red said looking out the window at the rain, "it seemed to come with the fog. Now hopefully it will go with it."

Chinook:

Doctor Williams said three British subjects had died, but actually four died. The fourth was only a few cells buried deep in Kathleen's womb, so small you would need a microscope to see it. However it was a life, and if events would have been different, Jimmy would have been a father.

Jimmy didn't remember exactly when Kathleen wasn't with him anymore. The dreams of her stopped and the dreams of his Mom, Dad and Becky started.

It was like just at one moment she was holding his hand and than she faded away. He couldn't feel her now.

It was at that moment that John Heuwit looked out the window of the small office and saw the fog had lifted. The wind had picked up and rain started to patter on the roof of the hospital.

John heard a small sigh from the vicinity of Jimmy's bed. He walked over to him and watched as his eyes flickered then started to open.

"Well, well, it looks like the Kraken Wakes!"

He felt his pulse and took his temperature. Both were almost back to normal.

"Airman Burns, can you hear me?"

17

Jimmy nodded yes. His lips formed the words, "what happened?"

"You have been a very sick man," said John.

He held his head and gave him a drink of water. Jimmy's head fell back and he went into a very deep sleep.

John called the nurse on duty and told her to report to Colonel Red that the patient had awakened from the coma and was sleeping quietly now.

Jimmy recovered quickly. Within a couple of days he was walking around the room and eating like he could never fill up his stomach. At the end of the next week he was ready to go back to duty. Colonel Smith was giving him his last physical.

"Airman Burns, I need you to masturbate into this cup, can you?"

"Yes sir, I think I can."

"You may find this a funny request, but as the disease went to your testicles we need to know if it damaged your ability to have children."

After Jimmy had done as requested, the Colonel told him to dress and go to the chow hall for his first real meal in almost three weeks, and then report back for his test results. Who should he meet at the chow hall, but none other than Sergeant Hopkins.

"Well you look a lot better today than you did last time I saw you. The next time you stick your weenie in some cunt make sure it is not diseased," he said. "You know we had to live in a small room with no smokes for two weeks all because of your fuckin' love life?"

"Sorry, Sarge. I think I got the worst of the deal though, but I will try to be more careful next time."

"Well there won't be a next time because they are ship'en you to Maguire as soon as they clear you here."

Jimmy's heart gave a jump. "Really!" he said.

"Yep, got the transfer papers on my desk this morning."

After chow Jimmy went back to see Colonel Red.

"Airman Burns, here are all your papers with the test results. You are leaving Mildenhall for Maguire in two days. Your Sergeant Hopkins has your orders.

"You will be put in the hospital at Maguire for more tests once you arrive stateside, so be ready for that."

"Ok sir, I just want to thank you and Major Heuwit for saving me."

"That's alright, son. By the way, I talked to your parents to assure them you were all right and would be home in about a month. Ok you're dismissed."

Jimmy snapped to attention, saluted and walked out of the hospital a happy man.

After Jimmy had been run through more never ending tests at

Maguire Air Force Base in New Jersey he was called into the hospital's Commanding Officer's office. He stood at attention while the General gave Jimmy a briefing.

"Airman Burns, you have been a vehicle for expanding medical science's knowledge of the diseases that ravage mankind. All your test results will be sent to the Center for Disease Control in Atlanta. You seem to have weathered this very well except, you could possibly develop a heart condition in your old age. This is something you should have the V.A. monitor as you pass fifty. Also you will never be able to have children. No live sperm were detected in your secretions. Other from that you have fared well, and you seem healthy. Good luck, dismissed."

"Thank you, sir." Jimmy was a free man.

Chinook:

Jimmy was ok physically, but mentally he would never be the same again. Most of the rest of his life he would hear voices and have dreams.

3

Jimmy arrived home at the end of March. He rode a bus from New York City's Grand Central Station to Chicago, where he stayed a week with an old buddy who had left England the summer before.

The buddy had gotten a job with United Airlines at O'Hare Airport. He took Jimmy out one day to look around. He tried to talk Jimmy into signing on with United, who was hiring baggage handlers, general maintenance and ground crew. They paid over six dollars an hour to start, but Jimmy was homesick for the West. If he hadn't been sick he probably would have stayed in Chicago.

His next stop was Minneapolis where another buddy had lived. When he phoned his house his dad told Jimmy that he was no longer there but had moved to Denver, Colorado. It seems his cousin got him a job with Coors Brewing company, and because of personal problems, he had to get out of the Twin Cities. When he got home, the girl he had loved and had written to every week for almost four years, was pregnant by some other guy. Jimmy then caught the bus to Cut Bank, Montana to see Steve Moore's folks. They were very worried that Steve would get sick like Jimmy, as they lived in the same room, and he had been in quarantine.

Steve said they wouldn't believe that he was ok so he asked Jimmy to stop to see them, if he could. Steve's Dad met him at the bus. He took him home, to a small modest house, and got him falling down drunk.

Two days later Jimmy, recovered from the drinking, left for Portland but now he understood why Steve liked to hang out at the pubs and drink. From Portland he caught a bus to Salem and then hitchhiked the thirty miles to Low Sky, where he called his dad, who flew down in the pickup to get him.

There were tears and hugs from his mother and sister, a big fried chicken dinner that night and Jimmy was home.

He hung out for about two weeks, helping around the farm, and doing some fishing when the trout season opened the first weekend in April.

One day while in Low Sky with his dad, he heard that the Flavor

20

Picked cannery, in Slayton, was hiring permanent workers. The giant cannery employed around two hundred year-round workers. At the height of the season, mid June to September, it had over one thousand people, working two twelve hour shifts seven days a week. It was the largest summer only employer in the area, and a boon to housewives, high school and college students, who all need the extra money.

Chinook:

The river valleys of Western Oregon are the richest farming areas in the world. Many varieties of berries, vegetables, fruits and grains are grown there. The abundance and variety is astounding, the farms and canneries, provide food for the world and jobs for the locals. In the mountains above the valleys large Douglas Fir, Cedar and Western Hemlock grow providing jobs logging the forests, and in the saw and plywood mills. The richness of the area is made possible because of the western winds that blow off the Pacific Ocean, bringing soft warm rain, in abundance, to this treasured land.

The next day Jimmy borrowed his dad's pickup, and went into Slayton, to apply for a job at the cannery. When he walked into the main office the lady there directed him to the employment office.

The door into the employment office was a screen door on a spring. When he walked in it slammed and the lady at the desk jumped from the noise. He was looking into the eyes of his old love Becky Anderson Skinner.

She ran from her desk and jumped into his arms, "Oh Jimmy," she said, "how glad I am to see you, it's been so long. I met your dad a few months ago in town, and he told me you were deathly sick! How glad I am that you are well now, it would be hard not to have you around, Jimmy. I consider you my closest friend."

After Jimmy had made out all the paperwork needed to apply for a job, Becky sent him to talk to the foreman of the warehouse, Jake Johnson. As it would take Jimmy about five minutes to walk out to the warehouse, she called Jake. She let him know Jimmy was on the way, and told him something about his background.

"We are buying more trucks and expanding our driver fleet," Jake told Jimmy.

"The board of directors found that it is cheaper and more efficient to deliver our own products to California, Washington, Idaho, Nevada, and the rest of the Western states than to contract to other carriers. So

21

we are hiring drivers as the new trucks are delivered. If you are interested we have a new truck coming in, in two weeks. I know you are just out of the Air Force, and we want to hire men who have completed their draft obligations. We would like you to start now, because we will train you and then send you in for your commercial license as soon as you are ready. Finally, Becky in the office told me you were the best, so the job is yours if you want it."

"It sounds fine to me," said Jimmy. "Do you mind if I ask how much it pays?"

"No, you will start at $105.00 a week, plus overtime, and then as you learn and get seniority you will go up from there."

"OK, Mister Johnson," Jimmy said, "I'm your man."

They went to the office to talk to Becky.

"Great, I'm glad you are coming here, Jimmy, I know you will like it."

He thanked Jake and after all the paperwork was finished Becky said, "I get off at six, Jimmy. Could I meet you at Rocky's tavern at 6:30 for a beer and a talk?"

* * *

It was about nine miles from Slayton to Low Sky. The road ran through farm fields, and Jimmy took his time getting back to town.

When he arrived he had still two hours to kill so he went over to the Low Sky High School to see if Mr. Bennet was still teaching there. Mr. Bennet was Jimmy's favorite teacher in high school and he wanted to see him again after all these years. He was gone for the weekend.

Jimmy walked down to the wall where they kept the pictures of the graduating classes. There it was under "1958," Becky, him and all the other kids that were in their class. It was one month shy of five years but it seemed an eternity.

As he was leaving school, he remembered the night he and Becky were buck ass naked in the front seat of his car, in this parking lot. A light shown in the window and there was the town cop, Chet. He could have had them in deep trouble, but he just said, "You kids get dressed and go home." Jimmy smiled. Dang, they would have been ruined if Chet had reported them; they had gotten lucky that time.

He remembered Becky naked; she was so beautiful, his heart skipped a beat.

He went down to the Shell station next. He called his Mom. "I'll be home late. Don't wait supper, I'm going to see Becky tonight. I know, Mom, it will be alright. Yes, yes it's ok."

22

His Mom hadn't liked he was seeing Becky; she reminded him of the last time they were involved.

Damn, this is a small town. He had known Becky a long time and he would likely see her a lot the rest of his life, he thought.

He knew his Mom was worried about him, but he was grown now and had to make his own decisions about who to hang out with. He was still kind of in love with Becky, and would not mind it at all if tonight led to her bed.

Pie Parkinson, a local football hero, who had graduated two years before him, now owned the Shell station. Jimmy shot the BS with him until it was time to go to Rocky's tavern to meet Becky.

When Jimmy walked in a voice from behind the bar boomed. "Jimmy Burns, well I'll be damned. I'd heard you were home. How you doing, boy?"

"Fine, Mr. Rocknell. Hey how's Sam doing, is he still in the Navy?"

"Yep, he is stationed in the Philippines and loves the Navy, just made Chief and looks like he's stayin' in for twenty."

"Hey, that's great. What about Susie, they ever get married?"

"Nah, when Sam left she moved to Portland to live with her Aunt. Last I heard she married some guy there and has a kid. What you like to drink, first one on the house to say welcome home. You stayin' in the area, kid, or you leavin' like some of the rest?"

"No, I'm staying. I just got hired over at the cannery in Slayton today, starting Monday."

"Bet your Mom and Dad are happy about that," he said.

"Well I haven't told them yet," said Jimmy. Rocky Rocknell handed Jimmy his Lucky Lager beer and walked over to an older man seated at the far end of the bar. Jimmy had never seen this person before he heard Rocky say, "Want another, Doc?"

"In a minute," the man called Doc said.

"Jimmy, come on over and meet the Doctor. This, Doc, is one of my son Sam's best buddies. He was eatin' at my house more than my kids did."

"Glad to meet you, Sir," said Jimmy.

The Doc looked at him and said, "Just out of the service, I can tell, still in the 'Sir' mode. Just call me Doc, son," he said.

Becky came in the bar just then. Rocky looked at her, then at Jimmy. He didn't say anything, but gave Jimmy a wink.

"Hi honey," said Jimmy. "Let's sit at this table where we can talk. Can I get you anything?"

"That Lucky Lager looks good, I'll have one of those," said Becky.

After they were settled they talked about their old classmates for awhile. Becky had kept track of most of them, and told him all the latest news. Jimmy was bursting to ask about Ralph Skinner, but didn't say anything. When he got their second beer Becky started to open up.

"Jimmy dear, I would like to apologize for the way I dumped you, and the letter I sent you when you were overseas and I was pregnant. I wished I could have brought back that letter after I sent it, and your reply served me right. Did you ever marry that girl?"

"No, she was never anything to me, just one date. I was so hurt I just used her name to hurt you back," he said. When he said that her eyes filled with tears and she took his hand.

"What about Ralph, did you two get married?" He knew Ralph never married her because his Mom told him, with a smirk, that Ralph left and never was seen again.

"No, I have never seen Ralph, nor has anyone else since that night I told him I was pregnant."

"Didn't he go to Seattle to work at Boeing with his brother?"

"No, his brother has never seen him either," she said. "I guess the thought of getting married to me made him so scared that he never stopped running. I did have a beautiful baby though. A little boy who makes me glad I'm alive. He is the sunshine of my life, and the spitting image of his father."

"Where do you and him live?" asked Jimmy.

"Oh we live with Ralph's Mom. When no one could find Ralph she invited me to stay with her until the baby was born. She paid all the expenses of the birth. After Sonny was born I was going to move home but she asked me to stay. She has that big house and Mom and Dad didn't really have room for the baby and I, so we stayed with her.

"She is so sweet, and she loves Sonny beyond anything. Ralph's brother is far away so she would be alone without us."

Damn thought Jimmy. He had hoped she lived alone. Oh well.

"Thanks for the beers, Jimmy. I got to go home and help Bessie with the baby, but I would like to have you over to supper one night."

"Thanks," he said. "I would like to come over, so I guess I will see you on Monday at work?"

"Sure, stop in the office and see me. Goodnight, Jimmy dear." She took his hand and brushed his lips with hers, and walked out the door.

Rocky looked over. "You two getting back together again?" he said.

"Nah, looks like friends for right now," replied Jimmy. "Did no one ever see Ralph again, or is he just hiding out?" Jimmy asked.

"I tell you, boy, that is one strange situation. The police came and looked into it and they questioned everyone in town, but they never found hide or hair of Ralph. Only God knows where that boy went to."

"I for one never liked the little shit much, always kind of a funny kid. I'm sure he went to Canada or some place and will never come back."

Jimmy said good night and went home.

4

Jimmy didn't sleep well that night.

He hadn't told Mom and Dad that he had been hired at the Flavor Picked cannery. He was restless, he was horny and he wasn't sure about Becky. He lay in bed and thought about her all night.

He fell asleep finally at about two A.M. and dreamed about Kathleen. The fog, Kathleen, Crawford Street, and finally in his dream they were making love.

When Dad's feet hit the floor the next morning, Jimmy woke up. His undershorts were wet and sticky so once again Kathleen had come to his rescue. He cleaned up and met Dad in the barn, where he was milking the cows. "Good morning son, how'd it go yesterday?"

"Uh, I got hired on at the cannery starting Monday, so I am going to need a car. Are you doing anything this morning?"

"Hey great, Jimmy. Well I was going to start disking the twenty acres, over by Mr. McCormick's place but that can wait. I saw in the paper that Valley Chev had a big car sale going on this week. We could run over there after breakfast."

They finished the chores, ate the breakfast Mom made, and went to buy Jimmy his car. Jimmy sat in the pickup thinking how nice it was that him and Dad were here, talking and doing things together.

They arrived at the Chevy dealer and started to walk back to the used cars. Dad was talking and then suddenly found he was walking alone.

He looked around to find Jimmy and saw him standing beside a brand new 1963, black, two-door hardtop Chevrolet Impala. Jimmy had just fallen in love again, out the corner of his eye he could see a salesman making a beeline toward him.

Dad tried to cut the salesman off, but he reached the lovestruck young man first.

"Pretty nice, isn't she, son. She looks good, drives good, and she is on sale today. Care to drive her?"

Jimmy climbed in, hardly hearing Dad explain to the salesman they were really looking for a used car. Oh damn, he didn't know any-

26

thing could be so beautiful. Red vinyl interiors, 327 V8 engine, radio, auto transmission, and power brakes.

Dad, with a sigh, climbed in the back seat. Jimmy touched the key and the engine roared to life, a deep mellow rumble came from the dual exhaust pipes. "She got twin manifolds," the salesman explained to Jimmy.

Jimmy went out on the road, touched the throttle and the car ran up to sixty in a flash smooth and purring like a kitten.

It was on sale; they wanted $2,495, marked down from $2995.00, today only.

Jimmy said, "I'll give you $2,300 cash, now."

"Well son, let me take this to the manager, and see what he says." A few minutes later, the salesman returned.

"Well, he says $2395.00 as we already marked it down, but I tell you what. You take it at that price and I'll throw in the Impala floor mats front and back." Jimmy's heart was racing, he was feeling numb, but he had to have this car. He opened his wallet and counted out two $1,000 bills, and four $100 bills.

Dad's chin hit his chest, the salesman raised his eyebrows. "I guess you weren't joking, son. Where did you get this much money?"

"Well sir, I just got out of the Air Force and I saved for almost four years, plus my rousting out pay for this."

"Oh," the salesman said. "Oh, a veteran. Well, Valley Chevrolet thanks you for your business and your service to our country.

"For veterans we have a little extra. We have here a certificate for free oil changes and two complete tune ups for the first 30,000 miles. We will put in four sets of seat belts for free so your friends and family can ride safely. Just remember us for your automobile purchases in the future. Ok, it will be about an hour for the paperwork, and while that is being done, our service people will install your seat belts."

Dad and Jimmy walked out to Dad's pickup. "Mom is going to have a fit when she sees that car, Jimmy. I told her we were going to just buy you a used car or an older pickup. Uh, do you have any money left?"

"Oh yeah, Dad, I have $338.50 left to tide me over until my first paycheck. Uh Dad, I want to give you and Mom one hundred dollars for room and board until I get my own place."

"No son. I want you to know that no matter what, you always have a home to come to. However, until you leave, I would appreciate you helping me around the farm." They smiled at each other. "But I'll let you explain to Mom about the car. Well no matter, I'll still get heck over it."

"Sorry Dad, didn't mean to get you in trouble."

"She'll get used to it shortly," Dad said as he climbed into the pickup. "See you at home. Now drive that thing carefully."

The first place he went to was Mrs. Skinner's house. He knocked on the door. "Uh, hi, Mrs. Skinner, is Becky here?"

Bessie Skinner was a medium-sized woman. She had a motherly figure and her hair was just starting to go gray. She held a little boy with curly black hair and blue eyes.

"Why Jimmy Burns, it is nice to see you after all these years. How are you feeling, dear. Your mother said you were very sick awhile back? I know she was very worried about you."

"Yeah, Mrs. Skimmer, I was pretty sick, but I'm alright now. I caught some kind of advance flu; they were never sure exactly what it was."

"Well dear, I'm glad you're better and home safe. Becky has walked down to Thorton's Grocery for a few things. She should be back in a while. Do you want to wait?"

"Oh thanks, but I'll go meet her."

He picked up Becky and took her for a ride in the new car.

"You like her, honey?"

"Wow, it's a nice car, Jimmy."

"Want to go to Slayton tonight to a movie."

"Sure, if you don't mind going to the late show. I put Sonny to bed at eight o'clock and maybe we could see the nine o'clock, if that's alright."

"Sure, see you at eight."

When he drove into the farm yard, his sister came running out jumping up and down. "Take me for ride, take me for a ride!"

"Come on, Mom, I'll take you too."

"Jimmy, this car seems new, is it?"

"Uh yeah, Mom. Do you like it?"

"Yes dear, it seems very nice. I thought your Dad said you were getting a used car."

"Ah, yeah, I was but then I saw this car."

"Hmmm," Mom said, and Jimmy thought, *poor Dad.*

*   *   *

After about two weeks Jimmy was fully trained in driving and loading large trucks. He was co-driving with the older more experienced drivers.

He was getting kind of desperate about Becky; she was warm and willing up to a certain point, then she would stop him just as he wanted to finalize his lovemaking.

She would say, "Sorry darling, it's not about you, it's about me."

He couldn't understand what that meant.

Once he started to get his paychecks he moved into Low Sky to a converted garage that the widow McDonnell owned, and rented out for a supplement to her meager income from social security.

It was about two blocks from Mrs. Skinner's house, where Becky lived; quiet and private. He could see it as a love nest for them.

He also, one night after he kissed her, asked her to marry him. "Darling, I love you. I desperately want you and I am willing to make little Sonny my adopted son, and raise him as my own."

She burst into tears. "Oh Jimmy, you are so sweet, and I love you, but, darling, I just can't just now. Please don't think bad of me. Could we just go on as we are for a short time."

This was a blow to Jimmy but she was so miserable he just said, "Sure baby. I'll wait as long as I have to."

Jimmy started to stop regularly at Rocky's Tavern when he wasn't on the road. Partially to keep his mind and other longings off Becky, and because it was really the only entertainment, other than sex and high school sports, in town. The Doc was always there, and after awhile they became friends.

Chinook:

Edward F. Baxter, Doctor of Clinical Psychology, retired.

He was born in Council Bluffs, Iowa and graduated summa cum laude from the University of Nebraska with a degree in Psychology. He wanted to be a psychologist so he enrolled at Cornell University in New York, for graduate work. Edward also studied Philosophy; he studied Marx, Schopenhauer, Nietzsche and Sartre. He also ran into the closed minded autocratic East Coast liberal thinking.

All the things he learned in childhood, morals, purity, fidelity and especially Christianity, were met with scorn and disdain.

Anyone who believed in God was considered weak and ignorant.

He was glad to return to the teachings of Jean Charcot, Joseph Breuer, and of course, Sigmund Freud. He found solace in Psychology, where you could actually help people.

Edward met a young girl, Jane Collins, attending Cornell from some obscure place called Oregon.

She was lovely—long dark hair flowed down to her waist, silken skin, breasts that pointed upward, green eyes, and legs that seemed to start under her armpits.

He was smitten, ran after her like a puppy and finally, after he finished his Masters dissertation, talked her into marrying him.

The first years of their marriage were bliss; she gave up school to get a job to support him while he finished his Ph.D.

After graduation he got an internship at Western New York Hospital for the Insane in Ithaca; she got pregnant and had a little boy.

Four months after the birth of their first son she became pregnant again and after this second child was born became a changed person.

She started to resent the fact he had an interesting and intellectual job and she was saddled with two screaming babies.

One afternoon he came home and she was gone; the note said she had tried but she was going back to Oregon. Her mother would take care of the children and she would return to school. He was devastated; after his internship was completed he left for Oregon.

He got a practicing position at Portland General Hospital in the trauma/psychiatry department.

After a few years, with another doctor on staff at PGH, he opened a private clinic. When he arrived in Portland she moved back in with him, but insisted on staying in school, declaring that she was never meant to be a mother.

Edward didn't just love Jane—she was his being, his all. So he gave her her every wish.

Fifteen years later he found she had been having an affair with her old high school sweetheart since returning to Oregon from New York.

During the summer clinic picnic, the new wife of one of his assistant psychologists asked the lady next to her who that woman with the lovely long dark hair was; she thought she knew her.

When told she was the wife of the head doctor, she just said "oh," and let it drop. But she watched the next day and out of the house across the street, at noon, came that same woman.

She made inquiries as to who lived there and found out that it was a divorced man who worked for Western Airlines at Portland Airport.

She watched for two weeks before she told her husband; she wanted to make sure she was right about that liaison.

Her husband knew how much Dr. Baxter loved his wife, and knew he had to be careful with any accusations.

"Dr. Baxter, I saw your wife today out in Milwaukee," he said.

"Oh," said Edward, "did you see her at the mall?"

"No, she was coming out of a house in my neighborhood."

"I see," Edward said. "Do you know who lives there?"

"No, I don't know him."

"Probably something to do with school," Edward said.

After Jane had graduated from University of Oregon at Portland with a Bachelors Degree in Psychology, she had taken a job as a school counselor in the largest high school in Portland.

After her sons started to school and she could no longer do this job full time, she became a station wagon Mom. She was still a backup counselor at the high school being called in times of emergency, or when the full time people were absent.

That night Edward asked his wife if she had been anywhere interesting that day. "No," she said, "just to school and back again."

The next week he asked their receptionist if he could borrow her car for the morning. He explained that his wasn't running that good and he had to go to the airport.

As he drove into the Milwaukee neighborhood of his assistant, she was driving out.

He sat at the stoplight and she turned left in front of him.

He looked into her face, she didn't look happy like he thought she would.

On her face was a scowl; he wondered if she and her lover had had a fight. More to the point, he reasoned she didn't want to return to her regular life after a morning of bliss with him.

His most hurtful thoughts were the things she had with her he had bought her. The coat she had on, for Christmas two years ago, and the car she was driving, last summer.

That night he asked her again if she had been out anywhere interesting.

"No, I have not left home all day," was her reply.

He kept all this in his heart and never let her know he knew about her affair.

Four years later the evening they arrived home from their youngest son's high school graduation, she told him they were through and she wanted him out of the house that night.

He packed a small bag and went to a motel; he thought it was just probably a little misunderstanding that would be healed in a couple of days.

The next day, however, a server with a subpoena arrived at his office—he was being sued for divorce.

That night he went to his house and all his bags were packed and in the garage.

Jane came out and said she had a restraining order against him for within one mile of the house, and would enforce it.

As he was leaving a strange car pulled into his driveway and a man got out.

He watched, at the end of the block, as his wife, the woman he had given his life to, ran down the steps of the house and into the arms of this new man.

They kissed, and opening the trunk of his car, got out his bags and carried them into HIS house.

Even after the problems they had had in their marriage the sight of her in another man's arms made him almost physically sick.

For the first time in his life he wanted to kill, and if he would have had a gun he would have went back and gunned the bastard down in front of her.

After the divorce he didn't want to live much. He sold what interest in the clinic he had left after the divorce, to his partner, and came to Low Sky where he would try to drink himself slowly to death.

*   *   *

Jimmy had returned early from a run to the Port of Vancouver, British Colombia. He and his partner delivered a truck and trailer of canned blackberries that were loaded on to a Japanese ship bound for the Orient.

Generally it took up to four days, round trip, to dump a load at Vancouver. Most times twenty-four hours to reach there, if Canada Customs at the border were backed up. Eight hours to a day and a half to unload, and than another twenty-four back, if U.S. Customs were backed up.

This time though, when they arrived at the cannery, at 6 A.M., the truck was loaded.

They left immediately, rolled through customs in two hours, and pulled on to the loading dock at the Port of Vancouver at two A.M. the next morning; it had taken them only twenty hours.

Generally the drivers got some sleep in the cab until it was their turn to unload, or if the wait was going to be over ten or twelve hours they would bed down in a motel.

This time they pulled right up to the ship.

Within minutes longshoremen were swarming over their truck. Within an hour the truck was empty and the documents for the cannery and customs signed and they were on their way back.

They took turns driving and sleeping.

At twelve noon, they were at the United Can factory in Everett, Washington to load up new cans for the cannery. They found out that the cans would be done and loaded by nine that night.

They left their truck with the loading dock foreman, walked across the road to the Puget Sound motel, ate breakfast and crashed until eight o'clock that evening.

By ten o'clock they were back on U.S. 99 headed south.

They drove all night and at ten the next morning rolled in to the parking lot of the warehouse at least twenty-four hours earlier than they were expected.

It was the first really warm day of the spring, over eighty degrees and summer was coming on quickly.

After putting his bags in his room he walked down to Rocky's Tavern and sat next to Doc.

"I'll have a Lucky Larger, Mr. Rocknell," he said.

"Ok, Jimmy boy, coming right up," he said. "How was the trip?"

"Oh not bad. We did it in just seventy-six hours, which according to our boss is some kind of a record. We got back in at ten this morning and I'm pretty tired."

He chatted with Doc for awhile and after his third beer said to him, "Doc, you understand women, right."

"Well, son, no man really, totally, understands women," Doc said, a small bitter smile on his lips. "And beware any man that says he does. You having trouble with Becky?"

"Well, I love Becky a lot and want to marry her. I even told her I would adopt her little boy if she wanted, but she just keeps putting me off. Says she loves me, says it isn't me, but her. I just don't understand."

Doc looked down at his glass. "Didn't the father of her child disappear quite suddenly?"

"Yeah, after the night she told him she was pregnant he left and was never seen again."

"Well, Jimmy, I think that is the problem. She hasn't let go of the possibility of his return and until he does or she hears from him the whole thing is unresolved in her mind. I'm afraid she can't move on with you until it is resolved. A girl like Becky just didn't give in to him, she probably loved him, or thought she did, and probably believes she loves him still. She blames herself for his leaving as he did; probably thinks she broke it to him too quickly or believes he felt forced into a situation he couldn't handle. She therefore believes he will return when he gets his mind straight. So until this is resolved with her you must either accept it or move on and find another girl with less encumbrances."

Jimmy hung his head. "I know, Doc, I know you're right. It's just that I want her now, and am finding it hard."

"Ah yes," mused Doc. "I was once young myself, and know the passions of love, and the sex drive of someone your age. I wish I could tell you something different."

"Mr. Rocknell, I'll have one more then I got to go to bed," said Jimmy. "Thanks, Doc, for the free advice. This is something I could never ask my folks."

After he drank his beer he went home, took a shower and plunged into a deep sleep.

*   *   *

He was walking through a thick dark fog. He could smell the diesel and coal smoke, and feel the chill damp on his face.

He could not see and ran into a post. Crawford Street was blazoned on the sign at the top.

He turned and feeling his way, he heard Kathleen call him. "Laddie, Laddie." He fought forward, then he saw her there, a small bundle at her breast. He felt frightened. What was she saying? "Come Laddie."

He couldn't get to her, she was just out of reach.

The noise was pulling him away from her; he heard his name, Jimmy, Jimmy. Slowly he came up out of sleep.

It was like climbing out of a dark well. The fog went away. He was in his bed and someone was beating on his door, calling "Jimmy."

He got up and looked at his clock. 6:45 A.M., "Jimmy darling." It was Becky.

He opened his door and stood there in only his undershorts. She glanced down quickly, then looked him in his eyes.

"Sweetie, my car broke down last night. I called Pie Parkinson, and he towed it to his Shell station but won't be able to have it done until this afternoon and I need a ride to work. Sweetie, are you, ok? You look a little frazzled. I was getting worried, it took you awhile to answer the door."

"Yeah, I just slept twelve hours straight and haven't got the fog out of the brain yet."

"Oh, dearest, I'm sorry, I'll get someone else to take me."

"No honey, that's fine. I want to go in today anyway. I need to get my paycheck."

She looked at him doubtfully. "Are you sure?"

"Yeah, I'm ok."

"Ok, sweetie, come over and I'll feed you breakfast before we go."

He took a quick bath and went over to Becky's. The smell of sausage, coffee and eggs when he walked into the kitchen perked him up and made him remember it had been almost twenty-four hours since he had eaten.

By 7:35 A.M. they were on the road, and now that his stomach was full he started to feel what he always felt, just lately, in Becky's presence—extremely horny. He reached over and took her hand; she glanced at him.

"Sweetie, would you like to come over for dinner Saturday night? I got a very nice ham at Thornton's Market and would like to make you a good meal. I don't think you have been eating very good lately."

"Well, I have a haul going out tomorrow morning, but it is only to Boise, Idaho so I should be home by Friday night. So you bet, I would be glad to come."

Becky was silent for about a mile. "Sweetie, do you remember Katie Overmars?"

"Of course," he said.

"Well she works for Thornton's."

"Yeah, as I remember she worked there in high school also," he said.

"She works in the office now and is in charge of the buying for the entire store, along with Mr. Thornton.

"We have become best friends the last few years, and I'm going to invite her over too, if you don't mind."

"Well, I would prefer to be alone with you," he glanced at her.

"I know," she said, looking down at her hands.

"But heck no, I always liked Katie. I used to tease her a lot when we were kids, and I haven't seen her since graduation."

"You know, Sweetie, she has really changed since high school. She has lost weight and wears her hair differently and she is really pretty now. Well, she was always pretty, always had that beautiful figure."

"Really," he said. "She always wore those dumpy clothes and was always slouching around. I didn't realize she had a good figure. Besides, I always had my eyes on you, never noticed any other girl."

She gave him a little smile. "Be serious. No, she was very shy, you know, but has gotten over that. She is much more confident about herself now."

They got to the cannery. He came into the office with her and she got him his paycheck.

"I'll come pick you up after work," he said.

"Oh, sweetie, you don't have to. I'll catch a ride back with one of the girls in the office. One lives in Lacombe and drives through Low Sky on her way home."

"Ok, then, I'll be leaving early tomorrow morning, so I won't see you until Saturday. Honey, if your car isn't fixed let me know tonight and you can drive my car. I'll be at Dad and Mom's today so call me there."

"Ok, how sweet of you, but Pie said the part would be in and he would have it fixed for sure this afternoon."

He looked longingly at her, said good-bye and went to help his Dad. That night Mom would make his favorite, a big fried chicken dinner.

The run to Boise went without a hitch. They reached there Wednesday afternoon late. They stayed overnight in a motel and unloaded their load of canned Blue Lake green beans into the local warehouse of Allied grocers early the next morning. Then they went to one of those large underground storage depots where potatoes are stored and loaded up cartons of potatoes, so at three o'clock that afternoon they were on their way to Eugene, Oregon with their truck filled with spuds.

The next afternoon they pulled into the Allied grocers warehouse in Eugene and after unloading headed up U.S. 99 toward Slayton.

They arrived at the cannery around eleven o'clock Friday night. Jimmy was back in Low Sky at right before midnight. He drank a beer and fell into a deep sleep. Saturday morning he awoke late and went out to help Dad after having breakfast at the Low Sky café.

Mom invited him for dinner but he told her he was invited out for dinner.

"Oh really dear, who invited you?"

"Becky did, Mom," he said.

He could see her face tighten with displeasure but he just kissed her on the cheek and left.

He took a long bath, shaved and brushed his hair. He was hoping Katie wouldn't be there and after an intimate dinner he could slip Becky into his arms with a chance of talking her into bed. Little did he know his life would change forever in just two hours.

5

Becky had a problem and had to think.

She couldn't go on the way she had with Jimmy. She knew what he wanted and on their last date she had let him go too far. He was terribly hurt when she stopped him.

She knew Jimmy loved her, wanted to marry her and would adopt Sonny. It was just that she hadn't resolved the thing about Ralph. She felt really stupid; she knew she would never see Ralph again. He had always had a dream of going to Alaska and he was probably up there now. In reality she blamed herself for his going.

Since she was a little girl she knew she would marry Jimmy when she grew up. The last year of high school they made plans to marry, after graduation.

Then Jimmy had gotten his draft notice, and rather than be drafted into the Army he enlisted in the Air Force. After Jimmy had left she felt let down and alone.

She flirted with Ralph the day of the Low Sky town picnic and he got up the nerve to ask her out. She encouraged Ralph to go further on each date and on the fourth date let him make love to her. They were both virgins and it was messy and painful and she had bled a lot.

Why did she do it? She couldn't say herself, but after a week she called him and they had another date.

They made love in the front seat of his pickup on a deserted lane and it went a lot better; in fact it was fun and daring. She felt loved, and a woman. It was after that date that she wrote the letter to Jimmy, breaking up with him, and saying she would marry Ralph.

Ralph had gotten a job at the Mill City plywood mill right after their graduation; he graduated on Friday night and started the graveyard shift on Monday night. He started at two dollars an hour, plus fifty cents an hour shift premium; that was one hundred dollars a week, a salary of almost astronomical proportion.

He would take Becky to Albany and Lebanon to eat and go to the movies.

Once he took her to see Fats Domino in a concert in Salem. Afterward they would go to their secret place and make love.

The second month into their love affair Ralph got his draft notice; Becky was really put out. How could all this be ruined again?

Because Ralph's mother was a widow and he her sole support [actually she also got some money from Jack, his brother, who was working in Seattle at Boeing, but they didn't disclose that to the draft board] he got a deferment to his draft notice.

Becky was ecstatic; now she knew he really loved her. The next month she missed her period. In a minor panic, she got a ride from her friend Mia and her boy friend to Salem, on the pretext that she was buying her mother a surprise present.

While there she slipped into a doctor's office and it was confirmed she was pregnant.

When she got back to Low Sky that afternoon she called Ralph. His mother got him out of bed and she told him she had to see him. They met and she told him. He seemed shocked, but he acted like he was very happy that they would get married as soon as possible.

She was a very lovely girl, and in Ralph's wildest dreams he never thought he could marry anyone the caliber of Becky Anderson.

Plus there was that extra incentive; he hated Jimmy Burns's guts, and it would be extra sweet to sleep forever with his girl.

They talked for hours until he had to rush to the midnight shift. She kissed Ralph goodbye and though she never saw him again, their affair still felt incomplete. Especially in light of the fact that they had a child.

Until this was resolved she couldn't go on with Jimmy.

This is where Katie Overmars came in the picture.

Katie had become her best friend after high school. Most of the kids they graduated with had left Low Sky for greener pastures at colleges or jobs in Portland.

They would have lunch, go shopping in Salem or just sit around and talk girl talk. Katie had always been shy and she needed Becky to help her socially.

Becky decided Katie and Jimmy would be a good match. If she could cause this romance to happen it would solve her problems with Jimmy and see her friend with a nice boy friend, or maybe even happily married.

So with this idea she set about the conquest.

Jimmy and Katie had known each other since first grade. They had never been friends but they were comfortable around each other;

so first on the agenda was to mention to each how the other had changed.

That was accomplished, and now they were both invited to dinner at her house tonight. This would be a no pressure—just friends togetherness sort of thing. Katie came over at six o'clock when she got off work; Jimmy was due at eight.

Katie helped Becky with dinner and she played with Sonny. They talked, as friends do, but Becky made sure the topic stayed on Jimmy. What a good job he had, what a great future, how sweet he was, and on and on.

Just before eight in walked the sacrificial lamb with not one clue as to his true mission there.

When Jimmy walked into the big kitchen an aroma of cooking washed over him—roast pork and fresh applesauce, and green beans with bacon on the boil.

Becky came to him and kissed him demurely on the cheek. "Did the trip go ok, Jimmy?" she asked.

"Yeah fine, no problems," he said. Just then he saw Katie sitting at the table with little Sonny on her lap.

Wow had she changed, her hair shorter and more blond than he remembered; a very brilliant red lipstick glistened on her full lovely lips.

She stood up holding Sonny as a shield between them and shook hands with him, "You're looking very good, Jimmy, being home must agree with you. I heard you had been sick when you were overseas."

"Yeah, I was a sick puppy for awhile but as you see I am fully recovered," he said.

Dinner was served and when Katie put Sonny in his chair Jimmy noticed that she had a great figure with an ample set of knockers.

The dinner was good; plenty of food, of which Jimmy ate more than both girls combined. The evening was pleasant with the friends casually chatting, mostly about things that happed in high school and where old classmates were now.

When Becky put Sonny to bed, Katie and Jimmy were left for about twenty minutes.

He noted she was a very pleasant and pretty girl, so different from that shy reclusive girl he had known in school.

But his mind was on Becky and he seemed a little distracted to Katie.

When Becky returned from bedding down Sonny the girls cleaned up the kitchen; they wouldn't let Jimmy help. After pie and coffee it was time to go.

Becky asked Jimmy to walk Katie to her car, which she had parked on the street in front of the house. She asked him before he left if she could ride with him to work Monday morning. He was happy to take her, as they had not talked that night and some things needed to be discussed between them.

On Monday morning the hammer fell!

Becky seemed cool and distant when he picked her up. "Jimmy dear," she said, "we have to talk about us. I cannot go out with you anymore. We can still be friends, I want for us to be friends. but we can't be anything more."

He almost took an oncoming truck head-on, as he looked at her with his mouth open.

"I, I, I . . . I thought you were going to tell me we could get married and start our life together," he said. "I know we have had a few problems sweetheart, but we can get by them. If I am too aggressive about making love to you I can be better, I can wait for that until we're married. I don't want to lose you again."

He sounded so wounded, so destroyed that she began to cry.

"Jimmy, I can't. It wouldn't be right for you to raise Sonny; he is not your child. I love Ralph, and even though he left me I can't marry you or anyone else. Please try to understand."

"I am sorry sweetheart, I can't understand. If I had that son of a bitch in front of me now I'd beat him to death for what he did to you."

"Stop it, Jimmy, stop it," she screamed. "You don't understand about Ralph and me, so just stop it."

He drove on, too stunned to say a word.

In a few minutes her crying stopped she shuddered and hiccupped. "It can't be for us, it wouldn't be fair to either of us to go on like this. I would like for you to ask out Katie. She would like to be your girl friend, she needs you, Jimmy, I don't."

They drove the rest of the way in silence, Jimmy glancing at her from time to time and she hiccupping and wiping her eyes, looking straight ahead avoiding his looks.

He left that afternoon with a truck and trailer full of blackberry cans bound for Southern California. When he returned two weeks later they studiously avoided each other for the rest of the summer.

Chinook:

State route 22 goes from Low Sky to Mill City. As the road climbs into the mountains it threads alongside the Thomas River.

About five miles from Low Sky the road now in a cutout carved by the river takes a sharp left hand turn.

If you stop in a pull out parking area across from the stream and walk to the edge you will see a large pool at the base of about a quarter mile set of rapids. From the road it is almost impossible to fish, as the elevated road bank drops straight into the river and a person would be standing in traffic.

There are barriers alongside the road at this point to keep errant cars from plunging into the pool below; that is except for one small area about as wide as a car where the bank was too steep to install a barrier.

If you walk down stream, however, you find a path that cuts down to the river; here is where men come to fish for steelhead trout.

The steelhead is a rainbow trout that migrates to the ocean. When it returns to its native stream to spawn after two or three years in the sea, men try to catch this silver rocket famed for its fighting abilities and delicious eating.

Joe Reed loves to stop alongside the Thomas River to fish for steelhead on his way home from the mill.

His shift ends at four o'clock and as he lives on a small ten-acre raspberry farm just outside Low Sky, he stops to fish one hour in the morning and most evenings. This morning he had stopped and saw the long dark forms of fish silhouetted in the clear aqua water.

Ah! he thought. *The first fish of the fall run that the Thomas is famous for.* At a quarter past four that evening, after work, he pulled into the parking area across from the pool.

He tied on his favorite lure, a wobble-rite he called "old gold." It was a battered old spoon that for some reason steelhead couldn't resist. He had caught more fish on that lure than he could remember.

He walked to the path and down to the pool.

From where he stood he couldn't cast to where he saw the fish this morning. It being late September the river was very low, probably the lowest he ever remembered. He found some large rocks exposed he hadn't seen exposed before; he jumped from one to the other until he rounded a protuberance in the bank of the road.

Now he had a full view of the rapids and sent his spoon in a high arc toward the head of the rapids.

He started to retrieve the lure. Half way across the pool the lure stopped; he raised the tip of his rod sharply waiting to feel the surge of a fish on the end of his line. The line gave then snapped back, sort of like he caught the limb of a sunken log. Damn he couldn't lose his "old gold."

41

He scrambled up the side of the bank to get a better angle to see what his lure was snagged on to. He pulled it, it pulled back. Finally he gave a hard jerk on his pole and the lure came free.

Breathing a sigh of relief he reeled it in.

There was something still on the barb of the hook. He lifted the thing up; well damn it is a rusted auto antenna. What the hell is that doing in the river? He climbed a little further up the bank to get a better look into the water. Just then the setting sun glinted into the water and he saw the roof of a pickup as plain as day.

Gasping, he returned to his car and lit out for the Low Sky police department and Chet the town cop.

Jimmy had gotten back late again from a one day run to Vancouver, Washington. The traffic coming and going over the Columbia River Bridge, while usually heavy, was particularly bad both ways today.

He was dead tired and after a beer and late night news on the TV he sank into a deep sleep.

He heard the banging. He thought it was a dream; someone was shouting his name. It sounded like Becky.

Unlikely! As they hadn't even looked at each other for over a month, ever since that ride to work.

It kept getting louder. He woke up—damn it was Becky. He looked at his watch; it was four in the morning.

She was screaming "Jimmy, Jimmy wake up," over and over. He went to the door; there she stood in her nightgown and robe, her hair a tangled mess and the tears streaming down her face.

"Jimmy, Jimmy please help us. They found Ralph and his truck at the bottom of the river."

Chinook:

On that morning almost four years ago Ralph had finished his shift. He was bushed; he had been with Becky the night before right up to about an hour before when his shift started.

He found it harder and harder to leave her now, and it was killing him. He loved her and wanted her more every day, but love and working all night was making him exhausted.

He was making mistakes at work because he was so tired and had just received a tongue lashing from the Foreman.

Well, he would get a good sleep today.

When he got home he saw his mom out in the yard. Low Sky had

42

been hit with a sharp wind during the night and a limb from the old Elm tree had broken off and pierced the roof above the kitchen.

He got out the ladder, climbed up and removed the limb. He went to the garage and got some tarpaper and tar. He cleaned off the ruined shingles and patched the roof. He didn't have any more shingles.

While eating breakfast his mom said, "Dear, the weather might turn bad. Could you get the new shingles today and fix the roof properly?"

After breakfast he got into his pickup and drove up to Lacomb shingle and shake mill for a bundle of shingles.

By two o'clock he had the roof fixed.

Mom made him some lunch, he took a bath and climbed into bed at three o'clock dead tired.

At six o'clock Mom woke him up. Becky was on the phone and insisted on talking to him.

He talked to her for awhile and promised to pick her up at eight that night. He went back to bed for an hour.

He got up, ate a sandwich his mom fixed and went over to Becky's. She told him about the pregnancy and they sat and made plans until eleven o'clock again.

He left for work.

He was having a hard time staying awake on the drive to work; the truck was warm so he rolled down his window. The cool air flooded the cab and refreshed him somewhat. He turned on his radio as loud as it would go to his favorite Country and Western station; the music jarred him and helped him stay awake.

He speeded up thinking, *If I can just get to work I'll be ok.*

The screech of metal on metal along the side of his truck awakened him; he felt he was flying. The last thing he saw before his head smashed into the steering wheel was the nose of the pickup crashing into the water.

He had fallen asleep just at the sharp left hand corner. His truck swerved to the left then right, going through the open part of the barrier, leaving two scrapes of blue paint at each end of the opening.

6

Jimmy dressed and took his car to Becky's. He ran up the steps and knocked on the door.

"Come in, Jimmy," Mrs. Skinner motioned him in.

She looked much worse than Becky and his heart went out to her; she had lost a husband and now a son.

"We are so grateful you can take us, we couldn't drive," she told him.

"It's alright, Mrs. Skinner, glad to be of help."

They walked into the kitchen; there sat Katie holding Sonny.

Sonny looked at him. "My Daddy has been drownded, Uncle Jimmy," the little boy said. He was not quite awake.

"Hi Katie, how are you?"

"I am doing fine, Jimmy, thanks for helping out. I'll put Sonny to bed again as soon as you all go."

Just then Becky walked into the room. She glanced at him and said, "Ok, let's go." Becky and Mrs. Skinner sat in the back seat. Becky had her arm around the shoulders of the sobbing older woman.

Her own face was white and death-like; they rode without talking, the engine making the only sound.

When they arrived at the scene there was a Highway Patrol car with his lights flashing blocking the highway.

Jimmy pulled up and stopped; he got out to talk to the patrolman.

"Sorry, sir, you have to take another road to Mill City. This road will be blocked here for at least two hours."

"Can we go up there and watch?" Jimmy asked.

The patrolman glanced at him with a funny look. "Uh, there has been a pretty bad accident, why don't you just drive around," he said.

"Yeah, I know, I have the person's mother and his wife in the car."

The patrolman walked up to the Jimmy's Chevy and shined his light in the back seat. He saw the ladies in each other's arms obviously disturbed and crying.

"Uh, ladies, are you sure you want to go up there. It won't be a pleasant sight."

"Oh, please, officer, we want to go, please let us," sobbed Bessie.

He turned to Jimmy. "Just pull in that turn out over there and stay with them, because if they get hysterical I want you to get them out of here."

"Yes sir," said Jimmy. He pulled into the turn out and helped them get out. They seemed a little more in control now that they were here. They had their arms around each other as they walked slowly past the patrol car.

A large tow truck was backed up to the opening in the railing lowering its towline slowly to divers waiting below on the bank.

Chet the Low Sky town cop was there with his car lights trained on the tow truck so the operator could see. The divers had a portable light stand with one strong beam shining into the river. You could see the light reflecting off the top on Ralph's pickup roof. It was a scene out of hell.

The divers took the towline and dove at the back of Ralph's truck.

Slowly the light over the mountains grew as dawn came on. In about thirty minutes one of the divers surfaced and yelled to Chet, "Have the tow guy take up the slack, ok, slowly." The operator engaged the winch; the line picked up the slack and became tight.

The diver yelled, "Ok hold it." The other diver surfaced.

"Looks like it will hold, tell him to start hauling it out but slowly, we don't want to break this cable."

The big winch started to whine; the tow truck squatted down as the weight of the pickup was felt. In a few minutes the tailgate of the pickup lifted above the water; then the bed, then the back window of the cab became visible.

The window was green with algae but you could see Ralph's skull through it.

It happened quickly. Bessie's knees buckled and she started to fall in a dead faint. Jimmy moved to her and caught her just before she hit the ground.

He looked at Becky—she was white as a sheet and shaking, her eyes wide and staring. "Becky, come on, we got to get Bessie out of here." He picked Bessie up in his arms and started toward the car. Becky was rooted to the spot but started to follow when he was half way back towards the car. He got them into the car and went to the highway patrolman.

"Excuse me, sir, do you have some smelling salts?"

The patrolman went to his car and brought him a packet. "Just break it under her nose," he said.

Jimmy broke the packet and Bessie snapped awake.

"What happened," she said.

"You fainted," Becky told her.

She tried to get out of the car. "I must go back."

Jimmy and Becky grabbed her at the same time.

"Mrs. Skinner, you can't go back, the policeman said you have to leave," he lied.

They got her seat belt on and took her home. When they got her in the house both Becky and Katie took her upstairs; in about fifteen minutes Katie came down.

"How's it going up there?" Jimmy asked her.

"It's ok, we got her into bed and Becky is in with her. She told me to tell you thanks, and we both can go now, she'll handle it."

Katie and he walked outside. He looked at his watch, "Six-thirty. Well, the café is open and I need a cup of coffee. Would you like one also, Katie?"

"Sure, I really need something. How did it go out there?"

"It was awful. Come on, I'll tell you over coffee."

They walked the two blocks to the café. After ordering coffee and breakfast he told her all that happened out at the wreck site, leaving out the part of seeing Ralph's skull. She started to weep a little. The waitress saw her tears and came over to ask if she was ok.

Jimmy then told her the story and knew by noon the whole town would know.

He walked her to her front door. They parted; she had to go to work and he was going out to help his Dad for the day.

Before he walked away she shyly took his hand and said, "That was a wonderful thing, you did this morning, Jimmy."

"Becky said you were a good guy. I see now that she was right."

He watched her go in her door and thought, *What a sweet girl. Maybe Becky was right, maybe she was the one he should date.*

He went to his car and drove out to his folks' farm where he retold the story for the third time for his parents.

The funeral didn't take place for over a week. The police had to question Becky and Bessie and the coroner had to check what was left of Ralph's body to find out if there was any foul play. Routine they said, on this kind of case, but the whole town buzzed with rumors and innuendo.

Finally the body was handed to the family. Ralph's brother Jack had been home helping Bessie and Becky since getting word the same day the body was found. He had taken over all things related to the ladies and Sonny so they didn't ask Jimmy for anymore help. Jimmy had a long haul to San Francisco and didn't get back until the day before the funeral. When he got home he went to see Katie at the Thornton's store. She filled him in over dinner at the café of all the things that had been happening since he had left. He asked her to go to the funeral with him and she accepted.

So began the courtship of Jimmy Dale Burns and Katie April Overmars.

Chinook:

One beautiful spring day in May 1919 a man and a very pregnant young woman knocked at the door of the Hill boarding house in Portland.

They had just arrived that morning on a ship from Poland on which they had left, almost three months before, from the port of Gdansk.

They had traveled through the Panama Canal which then was just five years old. They were a particularly beautiful young couple. They both had sky blue eyes and blond hair. She looked to be twenty-one, twenty-two, he around thirty. They couldn't speak a word of English, but through sign language they conveyed to the landlady Ethel Hill that they needed a room.

The Hill boarding house was a home for professional men. It had eight bedrooms, a parlor, where families or ladies could visit the men, and a smoking lounge. One large bathroom and a dining room with a table for eight. The private quarters for Mrs. Hill consisted of a bedroom, office/storage room, and a large eat-in kitchen. This kitchen was where Mrs. Hill took her meals and where she made and served breakfast and dinner for everyone living at the house.

There was a large back garden where the guests would walk or sit on warm summer evenings or on Sundays.

Mrs. Hill's husband had died about two years before. They never had children, and neither of them had living relatives; Mrs. Hill was terribly lonely. She couldn't turn this young couple away, especially since the woman was pregnant. So even though her house was full up, she moved the young couple into her bedroom and she moved into the storage room. The young man got a job on the riverfront in a salmon cannery, and also helped around the boarding house when not working at the cannery.

She could never pronounce their names in the Polish way, Wladyslaw, and Marciej, so called them Walter and Margaret. They seemed to accept that and so for about a year went on like this, all parties happy and Mrs. Hill no longer lonely.

About two months after they arrived, the baby was born. A beautiful little girl they named Ursula, Mrs. Hill thought it a horrible name but said nothing. It was a wonderful time for Mrs. Hill with the baby there. While she made the meals Margaret would sit in the kitchen with her baby at her breast and they would converse, the best they could. This way Margaret would learn English.

Mrs. Hill would help with the baby, changing its diaper and clothing, and bathing it. When the baby was ten months old Margaret weaned the baby from her breast and started working at the salmon cannery with Walter. Mrs. Hill now was in complete charge of the baby during the day and this started the best time of her life. She came to love this small blond creature without reservation, as much as if she herself had given it birth.

Then the tragedy struck.

A belt rubbing on a wooden beam in the upper loft area of the cannery caused a fire to break out. Smoldering in the attic it finally exploded to life engulfing the back half of the cannery where Walter and Margaret worked. They tried to run out the back of the building but the fire engulfed them and they died instantly. When they didn't come home that night, Mrs. Hill started to worry. Then the gentlemen guests came home from the town with the news.

Taking the baby Mrs. Hill took the tram, then walked down to the riverfront to the where the cannery was. She looked everywhere, talked to anyone who would listen but no one knew what happened to the beautiful couple from Poland. She waited a couple of days then went to the police station to see what she should do.

Officially the people killed could not be identified; the fire had been so intense that all that was found were some bones. The police listened to her story and told her they would make inquiries and to keep the baby until such time as they could find some relatives. A year passed and the police never contacted her.

One of her gentlemen guests was a young lawyer and with him she went back to the police. The police had no record of the young couple immigrating into the country. So it was concluded that they had entered United States illegally.

*   *   *

The young lawyer arranged for a temporary permit to allow Mrs.

48

Hill to keep the orphaned child, for otherwise the court would have put it in an orphanage.

The fiancée of the lawyer was the only daughter of a state judge; he was based in Portland. She pleaded with her father to rule on the case in favor of Mrs. Hill. When he seemed reluctant to award a baby to a woman who was sixty-four she begged him to visit the boarding house to see how wonderful a mother Mrs. Hill was.

After spending an afternoon at the boarding house he ruled that Mrs. Hill could adopt Ursula.

The name of the child was officially changed to April Hill; Mrs. Hill became a mother.

April grew tall and beautiful; she was a sweet hard working girl, but painfully shy. An intelligent person, she graduated at the top of her class in high school. Mrs. Hill was now eighty-two, and although she still had a twinkle in her eye she needed help with the boarding house.

April became manager and ran the day to day business. In February 1939 a young doctor moved into the boarding house. He had just graduated from the University of California medical school and was taking his internship at Portland General Hospital.

Chinook:

John Robin Overmars had grown up in Boise, Idaho. His family, from Ohio, had come west in the late 1850s on the Oregon Trail.

His ancestor's wife was heavy with child when they reached the treasure valley. They dropped out of the wagon train, and waited for the baby to be born.

There was a trading post there and the proprietor liked this young family and offered land on the Boise River for the help he needed running the store.

That young family became one of the leading families of the area and the baby was John's great grandfather.

John was very happy he had found a boarding house so close to the hospital, and the perk was the angel who ran it. It was Love at first sight. Holy cow, he couldn't believe it—this vision, this lovely sweet girl and she was free and single. He wondered about the local men; was there something wrong with them, were they all blind?

The first Saturday in September 1939 they were married. Mrs. Hill gave away her precious daughter and added a son-in-law. Her happiness knew no bounds.

Until the next June when her grandchild was born, then she fell in love all over again. The baby was a little girl and they called her Katie April. Katie was a picture, the apple of her father's eye, and the joy of her mother and doting grandmother. For a year and a half the family lived a near perfect life, then their world fell apart.

December 7, 1941, Pearl Harbor.

Within a month John joined the Navy as a doctor. At first he was stationed in Hawaii, where he helped with the wounded of the bombing attack and then later as the casualties poured in from the early battles of the war in the Pacific.

He hated being behind the lines, though, and in 1943 was sent to India. The need for doctors was high in the South East Asian Theater.

Early in 1944 the Japanese launched an attack into India. The hospital where John was working was overrun and he was wounded and captured. The Japanese Command needing doctors took him to Singapore and tried to force him to work in the hospital there. He refused to help the Japanese and was sent to a road gang along with local captured British troops and civilians. He almost died, his wound never properly healed and he was down to under one hundred pounds when the Japanese commander surrendered on August 14, 1945.

For the last two weeks before the end of the war he, along with the other captured troops, was forced to dig long trenches. The Japanese installed machine guns at the head of each trench; they all knew that they would be killed and that they were digging their own graves.

The day before the scheduled slaughter the order came from Tokyo to the Japanese commander that the war was over and he surrendered to the British consul.

April and Mrs. Hill had not known if John was dead or alive for almost two years. All the British and Americans would say is he was missing in action.

April had stayed in contact with John's family in Boise. Finally about October a letter came from the British Consul in San Francisco.

John was in a hospital in London; he was out of trouble and would be home before Christmas.

In tears of relief she called his mother and they cried on the phone for over ten minutes. When John came home he was not the same man that had left four years before. His personality had changed—he was now quiet, moody and introspective, where before he had been a smiling happy-go-lucky outgoing type.

For six months he seemed lost. In bed at night his need for April frightened her; he seemed like he couldn't get enough sex with her. Sometimes they made love twice a night. When finally he would fall asleep the dreams and the terrors would come. He would cry out, would yell, sometimes talk in a language totally unknown to her. April became pregnant the first month he was back. When the baby started to kick he slowly came out of his lethargy, but he was still restless.

He came home one day from the hospital and announced he had taken a residency in a small town called Low Sky where he would be the only doctor in the town. April and Ethel were ecstatic; they put the boarding house on the market and with the money purchased a large Victorian house on the main street of Low Sky.

The front parlor they made into a waiting room and the dining room into an examination room. They all five lived in the back. Mrs. Hill died in 1950 at the age of ninety-five. In 1954 the town council passed a resolution to build a hospital for John.

Katie wasn't as beautiful as her mother. She had plain blond hair, was chubby, and she was very shy. When she came to school, on the first day of the year that she was in the seventh grade, she had on her first bra. The boys all stared at her and giggled behind her back.

All the other girls either had flat chests, or just small bulges in the front of their dresses. Katie's front pushed out quite a lot, the beginnings of the large breasts she would have in maturity.

Katie had a crush on the Baptist preacher's son, Donald Manning. The boys dared, and double dared him to touch Katie's tits.

A Disney documentary, *Bear Valley*, came to the small local theatre in town. All the children from the grade school went to the movie as a field trip. Katie was pleased when Donald sat next to her at the movie. When the lights went out he slipped his arm around her and cupped his hand over her breast.

All the children, except Katie, knew what was going to happen. She didn't know what to do, the other girls were looking and the boys were whispering to one another. She sat frozen, and didn't resist Donald at all. After the movie, the teasing began. Some of the girls went to the teacher and told her what had happened.

The teachers split up the boys and girls into different classrooms and lectured them on proper behavior now that they were growing up. Katie was mortified; she retreated deeper into her shell. She started to wear baggy clothes to hide her breasts, and lost the few friends she had.

As she grew older she discovered romance novels. The author Susan Pink, who wrote the fifty or so famous flame novels: *Flame over Italy, Flame over Lincoln, Flame over France,* etc., became her favorite author. When her father came home and found her nose buried in some new book he would gently rib her, asking, "Good evening, Princess, which part of the world is burning tonight?"

When she became sixteen she became a part time cashier at Thornton's market. April and John discussed their daughter's problem, deciding that if she wanted to do this they would give her support.

They hoped, as she grew older, she would become less introverted and get more friends. April noted that she was painfully shy when she was in school, but became very much more open once she met and married John, and she had survived just fine. Katie missed the homecoming games and dances, and the proms. One of the less popular boys asked her to the senior prom, but she declined saying she had to work that night. When she was done with her job, chores or homework she would open a book and escape into thirteenth century Spain, or seventeenth century old California, etc., where all Ladies were beautiful and all Heroes charming, handsome, and brave.

All the while under those baggy, unflattering clothes Katie was becoming a very beautiful young woman, with an exquisite figure.

Marie Thornton, the wife of the owner of the market, took an interest in Katie. She was the third daughter of a surgeon in Eugene, Oregon, and when growing up always wore the best and most fashionable clothes. Her mother taught her taste and she had plenty of money to shop all the best stores.

When she was attending the University of Oregon she met Peter Thornton, the third son of the owner of the Eugene's two largest supermarkets; after graduation they were married. Each of Peter's brothers took over a market, so about five years after graduation Peter and Marie bought the old Low Sky market, expanded it and made it into the largest grocery in the area.

Peter and Marie had two boys and Marie never had a chance to hand down her knowledge of fashion and taste.

This is where Katie enters the picture. Marie liked Katie very much, thought her a sweet and lovely girl. She could never understand why her mother let her dress in such unflattering clothing; after all, April was the local doctor's wife and had money to dress her only daughter well.

Of course April herself could only be described as aggressively plain, a physically stunning woman but without the slightest taste in fashion. However Katie was always very clean, so Marie guessed April did take interest in her to the best of her ability. Marie then sensed that she was needed to fill the fashion gap.

When Katie graduated from high school she didn't want to go to University. Her parents tried to convince her of the fun she would have, not least the education that would prepare her for whatever course in life she chose. But she steadfastly refused to leave home. John and April threw up their hands and let her stay home; they figured that when she matured she might change her mind. Katie started as a full time cashier at Thornton's Market two months after graduating, spending the summer at her grandparents' home in Boise.

Katie's grandparents loved her very much and had called John and April to invite her for the summer. Grandmother took Katie to her hairdresser to have her hair done about a week after Katie arrived. "Gloria," Mrs. Overmars said to her in an aside, "cut her hair in a bob, with a wave on top and give her a blond rinse." Next grandmother took her to the cosmetics department of the Bon Marché. There she bought her a pink lipstick, a blush, and some face powder. The beautician showed her how to apply these beauty products and Katie was on her way to being a new woman. "WOW" everyone said, "what a difference, what a pretty girl!" This made Katie very happy so she decided she would keep this new look.

After Katie had worked for about a month Marie asked her if she and her mother would like to go to Salem shopping one day. Marie went shopping once a month, sometimes to Salem, which had a very nice if small downtown-shopping district, and to Portland when the major seasonal collections came out.

April had always greatly admired Marie Thornton and her beautiful fashionable clothing. She hoped to learn about fashion from Marie and also hoped she would influence Katie to wear nice stylish clothing. So in September the three women went to Salem for a day of shopping.

When Katie arrived home that night she arrived with four new dresses, three new pant and blouse outfits, new casual and dress shoes and most important new bras, panties, girdles and nylons. That night she sat her father down in the living room and gave him a fashion show. John was astounded; no longer was she his little girl. Before him strutted a lady he had never seen before, his baby, now a fully-grown woman.

A few months after the fashion show for her father, Katie heard Becky was pregnant and the father of the baby, Ralph Skinner, had abandoned her.

She went to see Becky, and they became close friends. The old Katie would not have gone anywhere near Becky, but her confidence was at a point now where socially she could handle a situation such as this.

The town had come down hard on Becky; she became the object of wagging tongues and harsh innuendo.

Mrs. Burns was the most vociferous of the local ladies. She was irked and humiliated that Becky could do this to her Jimmy. Up to this time she had liked Becky and her family, and was looking forward to having her as a daughter-in-law. The scandal of course changed this and she made sure, with rancor, that all the ladies she had any influence over dropped Becky.

Becky, who had always been a popular girl, took this excommunication very hard. Therefore she was very grateful to Katie.

After Sonny was born Katie would help her with him. They spent many a happy evening or Sunday afternoons playing, feeding and cuddling the baby.

After a year of being a full time cashier Marie had Katie promoted to dry goods manager and buyer. She would be in charge of all non-grocery items. These items included non-prescription drugs, party supplies, paper products, shampoos, skin creams and soaps. The Thorntons were very happy with her work, and Katie was happy with her life. She did not really need a boy friend; the only lovers she needed were between the covers of whatever "bodice ripper" she was involved with at the time. It was Becky, who taking advantage of their friendship, dumped her problem with Jimmy into Katie's lap.

The morning of the funeral Jimmy called his Mom and Dad and told them he was taking Katie and would see them there.

Jimmy's mother was very happy that Jimmy and Katie seemed to be hitting it off. She being the daughter of the town doctor and his beautiful wife was quite a jump up the social scale from the Andersons.

She was now glad that Becky had that trash Ralph Skinner's kid and her Jimmy could be in his rightful place among the best of their town.

It was a typical early October morning. A ground fog had risen during the night and by the time Jimmy had arrived at Katie's house was starting to dissipate into a beautiful fall day.

He knocked on the door. "Good morning, Mrs. Overmars," he said.

"Well, Jimmy, how are you on this sad day?"

"Fine, thank you. Is Katie ready, do you know?"

"I think so, dear. Would you like to come in?"

They had restored the old Victorian house that they lived in. Gone now were the traces of the waiting and examination rooms that he had visited as a sick child. It was beautiful—hardwood floors and thick wool rugs, with painted walls a cream color with light blue trim. It was so different from his parents' farmhouse, which was clean but plain. He would like a house like this one day.

54

Katie came down the stairs and she was stunning. She was dressed all in black, which suited the occasion, and also suited her with her blond hair and blue eyes. Her dress was plain and she had a small round hat with a net veil that covered her face. She was very sad for Becky and had been crying. She was so beautiful and sweet looking that Jimmy's heart gave a lunge.

The Skinners belonged to the Catholic Church and Jimmy had never been in that church before. It had an organ and high ceiling, with windows of colored glass like the cathedrals he had seen in Europe, but on a smaller scale.

Katie, being a Catholic, helped him stand and kneel at appropriate times during the mass. He was impressed with the formal Mass, the singing and the Latin, so different than the Baptist church he had attended with his mom, and where at age sixteen he had been baptized.

After the service they went to the small Low Sky cemetery for the burial. A tent had been set up over the casket and some chairs. Ralph's older brother, Jack, escorted Becky and Bessie. He had his arm around each of them and held them in a firm but gentle grip. It seemed to Jimmy that while Jack looked like Ralph in the face, he was a bigger man in stature.

When the graveside service was done, most of the people that attended the service went to Bessie's house where a lunch was provided.

The ladies of the community had volunteered to cook and dishes of food appeared for the mourners to eat. Katie went to Becky and gave her a hug. Tears rolled down both girls' cheeks and they kissed and cried together.

As Katie turned to Bessie, Jimmy, not knowing what to do, held out his hand to Becky. She took his hand and moved to him and gave him a long hug and a kiss on the cheek. "Dearest Jimmy," she whispered, "I never thanked you for taking us to the river that night." She looked at him and dabbed her eyes with her handkerchief. "I'll never forget your kindness."

He was touched. "Gosh, Becky, that was nothing, I was glad to do it."

He turned to Bessie, she took his hand and kissed him on the cheek also. "Thank you so much Jimmy dear, for that night you took us to the river. We could have never made it without you."

Jack took his hand and shook it too, thanking him for his help.

As he turned to Katie he noticed her eyes kind of shining as she looked at him. She was thinking, *Is this the knight in shinning armor I have been waiting for?*

55

He looked so handsome and vulnerable as he stood there. He was like Sir Oliver de Anjou, the knight in *Flame over Lincoln.*

Sir Oliver was in the service of King Steven of England, but he loved the beautiful Eloise of Kent who was the handmaiden of Maud the daughter of Henry the first and claimant to the throne of England.

The civil war raged on and Eloise and Sir Oliver were cruelly separated for twenty years; sometimes they would meet and the passion would flow. Sometimes there was only time for a kiss, or a few shared words of love. Finally the war ended and they were allowed to marry but by then she was thirty-nine and he forty-one.

Well, hopefully she would discover if Jimmy was the one before that.

After the condolences and lunch, they said their good-byes and Jimmy took Katie home.

7

Jimmy was going to Dad and Mom's after he took Katie home but he was just emotionally drained.

He had been to one funeral in his life and that was his Grandfather Burns when he was sixteen. Both his mother's parents had died when he was in the service and overseas so he hadn't had a chance to attend their funerals. He hadn't known what an ordeal it could be, especially since the person had been so young, and so widely known in the small town.

This was the first of his classmates, and first person of his age to die that he personally knew. All of a sudden it came home to him that not only old people like his grandparents died but anyone who could make a mistake, like Ralph did that night.

He lay on his bed and slowly his thoughts and fears of death were replaced with thoughts of Becky and what was going to happen now. Pretty much the bridge had been burnt between them, and now of course Katie was in the picture.

He thought about each one's pluses and minuses.

First Becky: he loved her still, he was willing at one time to overlook Ralph and take her with baby and all.

Physically Becky and Katie were very different; she was petite, had a beautiful face, jet black hair and blue-gray eyes. Though he had seen her naked a few times before he went away he had never made love to her.

The thought now of her naked body stirred him deeply; Becky was very beautiful naked. She had a nice shape with a firm belly and a round little butt with slender tapered legs. His only experience so far had been Kathleen; she had had a baby also, so he figured they would be the same physically, down there. He had noticed Becky had rather larger hips than before, and her belly bulged out slightly.

She had looked awful during the funeral, her cheeks white, skin shallow with red splotches, eyes red from crying, and hair kind of straggly.

Still when she thanked him, and hugged him, for helping them he felt a surge in his heart. The point was though she was the mother of another man's child.

She had slept with the guy he had disliked more than anyone in school and had rejected him.

He knew he could never have a child because of the sickness he had got from Kathleen; maybe if Becky would have had a child from someone he didn't know it would be different. Everyone would know forever that she had only Ralph's kid, and he wouldn't be man enough to father another child with her.

However, with Katie, people could assume it was her who couldn't conceive.

Damn, the resentment curdled in his chest. *He gave her plenty of chances.*

She could have stayed his girl when he was in basic training and tech school in the Airforce. It would only have been three months; he would have been gone, then they could have been married.

Then he gave her another chance when he came home and she shoved that in his face.

Maybe he should give up. Well, he resolved if she wanted to change her mind she could come to him this time and beg his forgiveness. Katie was a beautiful girl, but not as fine featured as Becky. Still she had a remarkable figure.

She was taller than Becky, who was five foot two; Katie was more like five foot six. She was a very sweet girl, had a good reputation and attended the Catholic Church regularly.

Her father was the doctor in town and that was a plus on the social scale. Also she was rich and her Dad and Mom would probably give them all they wanted in the money line. He didn't love Katie like he loved Becky, but he thought that a minor thing when weighted against the other advantages.

He thought he would keep taking out Katie and if Becky wanted him she could fight for him.

Katie, when Jimmy had brought her home, talked with her mother for awhile. She poured out her grief to her and her mother had hugged her and explained away the fright and sadness she felt.

When she felt better she went up to her room to think about Jimmy and Becky. She knew all about them, Becky had been Jimmy's girl all through school and it was always rumored they would marry after graduation.

Why they didn't, she would probably never know. She had asked Becky once why it had worked out with Ralph the way it did. Becky had just said, "I fell out of love with Jimmy, and in love with Ralph."

Well it really wasn't any of her business, so she just let it go and had never asked Becky to explain it further. Then Jimmy had come home and the romance seemed to pick up where it left off, with the small complication of Sonny of course.

Suddenly Becky started to talk up Jimmy to her, a swell guy, solid, good job etc. She was confused, but she had always liked Jimmy when they were kids. He had teased her a lot. While at the time it mortified her secretly she was glad he noticed her.

She was finding it rather nice to have Jimmy around now; they met for lunch and sometimes dinner at the café, when he was home.

She was very glad he had taken her to the funeral today. She wanted it to continue, but she guessed it was up to Jimmy and Becky to solve this troika. She would lay low, and let the others take the lead.

Becky was totally exhausted when finally the last of the people had left Bessie's house and the ladies had cleaned up for them. She had helped Bessie to bed and came down to say good night to Jack.

She had collapsed in his arms when he hugged her. She wept for a few minutes as he held her.

Then she pulled away kissing him on the cheek.

"Jack, dearest, thank you for all you've done for your mother and me. You have been an absolute angel for these two weeks."

"Gosh, Becky, I want to thank you. Mother relies on you and Sonny more than you know. I know her love for you two will help her pull through this a lot faster," he said.

They talked for a few more minutes, with their arms around each other's waists, then parted each to their respective bedrooms.

Becky got ready for bed, took two aspirins and lay there trying to sleep. Sleep wouldn't come at first; she stared at the ceiling and her thoughts turned to Jimmy. If she'd waited for a couple of months, and not have broken up with him, her future would be assured.

She would already be married to him, have a couple of babies, and the years ahead would not be filled with question marks.

Not marrying Jimmy when she had the chance could cost her a lot of grief and pain in the future.

She lay there thinking of the wedding she and Jimmy would have had. She in a long white wedding gown, all their friends and family there.

Chinook:

Becky's mother had been devastated, she had wanted her only

daughter to be married properly in a church and she, as the proud Mother-of the-Bride, would beam over the happy guests. Since almost from the moment of Becky's birth she had thought that day would be her happiest.

The shame of her daughter's out of wedlock pregnancy, the disappearance of the father and the resulting fallout, caused her to pull back from Becky. It's not that she didn't still love her; she just didn't trust her anymore.

That was why when Becky wanted to live with Bessie during and after her pregnancy she didn't say any word to the contrary.

After the wedding they would have been stationed in Europe, and she could have seen the great cities she had learned about in history and geography in school.

Just think, London and Paris, she thought, but she didn't know Jimmy would go there. Things could have been so different, for one Ralph would be alive and maybe married. Oh well!

Now, the immediate problem was did she want Jimmy back? Then the thought came to her, *What about Jack?* She knew he was attracted to her; he was taller than Ralph and had very powerful arms; when he hugged her she felt safe and cared for.

The best part was he had a very good job at Boeing and lived in Seattle; that could be the ticket out of Low Sky and Slayton which, just lately, she had grown tired of.

"Well," she smiled to herself, "she could have either Jimmy or Jack, if she wanted." With that thought she slipped into a deep dreamless sleep.

The next morning was Sunday; Jimmy arrived at the warehouse at seven A.M. to ready himself to take a truck and trailer load of canned vegetables to Denver.

He called Katie at home just before they left; he knew she attended ten o'clock Mass and would be up.

They talked briefly about the funeral. He made a date with her for when he would return. Dinner and a movie in Salem was suggested, and told her he would miss her.

Katie had just stepped out of the bath when Jimmy's call came. She was very thrilled he had thought of her, and quickly accepted the promise of a date when he returned in a couple of weeks.

What interested her the most was when he told her he would miss her, Sir Oliver always said that to Eloise of Kent when they parted, for the war swirled around them and they had allegiances to different sides.

They had kissed passionately of course; but this was a start and maybe Jimmy wouldn't go back to Becky.

While Jimmy was gone she would risk, discretely, probing Becky's mind on this subject. She went to Mass with a small smile turning up the corners of her mouth. When Becky awoke the next morning she went down to fix breakfast for the family.

She made a large hardy breakfast because Jack was heading home to Seattle after he had eaten.

Bessie came down with Sonny and they found they were all starved; they had been too distraught the day before to eat much.

After breakfast they followed Jack out to his car. He kissed Bessie and Sonny, and then took Becky into his arms. While he said his good-bye to her he noticed she pushed her body against his and his lips were met by her lips when he was going to kiss her cheek. He felt his cock quicken, and she must have felt it too because she gave him a smile.

As he drove away he thought, *Well, well, maybe I should look into this situation when the time is right.*

Becky had felt the movement down below when she kissed Jack. Now she knew he cared for her and if she wanted him, after a period of mourning, she would have him.

Her life was beginning to look more stable now!

Jimmy had a good trip out to Denver. While there he looked up his old buddy from the Air Force who worked for Coors. The buddy had just gotten married to the daughter of one of the Brew Masters and was really surprised and happy to see Jimmy. He thought he would never see him again.

They had a beer after he had finished his shift. He told Jimmy about the girl he had written to all those years back home in Minneapolis and that when he returned found she was pregnant.

He was devastated, had come to Denver and now was glad that it had turned out like it had.

He called his new bride and they invited Jimmy for dinner. She was a pretty little thing; black hair, blue eyes and they were obviously in love with each other.

Her family owned a house in a new ski resort called Vail, and they were into skiing in the winter and backpacking in the summer. Most weekends found them in the mountains. Her father had also got him into fly-fishing, what a great life he was looking forward to. They asked Jimmy about his life.

He told them about his sickness; he left out the part about

Kathleen, and his early discharge. He told them about his job driving all over the West and about Katie, leaving out Becky. When he left them they made him promise he would look them up each time he came to Denver; he promised he would.

When the depot had unloaded the canned vegetables from his truck, they loaded up sacks of toasted soybeans, due for Japan.

He headed for San Francisco, where a ship was awaiting him. He arrived home Friday evening one day less than the two weeks he was supposed to be gone.

He got back to Low Sky about ten o'clock that night and went to Rocky's Tavern for a cold Lucky Lager. Doc was in his usual place and they talked; they were becoming very close.

Doc gave him all the gossip that his "poor old mind could remember."

Nothing had really happened since the funeral, so all was quiet on the home front. Saturday morning he called Katie, and they made a date for that evening. He showered and went to see his Mom and Dad.

He was looking forward to the first real date with Katie.

He helped Dad load a steer on to his truck and they took it to the slaughterhouse, where it would be processed into meat for the house.

Dad said he was getting too old to slaughter his own animals anymore.

8

Chinook:
First Date: casual, non-kissing.

Jimmy cleaned and waxed his Chevy; he showered and went to pick up
Katie at her house.

He walked up to her front door; he was a bit nervous even though
he knew Katie's parents. He wasn't used to picking up a girl for a formal date.

Mrs. Overmars let him in. "She is not quite ready, Jimmy," she
said. "The doctor is in the living room, could you wait in there?"

"Sure, Mrs. Overmars." Jimmy walked into the living room, "Hi,
Doctor Overmars," he said.

"Hi, Jimmy, come on in and have a seat." The doctor put down the
paper he was reading. "I guess we men are destined to have to wait for
our women. How are your parents?"

"They're fine, sir, thank you for asking."

They chatted about the local fishing. The doctor had been
fly-fishing since a small lad in Idaho. When he had time now, which
was not often, he was usually seen on the local river pursuing trout,
steelhead or salmon, each to its season.

Jimmy loved to fish also but used natural bait: worms, caddis fly
larvae or salmon eggs.

This year's good steelhead season on the Thomas River naturally
led them to talk about the discovery of Ralph's body and funeral, and
then Katie walked in and all conversation ceased for a few seconds
while the men admired her.

She had on a light pink blouse and cream colored slacks, her hair
done up in a pony-tail with a cream colored scarf.

Jimmy felt decidedly underdressed, though he had on black slacks
and a light blue shirt. The quality of his clothes was "off the shelf,"
while hers were "designer."

Katie's parents saw them to the door. They each kissed her on the
cheek and wished them a good time.

They drove to Salem and ate on Main Street in a small restaurant called the Daisy Diner. They talked easily about old school friends, her job and his job. She was fascinated about all the places he had been.

After they finished eating they walked across the street to the Victoria Movie Theater and saw a comedy with Cary Grant, the title of which he could never remember after. He had her home at eleven o'clock that night. He opened her car door and walked her to the door. She gave him her hand. "Jimmy, thank you so much for the lovely evening. It's been so much fun."

He was touched by her heartfelt thank you, and picking up courage said, "I'll be gone all this week to California but would you like to go to the Candle Light Lounge next Saturday night for dinner and dancing?"

The Candle Light Lounge was considered the best restaurant in the area, a place where husbands took wives for anniversaries, or birthdays. They had a dance floor and a live band on weekends. Her mother and father had been there for all their anniversaries since moving to Low Sky.

She raised her eyes to his. "Oh yes," she breathed.

"Great," he said. "I'll make reservations for eight o'clock if that is all right, and I'll pick you up at seven."

"Oh yes, that will be fantastic," she said.

She went into the house and stood with her back to the door. Her mother called to her as she passed by her parents' bedroom. "Have fun, darling?"

"Oh yes, Mother, it was lots of fun."

She stood there for a minute. "Is something wrong, sweetie?" her mother asked.

"No, but Jimmy asked me to go to the Candle Light Lounge next Saturday and I don't know how to dance."

"Oh well," said April, "we will practice this week to my records, and by Saturday you will dance like Ginger Rogers."

Chinook:
Second Date: a first kiss date.

Jimmy got back the next Friday afternoon and was home in Low Sky at about five o'clock. He washed his face and went to Rocky's Tavern where he talked to Doc. "I have been seeing Katie Overmars lately," he told Doc.

"Yes I know," said Doc. "It has been the gossip of the week here.

64

Everybody who is anybody in Low Sky society has had nothing but Katie and Jimmy on their lips."

"Oh sure," said Jimmy, going slightly red.

"Hey Rocky, I think our latest lover here needs a beer to quench the fires of passion." Everyone in the bar laughed. Now Jimmy really did turn red.

Mr. Rocknell came over with a Lucky Lager, and slapped Jimmy on the shoulder. "That's alright, boy, these guys are just jealous, so drink this beer because you look like you caught fire."

The guys in the bar all doubled over with laughter, but in a few minutes it all died down, and Jimmy returned to a normal color.

He talked to Doc, played a game of pool with some of the guys there and went out to his parents' for dinner.

After dinner Dad asked him what he had planned for the next day. He said he had to go to Salem to buy a suit and new shoes because he was taking Katie to the Candle Light Lounge for dinner Saturday night.

There was a silence for a few seconds then his sister screamed, "Jimmy is in love, Jimmy is in love!"

"Hush up girl," said his mom. "Well I guess the rumors going around were accurate then; every busybody in town told me that you were going on a big date."

"I wonder how they found out so fast," said Jimmy.

"Well you know this town Jimmy," said his Dad. "Anything around here is news. I would like to ride to Salem with you. Could you drop me off at the livestock auction before you shop?"

"Ok, Dad," Jimmy said. "Sounds like a winner."

*   *   *

On Saturday morning Jimmy picked up Dad and they went into Salem. He dropped him off at the livestock auction and then went to Kenny's Men's Shop downtown. There he was fitted for and bought, a new blue suit, black shoes, white shirt and a conservative tie; navy blue with red stripes.

He found Dad at the auction and they had lunch at the café there.

"Uh, this isn't really any of my business son, " Dad shyly said, "but is Katie a serious girlfriend?"

"I don't know, Dad. I mean we have been seeing each other kind of casually for about a month or two and had one real date. I don't know how she feels about me, why?"

"Well your mother is very hot and heavy on you and Katie becoming an item. You know how she feels about Becky. Well, she ordered me to talk up Katie to you. I don't really know the girl, though, except her father and mother are very good people. Also she is a very pretty girl, the best one in town, that's for sure." Dad looked embarrassed.

Jimmy smiled gave him a pat on the back. "Ok, Dad, if Mom asks I'll tell her you did your duty."

A look of profound relief came over Dad's face. "Thanks son," he said.

Jimmy took Dad home and then went down to Pie Parkinson's Shell station and washed and cleaned up his car.

He filled up the tank and went home and got ready for the first formal date in his life.

At seven P.M. sharp he walked up to the Overmars' front door. Once again he was ushered into the living room where Dr. Overmars was sitting. They chatted about Jimmy's job; the doctor seemed very interested.

Katie had told her parents that he traveled all over the West, and had the responsibility of a large expensive truck.

Jimmy found that he liked the doctor a lot; they talked very easily together.

Katie then made her entrance with her mother following closely behind.

Jimmy almost gasped; Katie was simply the most beautiful girl he had ever seen. She had on a low cut red dress that showed her cleavage slightly without being vulgar. Her blond hair swept back in a way that made her blue eyes stand out. Red lipstick made her lips seem full and voluptuous. Her mother had brought her camera and Jimmy and Katie posed for a couple of snapshots.

The evening went like a charm.

Katie had never drank a cocktail but ordered and slowly sipped a sloe-gin fizz; her mother told her that was a sweet and mild drink and the one she always ordered when the occasion warranted.

Jimmy had a Tom Collins, and they ordered steaks which was the specialty of the house. After dinner they danced slow dances to the band, sitting through the fast dances. At eleven o'clock they left and half an hour later were on Katie's front porch. Katie didn't give her hand this time. She leaned slightly toward him. "Thank you, Jimmy, I had a wonderful evening," she said.

"Will you be gone next weekend?"

"Yes I am afraid so. I will be going to Los Angeles with a load tomorrow, then to Salt Lake City with a load of citrus, so they tell me, then back to San Francisco with a truck loaded with packages of salt.

"I am not sure when I'll return but I'll give you a call when I'm in Salt Lake City if you want. I should know better then."

"Oh yes, call me. I want you to come to dinner at my house. Mother asked me to invite you."

"Ok that sounds great. I'll be looking forward to it this entire trip."

He leaned forward slowly, to give her a chance to back away, put his hands gently on her shoulders and touched her lips with his.

She didn't back away but leaned toward him slightly more.

Her lips were warm and soft, they tasted of lipstick. His body exploded, but he didn't grab her like he wanted.

He pulled slowly back after the kiss and looked into her eyes. They were soft and limp. She sighed. "Oh Jimmy, be sure and call me soon."

"I will, darling," he said.

He walked to his car after she went in and closed the door.

His body seethed with passion; he didn't want to walk away and he wanted more of her lips, more of her smell, more of her soft skin, but that would come.

This next trip would be a long one and he wouldn't be thinking of Becky or Kathleen at all this time.

When Katie closed the door she leaned her back against it for a few moments. She was twenty-three years old and this had been her first kiss.

It was everything she had always thought it would be—soft, sweet and romantic, the kind of kiss heroes in books gave their ladies.

She had wanted Jimmy to kiss her more but she had gone in because she couldn't control this situation, and it scared her a little. She had always controlled any situation before but this was different, deeper, out of her grasp.

As she walked past her parents' room, her mother opened the door. "How did it go, sweetheart?" she asked.

Katie looked at her and smiled. "Wonderful, mother." She kissed Katie on the cheek and gently guided her toward her room.

They talked about the date, which waiter they had had, what food each had ordered, how good Jimmy danced and how her dancing had matched up, even though Katie had never danced before. How Jimmy held and helped her when she made a mistake.

When April got back in bed she laid there for a while wide awake, thinking.

John turned toward her. "I guess Cinderella has returned from the ball," he said stifling a yawn.

April looked at her husband. "Dear, do you like this boy?"

"Why yes, darling, he seems a fine young man. Why do you ask?"

"Well," said April, "I think we might be seeing a lot of him for the rest of our lives."

Before Katie fell asleep she knew she and Jimmy were no longer Lady Eloise and Sir Oliver.

She now was the Lady Charlotte de Ville, in *Flame Over France* with her blond hair and flashing blue eyes.

Jimmy was the Comte de Bourbon who was married to the dried up widow of the Duc de Burgundy, the Comtesse de Montreal, for political reasons. But he secretly loved Charlotte and stole her kisses when they could find time alone.

With a smile she fell into a deep sleep.

*   *   *

Jimmy didn't get home for over two weeks. He called Katie from Salt Lake City like he promised, and they set the date for dinner at her parents' house on the following Saturday night.

Chinook: The first dinner with the parents.

Jimmy came over early on Saturday evening. Dinner was to be at eight o'clock but they asked him for six.

When he arrived Katie met him at the door, gave him a quick kiss on the lips, a hug, and told him how much she missed him. She led him into the living room, where her Dad and Mom had a tray of coffee and cookies ready.

They were all interested about his trip and listened politely, while he reiterated his last two weeks.

After they had finished coffee Katie asked him to go for a walk.

They strolled the tree-lined streets of Low Sky. Katie had locked her arm through his arm as they walked. This signaled all the people watching that he was hers, and she could see his face from close up so she could observe his reaction to things she said. All in all it was a very satisfactory walk. She was pleased to confirm any rumors that might be circulating through the town concerning their status, now officially they were a couple.

Of course Jimmy had no inkling of the reason for the walk, he just thought it was a walk before dinner. He was very proud though that he was walking with the most desirable girl in town, the doctor's daughter.

"Aye, Laddie, you have cum up a wee bitty from me, have you no," the voice of Kathleen filled his head and made him jump. He looked around but Katie didn't notice his reaction. They returned to the house and the men talked while the ladies finished the dinner. After dinner the men returned to the living room while the ladies cleared the dishes and then served pie and ice cream before a crackling fire. Jimmy was very impressed with the formal, yet relaxed, atmosphere of the day, so different than he was used to.

After the pie and ice cream were consumed, Katie asked him to help her clear the dishes to the kitchen. She washed while he dried the dessert dishes, and when done Katie came into his arms. She raised her lips to be kissed, he pressed his lips to hers and moved the tip of his tongue slowly into her mouth. She hadn't expected that and her eyes flicked opened momentarily, but closed again while he tickled the tip of her little pink tongue with his. She was quite breathless after that kiss and he could feel himself start to harden down there.

He would have loved to go further but this was not the time nor the place, in her kitchen, with her parents two doors down the hall.

He looked over her shoulder and saw it was approaching ten o'clock by the kitchen clock. Kissing the tip of her nose he said, "Well, my darling, I think it is time to go." She gave him a small smile, took his hand and they returned to the living room.

He thanked her mom for the great evening and wonderful meal; he shook hands with the doctor and then Katie showed him to the door where they kissed again and said goodnight.

He walked out into the cold air of the night, his heart thumping and his blood racing. *Damn,* he thought to himself, *he could get used to this kind of living.*

Jimmy walked the few blocks to Rocky's Tavern. When he entered Doc was holding court at the end of the bar in his usual place.

"Ah, my son, they tell me you traipsed around the town with your lady fair on your arm this evening," he said smiling a rather suggestive smile at Jimmy.

Jimmy grinned. "Good news travels fast in this town I see."

Jimmy glanced up at Rocky. "Hey, Mr. Rocknell, get me a Lucky Lager and keep them coming."

Rocky Rocknell laughed. "Go get'em boy," he bellowed. "We need young love in this town, keeps the wagging tongues in business."

After Jimmy left Katie walked back into the living room where her parents sat. She sat in a big comfortable chair opposite them.

She must have been a bit flushed for her mother cocked an eyebrow at her. "Well, it seems we are proceeding apace here."

Katie flushed even deeper and sighed. "I don't know, Mother, he is a lovely boy, but we are just starting."

They both looked at Dad. "Oh no, don't drag me into this," said John. "It's up to Katie who she falls in love with, but I give my approval if this is the one you want, my dear."

Chinook: So the fish has been hooked, next he needs reeling in.

Jimmy left for Denver early the next morning, with a truck and trailer filled with canned peaches, cherries, pears and apricots. He spent the weekend with his old buddy, and his new wife, from the Air Force. It seemed the new wife was newly pregnant and his buddy had a smile wider than his face. He called Katie Sunday morning before she went to church, they talked for about fifteen minutes.

He told her the news about his friends and she sent her congratulations. Also he told her his mom wanted to have her over for dinner after church next Sunday; she told him she would call his mother and confirm the invitation.

Monday morning he drove to a large beef processing plant in Arvada, Colorado and they loaded up his truck with canned beef chili.

He headed up to Cheyenne, Wyoming where they filled up his trailer with packages of dried beef and jerky.

So filled he picked up highway US 30 and headed west.

Chinook: The first dinner with the other parents.

Jimmy was waiting outside the Catholic Church after ten o'clock mass on Sunday morning.

When Katie came out he took her to his parents' house for Sunday dinner.

9

She had been very nervous all week about this first formal meeting with Jimmy's parents. She had, of course, seen both Jimmy's Mom and Dad many times since she was a girl; however this would be different. She would be on display and she must impress them as best she could.

Family is very important to country and small town folk; family is not only love, acceptance and security but also recreation. You think about them, worry about them, plan your life around them and accommodate them in sickness and bad times, and they do the same for you.

So this was an important event for her, however a less important event for Jimmy.

While his family was very important to him he never for one moment thought they would not like anybody he chose for his friends, with the possible exception of Becky whom his mother seemed to loathe.

His mother would have learned to accept even Becky if she was the one he had chosen for his wife.

When they arrived, Buck, their farm dog, came up to the car. He was a large black, rumpled, Collie cross.

Dad said, when asked by strangers about Buck's lineage, "His mother was a Collie and his father was a fence jumper."

Jimmy told Katie to stay in the car. He got out and ruffled the big dog's ears. He went around to the passenger door to let Katie out.

Buck started barking as she stepped out of the car. "Don't worry, sweetheart, he is a good dog," he said.

"Come here, Buck, hold out your hand sweetheart."

Gingerly Katie held out her hand. Jimmy was holding Buck by the collar and said to the dog, "This is my girl, Buck, you protect her, not bite her."

The dog snuffled her hand then licked her palm, he started to wag his tail and she was initiated into Buck's pack.

When they walked into the house they came into a covered porch. On the left were two doors; one went to a large pantry filled with home canned foods and a very large chest freezer filled with meat. The other to a laundry room, with a washer and indoor lines for drying clothes in inclement weather.

They turned right and entered a large farm kitchen. The warmth and wonderful smells of cooking food rushed over Katie.

Jimmy's mom was bent over the stove stirring gravy; she straightened up as they entered.

His sister looked around the door from the dining room, with a big smile on her face. Katie extended her hand, "Mrs. Burns, how kind of you to invite me to your home," she said.

"Oh my dear how nice of you to come," she said wiping her hands on her apron, then taking Katie's proffered hand.

At that Jimmy's sister jumped into the room. "Hi, I'm Julia," she said. "I know your brother Mike. He is one year ahead of me in school; he is a sophomore and I'm a freshman."

Katie shook her hand also. "Would you like to come see my room?" Julia said.

"Just a minute, Jules," said Jimmy. "She needs to meet Dad."

Dad was sitting in the living room watching the Los Angles Rams playing the San Francisco Forty-Niners on their old black and white TV.

He stood up as they approached, he seemed a bit embarrassed. He didn't know exactly how to act before his son's girlfriend, especially one so pretty.

It turned out fine though. Katie stuck out her hand and he gently took it. She noticed how big and rough his hand was, so unlike her father's which was smooth.

She decided she would like this man a lot; he had gentle eyes, a soft smile and seemed shy.

After she was introduced to Dad she went off to see Julia's bedroom and that was where she still was when dinner was served.

She had not had a sister and found Julia fascinating. They talked as easily as if they had known each other forever.

The dinner was delicious: ham, mashed potatoes and gravy, corn, salad and for dessert apple pie with fresh made whipped cream.

Yum!

Katie felt stuffed. The men went into the living room to watch the last half of the game and Katie helped Jimmy's mom and sister clean up.

Afterwards they all sat in the living room and had a good chat.

Mr. and Mrs. Burns talked of her father; what a wonderful man he was and how they and everyone in the area were lucky to have such a brilliant and dedicated man for their doctor.

Jimmy and Katie left at about five that evening. Dad needed to start his chores and the milking of the cows.

Katie was charmed, she looked at Jimmy with soft dreamy eyes. "Darling, what sweet parents and sister you have, they made me feel is as if I were one of the family."

Jimmy smiled at her. "Thank you," he said.

He thought, *I don't think Mom would have been that sweet if you would have been Becky.*

He took her straight home. They sat out in the car for awhile in front of her house. He told her he was going to get a promotion of a sort. The company has bought another refrigerated truck and trailer combo, and wanted him to drive it. It would be more money and for trips of more than one day he would have a co-driver because they wouldn't be able to stop, at truck stops, like he did now and sleep.

She wanted to know how he would sleep then?

He explained how the new rig would have a sleeper attached to the back of the cab and they would stop only for eating and fuel.

"You know with the added money I'll be making I'll be able to afford a wife," he smiled at her.

Those words shot through her like a charge of electricity.

He saw she was startled. "Honey, I'm just joking. I didn't mean to panic you."

"Oh it's alright. I know you were just joking." She gave a little half-hearted chuckle.

"You know I am very expensive," she beamed. "You'll need a very large raise."

He leaned over and kissed her; all of a sudden the kiss was deeper than they both intended, a little shock went through them and they were both panting slightly when it ended.

He walked her to the door. "I won't come in. I am hitting the sack. I have to be at work by five tomorrow morning."

"Ok sweetheart," she said. "Where are you heading?"

"To Los Angeles. Were taking down a load of frozen peas, and baby lima beans and picking up a load of frozen orange juice in Escondido for the return trip. This is my first trip on the new truck and I'll have one of the older drivers for a partner. It should be interesting sleeping in a moving truck."

"Drive carefully," she said. "See you when you get back. Call me from California."

"I will honey," he said.

When she walked into the house her mother was waiting for her

73

and wanted to know all the details of her day at Jimmy's parents. She told her in depth what happened, but her mind wasn't into that now; she had to think of other things.

She went to her room after her mother was satisfied that she hadn't forgotten something important. She sat at her dresser and looked into the mirror. The "wife" word had been brought up. Of course it had been laughed off as a joke but she knew it was an exploration. It definitely needed some thinking on and a probe of Becky to see how the land laid there. She realized how important a development this was in her and Jimmy's relationship. First did she want to marry Jimmy? If she didn't it would be easier and kinder to break it off now.

Thank heavens Jimmy was gone for at least a week. She needed that time without him around to cloud her mind, to proceed with what would be the most important decision in her life. She lay down on her bed with her head whirling.

She realized they could no longer be Charlotte de Ville and the Comte de Bourbon; they had never married but remained secret lovers all their lives.

She was reading the latest of Susan Pink's novels, *Flame over Old California.*

The situation between Valencia Margarita Isabella de Segovia, niece of the Spanish Governor, and her dashingly handsome bodyguard, Juan Gonzales, was close to the same as theirs. He protected her when she left the hacienda, he was of humble origins, his parents were peasant farmers. Thinking she must hurry and read the rest of the book, she fell asleep.

Chinook: girding the old girlfriend in her lair.

Katie hadn't talked to Becky since the funeral, and that was over two months ago; already it was December.

"The time flies when one is so concentrated on one's own situation."

After work on Wednesday of that week she walked the two blocks to Bessie's house and knocked on the front door. Becky answered the door, and Katie's mouth almost fell open. She had to bite her tongue to keep from gasping.

Becky looked a mess, her hair was uncombed, she had no makeup on, her clothes were wrinkled and she looked like she had lost weight.

Becky's face brightened when she saw Katie; she rushed into her arms giving her a long hug.

"Dearest, how glad I am to see you. It seems ages since we talked."

Katie looked at her friend with some alarm. "Sweetheart, do you feel ok. Are you all right?"

"Come in," said Becky. "We must talk. Would you like some coffee?"

"Yes," said Katie, "I would."

When the coffee was made the two girls sat at the large table in the kitchen.

"I am afraid I have a problem," Becky started.

"Oh god, you're not sick?" gasped Katie.

"No, no, I am fine. I am afraid it's Bessie. She has not recovered from Ralph's death. Your dad has been seeing her but she doesn't seem to be getting better. You know she lost her husband just ten years ago and now with Ralph gone she seems to have lost her will to live. Your dad said she has deep depression. She can't watch Sonny while I'm at work so I have Mrs. McDonnell come in every day to baby sit. She needs the income and is glad to do it.

"Of course, that means more money out, but we are doing fine thanks largely to Jack who sends a check every two weeks. I am also doing all the cooking, washing, cleaning and what maintenance work I can so you see your friend exhausted with worry and work."

All this came rushing out like water out of a garden hose.

Katie had a deep rush of guilt here, she was so caught up in her own life she had cut her friend off in her hour of need.

She knew the main reason she hadn't seen Becky was she was stealing her boy friend and didn't really want to face her until she absolutely had to.

To save some face, and to salve her guilt, she said, "Oh darling, why didn't you call me. I would have been glad to help in anyway I could."

Becky gave her a little smile and shoved the knife in a little deeper. "Well, you have your own life and I know that a new romance takes lots of time and energy."

Katie's face turned the color of Rudolph's nose, she felt the knife twist in her stomach. "I, I . . ." she stammered.

Becky gave her another small wounded smile. "It's all right, dear, I gave Jimmy to you. You needn't feel like you took him from me, though it would be nice to have his strong back to help me now."

Katie took in a deep breath. "Well, he is home so seldom that we have very little time together, but I am sure he would help you anyway he could when he returns."

Becky eyed her with a rather sour look. "If you could send him over when he gets home I have some heavy stuff in the garage to move."

"Of course. I'll mention it to him when he calls me from Los Angeles tomorrow, or Friday. Now, is there something I could help you with?"

"Well, I hate to ask you for such a big favor, but could you talk to Mr. Thornton. I am afraid that I have rather a large bill with the store and it might be awhile before I can pay it."

"Oh sweetie, don't worry about that. I'll take care of it. I'll pay your bill. You concentrate on taking care of Sonny and Bessie."

Becky burst into tears. "How can I thank you Katie," she wailed.

Katie jumped out of her chair, kneeled by Becky and took her into her arms. "You are not to worry ever, do you hear me, ever. If you need anything you call me."

Becky hiccupped, sniffled and managed a small smile. "Thank you, my dear, I shall."

Katie called home and told her mother to have supper without her, she was with Becky.

She started to cook for them while Becky went to see about Bessie and get her ready to eat.

When Katie got home that night she lay on her bed before falling asleep. She thought, *Well I will help Becky any way I can but she can't have Jimmy back, he is mine. She had her chance with him twice.*

She smiled to herself. *Well I guess I have made my decision about our future!*

Katie then fell into a deep untroubled sleep.

After Katie had left, Becky lay in her bed. "I want Jimmy back. I need him now and Katie doesn't. He was always my boy friend and he loved me not her. Well, when he comes over to help me I know a way to get him back," for she was sure Katie was not giving him what she was thinking of. She smiled her little smile and dropped into a deep untroubled sleep.

It was eleven o'clock at night in California's Central Valley as the big truck rolled toward Bakersfield. Joe Wallis, his driver partner, was at the wheel.

Jimmy was in the cab sleeper in a deep untroubled sleep not knowing that 900 miles to the north his fate was being decided.

The next day in Los Angeles Jimmy and Joe watched as their load was taken from the truck into the huge freezers at Co-op Grocers warehouse.

The warehouse supervisor came up to them. "Guys, your load is ok, but you may have trouble with your refrigeration unit. We noticed a slight thawing on that last forklift load."

Joe and Jimmy climbed into the trailer. "Yep," said Joe. "She is blowing a bit warm. We had better call Jake at the warehouse. He won't be happy as this is a new rig." They called Jake at the cannery and told him the problem. He said he would call the dealer in Portland and get right back to them.

About thirty minutes later he called them back at the Co-op warehouse office and gave them the address of the manufacturer of the refrigeration unit. "Lucky for us they are made right there in LA," he said. "They are waiting for you, so just drive down there and they will replace the unit."

At the factory they were told that by tomorrow noon a new unit would be installed and they could have their truck back. They called Jake and he told them to have fun for the day.

The office manager took them to a rental car company and they drove across town to Redondo Beach. They got a hotel down by the beach and went swimming in the Pacific. That night they found a seafood restaurant on the beach with a view of the ocean. Back at their hotel they spent a good night in a real bed for the first time in four days.

Chinook: Buying a Christmas present for your girl, for the first time, is a very important undertaking for a young man in love.

After breakfast at their hotel the next morning Jimmy told Joe he needed to buy Katie a Christmas present, and this would be a good time to do it. They walked down the path fronting the beach to a shopping area, with stores mainly featuring souvenirs. Joe, having been married for almost forty years, gave the young man all the help he could.

They found a shop dealing in jewelry made from sea creatures and shells. Jimmy found a very beautiful necklace and bracelet set made from pink coral. He knew how much she loved the color pink. This set was kind of expensive and would take all his money. Joe, feeling sorry for the young man, told him to go ahead and buy it and he would loan him enough money to eat on until they got home.

So Jimmy made the purchase that he felt would ensure the continuance of his love affair. They picked up their repaired truck and headed for Escondido. There they were told it would be Saturday before they could be loaded now. As it was after four in the afternoon on Friday they decided to get a motel with a pool and spend the night in Escondido.

After dinner that night Jimmy called Katie from his room. "Hi sweetheart," he said, "how you doing?"

They talked for about fifteen minutes then Katie broke the news to him about Becky. She told him about her problems, especially Bessie not being well. "So darling," she said, "I felt sorry for her and told her we would help her clean out her garage on Sunday after Mass. Is that ok? She told me she needed a big strong man to lift most of the stuff she had and I know you're big and strong."

"Well I was kind of hoping we could spend Sunday together, you know just us. But you are probably right. She is our friend and we should help her out," he conceded. "Hope we can be loaded and out of here by tomorrow afternoon, or evening. We then go to Portland to unload this orange juice, hopefully we can be home late Friday night."

"Sounds wonderful, darling," she said, "How-bout a date Saturday. I have to do some inventory with Mr. Thornton Saturday morning. I should be free around noon. You could pick me up at my house around one and we could go into Salem. I want to Christmas shop for my family and yours."

"God, I miss you. I could use a kiss right now, baby. So I'll see you at one, I can't wait to get my arms around you."

Katie hung up the phone. She had told Jimmy a little white lie. She hadn't told Becky that "we" were coming. She had said she would tell Jimmy that Becky needed help. She had talked to mother and told her Becky wanted Jimmy to do a day of work for her. Mother cocked an eyebrow at her and suggested Becky could use both of them to help her. Katie had thought of this suggestion for a day or two and decided mother was right. She called Becky and told her Jimmy would be over after church on Sunday. Becky seemed very pleased. Katie just didn't mention that she would be coming with him.

The rest of the trip went very smooth for Jimmy and Joe, and they were back just before midnight on Friday.

Saturday at one o'clock Jimmy turned up on Katie's doorstep and they spent a very nice afternoon and evening in Salem.

It was so great just to be with her, Jimmy thought. *To hold her hand, to feel her lean against me, to make decisions on gifts together.*

They had dinner in Salem and arrived in front of Katie house at nine P.M. She let him kiss her more deeply than before. He was allowed to put his hand on her breast while they kissed. She then gently moved his hand to her back out of harm's way.

They would meet at eleven-thirty tomorrow morning then go to Becky's together. Jimmy went home and lay on his bed.

Katie's breast had been an electric experience; he was almost exploding with passion. Her breast was firm and full, and though covered by a bra, blouse and sweater it still felt wonderful.

The best part was she didn't jerk away or slap his hand or his face. After just a few moments she gently moved his wayward hand to her back.

Jimmy was so grateful that the love welled up in his heart; at this moment he loved Katie more than he thought possible.

He finally fell asleep, and as he slept he dreamed of fog and Kathleen. Kathleen came to him that night and in the morning Jimmy, though damp and messy, felt reborn.

Sunday morning at eleven he walked the couple of blocks to Katie's house to escort her to Becky's. Katie's mother came to the door. "Just go on to Becky's, Jimmy," she said. "She is not home yet. Mass was probably longer than Katie expected and she'll walk over in a few minutes."

"Ok thanks, Mrs. Overmars," Jimmy said, and walked to Becky's house.

When he walked around the back of the house Becky was standing there talking to the neighbor who lived just behind them, Mr. Rule. Mr. Rule owned Rule's Hardware, on Main Street.

His large delivery truck was parked in the driveway. "Ok, Mr. Rule," she was saying to the older man, "we'll put everything into the truck and whatever you decide you can use you can give the money to Bessie."

Mr. Rule had already decided to give Bessie one hundred dollars no matter what they put in the truck, because he knew she needed the money. He had tried to help her financially before but she would not take any money and this was a way to get past her pride. He had known both Bessie and her late husband almost all their lives and it hurt him to see her struggle, especially as he had all the money he would ever need.

After Mr. Rule turned to go Becky turned and saw Jimmy; smiling, she came to him and, giving him a hug, kissed him quickly on the lips.

"Jimmy dear, how nice of you to come to help me," she said looking at him with wide limpid eyes.

Jimmy didn't expect this warm of a greeting and jerked his head back just a little in confusion and surprise when she kissed him.

She noticed. "Jimmy, I want to apologize for that morning in the car when I hurt you so deeply. I just wasn't myself that day and I want us to be close again."

Looking down at her his heart gave a little jump.

"Can we be friends again, darling? You know I miss you terribly?"

Damn she was beautiful looking up at him; her lips slightly parted, her eyes imploring, her body pressing against him.

Just then Katie walked around the corner of the house, her eyes popped open so quickly they almost had whiplash. She took in the scene very quickly—her boyfriend in the arms of Becky. Luckily his arms were straight down at his sides and he had a rather stunned look on his face.

"Hi," chirped Katie. "I'm here. Shall we get to work?"

Becky jumped guiltily back from Jimmy; her face took on a rather sour look as she glanced toward Katie.

"Oh I didn't know you were going to come too, Katie," she said.

I bet you didn't, thought Katie. She said, "Oh, I just thought it would go faster if three were working."

After a couple of embarrassed seconds Becky recovered and led the others over to the garage. She opened the door revealing a large amount of lumber and junk stashed in there.

"We can load this on to that truck and then Mr. Rule will sort it all out and pay Bessie the money it's worth."

Jimmy pulled on his gloves and started to pull out the first boards; the girls attacked a pile of rusted small pieces of metal.

As they worked Katie noticed the difference in Becky since they last talked. She looked like the Becky of old. Her hair was brushed back from her face and tied with a scarf, she had makeup on, including lipstick, and even in her old working clothes she looked very pretty.

Katie also noticed something that she didn't care for. Jimmy had what looked like a light smudge of lipstick on his lips.

They worked for over an hour and slowly the garage emptied and the truck filled.

Chinook: The Rat!

When the garage was about half emptied Jimmy had taken a long board to the truck and both the girls were inside moving a big pile of rags and canvas. Just as Jimmy finished placing the board on the truck there came a blood-curdling scream from both the girls in the garage.

He turned to face the door when out ran Becky, white as a sheet. She glanced at Jimmy. "A rat," she shuddered.

"Where is Katie?" he shouted. Becky pointed into the garage.

Jimmy ran in the door and there stood Katie riveted to the floor.

He scooped her up into his arms and carried her outside. She was shaking like a leaf and buried her face into Jimmy's neck.

"Oh ugh, it ran over my foot. I felt its tail on my leg," she wailed. "Oh it was awful!"

Jimmy held her in his arms and kissed her cheek saying, "There there, baby, it's ok."

Becky, calmed down by now, had an unkind thought. *I think Baby is enjoying this moment too much.*

In a minute Katie was calming down so Jimmy put her down next to Becky.

"Stay here girls. I will deal with this."

He walked into the garage. On the wall was an old pitchfork. Taking it down he advanced toward the pile of rags. Slowly he lifted the edge with the tines of the fork. Out of the pile jumped a huge rat . It headed for the light at the door but foolishly followed the wall for protection.

Jimmy cut straight for the door and just as the rat reached it he plunged the fork into its back through its body pinning it to the floor. The rat screamed, turned its head to the fork, and baring long yellow teeth bit the tines.

Jimmy stepped toward it and crushed its head with the heel of his boot. The rat shuddered and Jimmy, lifting it on the fork, went outside.

The girls standing back from the door heard the rat scream and jumped into each others arms.

When Jimmy walked out with the still jerking rat stuck on the fork, they screamed again and turned away hugging each other all the harder. Jimmy smiling to himself, picked up a shovel that was resting up against the building and walked out toward an old garden plot.

He impaled the fork with the now dead rat into the ground and with the shovel dug a deep hole. He threw the rat's body into the hole and covered it up, packing down the dirt with his heel. It took him about ten minutes to accomplish this chore.

He returned to the garage, where the girls, now a lot calmer but with their arms still around each other, watched him return.

"If you don't mind, Jimmy, I think we will stay out here for awhile," said Becky.

"Actually," said Katie, "you couldn't drag me back in there." Katie said that with such force that Jimmy had to laugh.

"Oh you are a pig," they both said in unison, but they both laughed while they said it. However they didn't make a move to return to work. So Jimmy started to empty the garage by himself. Each time he lifted anything he looked closely for another vermin; he was scared of rats also, but would never tell that to the girls.

They stood there watching Jimmy work. Becky moved over to the truck to help as best she could with the loading, giving the garage door a wide berth.

After a few moments Katie felt a movement down by her feet. The rat still fresh in her mind she jumped, looking down she saw little Sonny.

"Auntie Katie," the little boy said.

"Yes my precious," said Katie kneeling down to look him in the eye and give him a kiss on the nose.

"I have a dried frog, would you like to see my dried frog?"

"I would love to come see your frog my love." She turned to Becky and said, "I am going to see Sonny's dried frog."

"Ok," said Becky, "but don't touch it. It's almost as yucky as that rat." Sonny took Katie's finger in his small hand and they walked off to the house.

"Where in the world did you get a dried frog, Sonny?" said Katie to the little boy.

"My Uncle Jack sent me dat frog," he said looking up at her. "He sent me a box wif' butderflies an' calipillers, an' somonders too," he said.

"Oh, good old Uncle Jack knows the way into the heart of a young man I see." They walked into the house leaving Becky and Jimmy alone.

Jimmy didn't see any more rats. He started to finish up the last pile of boards; by the time he was almost done Becky was back in the garage looking around gingerly.

She must have decided that there was no more danger, and soon was helping lift the last of the boards.

Finally the truck was full and the garage empty, Jimmy had found a large broom and swept the dirt and bits of wood lying on the floor out the door.

When he had finished he walked back into the garage to return the broom. Becky stood by him as he removed his work gloves. She moved to him before he could speak and put her arms around his waist.

"Thank you so much, Jimmy," she said. "No way I could have done this myself, what with Bessie being under the weather, plus of course that rat. You were my hero today," she cooed.

He placed his hands onto her shoulders and she cuddled closer to him; she turned her face up to his. He would have liked to hold her but was afraid Katie might come back; in spite of himself, he felt himself start to harden down below.

Becky must have felt it too for she smiled and lifted her lips to be kissed. He touched her lips with his, she pushed her mouth harder to his lips and ran her tongue into his mouth. They stayed like that for a minute, then Jimmy pulled back. "I am going with Katie now," he said. "I shouldn't be doing this."

"Oh sweetheart, I so want to make up for that awful way I treated you last summer. You could stay for dinner tonight. Afterwards I will make up for the years of hurt I have caused you."

"Well, Katie's mother is expecting us back for dinner tonight, so I can't stay," he said.

A look of irritation flashed over Becky's face. She recovered and said, "Last summer you asked me to come to bed with you. I foolishly put you off. Now I have all that behind me and I will gladly make love to you tonight if you want. Stay with me Jimmy, stay with me," she implored.

His brain was exploding. Dear god, how he wanted to stay with her.

Physically he ached for a female body but Jimmy was a good boy and he loved Katie. Now he would feel like a traitor if he had sex with Becky. In fact now he felt guilty for kissing her with Katie so close.

Why couldn't she have been this way last summer; he would have married her on the spot, if she had wanted.

"I am sorry, Becky, I have to go. We promised Katie's mother." He backed up from her and turned and walked to the house.

Becky stood there in the garage stunned, irritated and exasperated all at once. "Well damn him then," she muttered through clenched teeth.

Jimmy walked into the kitchen. Katie was playing with Sonny. He looked at her. "Are you ready, baby. I think we should go."

"Ok, is Becky coming in. I shouldn't leave Sonny by himself. Bessie is asleep upstairs."

Just then Becky walked in without looking at Jimmy. She picked up Sonny, using him as a shield. She looked at Katie, and said "Thank you for your help today. I couldn't have done it without you." Becky's mouth was a hard line. "Well I have to get some supper on the stove. Bessie and Sonny will be getting cranky if I don't feed them." She moved toward the door keeping Sonny between her and the other two. She held the door open as Jimmy and a very bewildered Katie walked through and across the porch. "Good night," Becky said to them and closed the door.

Katie looking stunned, slipped her arm through Jimmy's arm. "Ah, darling, what happened between you and Becky?"

Jimmy looked down to the ground as they walked carefully avoiding Katie's eyes. "Um, well, I think Becky wanted me to leave you and start dating her again."

Katie stopped. "REALLY," she said looking into Jimmy's face, "and what did you say?"

"I told her that I loved you and I couldn't."

Katie jumped into his arms. "And I love you too, my darling, my love, my hero."

Katie lay in her bed that night reading the last chapter of *Flame over Old California*. A smile twitching at the corners of her mouth. She thought, *I am Victoria, and he is my Juan.*

Just as Juan saved Victoria from the attack of the Mountain Lion, my Jimmy saved me from the rat.

Just as Juan forsake the advances of the beautiful daughter of the richest land owner to stay her bodyguard, so my Jimmy forsake Becky for my love.

Then she thought, *Mother was right when she suggested I go along with Jimmy to Becky's house. She might have taken him from me. Just as in* Flame Over Russia, *when Olga tried to steal Ivan from Catherine by using her body as bait.*

Her eyes got very big. *Do you think Becky would have given her body to Jimmy to lure him away?*

No, no, she thought. *We are friends. Becky would never do a thing like that. I am sure she was just checking to see if Jimmy was really in love with me.*

She snuggled under her goose down comforter. *She found Jimmy was in love with me,* and only me!

With the little smile still tugging at the corners of her mouth she fell into a deep untroubled sleep.

After Jimmy and the "Witch" had left her house Becky was seething. *Bastard,* she thought. *Bastard, bastard, bastard, how he could he take that little thieving witch over me.*

Why didn't he realize I was his real girl. I was here long before Miss rich bitch came on the scene.

She stomped around the kitchen as she made dinner for her family. "I was willing to give him something the virgin wouldn't. Maybe I should have stripped naked. I bet that would have changed his mind."

She threw a pan into the sink. "I am in love with Katie," she mocked in a falsetto voice. Just then the phone rang. She looked at it.

"Changed your mind, bucko. Want a little piece of me now, the virgin slap your face?"

She picked up the phone ready to tell Jimmy to take a leap. "Hello," she snapped. The voice on the other end hesitated slightly. "Ah hello . . . is this uh Becky? Hi, it's Jack."

In that instant Becky's attitude changed. "Oh, hello, Jack," she purred. "You know, it's funny, I was just thinking this minute how wonderful it would be to see you again. It seems like ages since you were here."

"Oh great, Becky, because I am coming down for a couple of weeks at Christmas and New Years. I know Mom isn't doing so well since Ralph's funeral and I thought maybe you could use a break, or some help with her."

"Oh Jack, how wonderful. We are so looking forward to seeing you. I know I'll be waiting on pins and needles until you arrive."

"Great," he said. "Could I talk to Mom?"

"Oh Jack, I am afraid she is taking a nap. Just wait, I'll go get her up."

"No, no, Becky, um I'll call her later or actually I'll be there in just a little over a week, so just tell her I'm coming, if you would."

"Oh yes, of course. Um, Jack could you say a word to Sonny? He is standing here."

"Sure, put my little buddy on."

"Hell'wo, Uncle Jack," the little boy said.

"Hello buddy, how's my favorite boy doing?"

"Tell him thank you for your dried animals," Becky coached.

"Tank you for my frog, Uncle Jack, I like him, but Momma doesn't an' need'er does Auntie Katie."

"Oh well you just hang on until I get there, buddy, then you and I will play with them. Could I speak to your Momma again?" Sonny handed Becky the phone.

"Ok Becky, I'll be there in about ten days. What would you all like for Christmas. I thought a tricycle for Sonny?"

"Oh yes, Jack, he would be so thrilled, also your mother needs a good warm winter coat. Anything you could bring for her in that vein would really be appreciated."

A stab of guilt ran through Jack's body. He knew they were poor and he should send them more money each month than he was now. "How about you?"

"Oh Jack, that is so sweet of you, but just seeing you would be present enough for me," she said.

"Ok gotta run. See you in a few days."

85

Becky hung up the phone. Any thoughts of Katie and Jimmy now far from her mind, humming a little tune she started to prepare supper again. That night alone in her bed she thought over the day. Now that Jack was coming she couldn't understand why she was so hot to have Jimmy back.

Well anyway, he would be sorry. Maybe she would give Jack what she was going to give him, she was sure Jack would appreciate her. She fell into a deep untroubled sleep.

Jimmy lay in his bed, his passion was up and his cock hard; he tossed and turned. Maybe he should have taken up Becky's offer, he could be with her now and maybe at this very minute he would be making love to her. He groaned, no, except for the sex, he didn't want any part of Becky. He really did love Katie and he really liked all the advantages of going with her.

It is just he had to do something quickly, he needed a naked girl in his arms. A girl to make love to. It was at that moment he decided to ask Katie to marry him. He would need to save for a ring. He would start saving his next paycheck. Jimmy tossed and turned and didn't fall asleep until the wee hours of the morning.

Chinook: Christmas; that most important time in the young couple's relationship is now here. Jimmy waits with a growing nervousness as Katie opens her present.

Jimmy and Joe returned home from Southern California the evening of December twenty-third. The next day, Christmas Eve, would be spent at Katie's parents' house. Jimmy was to arrive at their house at three in the afternoon.

They all sat in the living room around the tree, a fire burning in the fireplace, hot chocolate, cookies, cake and small minced pies for snacking on.

They all sat and chatted. Katie's Grandpa and Grandma were here from Boise for the holidays and the conversation ebbed and flowed gracefully.

Gosh, Jimmy thought, *how wonderful this all was.*

Grandpa and Grandma Overmars were very interested to meet Jimmy whom they had heard all about since arriving. He seemed a pleasant if unlettered young man who had, at least, a sense of manners that so many young people seemed to lack nowadays.

Grandpa and Grandma had wished Katie to marry a professional man, maybe a doctor, like her father.

Alas, according to their daughter-in-law, this young man was probably going to be part of the family. Well worse things could happen they supposed; if only he was a Catholic they may feel a bit better about him.

10

Dinner was finished about eight o'clock and after the dishes were cleared and the washing up done, the family and Jimmy started to open presents.

Jimmy had gotten for Katie's father a sweatshirt with "U-CAL BEARS," written on it in gold lettering. He had bought it when he and Joe had taken a load to the Oakland, California Docks.

He had called Katie to ok it before he bought it.

He had gotten her mother a sterling silver bell for her nic-nac shelf where she stored her finest possessions, and a Swiss Army Knife for her brother Mike. The knife had a spoon, a fork, a corkscrew, a scissors, plus all the knife blades. Everyone seemed very happy with his choices.

Katie had opened all the gifts she had received from her family. There was some very expensive clothing from her grandpa and grandma and French perfume from her parents. Jimmy had been worrying about his present, he had given small trinkets to Becky, for Christmas or birthday in high school, but never a major present to a girl that wasn't family.

Jimmy didn't realize, but this present was to be scrutinized very closely by Katie and her mother and grandmother to judge his taste, his commitment and whether he had the wherewithal as to the appropriateness of gifts to young ladies.

This gift would tell them a lot about the upbringing Jimmy had had, and the type of person he would be.

Otherwise cheap fake jewelry, gaudy clothing or personal items such as see-through underwear or negligée would be a death knell if he planned to marry Katie.

An inappropriate present and force would be put on Katie to stop seeing him. Katie had also wondered what present he would give her. She had never had a present from anyone other than family or close family friends. She took the package in her lap, looked down at it, and could tell he had wrapped it.

Taking off the paper she beheld a plain blue box with the small words, "Gifts from the Sea, Redondo Beach" written on it in fake gold lettering. She opened the box and gasped, lifting out the necklace she held it up. The lights of the Christmas tree shining off the pink coral made it twinkle; she put it around her neck and had her mother latch the clasp. Then she put on the bracelet and walked to where Jimmy sat. "Thank you, darling," she said, kissing him on the cheek. "It's lovely."

Behind Katie's back her grandmother and mother glanced at each other and gave a small nod. Jimmy had passed a major obstacle.

After the last present had been opened a dessert of apple pie with a rum sauce was served with coffee and they made ready to go to Midnight Mass.

The small Catholic Church was decorated for Christmas. A manger, with all the figurines of the Holy Family, shepherds and farm animals, was set before the Altar.

Around the rear of the Altar stood Christmas trees with lights the shape of angels on them.

The congregation had dressed in all their best clothing; it was a gala sight for Jimmy, who was used to a plainer sort of worship service.

After Mass he said goodbye to Katie, thanking her mother and father for a wonderful evening and, standing at attention, shook the hands of both her grandparents calling them Sir and Ma'am and wishing them a very Merry Christmas. He walked the three blocks to his room and prepared for bed.

After Jimmy had left them, Katie walked home between her father and grandfather; April and her mother-in-law walked a few steps behind the leading trio.

April glanced at Katie's grandmother. "Well, do you approve of Katie's young man?" she said.

"Yes dear, a very nice young man."

April sighed. She was glad there was harmony in the family.

Fifteen minutes later as Katie lay in her bed she thought over the best Christmas Eve ever in her life. She loved all her presents and especially the pink coral necklace Jimmy had given her. It was obviously very expensive and suited almost all her clothes; of course pink was her favorite color and Jimmy had picked that up without her ever mentioning it. The only way she could be happier was if Jimmy had given her a diamond engagement ring. But that would come she was sure. She glanced at her bedside clock. "Holy cow, one-thirty A.M." Well she would sleep until ten tomorrow. Jimmy would be spending Christmas day with his family but would be leaving for Oakland in the evening. She would see him next on News Year's Eve when he said he would have a surprise evening planned for her. She fell into a deep sleep a very happy girl indeed.

Becky and Jack had stayed up and talked late into the night. They had had a small intimate Christmas Eve supper, just the four of them. Sonny couldn't wait to get to bed tonight because, thanks to Uncle Jack, Santa would be at their house soon.

After Bessie had gone to bed they put out the presents Jack had brought from Seattle. Earlier in the week Jack and Sonny had gone to the mountains and had cut a small fir for their tree.

A few nights ago they had decorated it; it had been a very pleasant week with Jack here. Bessie had seemed better since he had come home and Becky was so grateful for him, for without him this would have been a very meager Christmas.

After they were done with placing the gifts they sat together on the old sofa. Becky snuggled under his arm. She would have gladly gone to bed with him but he just kissed her and sat with his arm around her.

About midnight they had went to bed, each to their own room.

Becky was worried that she no longer attracted men. She lay in her bed and thought both Jimmy and Jack had refused her advances just recently. Maybe she was getting old and unappetizing, though she was only twenty-three; maybe she was over the hill. She hadn't really gotten a present for Jack; she had planned to give herself to him for Christmas. *Oh well* she thought, *I still have a week to present him with his present.* She fell into a fitful slumber, knowing in a few short hours Sonny would be up to see what Santa had brought him.

Just before he fell asleep Jimmy reviewed what he thought was a very good day. He had scored on the present he had given to Katie and the rest of her family seemed pleased also with their gifts.

He had gotten a really nice wool shirt from Katie, which he would wear in the truck, and a sleeping bag from her parents to use in the truck's sleeper which could get rather cold at night.

He had fifty dollars already in the savings account he had started for the engagement ring, and he hoped to have enough to buy one for Katie by March.

He would go with his mom, dad and sister to his aunt's for Christmas tomorrow and then be leaving with Joe tomorrow evening for Oakland. All in all he had had a good Christmas. In his mind he tried to imagine Katie naked and fell asleep with the vision of her dancing behind his closed eyelids.

Chinook: New Year's Eve 1963.

Jimmy and Joe had arrived at the Slayton warehouse at two A.M. New Year's Eve morning. Handing the truck over to the warehousemen to clean and park the two tired drivers wished each other Happy New Year and headed for their homes. Jimmy awoke at noon and went to the café for breakfast.

He called Katie to come down and in a few minutes she slipped into the booth next to him.

"Oh darling, you are a lovely feast for my eyes, I have missed you so much. I really need to kiss you. How long will it take you to finish your food. We need to be alone for a bit."

He smiled at her. "Gosh baby, you get more beautiful every time I see you. How is that possible, the most gorgeous female in the whole wide world and yet you just get better."

She gave him a dazzling smile. "Oh I bet you say that to all the girls, handsome."

They chatted in that vein until he finished. "Let's go to my house," she said. "Mother is out with her woman's club and Father is going to be at the clinic all afternoon."

They walked through the front door of her house and as soon as the door closed she was in his arms, her tongue went into his mouth as they kissed.

He loved to hug Katie; he could feel her breasts pressing into his chest. With Becky it was different—when she hugged you there wasn't much to feel on top, she always pushed her pelvis into your crotch and then smiled at you if you had any reaction down there. He preferred to feel Katie's soft breasts rather than Becky's hard pelvic area. After a couple of long kisses she pulled her head back slightly and looking into his eyes said, "Ooh did I need that."

They walked into the living room, sat on the sofa, and between kisses he told her about the New Year's Eve Party they were invited to. The drivers, warehouse men, office staff and cannery mechanics had rented the whole Lotus Room Chinese Restaurant in Salem for the night. There should be well over one hundred couples there, and everything was included—music and food, party favors, noise makers and champagne at midnight, all for thirty bucks per couple.

"Wow Jimmy, that's expensive," she said.

"Hey, when you have the most beautiful girl in the world as your date, nothing is too expensive," he chuckled.

"Well you have to go now, sir. Your date has got to go to the beauty parlor. Hopefully Silvia will have an opening this afternoon." With that announcement, she picked up the phone. After talking a minute she hung up. "You may walk me to Silvia's, my sweet, she can take me now."

After a quick kiss they walked down to the beauty parlor and as he left her, he said, "Ok, pick you up at eight sharp."

Chinook: The New Year's Eve party. Every guy at the party will be envious of Jimmy.

Jimmy pulled up in front of Katie's house exactly at eight. He had on the only suit he owned—the one that he had bought in Salem. He had bought a new white shirt and electric blue tie that he had seen in a shop in California. Katie's mother let him in and he was talking to her father in the living room when she "entered" the room.

That was the only word to describe how she filled the room, how empty it was before she walked in. She had on a dress that followed every curve on her body; it had a high neck and sleeves that came down to her wrists. It was the color of the deep green one might see in a holly leaf or emerald ring. Around her neck was the pink coral necklace he had given her, and on her wrist the bracelet, her lipstick perfectly matched the necklace. Her blue eyes sparkled; her blond hair shone and had a different wave than she had that afternoon.

For a second he couldn't breathe; she looked like she just stepped out of a fashion magazine.

Her mother took a picture of them; he helped her on with her coat and they left for the party.

They arrived at nine o'clock and the parking lot was already half full. They had taken off their coats at the cloakroom and Jimmy marveled at how the fabric of her dress glowed and was so smooth to the touch; it was made of satin she had said.

They walked into the restaurant and every eye turned to Katie, some of the wives' and girlfriends' mouths dropped open. Jimmy spotted Joe and his wife Barbara, and he steered Katie toward them. After he introduced her to them the ladies went off to the restroom. Jimmy had never met Barbara before. She was a pretty woman now in her fifty-ninth year. She had beautiful silver hair and was as tall as Katie. Joe and Barbara had married right out of high school when they were both nineteen.

Jimmy remembered asking Joe how long he had known his wife. "Forever," he had replied. They had been born and raised on neighboring farms and had played together as children.

After the ladies returned from the restroom, they found a table to sit at. They were just settling down when who should walk into the restaurant: Becky on the arm of Jack Skinner.

Katie and Becky didn't see each other at first. Jimmy noticed that Becky looked a little bedraggled. Her hair needed to be cut, her dress had seen better days, and she had dark circles under her eyes.

Just then Katie saw them. "Oh darling," she said, "there's Becky and Jack. We have two extra seats at our table. Do you mind if I ask them to sit with us?"

When Becky saw Katie headed her way Jimmy saw her mouth give a small jerk, and it pulled into a straight line.

When Katie reached them she hugged Becky and over Katie's shoulder he saw Becky's face take on a sour look. After a few words Katie looped her arm through Becky's and led them back to the table.

Joe and Jimmy stood up as they approached and Jimmy introduced them to Barbara. Becky had seen Katie on the way toward her and Jack. *Damn*, she thought, *she looks absolutely fabulous.*

Becky had hoped to avoid Katie and Jimmy that night, she just didn't feel up to talking with them, but before she could move Katie was upon her giving her a hug. When Katie hugged her Becky could smell her perfume; it was light and delicate like a field of flowers, and it didn't come from a drug store.

Jack had given her a small bottle of cologne for Christmas, that next to Katie's smelled cloying and heavy.

She knew Katie had a rich family and all her income from her job at the Thornton's market went to personal things, but she started to feel a real resentment toward Katie. Katie then dragged her and Jack to the table where Joe and Jimmy sat with Joe's wife whom she had never met.

The band started and Katie and Jimmy went to dance. Becky started to drink a little heavily; she needed to drown her inhibitions. Barbara and Katie looked so good, she on the other hand felt like leftovers. Her dress was old and she was conscious of her hair needing to be fixed.

By eleven-thirty Becky was very drunk and she started to mumble a little. She had a small piece of food from the dinner in her hair.

Katie saw she needed to fix her lipstick which was smeared around her mouth, making her lips look lopsided.

Katie gently laid her hand on Becky's arm. "Sweetie, I have to go to the girls room. Would you come with me?"

"Bitch," Becky mumbled.

Katie let her hand slide from Becky's arm. "What?" she said.

"Bitch, boyfriend stealing bitch." Becky stood up none too steady. "I thought we were friends and you stole my Jimmy, you bitch," she now yelled at Katie.

Katie turned white as a sheet and stood there with her mouth open. Becky was just warming up.

Everyone within hearing now had turned toward the vociferous Becky.

"You come into my house, play with my little boy, call me friend, then you stab me in th' back, then you dress up to make me look bad and take my Jimmy. Give him back you slut."

Jimmy and Jack just sat there dumbfounded. Katie started to weave like she was going to faint.

Jimmy jumped up to grab her; as he put his arm around her she turned toward him and buried her face in the crook of his neck.

He was quite angry. "Becky, just shut up. If anyone is a bitch or slut it's you." Becky started to look green. Jack jumped up putting his arm around her. "Back off, man," he said to Jimmy.

Both men glared at each other for a few seconds then Becky broke the tension by puking all over the table. Barbara, who hadn't moved since the confrontation started, got the worst of it. Vomit ran down the front of her dress and made a little puddle in her lap. Everyone around the table got a little, and were jumping back when Becky's eyes rolled back in her head and she passed out.

In one quick movement Jack scooped her up in his arms; he took her to a clean table. At that moment the restaurant staff and owners jumped into action. They gave Jack a clean towel. He promptly started to clean up Becky. They hurried over to the table putting towels over Barbara's dress. The owner's wife took her to the ladies room, got her out of the dress and started to clean it with damp cloths. They grabbed the table and took it out into the parking lot through the front door, where they poured a bucket of water over it. Other staff brought a mop and cleaned the floor and chairs.

By now Jack had cleaned up Becky; he asked someone to get her coat. After putting on her coat he carried her to the door. He looked back, everyone was watching him. A small smile turned up the corners of his mouth. "I am really sorry about this, and so will Becky be in the morning. Good night." He turned and walked out with Becky still passed out in his arms.

The tension had broken and most people laughed, except Katie who was still pretty shook up.

Jimmy still had his arms around her; she pulled back a little. "I think I'll go clean up and see how Barbara is doing," she said, and she headed for the ladies room.

Needless to say that sort of killed the evening for our little group, but the rest of the people in the room started to celebrate as the clock ticked down toward 1964. The band struck up Auld Lang Syne, the lights dimmed and people started throwing confetti and blowing their horns and whistles, and singing along with the band, "Should auld acquaintance be forgot be forgot and never brought to mind . . ." After the singing stopped Barbara and Katie came out of the ladies room. Barbara was dressed in a white cook's uniform and carried her dress in a bag; she looked kind of cute.

Katie looked very forlorn. Jimmy put his arm around her shoulders and said good night to Joe and Barbara. They got their coats and left. They drove home in silence.

When they pulled up in front of Katie's house she started to cry. "Oh darling, I so wanted our first New Year's together to go well."

He took her into his arms and softly kissed her lips. "It's alright, baby, there will be plenty more," he said.

She started to hiccup and through her tears said, "I didn't even say Happy New Year to you or give you a New Year's kiss."

He gave her his hanky and after she blew her nose he took her into his arms again. "I love you, my darling, my sweetheart, my precious, my baby," as he said that he kissed her forehead, her eyes and her nose. Then he looked into her eyes and said, "Happy New Year, my love," and they kissed deeply.

Finally they pulled apart; they were panting like they had just run a mile. "Whoa," he whispered to her, "I think I had better walk you to your door. I might not be able to stop after another one of those."

They walked to her door. "Come over tomorrow, darling," she said. "Father and Mike are going to watch the Rose Bowl and we will have some lunch during the game."

She lay in her bed a few minutes later thinking about the horrid things Becky had said. She knew that Becky had been very drunk, in fact she had never seen anyone so intoxicated in her life. She had heard that people say things they don't mean while under the influence of alcohol.

Still she felt a little guilty. It was true that Jimmy had been Becky's boyfriend almost all her life. But she didn't start dating him until Becky had more or less dumped him and encouraged her to take him. Besides now it was too late; Jimmy was hers and she wasn't going to give him up. He loved her, she loved him.

She sighed. It was just like in *Flame over Italy*, the latest book she

95

was reading. The Contessa Maria no longer wanted to marry Florio the handsome young Captain of her father's personal guards. She had changed her mind because she had found out that Count Abruzzi, a man not handsome but rich and powerful, wanted to marry her. She arranged for Portia, her youngest sister, to seduce Florio. It was easy because Portia secretly loved Florio and carried out the seduction flawlessly.

Florio, in anguish, thinking he had betrayed Maria's love, asked her for release from his vow to marry her.

Maria, acting crushed, agreed to let Florio go so he could marry Portia. However before Maria could marry Count Abruzzi he was caught in a conspiracy to assassinate the King of Naples. He was beheaded and all his titles and land had reverted to the King. Now Maria, looking around for another husband, decided she wanted Florio back. However by now Florio had secretly married Portia and more than that, he loved her more than he had ever loved Maria. Also Portia was with child so Maria couldn't possibly have him back.

Katie wasn't with child but Jimmy loved her more than he ever loved Becky and Becky couldn't have him back PERIOD.

After saying her prayers, in which she thanked God for Jimmy and the New Year, Katie fell asleep.

But it was a restless sleep and she awoke tired and grumpy the next morning.

After Jack left the restaurant with Becky he put her in the car and took her home. Bessie and Sonny were, of course, sound asleep so Jack carried her up to her bedroom. He was going to just lay her on her bed and cover her over but her clothes smelled of vomit so he removed her dress, her garter belt and her nylon stockings. She lay now in just her slip; it was wet and smelled so he removed it also. She now was in just her bra and panties, but one of her breasts was half out of her bra and it looked damn uncomfortable so he removed her bra.

He lay her back down and looked for her pajamas. He found them under her pillow and was about to put them on when he stopped to admire her. Her arms were spread wide and her hair was curling around her face.

Damn she was a beautiful woman. Her breasts were small but they were nicely shaped with small dark nipples, just big enough for a good handful. She had a slim waist and beautiful rounded hips with lovely tapered legs ending in small finely shaped feet.

He was never really close to his brother Ralph but now he thought, *Damn Ralph you had a lot better taste than I thought you had. I bet you*

96

hated to die and leave this little baby. He put on her pajamas and slipped her under the covers. His love life was in a mess right now, but when he got it taken care of he was going to come back and claim this little honey for his own.

The next morning Bessie made him breakfast and he was on the road at nine o'clock. Becky didn't wake up until almost noon, her head pounded so badly that she almost vomited again.

She slowly crawled to the bathroom and peed. She stood up with the help of the sink and splashed water in her face. She had enough strength to drop an Alka-Seltzer into a glass and found if she moved her head slowly she could function.

She went downstairs and Bessie gave her some coffee; she couldn't eat at all and also almost threw up the coffee.

Slowly the night before came back to her. "Is Jack up yet," she asked Bessie.

"Oh dear, he left three hours ago on his way home," said the old lady.

"Oh god," said Becky holding her head. "I am afraid I made a big fool of myself last night, probably lost friends forever."

"Jack said you got kind of sick last night but you probably would be ok this morning. He checked you before he left and said you were still breathing and I should just let you sleep."

At about one o'clock the phone rang. Bessie answered and said, "Yes, she is up and looking ok, ok just a second. Becky, it is Jack and he wants to talk to you."

"Hi, Jack, I am so sorry . . . oh I don't feel very good but I'll live I suppose. Jack," she lowered her voice so Bessie wouldn't hear, "did you put me to bed?"

"Oh I wish I could have been awake. I had planned a New Year's present for you. When you come back I'll be here . . . ok, so hopefully you'll be back by next summer, couldn't you make it a little sooner . . . yes, I suppose. Where are you now, . . . Longview, Washington? Well drive carefully, sweetheart, see you as soon as you can get back." She hung up the phone and started to cry.

Chinook: Becky had hoped to right the wrong she felt she imposed on Jack. She hoped to see him in just a few months. In reality, she wouldn't see him again for almost four years.

Jimmy went home after dropping off Katie and fell into a deep sleep.

He was back at Katie's by noon the next day. A small table was set up in the living room and on it were various salads, fruit, cold meats and bread to make sandwiches.

Katie and Jimmy sat together on the sofa during the game and her parents sat in armchairs. Katie was subdued since he had arrived; he didn't ask her why but thought it was probably because of last night. He wished he could hold her and kiss the sadness away but couldn't in front of her parents.

He held her hand through the first half of the game; she had squeezed his hand back to let him know she appreciated his concern and warmth. During half time they all ate and after they had finished Katie seemed to perk up. During the third quarter the phone rang and Katie left the room to answer it. She didn't return until the fourth quarter; when she did return her eyes were red like she had been crying.

Her mother glanced at her with concern but said nothing. She had noted Katie's lethargy this morning but had put it down to a spat between her and Jimmy. When Jimmy arrived at noon everything between them seemed normal, so she had put that thought aside and wondered what had gone wrong the night before.

Katie sat down by Jimmy, took his hand in hers and cuddled against him as if she was seeking warmth and comfort. She gave a little shiver and a small hiccup but then seemed to be ok the rest of the game.

After the game the young couple went for a walk before dinner. Jimmy put his arm around Katie and said, "Baby, did something upset you during that phone call?"

"It was Becky. She called me to apologize."

"Well she should have," Jimmy ventured. "She had absolutely no right to say those things to you, at all. Especially you, the sweetest person on this earth!"

"Thank you, darling," she said. "I'm not terribly sweet I am afraid. I wasn't very charitable to her I am sorry to say. It wasn't the names she called me so much as her saying I stole you from her, and her wanting you back. We rather discussed that at length. She apologized about that saying she had already made a pass at you and you had rejected her telling her you were going with me."

Katie stopped and looked him straight in the face. "When did she make a pass at you, and what did she say?"

Jimmy looked down at the ground and hesitated.

Katie said, "Darling, I know you don't want to talk about it but we must not hold secrets from each other. We have to be open to one another, or we will never have a complete love, so please tell me."

"Well it was when we were helping her clean Bessie's garage. You had went into the house with Sonny and I was finishing up and putting the broom away. She came to me and I thought she was just going to thank me with a kiss on the cheek. Instead she put her arms around me, kind of rubbed her body on me, kissed me rather hard and told me she wanted to go to bed with me. Also that she wanted me back and wanted me to dump you, saying I would not be sorry if I did."

Katie stiffened and said, "And what did you say."

"Well I told you that night that I told her that I couldn't because I loved you."

Katie relaxed. Her eyes became rather large and limp. She came into Jimmy's arms. She pressed her lips to Jimmy's ear and said, "Darling, I love you more each second, each minute of each day. Don't worry, she will never make a pass at you again."

Chinook: Jimmy and Katie finished their walk much more light-hearted than they started.

Their young love survived yet another potential roadblock, as all young love must if it is to mature and grow. Jimmy was now totally committed to Katie. He was saving for the ring, Katie obviously loved him, and he loved her more than he thought he could love anything or anyone. So he took the next step, he was going to become a Catholic. He started attending Mass with Katie whenever he was in town. They joined a group of young Catholic couples that were committed to each other but not yet married.

11

The Priest of St. Thomas, Father George Road, had started this small group and they met on Friday nights. Generally the girls made cookies and cakes, the boys would bring soft drinks and they would socialize. They would talk about problems young people have, and how the church would fit into their lives, and what was expected of Christian couples not yet married.

It was a very relaxed time for Jimmy and Katie and they really enjoyed these Friday nights. In February Jimmy told Katie he wanted to be a Catholic.

"Oh darling, that is wonderful," she said, "but how will your parents take it? You know, darling, you don't have to become a Catholic to marry me, it's just that our children would be raised Catholic if we'd have any."

"I know, baby," he said, "but I really like going to Mass, I even like the Latin. Could you set me up a visit with Father for next week?"

So Jimmy and Katie had their meeting with Father Road. During the meeting Father asked him if he now attended any other Church.

"Yes, Father, I go to the Baptist church with my mother at times."

"Well," said Father Road, "Pastor Manning is a friend of mine and a very good man. Of course he is no match for me in chess but I will inform him of your intention. Tell me, Jimmy, did you get baptized by Pastor Manning?"

"Yes, Father, when I was sixteen."

"Are you sure you want to become a Catholic. It can be a rather rigorous faith at times, what with early masses and fasting," intoned Father Road.

"Yes Father," said Jimmy. "I hope to marry Katie someday and I want to be the same faith as her." So Father Road set Jimmy up with reading material and instructions in the faith.

With Jimmy wanting to be a Catholic Katie's happiness soared.

Jimmy's Mom and Dad had a few reservations but as he was a man now he had to chart his own way, and they wished him the best.

Katie's parents breathed a sigh of relief; they were very happy that

Jimmy decided to become a Catholic. It could be a lot less strain on a young relationship when the couple was of the same faith.

At the end of March Jimmy called Doctor Overmars and asked him if they could get together for a talk.

"Do you mean professionally, Jimmy?" asked the doctor. "Do you feel bad?"

"Oh, no, Doctor," Jimmy replied. "There is just something I would like to discuss with you."

So they made a date for lunch one day. Jimmy's stomach was flipping when he met the doctor at the café.

They made some chitchat and when the food came Doctor Overmars said, "So what do you have to ask me, Jimmy?"

Jimmy swallowed hard. "Doctor, sir, I love K-Katie very much and, and I was wondering if I could ask you for her hand in marriage."

The doctor tried to look serious but a large grin split his face. "Of course, you may marry my daughter, my son." He reached his hand across the table to the nervous young man, and shaking his hand he said, "Welcome to the family."

"You know, Jimmy, if I would have said no, both my wife and daughter would have killed me," the doctor chuckled. "We all like you very much, son. You will be a fine addition to our family. I guess I am supposed to keep this a secret?"

"If you wouldn't mind, sir. I plan to ask her to marry me in about three weeks."

By the second week in April Jimmy had enough money saved for the engagement ring. When Joe and he had gotten back early that week from a trip to Vancouver, B.C., he drove to Salem to buy it. He went to Robinson's Jewelers where he knew Dr. Overmars bought jewelry for his family. Even though Katie and him had never spoke especially about getting engaged he knew about what kind of ring she wanted. On their dates if they walked past a jewelry store they would stop and Katie would point out rings she liked or admired. He knew she wanted a solitaire diamond. When he arrived he told the salesman what sort of thing his fiancée, to be, wanted, and how much he had to spend.

The salesman brought out a set that wasn't displayed. The set had a plain gold wedding band and the diamond ring was a one carat square cut solitaire. The two bands locked together to form a pair.

Some young man had ordered the set about a year ago but before he could pick up the ring his bride to be, called off the nuptials.

Jimmy could have it for six hundred, just what he had in his

101

pocket. The next thing was to set up the engagement evening. He called the "Top of the Benson," the best restaurant in Portland.

The "Top of the Benson" was just that, the top of the biggest and best hotel in the city with views of the city, mountains and river.

He explained to the Maitre d' the reason for the reservation, and the date he wanted the table.

"Ah yes, sir, that date is open for a table for two by a window. We do many engagements. One very romantic thing we do is at dessert time your waiter will bring out a covered dish. Under the lid is a mound of crushed ice with your diamond ring perched on top. Your server will set the dish before the young lady and will raise the lid revealing the ring. Would this be satisfactory for you sir?"

"Yes, that sounds really nice," said Jimmy.

"Ok sir when you and your fiancée come that night just slip me the ring and we will take care of the rest. My name is Mr. Parsons, and I thank you, sir, for thinking of the Top of the Benson."

So all was set for the momentous occasion.

Before he left on a long trip he said to Katie on their Sunday afternoon walk, "Baby, isn't it close to our six month anniversary?"

"Yes, darling," she said, "it will be six months since our first date next weekend. Why?"

"Well, how about a real dress-up date. How about we go to Portland to a really fancy restaurant? You know it's been awhile since we dined and danced."

Her eyes brightened. "Oh darling, that would be so romantic and fun."

"I'm afraid it will be a week late from the exact date of our anniversary because I won't be home next weekend," he apologized.

"Oh dear," she sighed. "I won't see you for two weeks?"

"No, we leave for Phoenix tonight, then to LA, then San Francisco, then Eugene then home."

"Well, darling, the last kiss I give you tonight will have to be a good one so you don't forget me."

"Ha," he laughed. "Like I could forget a cute little number like you. However I will take that kiss anyway."

Katie lay in her bed that night looking at the ceiling. *Gosh,* she thought. *I will have to go to Salem to get just the right dress and shoes for the night out, and my hair is a mess. I had better get an appointment with Silvia for next week.* She sighed. *It was so fun having a boyfriend and being in love. How did I ever live before Jimmy came into my life I would like to know?*

*   *   *

The trip went very routinely for Joe and Jimmy. They were a good driving team and enjoyed each other's company, which is very important when two men are cooped up in a small space, like a truck cab, for days on end. They arrived back at the warehouse at two A.M. Friday morning.

Katie and her mother had two weeks to prepare for the big date. They had lunch and a whole day of shopping in Salem, and they both went to the beauty parlor together to get new "do's." It was such fun for them both; they had never been closer in their adult relationship.

April wondered if maybe something big was going to happen on this date. She probed Katie, nothing there. She, offhand, asked her husband if he knew the reason for the occasion. He just shrugged. Well, there was something in the wind and she must be attuned to it.

Jimmy arrived at Katie's house at six P.M. sharp on Saturday evening.

He had returned from his men's shop in Salem just hours before. The salesman there had talked him into a new look for spring. Instead of a new suit he had on a navy blue blazer with tan, almost cream-colored, trousers, black shoes, a light blue dress shirt with cuff links, and dark blue tie with a conservative red stripe.

When Katie's mother opened the front door she sucked in her breath. "My," she gasped, "Jimmy, you look very handsome."

"Thank you," he said. "Do you think Katie will approve?"

"Yes, my dear, I think Katie will be very pleased." Just then Katie entered the room. She had on a black dress that was covered in sequins whenever she moved, she kind of twinkled. She had on his Christmas gift, the pink coral necklace, and a small pink jacket that matched the necklace was over her arm. Her handbag, gloves and shoes were matching black shiny leather, her hair gleamed blond with a new wave that swept softly across her forehead.

Her mother helped her on with her jacket and gloves, then she took a picture of them both. Katie had a dark mid-length mink coat that her Grandmother had given her two Christmases ago, Jimmy helped her on with that and they were on their way. All told it was about sixty miles from Low Sky to Portland; once you got through Salem you picked up the new freeway that took you into downtown.

They arrived in front of the Benson at exactly seven fifty-five. The valet opened the doors of the car and they entered the lobby and up the elevator to the restaurant. The cloak room girl took Katie's mink coat, and they stepped up to the Maitre d'.

103

"Good evening I am Mr. Parsons," he said. "May I have the name, Sir?"

Jimmy gave him his name. "Ah Miss Overmars and Mr. Burns." He snapped his fingers at the waiting Captain and told him a table number. "Welcome to The Top of the Benson," he said smiling at Jimmy.

As Katie started to follow the Captain Jimmy slipped the box with the diamond ring into Mr. Parson's hand. The Captain seated them with a wish for a lovely evening.

Katie looked at Jimmy, her eyes shining. "Oh darling," she breathed, "how wonderful it all is."

They looked out over the city with the lights in the buildings and on the street coming on as the sun set over the mountains to the west. As they watched the orange light of the setting sun turned to darkness and the city began to glow. The neon signs of the theaters and restaurants below them illuminated the streets in reds, greens and blues.

They turned as the waiter came to their table and introduced himself to them. "Good evening, my name is Stefan. I will be your waiter tonight. Could I get you anything from the bar?" he asked.

Jimmy ordered a split of champagne and two glasses, explaining it was their anniversary.

"Very good, sir, could I suggest our house champagne. It's a French vintage and a bit sweeter for the lady's taste."

"Yes, that sounds fine," said Jimmy. The orchestra in the corner of the room started to play an old favorite. "Shall we dance, baby," he purred at her.

She gave him a dazzling smile. "It would be a pleasure, darling."

As they danced Jimmy started to sing quietly in her ear, along with the orchestra, "It seems we stood and talked like this before. We looked at each other in the same way then but I can't remember where or when. The clothes you're wearing are the clothes you wore, the smile you are smiling you were smiling then but I can't remember where or when." Katie sighed and cuddled closer into his arms as he continued. "The things that happened for the first time seemed to be happening again, and so it seems that we have met before, and laughed before, and loved before but who knows where or when."

The music stopped, Katie looked up into his eyes. "Darling, I didn't know you could sing, and you have such a lovely voice."

"Well I am afraid I might not have gotten the words right, but thank you, baby, I am so happy I could sing for you all night."

When they arrived back at the table the waiter had brought their champagne. He poured it into their glasses. They lifted their glasses, clinked them together and toasted to a wonderful evening, and so it was.

After they had finished their entrée Jimmy said to her, "Baby, I took it on myself to order a special dessert for us. I hope you like it."

"Oh, darling anything you have done tonight couldn't be anything but wonderful."

Jimmy gave a small wave to the waiter and with a flourish the pastry cook, with his tall white hat, swept through the restaurant, a silver tray covered with an ornate lid balanced perfectly in his upraised hand.

Katie saw him coming; all the other patrons of the restaurant saw him coming. She remembered thinking, *Oh a special anniversary cake.*

He approached their table and with an exaggerated bow said, "Miss, may I place this in front of you?"

"Please do," Katie exclaimed.

Now everyone in the restaurant were craning their necks to see what was happening.

"Miss, I will remove the lid with your permission," he said.

"Please do," Katie said.

With another flourish he removed the lid and stepped back.

Katie was astounded there was no cake, only a gleaming round pile of shaved crystal ice.

Then she saw the diamond on top. Totally unprepared, her hand flew to her mouth. She screamed, "Oh my God."

She turned toward Jimmy who was now on his knees beside her chair. "My darling, my love, will you marry me?"

"Oh yes, oh yes a thousand time yes," she said and burst into tears.

Jimmy stood up and she rose from her chair; he took her into his arms and whispered into her ear, "My baby, my love, how much I love you, no one can understand."

Everyone in the restaurant was applauding. Some of the ladies were daubing their eyes with hankies, and the restaurant staff was smiling.

Suddenly Katie and Jimmy realized they had the attention of the entire restaurant and blushing sat down in their chairs.

Jimmy still had hold of her hand and he picked the ring off the ice and slipped it on her finger. Tears welled up in her eyes again; she looked at her hand with the big diamond sparkling there.

The band struck up a tune and they rose from their chairs and going to the dance floor started to move with the music looking deeply into each other's eyes.

The restaurant patrons let them dance a few minutes alone, then other couples came up one by one. As they passed Jimmy and Katie they congratulated them; the newly engaged couple thanked them all.

When the band stopped playing they returned to their table; the management of the restaurant had given them a small cake with pink frosting. The waiter served them but they were too excited to eat more than a few mouthfuls.

Jimmy called for the check; he left a very large tip.

As Katie was retrieving her coat from the cloakroom Jimmy went to Mr. Parsons and thanked him profusely. "It was a wonderful evening," he told him. "I will be forever grateful to you and your staff."

Mr. Parsons shook his hand. "It was our pleasure, Sir," he said. "I hope you both have a wonderful life together and come to see us now and again."

Katie cuddled under his arm on the drive home; they listened to the radio and didn't talk much, words would come later.

When they reached Katie's house she said, "Please come in, darling, I want us to tell my parents together."

"Um," Jimmy said. "I think your father knows already. I asked his permission to marry you almost a month ago."

"You asked my father for my hand?" She looked into his eyes. "Jimmy, can you get anymore perfect?"

She kissed him very softly and deeply.

When Katie let them into the house she called upstairs, "Mother, Father could you please come down, we need to talk to you."

April was just drifting off into sleep when she heard Jimmy and Katie pull up in front of the house. She went to the window and saw them both come to the door, so she was putting on her housecoat when Katie called to her. She shook her snoring husband and said, "John, the children want us, put on your robe."

When she first saw Katie's flushed face a shock ran through her body and she thought, *they have been in an accident of some kind.*

She came quickly down the stairs and on reaching the bottom she heard Katie say, "Mother, oh Mother, I am engaged and will be married." Then Katie was in her arms crying and laughing at the same time.

April started to cry also and reaching out pulled Jimmy to them and they both put an arm around him.

Jimmy looked up just as his father-in-law to be stepped out of the bedroom with a big grin on his face; in a second he was shaking Jimmy's hand.

Katie then moved into her father's arms, kissing him on the cheek. "Jimmy told me he asked you for my hand in marriage a month ago.

You know I would have never spoken to you again if you would have said no!"

April looked at her husband with her mouth open. "John, you knew about this for a month and never told me. You are a beast."

April looked at her daughter. "Sweetheart, did you get a ring?" Katie raised her hand toward her mother; the diamond flashed a bright red deep inside, as it moved in the light of the entry hall.

Just for one second April felt a stab of apprehension from the startling red, then the hand of her daughter was in front of her face and she could see the diamond up close.

"Darling, how beautiful, what a gorgeous jewel. Jimmy, you not only have exquisite taste in fiancées, but also so it seems, in gems."

"Thank you, mother-in-law to be," Jimmy smiled, and bowed from the waist.

April giggled. "Is he always this sassy, Katie?"

"Oh yes, mother, always," she put her head to one side and said in her most affected voice, "but we'll change all that once the wedding bells ring."

They all had a good laugh at that.

An hour later Katie lay alone in her bed. She raised and lowered her new diamond in the light of bedside lamp. It twinkled and flashed blues, greens and reds; it made her heart thump and she caught her breath. It was so beautiful and all so wonderful. This night was better and more romantic than any love story she had ever read about in the flame books. She was so happy she didn't even feel animosity for Becky anymore.

She had been quite cross about Becky; she had offered Jimmy her body to take him away, but now that threat was gone and Jimmy was hers forever. Becky was her only friend really, and she would need bridesmaids when the wedding came. Now that Jimmy could no longer be stolen she would forgive Becky and they could take up from where they left off.

She snuggled down into her bed; in the morning after Mass Jimmy and she would go to his parents' farm and break the news to them. "Sigh, I am a very happy girl."

For some reason, all day, Becky had been cranky and out of sorts. Even now she lay in bed and tossed and turned though it was late. She felt that she had lost something, things just didn't fit; everything was an irritation, sort of like her period was coming on. Well, maybe she would feel better in the morning, but sleep would come hard tonight.

Jimmy lay in his bed emotionally and physically exhausted; he felt like he had run ten miles. He was very happy now that the engagement was started, and that Katie was so thrilled and happy. However he needed her physically; now he wanted her in his arms; he wanted to make love to her.

Then he felt the soft dampness of fog on his face, the smell of coal smoke filled his nostrils.

"Hello, Laddie," Kathleen smiled down from above him.

She was alone, the bunch of rags that she had been holding to her chest the last few times he had seen her were gone. He held out his arms and she came to him. In a few minutes he was relieved of that terrible pressure, that gnawing ache in his loins, and he fell into a deep sleep.

12

The next morning Jimmy was at Katie's house at 10:00. April had invited him the night before for breakfast.

After breakfast, the newly engaged couple would go to eleven o'clock Mass, then to Jimmy's parents to break the good news to them.

When they arrived at Mass Katie took off her gloves and held her hand in such a way that everyone could see her new diamond. She knew that it was probably a small sin to flaunt her ring at church, but she was so excited and happy she could not help it. She said a quick prayer for forgiveness.

Everyone quickly saw the sparkling gem and after Mass she was surrounded with chattering girls oozing envy and congratulations.

Becky had had a terrible night, she had finally fallen asleep around two A.M. At six A.M. Sonny had crawled into bed with her. "Mommy, I don't feel good. I feel I going to fro-up."

She took her sick baby to the bathroom; he didn't throw up but he did feel warm to the touch. She gave him some of the medicine that Doctor Overmars prescribed when he last had a cold. That seemed to settle him down a bit, but now he was hungry.

When they left the bathroom she caught a glimpse of herself in the mirror. *Lord, I look like I am fifty,* she thought.

After feeding Sonny she put him back in bed and went for a bath; she was feeling decidedly scruffy. She needed a haircut but couldn't afford one just yet with all the bills they had; they were just making it. Thank heavens Jack had doubled his monthly contribution to them. Bessie had never returned to health since Ralph's funeral, and the doctor bills were creeping up.

At exactly twelve noon the phone rang. It was Betty Freely, the town's gossip with the news about Katie's ring and engagement.

"I'll tell you, Becky," she warbled, "that thing was big enough to choke a horse and boy did she flash it around."

Becky listened with mounting shock, so Jimmy had totally abandoned her. She knew she had pushed them together last summer, told Katie to take him, but she didn't mean forever. She just wanted him off her back until the Ralph thing was resolved. She went to her bedroom, locked her door and just lay on the bed too exhausted to even cry. She felt anger rising—she needed Jimmy more than Katie now. When she joined the Cannery office staff she was making forty dollars a week, now after three years she was making fifty a week, a twenty-five cent an hour raise.

Jimmy had started at one hundred dollars a week, now in just over a year with the company he was making three hundred. She didn't begrudge him that money, she knew he was the best driver in the company. That he was on the road for weeks at a time and was home sometimes only for one weekend in two. But had Katie not stolen him she would be the one with the ring and the money; maybe she would already be married to him and be pregnant.

She clenched her fists, damn her, and damn him. She felt actual hate for them both. However she was too tired to maintain this emotional high and slipped into a troubled slumber after a few minutes.

When Jimmy and Katie arrived at his Mom and Dad's farm Katie, at the suggestion of Jimmy, turned her diamond around so when she cupped her hand it couldn't be seen. They wanted to surprise them; Jimmy had not mentioned anything to them about wanting to marry Katie, so it would be a quite shock to them. They only knew that Jimmy had called on Saturday morning and invited themselves to Sunday lunch.

When they walked into the kitchen Jimmy's mom and sister Julie were cooking. Katie hugged them both and asked if there was anything she could do to help; within seconds she was setting the table.

Jimmy walked into the living room where his Dad was having a nap in his chair, his head bent over the Sunday paper, which had fallen into his lap. His father woke after a few minutes and they talked about the farm and Jimmy's job. In about half an hour the ladies called them to lunch. Katie sat down at the table and laid her hands in her lap. They all bowed their heads and Dad said grace which was a ritual that Jimmy's family followed at all meals taken at home. While the prayer was being said she turned the ring diamond right side up. They were chatting amiably amongst themselves when Katie passed the mashed potatoes to Julie. The big diamond sparkled as she moved her hand. Julie froze staring at her finger, then let out a shriek. Jimmy's Mom and Dad jumped in their chairs, his Mother almost dropping the green beans.

"Julie what the heck . . ." exclaimed her dad, then following her gaze saw the ring. He looked at Jimmy who had this big goofy grin on his face, then to his wife, whose mouth was open in a stupefied fashion, her eyes locked on the sparkling gem.

Then everything started to move at once. Julie and Katie stood up from their chairs, at the same time Julie jumping into Katie's arms. Jimmy's mom rushed around the table to join the hugging.

The tears of joy were flowing. Jimmy looked down the table to his Dad who was still stunned and not moving, but looking in wonder at the crying, laughing women.

Jimmy got up from his chair and walked around to his father, laying his hand on his dad's shoulder. He said, "Well, Dad, looks like you are going to have another daughter soon." His dad looked up at Jimmy stood up and gave him his hand.

"Congratulations, son," he said shaking Jimmy's hand, "I guess I am."

Then Katie moved over to her future father-in-law and gave him a hug.

"Sorry, Mr. Burns, I hope we didn't scare you too much."

"Oh no, my dear, I am very glad that this young scalawag here had the sense to ask you to marry him, but please call me Norm."

"Ok Norm, would you mind too much if I also called you Dad?" she implored.

"No, no, that would be fine," he said blushing slightly.

They all moved back to their respective chairs to finish lunch but the only subject discussed the rest of the day was the engagement and the coming wedding.

Katie told them of the engagement dinner at the Benson in Portland and how romantic and wonderful it had been.

Julie listened, her eyes large and limpid. She looked at her brother. "I didn't know you could be romantic, big brother."

"Sure Jules, I can be lots of stuff you didn't know. I am a man of mystery." Everyone laughed at that.

Katie told them she hoped the wedding would be either in July or August, that she hadn't talked to the priest yet to see which dates were open.

She looked at Julie. "Dearest, would you be one of my bridesmaids?"

Julie jumped. "Me?"

"Yes, my dear sister," Katie said. She was becoming very fond of both Jimmy's mother and sister, thinking of them as relatives already.

"Oh yes, Katie I would love to be one of your bridesmaids, and your sister," the young girl bubbled, her shining eyes shinning even more.

"Good, I shall need lots of help from you both on this wedding. I hope you won't mind me calling on you whenever I need help."

"Oh no, we shall be glad to help in any way," they both said in unison.

Chinook: Thus started the biggest social event in Low Sky in many years, and the ladies of the Burns family would be the envy of the community.

Jimmy and Joe left that night for a trip to the midwest, their truck and trailer filled with frozen packages of strawberries, blackberries and raspberries. They would be gone two weeks, returning with a truckload of corn fed prime steaks and beef for the restaurants of Salem, Portland and Eugene.

Doc had a ritual he preformed every morning; he would awaken at nine-thirty, bathe, shave and at ten-thirty walk into the doors of the café to have breakfast. He was very popular with the cook and waitresses at the café. They could always count on him to be cheery and have a joke to tell them. He was also a big tipper, and that was rare for a small poor town.

So the Tuesday after the engagement, which was the only thing the girls at the restaurant wanted to talk about this morning, was no exception. After breakfast, and two cigarettes with his coffee, he walked the two blocks home to go to the bathroom. Then at noon when Rocky Rocknell opened his bar he would go to his seat at the far end of the bar and order his first scotch and soda of the day. There he would sit until eleven o'clock that night when the bar closed, one o'clock A.M. on Friday and Saturday nights, leaving his stool only to pee.

Today though a different thing happened, just after he had seated himself he heard Rocky's voice bellow.

"Doctor Overmars, sir, how are you this fine spring morning?"

"I am very fine, Rocky, maybe you have heard of our glad tidings this weekend?"

"Oh yes, sir, that's all we have been hearing since Sunday afternoon," Rocky pontificated, "congratulations to you and your lovely wife and daughter. I've known Jimmy since he was knee high to a toad, good kid, and his family are good people too. Could I get you something to wet your whistle with, Doctor?"

"You know, Rocky, it has been years but I think I would like an Olympia beer."

112

"Said and done, sir," Rocky boomed.

Doctor Overmars moved down to the end of the bar where Doc was sitting. "Excuse me, Doctor," he said. "I am John Overmars. Would you mind if I sat with you for awhile?"

"Certainly, Doctor Overmars," said Doc indicating the chair next to him. Holding out his hand he said, "I am Edward Baxter and I am very happy to make the acquaintance of the most revered man in this community."

"I thank you for that, Doctor, however I am just a small town doctor and there are a lot of things I don't know, especially about mental problems. That is why I am here today to talk to you. First, are you the Doctor Baxter that was part of the prestigious Baxter, Bauer, Reiker Clinic in Portland?"

Doc looked at him. "Yes, Doctor. Doctor Bauer and I founded the clinic, and then later we brought Doctor Reiker into the partnership. However I am no longer associated with the clinic. My ex-wife now is the Baxter in the partnership. She got my share of the clinic in the divorce."

"I see. Well, their loss is maybe our gain." Doctor Overmars smiled at Doc. "We can't talk here but if you could come to my office this afternoon I would like to ask you about a patient that I am very worried about, and can no longer effectively treat."

"Yes," said Doc. "I could do that. What time?"

"I have an opening for about an hour at three o'clock, so barring an emergency, I shall await you at that time."

Doc smiled and nodded his head. "I will be there with pleasure, Doctor Overmars."

By three o'clock Doc had finished his Scotch and soda and waving to Rocky said, "I'll be back later, keep my chair warm."

"Ok Doc," boomed the big bartender. But Doc was wrong—he wouldn't be back for some time.

Doc walked into the small hospital at five minutes after three and spoke to the receptionist. "I am here to see Doctor Overmars."

"Oh," she exclaimed, "so you're the famous Doctor Baxter. I thought you were just a jolly old drunk that we would always see at Rocky's."

"Jolly? I always thought myself as acerbic rather than jolly," he said with a twinkle in his eye.

"Huh?" said the receptionist. "Oh just go on in, he is waiting for you."

Chuckling, Doc knocked on the office door. "Come in," the voice behind it said.

"Doctor Overmars, I am here as previously agreed."

John smiled, extended his hand in greeting, and indicated the chair in front of his desk with his other hand. "Have a seat, Doctor Baxter, but please call me John."

"I shall sir if you call me Ed," said Doc.

John Overmars knew he was going to like Ed Baxter a lot. The one thing he missed as a small town doctor was the dearth of other professional colleagues to talk to, and he hoped that Ed would take up the offer he was about to make to him. "Ed, would you mind if I asked you about your background, professionally of course."

"Sure John. I graduated from the University of Nebraska with a degree in Psychology, did my Masters Dissertation at Cornell in Psychoanalysis. I received my Ph.D. in Clinical Psychology at the University of Pennsylvania. I did my internship at Western New York Hospital for the Insane in Ithaca, New York, and for personal reasons I came out to Oregon and got a job at Portland General, until Bob Bauer and I opened our clinic. I did a lot of trauma work at Portland General, but being a psychoanalyst is my first love. Bob is a psychiatrist and Joe Reiker had his Masters in occupational therapy and his Ph.D. in psychotherapy. So as you see, with our staff, we handled a broad range of mental, physical, and psychoanalysis problems."

John sat for a minute; it seems his prayers had been answered. He had of course, checked out Ed Baxter before he talked to him and everything he had learned about him was confirmed here.

"Ed, I have a problem. My knowledge runs up against a wall once I leave the physical side of human sickness," John leveled with him. "Every year there is more and more mental work here and I can't handle it. I send most of my bad cases to a clinic in Salem but that is a hardship to many of my patients."

John held his breath. "I would like to offer you a practice here in our hospital. We have an extra office where you could work from and we need a psychologist very badly. I know you can't prescribe out of your field but I would take your suggestions for medication if it was needed," John crossed his fingers under his desk. "So I am offering you this position to work with me to better the lives of the people in our area. As you know the area is growing especially as gentleman farmers move out of the city to find a better life for their families, so what do you say?"

Ed sat there rather stunned. "Well, you know, John this a shock. I just expected you to ask me a professional question not offer me a position." Ed sat for a while looking down at his lap, then he said, "You know I was getting rather bored sitting at Rocky's every day. There are

114

some rather colorful characters with some rather interesting psychosis that frequent Rocky's. Having said that I believe I have just about sucked that venue dry as an intellectual pursuit. I accept your offer. I should be up and running in two weeks, how does that sound?"

A large smile lit up John Overmars' face; he stood up, offered Ed his hand and said, "Doctor, that sounds just fine. Welcome to the firm." The two men chatted for a while, then Doctor Overmars' demeanor got serious.

"Ed, the reason I looked you up in the first place was because of Bessie Skinner. Since her son Ralph was discovered in the river she has been slipping down hill."

"What are her symptoms, John?"

"Sleeping all the time, weeping constantly, saying she doesn't want to live, the light has gone out of her eyes. Basically it seems like she does want to die. I keep giving her tranquilizers in ever stronger doses but she doesn't improve. I have tried to get her into the clinic in Salem but she refuses to go, so I'm at wits end."

"Well, of course," Ed said. "I haven't seen her, but maybe medication is not the answer. I had better get on this one right away. When do you see her next?"

"Well, generally on Thursday mornings she has been coming in."

"Ok, when she comes in just send her to me."

"Thanks, Ed, I think we will work together well."

The men stood up and shook hands, then Doctor Edward Baxter went home to prepare himself for the continuation of his work.

Wednesday morning Ed came into the hospital. He brought books, charts and psychological tests he had stored and not looked at since turning up in Low Sky.

He installed shelves, found a file cabinet in another room that wasn't being used, hung charts and his diplomas from the various schools he had graduated from. By noon the office looked like he had been in there for years, and it looked very professional. The only thing he lacked was a comfortable chair for his patients to sit on but that would come soon. After lunch at the café he got out Bessie Skinner's file. He read the physical and mental history of Bessie page by page. She had had some problems with her health—after Ralph was born a small infection that required a couple days of hospitalization. She had taken some mild tranquilizers when her husband died, but mostly her chart showed a strong healthy woman.

That is until Ralph's body was discovered; her health had deteriorated steadily since then. Ed found a telephone number for Boeing in

Seattle and a name "Jack Skinner Jr.," under the heading "who to call in an emergency." He called the number and within a few minutes a man answered who said he was Jack Skinner.

"Mr. Skinner my name is Doctor Edward Baxter, and I, with Doctor Overmars' recommendation have taken your mother as a patient. As you are the named person to contact I would like to go over with you some recommended procedures I am contemplating."

"Ok doctor, I have a few minutes, shoot," said Jack.

"Thank you," Ed retorted. "I would like to put her into the hospital in Portland for two days for a complete physical, to see if there is any medical problems associated with her illness."

"Ok Doctor," replied Jack. "If you feel that is necessary."

"Yes, Mister Skinner I do. Now this won't be cheap and I don't know her resources but if there are any problems I can get it paid for by the Oregon medical aid program."

"Doctor, that won't be necessary. If I give you my address could you send the bills to me?"

"Yes, we most certainly can, and thank you, so if you hold on I'll put you in touch with our billing department and they will take your address down, so hold on just a minute." Ed walked to the billing office and told the clerk that the son of Mrs. Skinner was on the phone with an address for her to bill to.

Ed sighed. That went much easier than he had hoped; when a line opened up he called Portland General and made an appointment for Tuesday and Wednesday of the next week for the admission and testing of Mrs. Skinner.

He messed around with his office to get it looking better, read up on depression a bit, went to the café for dinner, then home.

The next morning he was in his office an hour before Bessie arrived reading over her chart again to make sure he had missed nothing. When she arrived she was brought into his office and he was taken aback. Even though she looked haggard and had lost a lot weight she was truly a beautiful woman—raven black hair flecked with silver and large brown eyes that looked very sad.

They seemed to hit it off immediately; he explained who he was. That he was a psychologist made her pause just for a second.

He quickly assured her that she wasn't crazy. He explained how Doctor Overmars was worried about her and thought that he, Doctor Baxter, could help.

The interview went smoothly; she protested a bit when he told her about going to the hospital in Portland; "My lands, doctor, that would be very expensive."

He assured her that her health was worth it. He asked her if she could get to Portland; she told him about Becky and gave him her telephone number.

After she left he called Becky at the cannery. He told her who he was. "Oh yes, doc, how are you? It's been a long time since I have seen you. I don't get around Rocky's much anymore."

"Miss Anderson, I have taken over Mrs. Skinner as a patient and I need to get her to Portland General hospital next week for two days. Can you take her?"

"Oh doc, I don't think I can get the time off," Becky replied. "Um, I don't know how we can do it."

"Well, with your permission," said Ed, "I can take her and then bring her back. I used to live there. Also I want to be there for the examination anyway."

"Oh yes, doc, that would be great. How can I thank you."

"Well, Miss Anderson, my thanks will be to see Bessie get better."

And so it was set. The next Tuesday morning at seven Becky brought Bessie to the hospital. There she helped get Bessie in the back seat and strapped in with the lap belt. She was decidedly drugged. "How many tranquilizers did Mrs. Skinner take this morning?" he inquired of Becky.

"Her usual, doc. She takes one of the new blue ones Doctor Overmars prescribed for her. I give it to her each morning and she then sleeps until noon."

"I see," said Ed. "Thank you." Becky leaned over Bessie and kissed her on the forehead.

"I will see you Wednesday night, dearest. Just relax and do what the doctors want. Ok?"

The groggy older lady nodded her head and Becky closed the car door. The drive went without incident, Bessie slept the entire way. At nine A.M. Ed pulled up to Portland General. He called for a wheelchair and took Bessie to Patient Registration, there she was taken to her room while Ed filled out the pertinent paperwork. After asking for the name of the doctor who would be in charge of Bessie's examination Ed went to see him to fill him in on the facts of the case. Ed had worked with this man before years ago and knew him to be a good thorough doctor.

After all was arranged Ed went across the street to his old clinic to see Bob Bauer. The receptionist jumped up when he walked into the building. "Oh my god, Doctor Baxter, you've come to visit us, how nice to see you."

"Thanks Susan," he exclaimed taking her hand. "How nice to see you. Things look about the same around here."

"They are about the same, but we miss you a lot," she said emphasizing "a lot."

He caught the inference, smiled at her and asked, "Is Doctor Bauer in?"

"Oh yes, he will be with a patient for about another hour, I am afraid."

"Ok, that's fine. Ah, I have to go get a place to stay but I'll be back to take him out to lunch at noon, so could you tell him?"

"I most certainly will, Doctor Baxter. Er, there isn't any possible way you would be coming back here is there?"

"No, I am afraid not, Susan. I have a practice at a small hospital in a country village called Low Sky. I think that is all I need right now."

Susan gave him a little smile. "Ok, Doctor Baxter, I'll tell him about lunch."

Ed checked into the Town Center Motel about a block from the hospital, and at twelve o'clock sharp walked back into the clinic's reception room. Susan glanced up with a smile on her lips, pushed a button on the intercom and said, "He's here, doctor." Within about three seconds the doors that led to the examination rooms banged open and out bolted Bob Bauer.

"Damn, Ed, you're a sight for sore eyes, welcome home," he said grasping Ed in a big bear hug.

The questions came fast: "Are you here for good, have you moved back, are you thinking of opening another clinic?" He held Ed at arm length with his hands on Ed's shoulders. "Well damn it, you are looking good. Bit lighter maybe. This place you disappeared to must suit you."

Ed was just standing there with a big goofy grin on his face. "It's nice seeing you, Bob. Let's go have lunch and I will catch you up on the last three years."

Doctor Bauer looked at Susan. "Cancel all my appointments for the afternoon, transfer those that can't be put off to Doctor Reiker and tell Mrs. Baxter, if she asks, that I'll be back tomorrow morning!" With that exclamation the two men walked out the door and headed for the Breakfast Club restaurant.

The Breakfast Club was a restaurant for members only, catering mainly to business and professional people. For a yearly subscription fee a businessman could bring a client or reserve a whole room for a meeting. Many a deal was worked out over a steaming plate of ham and eggs or the steak and crab lunch.

After they were seated Ed began to tell Bob about his life since that day three years ago when he cleaned out his desk, bid everyone good-bye and walked out the front doors of the clinic.

Bob listened with rapt attention as Ed talked about leaving Portland, heading south, not knowing where he was going, but looking for a place to heal his battered mind and soul. How at Salem he had, for some reason, turned left and headed for the purple Cascade mountain range on the eastern horizon. How, as he drove and climbed toward the mountains, the land had changed to farms with orchards. How the slopes of the hills were covered with firs marching up to the high mountains with the tops, of snow-capped peaks, pushing up into the blue sky. How when he reached a town by the name of Slayton he had turned right and wandered down a country road through lush fields filled with every kind of berry and vegetable. Strawberries, raspberries, blueberries, sweet corn, green beans with vines growing up six feet high on strings wrapped over wire strung from poles at the end of each row. Fields of carrots, small yellow potatoes and hops for brewing beer. How he topped a hill and dropped into a valley with a Victorian village, "built in 1880's" so the sign said, nestled between the hills with a small river running through the middle of it. The sign went on to say "The Home of 500 happy people." In this village he found an old bar run by a jolly robust sort of gent and right across a side street from the bar a small one bedroom house to rent.

A good place he thought to stay and drink himself to death.

How after a while he gave up the "drinking himself to death routine," because he wasn't really a big drinker.

How he had presided over some rather eccentric and colorful locals who frequented the bar from opening to closing. Finally how the local M.D. had talked him in to opening a practice in the town hospital and that was why he was here. He had brought a patient to be given a complete physical before starting her mental recovery.

Bob looked at him with his eyes wide open. "Gosh, Ed, what a story. I was afraid you had driven off into a canyon somewhere and some day I would have to identify the car and what was left of the body."

"I wish you had written or called me to let us know you were alive."

"Well, Bob, as you know, after the divorce I was trashed, emotionally I was burnt up. As Jane got my half of the clinic from the Judge I had no reason to stay, and I just had to purge some demons. Speaking of Jane, how you getting along with her?"

Bob looked up at the waiter approaching with their food; after the food was placed on the table and the waiter retreated he looked down at his plate. "Well," he started, "she is a worker and the clinic is doing fine. The problem is she has such a caustic personally that we all find her extremely hard to be around. She got licensed to be a therapist by the state and has a large patient log of mostly frustrated, oversexed, or undersexed housewives. That business brings in a lot of money and keeps her off our backs for the most part. Just a year ago I tried to buy her half of the clinic but it was a no go, she likes being a therapist and telling people what's good for them."

Ed smiled. "Well if it wasn't the patients it would, in my absence, be you and Reiker." They both had a laugh at that and spent a pleasant afternoon talking about old times. They went to a local pub after lunch and got slightly potted. Ed went to the hospital after he had eaten dinner to check on his patient. She was doing fine and was asleep now. He arrived at his hotel room about eight o'clock, had a shower, watched the local nine o'clock news on the old TV in his room and fell asleep at ten.

The next morning he breakfasted at the motel restaurant and then went to the hospital. He talked to the doctor in charge of the Bessie's examination; all tests so far had been negative, no problems at all. She would be released at three o'clock this afternoon. He walked over to the clinic again to see Bob one last time.

When he walked into the reception area he stopped dead in his tracks. There she was talking to Susan, Jane, still the most beautiful woman he had ever seen; the long dark hair spilling down her back, the trim tapered legs disappearing into the hem of her just above the knee skirt. After all the hurt and frustration she had caused him it was still there, the ache, the passion, the yearning, and yes, the love.

He knew that if she turned and seeing him ran to his arms now and asked forgiveness he would take her back; he would have no choice. Susan glanced past Jane as she stood checking her schedule for the morning. Following Susan's gaze Jane turned and saw Ed standing there.

For one moment her heart stopped, and she felt a flash of fear. Was he a ghost, was he here to take her away to hell? Then she shook her head. *You must be getting stupid in your middle years,* she thought to herself. No one had heard a thing from him for three years, she knew he would have never called her but the boys hadn't heard from him either. He looked real enough, so she said, "Well well, the prodigal son has returned." A small sardonic smile twisted her lip slightly. "Not eating many husks with the pigs I see, more like prime rib maybe. I wonder where you came from," she wondered aloud, "where have you been?"

Ed looked back into that heavenly face, his knees almost buckled. "I wouldn't think that you could possibly care what happened to me," he mused.

120

Her eyes flashed like a hard green diamond, her lips slightly curled. "So it starts already, Ed. It seems we can't be in the same room together.

"However, I am glad you're not dead, for what that's worth." Saying that she turned and walked through the doors into the examination rooms and was gone.

He had to fight himself not to run after her; damn would he ever get over her.

Susan was embarrassed. She glanced at Ed and saw the stricken look on his face. She cleared her throat. "Would you like me to call Doctor Bauer, Doctor Baxter?"

"Yeah, thanks Susan, if he is not busy."

Bob, Bill Reiker and Ed had lunch together. After lunch Ed went to the motel and checked out. He moved his car to the hospital entrance and went in to have the last talk with her physician.

"Well, Ed, she is as fit as a horse. Her only trouble was she was dehydrated, but we re-hydrated her with eight bottles of saline drip. She is almost ready, she is awake if you want to see her now." As they walked up to her room her doctor said, "My suggestion would be to monitor her fluid intake and of course take her off those sedatives she was on."

"Thanks Mark," Ed said. "I was fairly sure she was ok physically, but I had to be totally sure before I started her treatment."

They loaded Bessie into the back seat and at five o'clock Ed pulled up in front of her house. She talked to him on the way back, and had watched the passing scenery from the window of the car making comments now and again.

Ed helped her into the house and saw her seated in the kitchen before he left. He asked the babysitter to have Becky call him at the hospital as soon as she was back from work. He had just returned to the hospital and was updating Bessie's file when the phone rang; it was Becky. He told her that Mrs. Skinner was just fine physically, that she was to throw away the blue pills and instill in Bessie the need to drink a lot of fluids during the day.

He would start to see her on Friday at ten o'clock and would see her three times a week at first, and then as she progressed once a week.

Becky hung up the phone, she was very happy that Bessie was going to be all right. A ton of weight had just been lifted from her shoulders and already she felt better than she had since Ralph's body was found.

13

Chinook:

It was a good thing that Becky was feeling better. On Saturday she would have a surprise visit from Katie and she would need all her strength for what Katie would ask her.

Katie's life had been busy since "THE ENGAGEMENT." She had talked to Father Road and the big day was set for the first Saturday in August.

Jimmy's indoctrination into the church would be finished in July. His first Confession, conditional Baptism, and first Communion would follow the next Sunday.

A person can only have one baptism in their life for original sin. Jimmy had already been baptized in the Baptist church, so this one would be conditional and executed just in case an error was made the first time.

Katie and her mother were very happy that Jimmy would be a Catholic by the wedding; this way the newly married couple could have a Nuptial Mass.

Things were not perfect though and Katie was worried. She wanted five bridesmaids; she had Jimmy's sister and two of the girls from the young unmarried group at church. Her cousin from Boise was going to be her maid-of-honor. The maid-of honor and Jimmy's best man had to be Catholics because of the Nuptial Mass; the rest of the group didn't matter, they could take a seat during the Mass.

Her only hope then was Becky. Becky who had been and hopefully still was, even after their small misunderstanding over Jimmy, her best friend.

Saturday morning Becky had woken early and just ran a brush through her hair and slapped on a pair of dirty jeans and a wrinkled blouse. She was going to clean house in the morning and then work in the flowerbeds and weed around the daffodils in the afternoon.

Sonny and Bessie were fed breakfast and now that Bessie was

starting to feel better she would look after Sonny, which would give Becky the freedom to do the chores that had been building up all winter.

At about eleven A.M., Becky was in the middle of cleaning the kitchen windows, when she thought she heard a knock on the front door.

Well Bessie was playing with Sonny in the front parlor, they could get it, she thought. She heard the door open and Bessie say, "Oh hello, dear come in." Then Sonny started yelling, "Auntie Katie, Auntie Katie." Becky was so surprised she dropped her cleaning rag.

She heard Katie say, "Hello, my sweet little one, is your mommy home?" Then, "How nice to see you Bessie, you look so well!"

Becky was rooted in her tracks. "Thank you, my dear. Oh what a lovely ring, can I see it? Gosh it is so beautiful. Did you come to see Becky?"

"Yes," Katie said.

"I will get her. Just wait a second, dear."

Bessie appeared in the kitchen doorway. Becky could not have looked worse; she had a black smudge of grease on her nose, from when she cleaned the oven, her hair was a mess and the clothes that she had shoved on when getting up were now more disheveled and dirty than ever.

"Katie is here to see you my dear," said Bessie with a small smile.

"Ok, I am coming," Becky pulled off her yellow latex gloves patted her hair and walked out into the parlor.

Katie looked like she had just stepped out of the latest spring issue of *Harper's Bazaar*. She had on a simple white cotton dress with yellow daisies scattered over it, a yellow sweater and on her feet yellow pumps, all of course matching perfectly. Her blond hair glowed and was cut to perfectly frame her lovely face. Becky would have died with embarrassment if she hadn't been so stunned.

Katie crossed the room and took her hand; the ring caught the light and flashed fire. "Dearest, I have come to ask you a very important question, could we sit down?"

Becky just stared at her, her eyes then moving to the ring. Bessie moved quickly to usher the girls to the sofa in the front parlor.

When they were seated facing each other Katie said, "I would like you to be one of my bridesmaids."

That focused Becky's attention and her eyes narrowed slightly. She opened her mouth and in a voice she almost didn't recognize as her own, she blurted, "But I could never afford a bridesmaid's dress, especially one nice enough for your wedding."

Katie smiled at her. "Oh dearest, don't worry, I will pay for your dress. I just want you with me on that day."

Becky just stared at her. Bessie quickly added, "Oh Katie, that would be wonderful. What will your colors be?"

"Rose Pink and Cream," Katie quickly said turning gratefully to Bessie. "All the bridesmaids will be in Rose Pink with, I think, cream colored camellias in their bouquets. Becky, with her dark coloring, would look lovely in pink, don't you think?" she said turning back to Becky.

"Oh yes, dear," Bessie was quick to utter.

"So, my dearest, would you consent to be one of my bridesmaids?"

Becky, overwhelmed, nodded her head yes.

"Oh thank you," gushed Katie, taking both of Becky's hands in hers. "Two weekends from now we all have an appointment in Salem for our fitting at the Capital Bridal Shop. Could you come with me then?"

Once again Becky nodded her head yes.

"Oh this is all going to be such fun," Katie said rising.

She walked over to where Sonny was playing with his truck and said, "Sweet one, would you like to be in Auntie Katie's wedding also? Auntie Katie and Uncle Jimmy would like Sonny to be the ring bearer," she said turning to Becky and Bessie.

"Oh how wonderful," said Bessie and Becky just nodded.

After Katie had left Becky sat riveted on the sofa for a few minutes; slowly she could feel the heat rising in her face. She walked out to the kitchen, picked up the old cracked cup she had been having coffee out of and slammed it into the wall.

Bessie quickly took Sonny and his truck and went out into the yard shutting the door.

"The gall, the absolute gall," Becky fumed. "Stealing my man then asking me to be in her stupid damned wedding. The slut, damn her." Becky kicked the window washing bucket, hurting her toe, she hobbled up to her room, crawled into her bed and cried herself to sleep. All the chores she had to do, forgotten.

Jimmy arrived home later that same afternoon. He called Katie and took a bath, then he went over to Katie's house, picked her up and they went to dinner in Salem.

She told him about her visit to Becky to ask her to be one of her bridesmaids. "I thought when I first arrived that she would refuse me, she seemed a little cold. But after awhile she seemed to soften and consented, so I am quite happy about it. After all, it was Becky who broke

124

up with you originally; and how glad I am she did," she smiled at Jimmy. "It wasn't like I had stolen you directly from her arms because you both had stopped seeing each other three or four months before we started dating."

"So you are friends again?" Jimmy inquired.

"Yes darling, I think so. We have a few more bumpy roads to travel but I believe we will be fine."

After dinner Jimmy found a place to park on a hill overlooking the city. After they had been kissing for a few minutes Katie felt Jimmy becoming a bit passionate. He started to slip his hand up her leg and his kisses moved down to her cleavage. She didn't stop his hand or his kisses.

She gently stroked his hair; kissing his forehead she said softly, "Darling, if you want me, I won't stop you, but it would be better to wait until we're married."

He stopped. "I know, but I love you so much, and I want you so much."

"I know, darling. I want you too, but it is a sin, the sin of fornication, and God doesn't like us to sin."

"A sin? How could my making love to you be a sin, it would be heaven."

She smiled. "Ah darling, I do so want to be a virgin on our wedding night. It is only four more months to wait, then you can have me all you want, forever."

"Four more months," he groaned. "Darn that sounds like forever. I don't think I'll make it. I think I will explode after tonight."

She laughed. "Why sir you do make a girl feel wanted." She batted her eyeslashes at him. "I am sure you will make it just fine. In the meantime, you don't have to stop kissing me."

After a couple long kisses she squeezed him tightly in her arms and whispered in his ear, "They say that marriages are made in heaven, and I am sure that heaven meant us to be married, my love."

"I think you are right, baby. I know it will be heaven when you are totally mine."

They left their hill and cuddled together in the front seat as they drove slowly back to Low Sky.

Chinook:

Jimmy was totally in love with Katie, with a kind of love that a few months ago he didn't know existed, that he didn't realize he could be consumed with. He knew now what that phrase "Thee I will worship with my body" meant. Though with not only his body but also with his mind and his being. The cool water of Katie naked and submissive in his arms would be the only salve to slake the fire that was pent up in every one of his cells. He no longer needed or thought of Kathleen. She hadn't visited him for a while, though one night he felt the cold dampness of fog caress his cheek as he fell asleep; she kept watch over him.

A week before, as he sat unnoticed in his car, he had watched Becky walk down Main street. It was the first time he had seen her in months. She looked washed out, her face tired and her feet dragging. If he had never known her he would have thought her forty-four not twenty-four. He couldn't believe that less than a year ago he had been in love with her, ready to defy his mother and the town gossips, to marry her and adopt Sonny as his own. He felt a slight revulsion as he looked at her now and thanked his lucky stars he was with Katie. He knew this was an uncharitable feeling. Slowly the Catholic training he was receiving was changing him. He would have to mention this uncharitable feeling, for another person, in his first confession.

He was trying to turn the open lust he felt for Katie into a softer love that protected her. He had to convince himself that she was more to him than an object of lust, not just a body to slake his cravings. That a marriage wasn't just for sex but to help each other attain heaven, and to create children. That is why, Father explained, they couldn't practice birth control once they were married.

The realization that he was sterile was a knife in his heart. He hadn't told Katie that they would never have children.

She had mentioned, in an early stage of their relationship, that all children she brought into the world would be raised Catholic. Now since he was becoming a Catholic that was a moot point and she had not talked further about having or even wanting children.

He was a coward; he couldn't lose her so close to having her, so he held his tongue and someday, he told himself, if she really wanted children they could adopt. This sin of omission, though, still flooded his heart with guilt. Some day he knew he would have to confess this terrible lie and do a long penance, but for now it had to be kept hidden.

So the days passed and the time was soon upon them when Jimmy became a Catholic and the wedding day arrived.

The Overmars' house was in pandemonium; it was the Friday morning before the wedding day.

John Overmars and his son Mike were keeping out of the way as much as they could. Mike said to his father at breakfast, "Gosh Dad, I'll be glad when this mess is over. I miss my bed and that sofa isn't the best place to sleep."

"Well son," said John with a sardonic smile on his face, "this is the time that women take control and it's best that men just try to stay clear and to quickly do as they're told." John reached out and rumpled his son's hair. "Remember this will pass soon."

Just the day before at the clinic John had asked Edward if he could spare a room for Mike and himself, and even though Edward laughed, it was not totally a joke.

*   *   *

Jimmy had moved out to the farm after his last trip, which had been to Denver. His Air Force buddy and wife had been invited to the wedding but she was almost ready to have their first baby. In fact she had it the evening Jimmy and Joe left Denver, their truck loaded with sides of prime beef.

Jimmy and Katie had obtained a small two-bedroom house just beyond the grade school playground and would move in after their honeymoon. They had rented the house two weeks ago and Katie along with her mother and a hired man had cleaned and painted the inside and outside of the small house.

The new curtains had arrived just yesterday but lay in the front room of the little house ready to be hung by April and the hired man while the young ones were away. Hopefully the new furniture would arrive before they returned, but there was no time to worry about that now. The night before the wedding April had finished in the kitchen; everyone in the house had gone to bed in anticipation of the big day. As she walked past Katie's bedroom door she noticed the light still on.

She knocked and said, "It is your Mother. May I come in?"

Katie had been hanging her dress when walking past her full-length mirror in her bra and panties, stopped to look critically at her figure. She had turned slowly looking herself over.

This was the sight in a few short hours that Jimmy would look upon. Would he think she was pretty, would he be glad he married her, will it have been worth the wait?

She slipped off her bra. She had always thought her breasts were too large for her figure. She remembered when Becky had first become her best friend; Becky had told her all the girls in high school had been envious of her breasts and figure. One had even said, "Why can't I have those tits and she have mine; she is never going to use them anyhow." At the time that really had made her angry, but Becky just laughed it

127

off. She then slowly turned focusing on her hips and butt. "Sigh," she wished her butt was not so saggy and her legs longer, however she was pleased with her stomach, "nice and flat." That was the way she stood when she heard her mother's knock.

"Yes come in, mother," she said. April opened the door and slipped into the room. There she observed her beautiful daughter standing before her mirror naked casting a critical eye on her body.

The years slipped away, she thought. When she stood in front of the mirror the night before her wedding wondering if John would think she was pretty.

Katie had a much different figure than April. April was taller with a more boyish figure. Katie had taken after John's mother with a more voluptuous, more curvaceous figure. April sat down on Katie's bed. Katie turned away from the mirror and putting on her robe sat next to her beloved mother.

April glanced up. "Darling, you are a grown woman and you don't have to answer this but have you and Jimmy . . . err . . . had . . . um . . . relations?"

Katie turned slightly pink looking down. She said, "No mother, I am still a virgin."

Taking a deep breath April said, "Do you know what Jimmy will want to do to you tomorrow night?"

"Yes mother, I think I know. I have never seen a naked man except in a drawing in biology once, but I have overheard girls tell what their boyfriends did to them."

"Well dear, I am sure Jimmy will be gentle and kind to you, because it is so obvious that he adores you. It may hurt a bit, my dear, when he loves you the first time, so be ready for that. It won't be his fault, but ladies have a skin over their opening that needs to be pierced by the man.

"The women of our family love their husbands and they let them have their bodies when they are asked, but we only let one man do that special thing to us. Gran had only one man, I have had only your father and I know you will only let Jimmy do that as long as he lives. Other women let men other than their husbands have that special thing, but it is not our way."

"Mother," said Katie avoiding her mother's eyes, "is it fun?"

April looked at her daughter. "Oh yes, darling, it is fun. It is romantic and sometimes it is glorious."

Katie glanced at her mother and watched as her eyes took on a faraway look like she was seeing the past. "But it is more, much more than that. It is having him in your arms safe and warm knowing that he is not out in some foreign country with bad people trying to kill him. At some bar late at night patching up a drunk that has been shot, or on the road during a storm going someplace to deliver a baby. Knowing that he is safe with you, safe warm and loved, is worth more than all the riches any person could accumulate in ten life times." April halted. "Oh well, I guess I got carried away a bit there."

Katie looked at her mother, her eyes shining. "Oh Mother, I never knew you felt that way about Father."

"Your father is my life, darling. Well you need your sleep and I should go now, big day tomorrow."

"Mother, there is one more thing I have to ask you before you go," said Katie looking into April's face.

"What darling?" inquired April.

"What's it like to be pregnant and have a baby?"

The question rocked April, with all the preparing and planning she had missed one thing her baby was going to be loved and maybe within a year she was going to be a grandmother. April's eyes filled with tears and she moved into Katie's arms and started to weep. "Oh my dear, my baby."

After twenty-four years of being comforted a hundred times with hurt knees, elbows and feelings the roll was reversed and Katie comforted her mother as she sobbed gently in her arms.

Jimmy was now a fully active Catholic. During his first confession he had mentioned having slept with a prostitute when overseas in the Air Force. He thought he heard Father suck in his breath slightly, but actually Father was stifling a small yawn; he hadn't slept well the night before.

So absolution was given and Jimmy could fully concentrate on his upcoming wedding with Katie.

Becky had by now forgiven Katie; actually she was now very happy to be in the wedding. She had received her bridesmaid's dress from Katie and it was the most beautiful dress she had ever owned, and she did look gorgeous in it.

Katie, Becky and the rest of the bridesmaids had gone to the beauty parlor the day before and had their hair done. Katie paid for them all and Becky even got a new pair of matching pink high heels from Katie.

The morning of the wedding Becky put on her new dress. *Wow*, she thought, *what a pretty girl I am!* She turned slowly in front of her mirror. *Eat your heart out, Jimmy Burns, you could have had me but now it's too late, so poo on you!*

The wedding was long, as most Catholic weddings are, but it was lovely, the biggest thing to hit Low Sky since the new high school opened twenty years ago.

The reception was held in the IOOF hall, on Main Street. The food, which was plain but very good, was catered by a group of women from Slayton that did weddings all over the area.

In the main it was a perfect day, the groom nervous, the bride radiant and beautiful beyond words. Jimmy's mother and sister were as proud and happy as two people could be. Jimmy's dad just stood with a big grin on his face accepting congratulations from everyone. He never stopped marveling what a lovely daughter-in-law his son had caught, if the truth be told he was just a little in love with her himself.

Chinook:

Once the cake had been cut and eaten, the dancing started with Katie and Jimmy leading off.

Katie's Father interrupted in a few minutes and Jimmy danced with April. Then Jimmy's Dad with a bit of prodding broke in and danced with Katie and Jimmy with his mom, and so in ever widening circles everyone danced with Katie and Jimmy.

Finally Jimmy danced with Becky. At first she was silent, not catching his eye, looking at everyone but him.

Finally, just before he was going to move on to Katie's cousin, Becky kissed his cheek. "You and Katie were meant for each other," she said.

"Becky I . . ." Jimmy stammered.

"No Jimmy, I have been thinking, if we would have been meant for each other it would have worked out but it didn't, so let's leave it that way, but we will be lifelong friends, ok?"

"Sure Becky, we will always be buddies!"

"That's it, Jimmy, buddies, that's what we will be, buddies." Then Becky gave him a little punch in the shoulder. "But you had better make her pregnant soon or I'll wonder about you BUDDIE!" Then with an arch of her eyebrows and a quick smile she turned and walked away.

Jimmy went to find Katie's cousin.

Jimmy's mom had been watching Becky and Jimmy dance; when she saw Becky give him that small punch and walk away she could not help but smirk. *Ha, ha,* she thought and smiled a triumphant smile.

Katie stood on the stage of the hall and threw her bridal bouquet to a waiting throng of girls. Becky stationed herself in the middle of the throng and as the bouquet floated down made a quick jump and snatch and claimed it for herself. *It is now time for me to move on and this is the start,* she thought.

Katie and Jimmy went to her house to change and then kissing their mothers, fathers, and siblings goodbye drove to the Benson Hotel in Portland for their first night together.

Chinook:

Men say the four most important times of their lives are, their birth, marriage, birth of their children and their death. For Jimmy tonight would be a very major milepost. The night when he would see his love naked for the first time and hold her in his arms. Would he be up to the task, would she enjoy his lovemaking? Katie was a virgin and Jimmy a near virgin; he wasn't really sure how girls were constructed between their legs. He had had Kathleen twice but never had looked down there so he was going in blind as it were.

When they undressed each other he couldn't believe how beautiful she was. He had seen Becky naked and Kathleen naked but neither could hold a candle to his wife. "Wife"—how strange that sounded. They fumbled around and accomplished the deed all right, so the marriage was consummated exactly three hours after they had left home. Like most young couples on their wedding night there was a little pain and blood on Katie's part, and a small amount of pleasure and relief on Jimmy's part. Then they fell asleep in each other's arms, exhausted.

The next morning when they awoke they tried to make love again but it was too painful for Katie, so they kissed and chatted calling each other, "wife" and "husband," tasting the words. Jimmy slowly moved his hand over Katie's naked body marveling how soft her skin was and how warm and beautiful she was. They showered together, put on the big fluffy robes the hotel provided and called room service for their first meal together as man and wife. After breakfast it was Katie's turn to explore Jimmy; after a bit of hesitation she touched his penis for the first time, marveling how hard it was. So bit by bit they found out about each other just like millions of generations before them had done on the first few days of wedded bliss.

After a week they came home. Katie was better now and they made love every moment they could. They pulled up in front of their first home and Jimmy carried Katie across the threshold of their little house. Two days later Jimmy had to leave for two weeks; he bravely held Katie in his manly arms and comforted her as she cried, promising to call her every time the truck stopped, telling her he would count the seconds until they were back in each other's arms. Katie would start back to work tomorrow but tonight would be unbearable without her Jimmy.

So they parted for the first time, a lump of pain in Jimmy's chest and throat, and tears running down Katie's cheeks. After Jimmy left Katie fixed her makeup and walked the few blocks over to her parents' home, no longer hers she thought, to see her mother. They had lunch together and talked about the little house. All the furniture hadn't arrived yet leaving Katie and Jimmy with a bed and kitchen table with four chairs as their total furniture.

Katie told her mother what a lovely honeymoon they had had. After leaving Portland they had driven down the Oregon coast road stopping whenever the notion came upon them.

14

The manager of the store where the furniture had been ordered, called April just that morning and told her the load would be at the house Wednesday morning or by Thursday morning at the very latest. Katie was very thrilled because that meant everything would be in place when Jimmy arrived home.

When the furniture arrived Katie and April worked for the best part of a week to make the house perfect.

The hardest thing that Jimmy had done in his life, so far, was leaving Katie that morning knowing he wouldn't see her for almost two weeks. The pain in his chest was almost unbearable.

Jimmy drove first that morning and Joe sitting in the passenger seat looked with sympathy at the young man, remembering the first time he had left his new bride. However Joe, who had joined the Army, was off to basic training and wouldn't see Barbara for at least two months. The hardest part of course was that Barbara was two months pregnant with their first child; he closed his eyes and recalled how he begged her to take care of herself while kissing her tear-streaked cheeks and sweet salty lips. Well thank heavens for her parents, whom she stayed with during his absence. Because Joe had gotten Tank School, right out of Basic, in Texas, and hadn't returned home for four months. He remembered coming home to a wife who had grown much larger in the middle, how beautiful she was, and after they had made love that night how he stroked her swollen belly and felt his son move in her womb for the first time.

Just then the truck lurched as Jimmy slammed on the brakes almost striking a car in front of them who was signaling for left turn. "Damn, Jimmy, you want me to drive?" Joe said looking askance at the young man.

"No, it's alright, Joe, my mind was somewhere else for a moment but I'll be alright now." Joe looked hard at his companion. "Are you sure? I can wheel this buggy for awhile if you want. We want to make sure you get home alive otherwise pretty Katie would never forgive me."

Jimmy smiled. "I will be fine now, thanks for your concern."

"Well it's kind of my concern too. I want to live to be a grandpa again."

Chinook:

So it went for the young couple, as it has for countless young couples. When Jimmy arrived home in two weeks the little house was finished and furnished. He barely noticed though, having eyes only for his beautiful young Bride. April thought they were so sweet; they couldn't be apart for more than a few minutes and when they were together were touching all the time. Jimmy would have her hand in his or his arm around her; Katie would lean against Jimmy or would snuggle under his arm while standing or sitting. April was very happy for them—they seemed so suited to each other and any misgivings she might have had about their marriage vanished.

Each time Jimmy left it became easier for them to cope. Now a year had elapsed and their lives were sorted out.

Katie was sometimes lonely when Jimmy was on the road; she spent a lot of time with her parents, actually staying in her old bedroom overnight at times.

She also became fast friends again with Becky. Most Saturday mornings they would go shopping or have lunch and once took Sonny to the zoo in Portland.

April hoped Katie would soon be pregnant; she thought Katie would be better for it and it would cement a marriage that was fragmented because of Jimmy being away so much. Each time Jimmy returned home, he wanted to make love to Katie as much as he could. Katie was starting to resent his urgency just a little.

Yes, it was kind of fun having Jimmy make love to her; she felt warm and protected in his arms, and she liked him making a fuss of her and he always brought her little presents. That was all ok but she really didn't enjoy the physical part as much as Jimmy seemed to. It was somewhat messy, and sticky; she was naturally a clean person and she always took a bath when he was done having sex with her. So it seemed to her she was either under Jimmy or in the bathtub the entire time he was home.

Another thing was bothering her. All the girls she knew got pregnant within a few months of being married. Mother had gotten pregnant with her soon after marrying Father. Becky had gotten pregnant with Ralph soon after dating him and they weren't even married. It was not as if Katie pined for a baby but she had a romantic notion about giving Jimmy a child and she felt she was letting him down.

Jimmy, to his credit, never mentioned them having a baby so she was under no pressure, but a baby was something all lovers had when they got married; anyway, in all the *Flame* books they did, and those books were her guide to love and life.

Jimmy had two weeks vacation this year, so on their anniversary they spent it at her Uncle Bob's ranch in Idaho.

They reconnected. Jimmy didn't seem to be as urgent to make love to her every second and sometimes they would pack a picnic and ride horses out to a stream and wooded area where Jimmy would fish for trout and she would sunbathe. She would remember that vacation for along time.

Jimmy would be very attentive to her; they would have their picnic they would talk, hold hands, and he would stroke her hair.

Sometimes at home he would sneak up behind her and grab her breasts; she didn't like that, he didn't do that here and that made her happy.

Jimmy was so in love with Katie. He just couldn't let her go. When he came home from a long trip he made love to her as much as physically possible. He thought she liked it and wanted him the same as he did her. When they made love she would look into his eyes, smile and stroke his hair, sometimes when they had finished she would sigh and kiss him asking if he had enough.

He also felt guilty about being away from her so much. So he made love to her to show her he loved her. He liked to sneak up behind her when she was doing another task and surprise her by hugging her and fondling her breasts, kissing her on the neck or running a hand over her stomach. When he would grab her she would gasp and push back into him or jump; he thought she liked it. He liked it; the feel of her breasts in his hands would always drive him crazy with lust. She never complained, only asking him if he had enough or if he was happy with her, he never suspected she wasn't totally happy.

On the last day of their visit they left just after lunch, thanking Katie's aunt and uncle for a very nice stay.

Katie was the happiest she had been since their honeymoon. They stayed overnight at Bend, Oregon and Jimmy was just as he was on the ranch, attentive but not sexual, loving but not demanding. That night in their motel room they fell asleep in each other's arms, both exhausted but calmer, and more attuned to each other than they had been for a long time.

They arrived home. The next morning Jimmy had to leave at six

A.M. He insisted that Katie not get up that early, so they made love that evening. He was very gentle with her, letting her control the situation. It went very smoothly and Katie felt they had entered a new phase of their relationship, and she was very happy until he arrived home again two weeks later.

They then slipped back into the old routine and Katie's balloon burst. She resigned herself to his ways, not wanting to hurt him, but once again she felt used rather than loved. Jimmy left on that Monday morning.

Katie walked the couple of blocks to work like she always did. This morning however she saw a movement ahead of her just to the right of the sidewalk in some long grass. She stopped and the moving grass revealed itself as a small mouse. The timid creature moved to the middle of the sidewalk twitching its tiny nose, looking around with black shining eyes. Katie stood frozen to her spot not moving a muscle.

The bush just behind the long grass exploded; a large tiger striped cat, which neither Katie nor the mouse had noticed, enveloped the mouse impaling the helpless small creature with its claws.

Katie screamed. The cat, looking at Katie, for the first time, laid back its ears, hissed, turned and sank his fangs into the mouse. Getting a good hold on the struggling prey the cat then ran off with the mouse dangling from its jaws. Katie was shaking all over, she was almost ill. Starting to cry she ran home; she sat on her sofa sobbing and shaking for some time. She had never seen anything die before.

When she was a small child she had found a dead bird in the backyard; that had upset her very much. To calm their little girl Mother and Father had had a funeral for the bird, burying it in the garden with some prayers.

This sudden death though had shaken her to her roots and she didn't know why. Finally calming herself she went to work and removed it from her mind until that night before falling asleep.

All alone in her bed she remembered the small mouse's death with a shudder. She felt empathy with the creature; it was pounced on and she felt pounced on also every time Jimmy came up behind her and grabbed her. Why should she have to feel that way, afraid to turn her back on him? She made a vow before falling asleep to ask Jimmy to not do that anymore.

It wasn't like she didn't like to be in his arms. She just didn't liked to be pounced on. If he loved her, he would listen and not do it anymore. So Katie was the first to lay down guidelines in their young marriage. Their relationship was starting to mature, starting to move from the romantic to the pragmatic.

Jimmy would be hurt for awhile but he would alter his ways because it was practical to do so, and because he liked living with Katie and wanted her to be happy.

Becky lay in her bed that night also, thinking about Katie and Jimmy. Although she had made a vow to move on she was still terribly jealous of their relationship. They seemed so happy, they had the perfect marriage. She could have had the perfect marriage with Jimmy but for Ralph. Why hadn't he just stayed away from her; she would have never gone out with him unless he had asked her. It just wasn't fair, why didn't nice things ever happen to her. Becky dropped into sleep, her jaws tight and lips thin.

Jimmy had driven all day while Joe had slept on and off. They were on their way to Kansas City with a truck and trailer filled with frozen vegetables and berries. Now as they entered Idaho Joe had taken over and Jimmy was in the sleeper thinking about Katie. How much he loved her and how he could not understand how he had lived without her. To be celibate again would be like being plunged into hell. He lay with his eyes closed and pictured her in his mind naked. He could reach out and almost feel her nipples under his fingers, the soft skin on her belly and the soft down between her legs. He woke up just as he ejaculated in his underwear; sheepishly he reached for some Kleenex and cleaned up his mess as best he could. He stuffed the wet Kleenex into his jean pocket hoping to get rid of them at the next stop. He lay down again smiling to himself. *Gosh it has been only twenty-four hours since I have made love to her and already I have had a wet dream, oh Katie what you do to me.* With that thought on his mind he fell asleep again.

*   *   *

Chinook:

Lay your right hand on table palm up. Spread your fingers and point the tips to the west. Curl your little finger and ring fingers into your palm and cover them with your thumb. There you have the valley of the Thomas River. The fingers covered by the thumb are the mountains, the Thomas River enters the Valley at the web between your index and second fingers where it falls for over one mile in a series of rapids and calm water to finally plunge into the pool where Ralph died.

The river meanders through the Valley dissecting Low Sky with

137

approximately one third of the village to the south and two thirds to the north of it.

Almost one million years ago a glacier moved down between the ridges from the higher mountains carving and smoothing the valley we see today. When the glacier reached the large joint of the second finger a spur of it moved south cutting a quarter mile opening into the ridge which men now call the Richardson Gap. The cleft was named after a pioneer family that homesteaded the gap in the early 1870's. Today you can still see the original house and barn Fred Richardson had erected some ninety-three years before. Above the old farm rises a shear cliff one thousand feet into the sky. When you leave Low Sky and travel east on Highway 22 in about one and a half miles you approach the Richardson Gap Road. Turning south you pass through the gap and once past come to a crossroads with Route 1 Road. If you turn east on this road you will be traveling up the side of your hand, with the mountains looming to your left and to your right a small river known locally as Crabtree Creek.

Jimmy and Katie had been married just over two years now and they had settled into a routine. Jimmy no longer pounced on Katie as he once did. If he wanted to make love to her he asked her. If she felt like letting him she said yes. If she didn't, she said no. It seemed to Jimmy the "no's" were coming more often. Generally she would let him make love to her when he first arrived home from a trip unless she didn't feel good or if she was in her period. After that though she wasn't terribly receptive to him, unless he was home at least four days, then she might consent again. Jimmy resigned himself to this new regimen though he could have used more sex than he got.

Katie was getting restless. She had almost given up the thought of babies and was thinking about houses and land. One day as she was counting inventory at Thornton's, she overheard a couple of farmers chatting about a place for sale out on Route 1 Road. It seemed a farmer, a Mister Tremble and his wife wanted to retire and move close to their married daughter and grandchildren who lived in Portland. He had sold off five hundred acres to his neighbor. But the neighbor didn't want the house, barn or the pasture, consisting of about twenty acres, that the home place sat on. Mister Tremble had tried to sell it for about six months but no one seemed to want to live that far out. Katie went up to the farmers and asked for the address of the place and received it from them, 230 Route 1 Road.

Katie thought she remembered Route 1 Road. Every summer since she was a baby her family had at least one picnic out at a small isolated county park called Roaring River Park which was about five or six miles up Route 1 Road. The park was located at the place where Roaring River merged with Crabtree Creek, "the only place in the world where a river ran into a creek," so said Father. There were places to paddle for the children and some good fishing for Father.

Katie loved going out there as a child; the family usually had the park to themselves and they always had such fun. A few months ago Father had said, one night at dinner, "If you and Jimmy want to buy a house I will help you kids with the down payment." Jimmy was gone for two weeks so that night after work Katie went over to her parents' house and asked Father if he would go with her to see the farm that was for sale. Father had been out to that farm once before when a horse had kicked Mister Tremble and had broken his leg. He remembered it as a beautiful place. Father called Mister Tremble and asked him if he would be at home Saturday morning as they would like to look at his place and the appointment was set.

The next night Jimmy had called from Albuquerque, New Mexico and she told him about the farm and he had seemed excited about it. Together now they both made over four-hundred a week and their bank account was over five thousand dollars. Saturday morning arrived and Katie and her father drove out to Mister Tremble's farm. Almost two miles up the Route 1 road they saw a mail box with 230 on it. They turned left and crossed over a bridge that spanned a small brook. The lane to the farmhouse was well graded and graveled but they couldn't see the house until the car climbed a small rise about ¼ mile from the Route 1 Road. It was a beautiful setting. Almost an acre of lawn ran from the top of the rise to the house. To the left of the house was a garage, beyond that a large shed where a tractor, combine, farm truck and other machinery were stored. Straight behind the house was a vegetable garden and just beyond that a large white barn sat. The Trembles met them on the drive. Father introduced them to Katie and they went into the house.

The house was gorgeous, built at the end of the Depression it was as solid as a rock. They walked through a large eat-in kitchen, very like Jimmy's mother's kitchen, which Katie loved. The whole front of the house was taken up with a formal dining room and living room or parlor with a large brick fireplace in one corner. Katie could see, in her mind's eye, a large Christmas tree set up there next to a crackling fire. All the floors were hard wood, waxed and buffed with a golden glow.

Katie was in love; the older adults took a seat and invited Katie to look around on her own.

"If you have any questions, dear," said Mrs. Tremble, "just give us a shout." Katie wandered slowly through the house. A large old-fashioned bathroom was on the ground floor along with the main bedroom. Between the bathroom and the main bedroom was a stairs to the upper floor. The door had panes of glass set into it so the large window on the first landing let light into the hallway. She climbed the stairs and found two more medium sized bedrooms, with a smaller bedroom between them. *Humm* thought Katie looking into the small bedroom, *perfect for storage.* Large windows let in plenty of light. The rooms all had beds in them but were otherwise empty as the older couple's children had long since left home. The rooms were quite dusty and all could have used a little paint. There were no signs of dampness or mildew, that meant the roof was in good shape.

Katie came downstairs again and as she started to go out though the kitchen old Mister Tremble joined her.

"Come outside, Mrs. Burns," he said and "I'll show you around." They walked out into the large covered screened porch that they had used to enter the house but this time they turned right and went down the stairs and out on to a small path. The path led to a medium sized chicken house.

As they entered Mister Tremble told her she could keep around two hundred chickens in this house.

About twenty chickens lived there now and they scattered, squawking as the people walked in. He then showed her the fenced in yard where the chickens spent the daylight hours, pointing out that the fence was sturdy enough to keep out coyotes and foxes. After they left the chicken house they turned right and following the small path again down the side of the garden entered a pigsty.

"This pig barn will hold three sows and their piglets and they have a nice fenced yard to run in. We also keep a fatting pig in here for our home meat." He smiled at her.

Katie gave a little shudder. "You mean to fatten them up for slaughter?"

"Yes, Mrs. Burns, we generally have half a pig for our freezer and sell half to someone in town."

"Oh I don't think I could ever kill anything," exclaimed Katie.

"Oh we don't kill them, we take them to Gingham's slaughter house just outside Low Sky and they do it for us. Also they package the meat, and make it ready to put into our freezer. So by selling the side of the pig, we pay for the cost of rearing it and the slaughter of it so we get free meat plus a small profit."

"Oh," said Katie looking interested.

Mister Tremble smiled to himself. *She'll make a farmer yet,* he thought. Next they went into the big barn.

Instantly Katie liked the barn; it seemed warmer than outside and the smell of hay, cows and horses filled her nostrils.

"All our animals are gone now," explained Mister Tremble. "We sold them all off when we sold the land but this barn will hold twelve milk cows and there are boxes for three horses. We also have a room where we keep the calves after we take them from their mothers and in here," he said pointing to an empty room with a door leading out to a small fenced area, "is where we fatten a steer each year for the house."

Katie looked at him with an inquiring glance.

He smiled again. "Yes, Mrs. Burns, the same applies here as to the pig." Mister Tremble then led the way up a ladder into the haymow. Most of the hay was gone. "We also sold most of our bailed hay, but you could rent out this mow very easily, most farmers always need extra hay storage."

They walked over to a small door. As Mister Tremble opened it they looked down on the house and the machinery storage shed.

"You see the tractor, combine, truck and implements in that shed?" he asked.

"Yes," Katie said.

"Well, they are not owned by me. I sold all my equipment when I sold the land. That stuff belongs to a farmer down the road who rents the shed from me. So you see even if you don't farm you can have a good business renting out storage space, and pasture to horses or other farm animals. You can also raise your own meat, have your own eggs and plant and harvest your garden. When you raise your own food it tastes so much better, and is so much better for you than the stuff you get in the stores nowadays," he said, giving her a side glance.

"Last but not least," he said leading her to the rear of the mow. There he pushed open one of the huge double doors that dominated the north end of the barn. "These doors are where they bring in the hay," he explained to her, "but look at this view."

As the door swung open there appeared a panorama that made her suck in her breath. The pasture, an emerald green, swept out to a fence that determined its boundary. Just beyond that fence giant firs climbed up the sharp flank of the mountain so dark a green that they were almost black. The door opened more and she could see a cleft in the ridge to the right of the main bulk of the mountain.

"That canyon is where our brook comes from," he said, pointing out the small stream that ran through the pasture and down below the house. "If you ever want a change of pace for dinner just get your husband or father to drop a line with a worm on a hook in that brook, it is full of native rainbow trout; they are just pan sized and so tasty."

The door finally finished its slow sweep and there above the dark green of the ridge stood the snow-capped top of Mt. Franklin white against the blue of the sky.

Katie slowly let her breath out. "Oh Mister Tremble it is so beautiful here."

"Those trees up there is government timber, probably known to you city folk as National Forest, over the years they have logged some of it but they always replant soon after so you will always have a good view of trees and mountains."

Mister Tremble and Katie went back to the house. Her father and Mrs. Tremble were still sitting in the parlor gossiping about the local society.

John looked up when they entered the room. "Well honey, have you seen everything you wanted to?"

"Oh yes, Father," she said.

"Well Bill," said her father to Mister Tremble, "could you give us the price you are asking for this place?"

"Well Doctor Overmars, I believe I will take twenty-one thousand."

"That seems a fair price, Bill, we will discuss it with her husband and get back to you with in the week, if that is ok?"

"That is fine with me, Doctor." The good-bye's were said and Katie and her father drove back to Low Sky not saying much, but buried in their own thoughts.

When they arrived home Mother had the evening meal on the stove. While she cooked Father and Katie sat in the kitchen talking to her while sipping mugs of hot cocoa she had made them.

"Well then, I guess you both seem sold on the place," she said.

"Except there are two things I want to change quickly," declared Katie. "One is to update the bathroom and another is to replace that old wood furnace with a modern oil burning one and maybe updating the ducting as well."

"Yeah," said John, "Mrs. Tremble told me that the furnace was original with the house and they were having increasing trouble with it."

The farm was the main topic through dinner. As Katie was leaving to go home, John said to her, "Well honey, Mother and I have some money we want to invest. What we would like to do is be your finance lender, we would loan you the full amount. What would happen, is we would go to an escrow company, and for a small fee they would handle the paperwork. They would issue you payment notices every month, handle escrow accounts for taxes and insurance, if you and Jimmy so desire, and then pay us every month."

"That way everything would be handled legally for tax purposes, because now you will be able to take all your interest paid off your income tax."

Katie looked at her parents. "Oh Mother and Father, that would be so good of you. As soon as Jimmy calls I'll let you know."

As Katie lay in bed that night her head swirled. "Gosh, I am going to be a landowner, heck a land baron," she giggled to herself. She thought of the things Mister Tremble told her about making money and she had, for the first time since she had been married, a goal to work for. This is the first of the things she and Jimmy would own, someday maybe they would own a part of Low Sky, or maybe many more farms making lots of money. *Maybe I will have a Cadillac*, she mused, *all rich people have a Cadillac*. Katie fell asleep with the thoughts of power and wealth dancing in her head.

Becky lay in her bed tossing and turning. *Even with the extra money Jack is sending us we still don't seem to have enough money to cover all the expenses every month*, she thought.

I just got to have a raise. I have been there four years and only ever had one small raise, all I need is ten dollars more a month, we could break even then. I have to ask for a raise, will I have the guts to do it?

Jimmy lay in the sleeper of the big truck, his eyes heavy, his belly full. They had just left a truck stop on the outskirts of Flagstaff, Arizona, where they had eaten, showered and loaded up the fuel tanks with diesel.

Joe downshifted as the big truck pulled out on to Route 66 and started to climb the hill west of town, the headlights parting the darkness.

Jimmy put his arms around his pillow, he pretended it was Katie. He needed her badly, he could almost taste her skin, but he fell asleep with his longing unabated.

Jimmy woke up just before they reached Barstow, California. After breakfast he called Katie; she had just gotten up but was all excited about the farm and told him her parents were loaning them the money to buy it.

Well, he didn't really understand everything she was on about, but he could deny her nothing and gave his blessing to the transaction.

He told her he would be home by the weekend and to ready herself because he was very in need of her love.

143

She seemed to be in a very good mood and purred that she couldn't wait to be in his arms again.

This made Jimmy very happy. He thought, *Gee we ought to buy more farms.*

Joe climbed into the sleeper; Jimmy would drive the truck to Escondido, where they would unload the sacks of pinto beans and chili they picked up in New Mexico and load up frozen orange juice for the trip home.

The transactions, with all parties involved with the farm, went quickly. Because Jimmy and Katie didn't have to be approved for a loan within five weeks the young couple took possession of the farm and Katie had the work started on the bathroom and furnace.

By the end of October Jimmy and Katie had started to move into their new home. All the furniture had been installed before the first big rains and storms started in early November.

Their first night together in the farmhouse was a beautiful night. The last night of a full harvest moon before it started to wane. They sat on the front porch, their arms around each other; the golden moon lighted the mountains and fields as almost midday.

"Oh darling, I am so happy, it is so beautiful out here," Katie whispered into Jimmy's ear. "It seems to me we are really starting our married life just now," she said stroking his cheek with her fingertips. "I mean I was happy in our first little house but this is really ours, maybe now I will get pregnant."

She didn't notice the almost imperceptible stiffing of Jimmy's muscles. "Gosh, baby, it's alright, I really am complete with just you. If we don't have a child I'll be just fine."

She turned and kissed his lips. "I know, darling. You know, darling," Katie mused, "we are envied, many people I know want what we have, but it would be kind of completing our . . ." her talking stopped as he slipped his tongue into her mouth.

As they kissed the wind started to blow, when they finished they looked up and noticed the moon was already blotted out by the fast moving storm clouds. Arm in arm they went to their bedroom and made love as the first wind-blown raindrops rattled against their bedroom window.

After they had finished Katie went off to take her bath; Jimmy lay in bed, he felt completely satiated and totally in love with Katie.

How had he lived before he married Katie, he couldn't fathom. Their love life had taken a bad turn but was now on track again. With a satisfied smile on his lips he drifted into sleep.

Katie lay in the bathtub. The hot clean water and the scented soap she was using warmed and cleansed her body and soul. *Maybe I got pregnant tonight,* she thought. *Jimmy has made me very happy, I have been a little mean to him.*

She sighed, *Now I have my farm I vow to treat him better, it will cost me nothing, except maybe a little time.*

Becky lay in her bed with Sonny. He had had a bad dream and she had brought him into her bed to calm him. She looked down at his sleeping little face, and worried about money.

It seemed she always worried about money now. She had finally gotten up enough courage to ask for a raise.

The office manager turned her down flat. "Becky," he said looking up to the ceiling, "the only way I can give you a raise is if you get promoted, and we haven't any openings now."

She looked at him her eyes starting to brim with tears.

Quickly he said, "Carol, the manager of Accounts Receivable is pregnant, as you know," he looked at her now, "and she has told me she plans to quit when she is six months along.

"If you are interested," he continued, "I couldn't pay you as much as she makes but it would be a five dollar a week raise for you if you're interested?"

Gee, she thought to herself, *that is four months away.* "Yes, Mr. Roman, I would be very interested, thank you."

So getting through four, five months actually, until the raise came into her pay slip would be hard but she had no choice.

She leaned forward kissing Sonny on his nose. "I think, my precious lamb," she whispered, "that I wouldn't have these money problems if it weren't for you. If I would not have loved your father and gotten pregnant with you I would be married to Uncle Jimmy and you would be rich and have a father. But as it turns out, Auntie Katie has Uncle Jimmy, and all that money." A smile stole across her lips. "Of course I wouldn't trade you for all their money. I know Auntie Katie with all that money doesn't seem to be able get one of you. I believe she would pay a lot of her money to have one just like you." She cuddled Sonny up to her, closed her eyes and fell into a deep untroubled sleep.

Katie and Jimmy had been in their new farm for almost seven months now; her farm business was perking along. The pasture was let; a farmer over by Low Sky had ten milk cows grazing there and used the barn for milking. Each night and morning he or his son would come and milk them; they would give Katie a quart of milk as part of the deal each morning.

145

Jimmy had received a very large raise on his fourth anniversary with the company. He was now making eight hundred dollars a pay period, a very good wage for 1967. Katie quit her job with Thornton's, and became a full-time housewife, and farm manager.

The farm rentals were bringing in over one hundred a month so the young couple were rich beyond their wildest dreams. It was April and spring on the farm; one of the milk cows had just had a new calf. Katie noticed it the first day that it was born. She ran out to the pasture; it was lying in the grass and when she approached stood on wobbly legs. When she put her arms around its head it nuzzled her looking for a teat. Its nose bumped her breast, rather hard, she drew back, and put her hand on its muzzle.

The calf started sucking her fingers. "Oh dear little thing, I think you need your mother, there is not much nourishment in my fingers." She extracted her rather wet fingers from its mouth and guided the baby toward her mother, the cow turned her neck and with her head guided the wobbly baby toward her udder. Within a few seconds the calf found what she was looking for and started to suckle.

Katie stood there for a few minutes watching the calf suck; it kept driving its nose into the cow's udder. She wondered if it hurt the mother, but the cow didn't seem to mind. Later in the day she called Jimmy's mother to ask her a question about baking bread. Jimmy's dad answered the phone and as she waited for mom to come to the phone she told Jimmy's dad about the new calf.

She asked him about the calf driving her nose into the udder.

"Oh, that is a natural action for young calves and lambs," he explained to her. "It's a signal for the mother to let down her milk. However when you are around calves you must be careful because they can give you a butt in a very tender place."

"Thanks Dad," Katie said, "I'll remember that."

Her breast had a tender spot where the calf had butted her and a bruise was beginning to form on the inside of her left breast. Slowly Katie was becoming a farm girl; every day she learned something new, and it was fascinating.

Jimmy was home for five days this time and when he had just left Katie called Becky to see if she wanted a Saturday shopping and lunch. Being on the farm was wonderful but she missed just walking a few blocks to find female companionship. She was just a bit lonely even though she called Mother every day. So on the first Saturday in May she picked up Becky.

She was supposed to arrive at ten o'clock but she arrived fifteen minutes early so she could play with Sonny. Sonny brought his latest toy from Uncle Jack and sat upon her lap.

"See dis, Auntie Katie, it's a twuck. See dis wheel, it turns."

Katie hugged the little boy and kissed his cheek. "I see, my pet, my, that is a very nice truck."

He wouldn't be sitting on her lap much longer. He was five years old and growing like a weed.

Katie hadn't seen Becky for two or three months; she met her one evening shopping at Thornton's Market. They greeted each other then went to the cafe across the street for tea and a chat. She was definitely depressed then; sad, tired and somewhat grumpy with life in general.

Now she seemed livelier, more like the old Becky she had been before the discovery of Ralph's body.

Katie talked on the way to Salem about the farm, but once they had been seated at the table at Frederick's Restaurant it was Becky's turn.

"First of all," she beamed, "I have been promoted, and been in the job for just over a month."

"Oh darling," gushed Katie. "Jimmy, that pig, didn't say anything about it. If he would have I would have sent you flowers or a card or something."

"Oh I am not sure Jimmy knows about it. I really don't deal with the drivers anymore. I am the Accounts Receivable manager now."

"Gosh, tell me all about it," Katie gushed. "Do you like it, are you in charge of many people?"

"Yes, I love it. I was getting so bored with payroll, and ours is the biggest section of the office. I have five girls working for me, PLUS I got a raise which we desperately needed."

Katie was looking at her, her mouth open and eyes wide.

"Bessie is so much better now that Doc has been working with her. She seems to want to live again and she can take care of the house and Sonny; that is such a very large weight off my shoulders."

"Oh darling, I am so happy for you," said Katie. "It seems ages since you have seemed this happy."

Becky's eyes enlarged. "Now the big news. Just before I moved to Accounts Receivable we hired a new driver, and I mean, my dear, he is a dish. He seemed to like me so I am hoping he will ask me out."

"If he hasn't asked you out, maybe he could be married," said Katie.

"No, he is not. I made sure when he filled out his paperwork. Gosh, he's just super; tall, auburn hair and his eyes when he looks at me my knees buckle."

147

"I never saw anyone matching that description around here before," said Katie. "Is he local?"

"No he is just out of the Army and from Florida. I asked him what he was doing in Oregon. He just said he had never been in this part of the country before and wanted to try it."

Chinook:

So the girls chatted, gushed and ate lunch all afternoon like girls do, but Katie was more interested in this new arrival than she would care to admit.

Katie didn't hear anymore about the newest interest in town until Jimmy came home a couple of weeks later.

At the dinner table the night he arrived Katie opened the conversation with, "Um, when Becky and I had lunch last Saturday she said the company had hired a new driver?"

"Huh, oh yeah, he seems like a nice guy. I met him just before the last trip. I guess he is settling in."

Katie was silent for a few moments. "Um Becky said he just got out of the Army and was from Florida."

"Hum I guess," said Jimmy.

"I was thinking maybe you could invite him over for a Sunday lunch if you wanted, and we could have Becky, Joe and Barbara and some of the other families so he could get acquainted?"

"Yeah, honey, that sounds like fun. I really don't know him that well but I'll ask him."

"Ok darling, I'll clear a date with Barbara and Becky and let you know when to invite him."

Chinook:

So the line was cast into the water. Katie had a feeling that this poor fish was just the ticket for Becky and she wanted to be there when the hook was set.

Katie called Barbara and Becky. Barbara and Joe couldn't make it, they usually had family obligations, and as Joe was home so few weekends she wouldn't commit them. Becky was sure as she had almost all Sundays open, except she couldn't come until Bessie returned from church which was almost one o'clock every Sunday, so she could babysit Sonny.

"Oh my dearest, you could bring Sonny. We would be glad to have him. Jimmy would show him the animals."

"Well," said Becky, "I don't think springing Sonny on Dom would be a good thing. He hasn't asked me out yet and I don't want to scare him off."

"Ok," said Katie. "The boys will be home the first weekend in May. Why don't you invite, um Dom, for that Sunday and give him the directions out to our farm."

"Well, I could show him, we could come out together," said Becky.

"Oh dearest, I thought as you won't be out until after one you could have him come say at twelve and that would let us get to know him a bit and Jimmy could show him around the farm."

"Oh well, ok" said Becky sounding a bit dubious.

"Well, dearest my thought is," Katie intoned, "we would have all that introductory stuff out of the way and when you arrive we could concentrate on you and him without Jimmy dragging him off to see the trout stream or something. You know, just as we started to weave our trap."

Becky giggled. "Good thought my love. My, my we are devious women."

"All is fair in romance, my dearest," chuckled Katie. So the date, and the stage were set to start to change the status of Dom from single to boyfriend and possibly husband one day.

The Saturday afternoon before the Sunday lunch Jimmy had just returned from helping his Dad. When he walked into the kitchen the smell of baking pies filled his nostrils.

"Yummy, oh baby, that smells good."

"These are not to touch, young man, they are for tomorrow."

"So I see," smiled Jimmy. "This Dom guy is going to get the whole home cooked extravaganza. Do I see the domestic web being gently woven around this poor soul?"

"No," said Katie. "I am helping Becky to get aquatinted with him in a comfortable setting."

"Hum, but isn't this your mother's famous blackberry cream pie recipe, the one that tipped me toward a married life?"

Katie put her hands on her hips and pushed out her bosoms. "I think this is what tipped you toward a married life, this here body!"

"Better than blackberry cream pie," said Jimmy with a wink.

They went to early Mass on Sunday morning and by the time

149

Dom's car pulled onto the farm lane the kitchen was filled with the heavenly smell of cooking roast and newly baked bread.

Katie watched with interest as Dom got out of his car. *My, Becky was right. He is tall,* she thought. She called Jimmy, "Darling, he's here." When Dom knocked on the front door they both were there to greet him.

"Darling, I'd like you to meet Dominic Stanza."

"Very pleased to meet you, Mrs. Burns," he said in a soft southern accent. He reached out his hand to take hers. "Please call me Dom, I cannot abide Dominic."

He lifted his eyes to hers. Katie couldn't breathe. Her knees felt weak. The thought, *What a gorgeous man* flashed through her brain.

She felt the firm, gentle grip of his hand and almost gave herself away when she blurted, "So, so nice of you to come."

Chinook:

Marcus Tra-Janus Cassius sat under a tree to shield himself from the intense noonday heat. Even in the shade he could feel the sweat trickling down his skin under his thin woolen shirt. His armor had been removed and was lying beside him.

Around him almost one thousand Roman troopers, comprising two cohorts, did the same. It was the middle of the summer of the year 117 A.D. and the Emperor Trajan had ordered them north from Adrianopolis, capital of the Roman Province of Thrace.

Four days and nights of forced march had now deposited them on a mountainside in Upper Dacia. They had reached this destination just a few hours before.

Their Centurion had told them to sleep as best they could, for they might be called into battle at any time. They could hear the battle raging beyond the ridge to the right.

The Dacian King had fought for almost ten years to rid his country of the Romans. His army had fought with fierce stubbornness but the end was near. The last of his army was now fighting in the valley beyond the mountain they rested on.

Marcus lay with his head resting on his breastplate, his eyes were closed. Behind the lids he saw his home in Gaul; the vineyards climbing the hills above the river, the warm sun cooled by a breeze off the sea. His golden-haired mother standing in the courtyard of their villa looking out over the hills, to see if his father was coming, as she usually did in the evenings.

Even though his nostrils were filled with the scent of the pines that covered these foreign mountains he could still smell the scent coming from the grape crushing tubs below the villa. He could see the slaves turning the great handles that crushed the grapes and sent the sweet juice pouring into oaken vats.

His father had been an officer on the staff of General Trajan during the German campaigns; in fact had been wounded by stepping in front of the General and taking a spear meant for him. He therefore saved the life of the great man. For this act of heroism Trajan gave the farm in Gaul to him.

His father had married his third wife, Marcus's mother, soon after he had arrived to claim his farm. She was of the Aedui people who lived in the region. He first saw her as he traveled through her small village just by the river; he was fifty-nine and she was eighteen, the daughter of the headman. He was struck by her beauty, eyes the color of the sea and long golden hair to the middle of her back. Just nine months after they were married she bore him a son who he named after Trajan. That was how Marcus got his name.

His mother was tall, actually taller than his father. His father, a Roman citizen born in Capua, was only five foot eight inches tall, but he was a powerful man of wide shoulders and thick muscular arms. Marcus inherited his father's shoulders, muscular arms and his dark eyes, but his mother's golden hair and height.

He had left home five years before, at the age of eighteen to join the legions. His father had died just six months before at the age of seventy-eight.

His mother had re-married just three months after his father's death to another, younger ex-soldier. She became pregnant at the age of thirty-seven and Marcus decided it was time to seek his own life. She had tearfully begged him to stay but the thirst for adventure ran through his veins.

This is how he found himself on a mountainside in Upper Dacia. He must have fallen into a very deep sleep, for the next thing he knew someone was kicking his feet and yelling his name. The warriors of the Dacian army had broken through the lines of the Romans and were now attacking from the rear also.

They quickly donned their armor and filed over the ridge and down into the valley. The noise of the battle grew louder as they descended the slope. In about two hundred yards they broke from the trees and before them was a valley with a river running through it. They stood dumbfounded; their mouths open and eyes staring. The whole of the valley was covered in the bodies of horses and men.

They could see the phalanx of the Roman troops moving, hacking their way through what seemed endless screaming savages. Their Centurion was soon yelling at them to form a square. Spear men to the outside, sword men to the inside, shields up to their chins forming an almost impenetrable wall they marched in rapid time down to the fighting.

Marcus had been in training for this situation for years but the reality of war and death so close at hand made his heart feel like it would jump out of his chest. Fear gripped his brain and he had to fight himself to hold his position in the phalanx. To the count time of their march the men started to beat their shields with the butt of their swords. Once that happened Marcus felt better and he marched out with his companions. All of a sudden they were attacked; Marcus had a vision of a thing that didn't seem human, its face was covered with red and black paint, its mouth open screaming.

The thing seemed to come at him through the air; he raised his spear and the thing impaled itself on it.

The weight of the attack pushed Marcus back into the square, the thing on the end of his spear made him stumble and fall on his back. The thing then slid down the shaft toward his face, its mouth was open and he could see the life leaving its eyes.

Just when its face was six inches from his a gush of blood came from its mouth and his face was covered in the warm sticky substance.

He couldn't see or breathe, the blood was in his mouth, nose and eyes. People were treading on him, he couldn't move.

All of a sudden the fighting moved away from him. He pushed the thing off him, the spear still protruding from its stomach, rolled over and vomited—that cleared the blood from his mouth. He wiped his eyes with his sleeve so now he could see. He didn't try to remove the spear from the dead body; he instead pulled his short heavy sword from its scabbard and rejoined the phalanx. When he reached the shield wall it opened and he was back in his place.

How long the battle went on then he could not say, only in what seemed an eternity he heard a mounted officer yell, "the King is fleeing the battle."

Marcus turned and looked in the direction the officer's sword pointed. He saw a chariot with two men in it and a mounted group surrounding it heading down the valley.

Just then there was a thud beside him. Swinging around he saw the officer laying at his feet, an arrow through his neck. He still had the reins from his horse in his hand. He looked at Marcus—his eyes staring his mouth moving like he was trying to talk. Then his face went slack and Marcus grabbed the reins of the now shying horse.

Putting his sword back into the scabbard he mounted the horse, wheeled and took off after the chariot. An arrow nicked his ear, a sword blade glanced off his stirrup but soon he left the battle behind. It got very quiet; he could only hear the drumming of the hoofs of his mount. He turned along the river for he saw that the chariot would have to cross it further up the valley. He glanced over his shoulder—other mounted Romans were in pursuit of the King but they were far behind him.

He lay flat along the neck of his horse. This was the way he would ride at home, when the local men held races. He and the beautiful black horse from far Cappadocia, his father had given him at the age of fifteen, would fly to the finish line far ahead of the others. The mounted guard of the King didn't see him coming; they were too busy looking back at the pursuing Romans. Marcus also had the advantage of being low along the river where trees, brush and banks shielded him from the guard's sight.

When the chariot of the King crossed the river Marcus was among the guard instantly. He knew he had only seconds to stop the King so he had aimed for the neck of the closest horse pulling the chariot.

He had his sword ready; he plunged through the stunned guards, swung his sword and buried it in the joint where the horse's head attaches to its neck. The horse went down like a sack of flour, the chariot running over its trashing body throwing the King to the ground and his death by a broken neck.

A sword had glanced off Marcus's helmet and he rode on back to his cohort stunned and bleeding down his back from a cut under his helmet. He managed to reach them before he fell off the horses back into the arms of cheering comrades.

As soon as the warriors of the Dacian army saw their King captured they melted into the nearest forest at hand and the battle and war was won. Marcus was not badly hurt; by the next day he joined the others in the Roman army to round up and burn the dead. Many giant fires were lit with logs and the dead were stripped of their belongings to be returned to their families and their bodies burnt, or buried where they had fallen.

It took almost a week to clean the battlefield of the fallen. On the morning of the sixth day the Centurion, who was in charge of the clean-up, lined his men in twos and started the long march back to Adrianopolis; this time the march wasn't forced and in six days they saw the city from a hill.

Marcus had fallen in love with a Thraceian serving girl who was a slave at the local Roman governor's house. Her parents had sold her to the Governor because they were too poor to raise her. When she first came to the house she was skinny and sickly, but now at the age of sixteen she had blossomed into a lovely creature.

She was small still, no more than five foot in height, but she had long silken hair that fell to her tiny waist. It was as black as the night and soft to the touch. Her skin was an olive color, clear and smooth, but it was her eyes that captured Marcus.

The pupils were a light blue, so light a blue that they were almost white, and when she turned them on Marcus his knees melted.

After they were home almost three months he was called into the presence of the great Praetor of Rome who was visiting Thrace.

"You are the son of Claudius Cassius are you not?"

"Yes sir," said a very nervous Marcus, who stood at rigid attention.

"The bravery and devotion to duty you showed during the capture of the Dacian King has reached the ears of the Emperor. Whom at this moment recuperates from an illness in the province of Cilicia as he travels home from India," the Praetor said smiling at the sweating young man.

"It seems your father saved the life of the Emperor many years ago and he now sends you greetings and grants your heart's desire."

Marcus stood tall and said, "Sir, I want the slave girl Celius in the house of the Governor for a wife. I also want the land in the valley where we defeated the Dacian King for a farm and the rights to all the water in the river that flows through that valley."

The Praetor raised his eyebrows and pursed his lips. "Young man," he started, "do you realize you can become the adopted son of the Emperor, I believe that is what he wants."

That rocked Marcus back on his heels. "I, I," he stammered, "I want to thank the Emperor for so great a gift but my desire is to have a farm and raise horses that come from Cappadocia."

So his wish was granted and Marcus and Celius were the first to live in the valley of the Theiss River, where they raised five sons and one daughter. Their horses became famous throughout the empire; known far and wide for their speed, stamina and beauty. Marcus died in the arms of his wife on the day of his seventieth birthday.

In the year of 256 A.D. the Romans were driven from the valley of the Theiss River and most of Upper Dacia by the Goths. But by then the blood of Marcus and Celius was flowing in the veins of hundreds of people in that region and was soon mixed with that of the Goths.

In the year 446 A.D. Attila the Hun, known as "Ethele," meaning scourge of God, by the people of the valley of the Theiss, swept out of the Caspian steppes with his hoards and mixed their blood with the people of the region.

By the year 454 Ethele was dead and the Huns gone from the valley.

Germanic tribes moved back into the region but the blood of the Huns stayed.

An Asiatic people called the Avars drove out the Germans in the fifth century. For 250 years they controlled the area—leaving almond eyes and honey-colored skin as their legacy to the gene pool of the valley.

A Slavic tribe called the Moravians displaced them.

Between 791 and 797 the Frankish Emperor Charlemagne conquered the valley and the Franks controlled that area until 896.

That year the Magyars swept in from beyond the Ural Mountains of Russia. They were a people of unknown origins; suffice it to say they were tall and had red hair, and were the final ancestors of the people we now find in that small valley of the Tisza River, in the modern country of Hungary.

They are a beautiful people, tall with hair color ranging from strawberry blond to sunset red to auburn. The men have broad shoulders and strong muscular arms; the women high breasted with long legs. They all have honey-colored skin with freckles; almond eyes with pupils that are such a light blue they are almost white.

In the summer of 1912 an event of some magnitude was to take place. The oldest son and oldest daughter of the two largest farmers in the valley would be married. The people of this small valley loved to make merry. They feasted, danced, played music and drank as much of the local wines, as they could, at any provocation. Especially during local saint days, weddings or births of children.

This occasion was special though because it also had economic implications for the valley. The combining of the two largest farms in the valley could do nothing but herald a new era of economic vitality for the people of the area and the small village of Duna. Mihaly Tarpa had, from his first recollection, always loved Maria Tarpa. They were, within one week, the same age and cousins. They had always played together as children, their homes only a few yards from each other in the village. Both the families supported their coming union and their respective fathers rejoiced knowing that when they died their farms would be joined into one.

Mihaly had a secret though that he hadn't told anyone but Maria. Five years before, when he was fifteen, a letter had arrived from his fa-

155

ther's younger brother who lived in America. The letter raved about a place called New Jersey, where milk and honey ran in the streets and gold lay on the ground for anyone to pick up, or so the letter hinted. In the return letter his father had written, Mihaly smuggled in a note to his uncle telling him he would like to see this land of milk and honey one day.

One year later a letter just for him came from his uncle in faraway America. His uncle said that if Mihaly would come and look him up in a village called Trenton he would give him a job, "probably picking up all that gold," he told Maria.

Mihaly could have never told his father he planned to leave as soon as he married and Maria was sworn to secrecy. Maria didn't want to leave the valley and her mother and father, but she loved Mihaly and as he would be her husband she would submit to his wishes. Maria was also two months pregnant with Mihaly's child, so there was no turning back now.

After a traditional wedding the newly married couple were escorted through the village by all the young people and deposited in the house their parents had built for them.

They lay in bed. Mihaly held Maria tight in his arms as he listened to the sounds of the celebration and she wept as if her heart would break.

The next night they left the valley forever. Mihaly put a letter to his father on the marriage bed and the young couple slipped away in the night. After they departed the valley they followed the road to Budapest. This was the same road that Marcus Cassius and his Thraceian bride Celius had traveled to the valley on one thousand eight hundred years before.

Rico Stanza maneuvered his truck through the traffic on Trent Avenue. It was the fifth of May 1938 and the first warm day they had had in Trenton that spring. He pulled up to a stoplight and sat impatiently as a crowd of pedestrians crossed in front of him. Suddenly his heart stopped; he couldn't breathe because before him walked an angel, a girl so beautiful he couldn't believe she was real.

She was tall, about five foot ten. Her young breasts pushed her blouse out in front of her causing a slight gap where it buttoned down the front so he could just see a bit of her bra. Her feet encased in high heels started the sweep of her glorious ankles and legs to where they disappeared in her skirt just below her knees. Her hair was auburn and hung down to the middle of her back, and as she walked the noonday sun flashed fire through it.

He gave a wolf whistle; she turned to look at him, a small smile playing on her lips. He could feel his cock start to harden; this was the girl of his dreams. When completely across the intersection she turned into Diana's luncheonette.

Quickly he found a place to park his truck, and ran back to the luncheonette. He found out her name was Angela Tarpa, and she was nineteen years old. She worked in her father's office just a block off Trent Avenue. A year and three months later they were married.

Angela Maria Tarpa was the youngest child of Mihaly and Maria Tarpa. Their first born was a son, who was now twenty-five, married and working for his father. Next came Angela's older sister Bena, a beauty who had won a Miss New Jersey contest just two years before, and now was engaged to the son of the owner of The New Jersey Bank.

The Tarpas were quite rich; they owned a small cable manufacturing company down on the Delaware River harbor. During the World War they made a lot of money selling cable to the U.S. Navy and Uncle Franz retired and moved home to the small valley by the Tisza River.

Mihaly had taken over the running of the company and now his son, Franz, was with him in the business. Rico was offered a job at the company, but he had another dream, which he confided to Angela, just before they were married.

*　　*　　*

His mother's brother, a black sheep of the family, had moved to Florida many years ago and became a fisherman.

After the World War the sport of fishing was growing in the islands off the Florida coast. Rich men from New England, New York and the midwest were flocking to the abundant waters of the Gulf and Atlantic to catch tarpon, snook, barracuda and red fish. Rico's uncle had bought a small island in an area called Ten Thousand Islands, on the southwestern tip of the state. He had built a small fishing resort on this, "chunk of coral and sand," as he called it. Having never married, he had been in touch with Rico for months trying to lure him south.

A few years before the U.S. Congress had passed a bill to make the southern tip of Florida into a huge national park called The Everglades and his uncle was very enthusiastic for the growth of the sport fishing trade. Angela didn't want to leave Trenton and her family, especially her mother and sister. However she did love Rico and as he would be her husband she would submit to his wishes. She was also sure she was pregnant with Rico's baby, as she had missed her last period, so there was no turning back now.

157

They had a very large Catholic wedding; six hundred attended the church and more at the reception. Mihaly and Maria spared no expense and it was a wonderful day. After they returned from the honeymoon the family took them to the train in Philadelphia and sent them off to Florida with many tears flowing. When they arrived at Rico's uncle's resort they found that it was just a cabin, so the work started to make it a home and a true resort.

It was October the second, 1951. Dominic Stanza, who was now almost eleven and a half, stood on the end of the dock waiting as the float plane with the new guests taxied up. Up by the house Papa and R. J. [Rico Jr.], his younger brother, were bringing down the bags of the departing guests. As the float of the plane touched the dock Dominic deftly and snugly secured it to the turnbuckles on the dock, and the new guests started to deplane. First a smaller rather dark man, with a New York accent got off, then a very large very white man followed.

Dominic had never seen a man so white. He had pale yellow hair and blue eyes, even his eyebrows were pale yellow. His skin was almost translucent, you could see the blue of his veins running up his arm. He spoke with a heavy accent, almost like his grandfather Tarpa, but more clipped; it was like the man was speaking in his throat not his mouth.

Klaus von Horst at fifty-two years, was the most powerful and influential man in German banking. He was the latest inheritor of his family's control of the Horst Bank that held the purse strings of the German Government, which they had financed for almost two hundred years. A disciplined, sophisticated, man of the world, he had two vices, beautiful women and fishing, both of which he indulged every chance he got.

Klaus was born with a fly rod in his hands. He had fished the trout and salmon streams of his family's estates since he could walk. At the age of sixteen he discovered his other vice.

His father had called him into his den one evening. "Klaus, it is time you became a man," his father proclaimed. "You will come to my office tomorrow at the end of business, so don't be late." With a flick of his father's hand he was dismissed. The next evening he waited for his father in his outer office, the old man came out and took him to his limousine. They drove from the Mitte district of Berlin, where the bank offices were located, to a quiet street in the Lichtenberg district where they entered a building whose heavy Prussian architecture gave it a rather ominous feel. Once through the front door they were greeted by a sophisticated older gentleman, who very formally welcomed them with a deep bow. Taking their wraps he escorted them into rather an

158

ornate, larger room where the color scheme tended to red walls and gold trim.

The combined smells of cigars, food and perfume washed into Klaus's nostrils. Men in dark business suits were seated at the tables while ladies with low cut gowns displaying large cleavages circulated through the room. One lady spotting his father came to them and taking his father's arm led them to a table. Klaus's father exchanged a few whispered words to the lady. She appraised Klaus with a small smile flitting around the corners of her mouth and an arched eyebrow. Inclining her head in assent to Klaus's father she disappeared.

Klaus's father, brought up in the Old Prussian way, had never shown much warmth to his children, always expecting them to be quiet and well disciplined in his presence. Now, as they ate their dinner, he talked to Klaus as he would an equal; a business partner or a friend.

At the end of the meal, he said something curious to Klaus. "Son, now that you are becoming a man you will feel passions for the girls that you associate with. You may want to kiss them or touch them, that is normal. But, son, you must not despoil these young ladies for they will be the wives of powerful men one day and they must come to their husbands virgins."

Klaus turned a deep red; he mumbled something to his father and looked around to see if others had heard. Of course he knew that men had sex with women and that they had babies because of it, but he didn't understand how it happened. The boys in his school had bragged about having sex and how and what they had done; it didn't sound particularly inviting. When he was still in the nursery he had taken baths with his sisters but couldn't remember anything about how they looked naked.

His father continued. "When you have these urges I want you to come to this place and don't worry, it will be taken care of."

Just than he felt someone at his elbow; he looked up into the blue eyes of a young woman not much older than himself. She introduced herself as Helga; she spoke German with a funny accent.

He looked back at his father who said, "Now go with this young lady."

"But, Father, I . . ." Klaus was aghast. His father sat up very straight with that look that brooked no dissent, and said, "Go Klaus."

*   *   *

Klaus was introduced to the world of sex, which he found he enjoyed very much and with a lot of practice became quite good at. In the

159

coming years he visited Helga and the other girls there a lot, until he was married at the age of twenty-five.

His wife was a lovely girl with sky blue eyes and hair the color of spun gold. Klaus loved her very much and respected her more. She was fragile and petite and after four children in six years almost died while giving birth to their last child. The doctor had told him she would die if she had another child, so Klaus returned to the dark Prussian building on the quiet street, in the Lichtenberg District, on a regular basis.

Over the years he had had a number of discrete affairs, most with disenchanted wives of business colleagues, and during the war with wives of men at the front. Klaus had a philosophy, he only had sex with whores or married women; that way if they became pregnant someone else could deal with the problem.

He knew he had made Helga pregnant because she had disappeared for about five months and then one day returned as if nothing had happened. In actual fact his father had paid Helga rather a large stipend and saw to it that a middle class childless couple adopted the baby. Some of the wives he had had affairs with "became with child," and at least three unsuspecting husbands were raising his blow-by.

Now he stood on the balcony of his room looking out over the crystal clear water and islands marching out to the Gulf of Mexico. After lunch they would go fishing for snook around the nearest islands. At lunch he saw for the first time the wife of the owner of the resort. He was stunned at her beauty, the honey-colored skin smattered with freckles, auburn hair done up primly in a roll at the base of her neck. She wore a loose fitting print dress but even that couldn't hide the movement of her breasts under the cloth.

"She must not wear a corset or brassiere," he mused to himself. He tried to keep his mind on what the other two men were saying about the fishing that would start within the hour, but he couldn't keep his eyes off her. When she served him his bowl of conch stew he could smell her aroma, not of perfume but of soap and musk; his pulse quickened and his mind reeled.

The men had a good afternoon; they had caught a mixture of both snook and red fish. They retired to their respective rooms after dinner for tomorrow would be a long day of fishing. They were going to target tarpon and Klaus was very interested to catch, for the first time, the silver fish he had heard so much about.

They left the resort just after six A.M., for half an hour they flew over the water on the boat. The boat was large—over twenty feet long and the propulsion was an airplane propeller. To Klaus the speed was incredible, it seemed they were flying over the water, not touching it at all. Just as they neared the open gulf Rico powered down and swung the boat along a reef. Klaus looked into the water; it seemed incredibly shallow for being out so far at sea. The water was crystal clear and he could see small fish darting around. Rico took up a pole and started to push the boat along the reef. He explained to the men, "look for movement ahead in the water or the sight of fins and tails breaking the water." The day had been overcast when they left the resort but now the haze was burning off and the temperature was beginning to climb.

About an hour later they saw the first fin break the water, then another and another. Soon the water fifty feet ahead of them was boiling with feeding tarpon. Rico handed Klaus a long heavy fly rod; on the end of the line was a green and white streamer six inches long.

Under Rico's direction he deftly cast just to side of the feeding tarpon. One strip, two strips: suddenly a dark flash behind the streamer. He felt the hit and sharply raised the tip of his rod, the fish felt heavy on the line and what Klaus had stripped flew through his fingers. The water exploded into a million droplets, out of the middle of this rainbow rose a fish the likes of which he had never encountered. Like a silver daemon it hung in the air; the sun off its scales was almost blinding, then it was down in the water again and his reel smoked as it ran. For what seemed an eternity the fight went on as it had started. Klaus's arms grew weary, but the fish never gave an inch.

Then as suddenly as the fight had started he felt the fish give way. Klaus brought it to the side of the boat; it lay in capitulation and Rico grabbed the gaff ready to plunge it into the fish.

"No, please no," yelled Klaus, "give me your pliers please," he said to Rico.

Kneeling down on the deck of the boat Klaus pulled out the hook and put his hands on the fish.

"A creature this beautiful, this magnificent should not be destroyed," he spoke softly almost to himself. Grabbing the fish down by its tail he slowly moved it back and forth in the water trying to move as much water as he could through its gills. Klaus had big hands but they didn't reach around the belly of the tarpon.

"Be careful of the gill plates, sir," Rico advised him, "they can give you a nasty cut."

Then with a flick of its tail the fish was off. They watched his fin streak across the water for a second and then he was gone.

Klaus looked at Rico. "How much do you think he would veigh," he asked.

"Seventy to seventy-five pounds I'd say," said Rico.

"Yah, a beautiful animal he vas," Klaus slipped into a deeper accent. They caught more fish after that but none matched the first one for weight. The day was hot even on the water; it must have been close to ninety degrees. Around four in the afternoon Rico noticed that even with a large hat on Klaus's white skin was very red.

"Gentlemen, I think we should call it a day," said Rico.

"Yah," intoned Klaus, "I am getting very tired."

When they returned Klaus took a long cool shower. Angela gave him some skin cream for his face and arms where they had been exposed to the sun. After dinner the men went out to the veranda at the rear of the resort and the dark man from New York brought out some Cuban cigars and a bottle of Johnny Walker Scotch. The men smoked quietly and slowly sipped at their Scotch not saying much as the sun set over the gulf. Just at dark Klaus excused himself to bed. He found Angela in the kitchen and thanked her for her dinner and skin cream. He then fell into a deep dreamless sleep.

*   *   *

The next morning Klaus didn't feel well. Even though he had had a good rest during the night his face, arms, hands and knees were still rather red from sunburn and sore. The long day had taken a toll on him and because this would be another long day he decided to stay at the resort. Soon Rico, the dark man from New York and R.J., who loved to go on the boat, left and he was alone with Angela and Dominic. Klaus sat in the dining area which was part of the large room that included the kitchen; he sipped his coffee and watched Angela bustle around doing her chores.

"Ah she is a most tempting young woman," he mused to himself. He didn't feel that bad about missing a day of fishing.

Angela had always been benevolent about living at the fishing camp. Rico loved it; it was a very good environment for her children and she had pride in what they had built together the last twelve years. Rico's uncle was a good man; she had liked him from the very first. He had always been a confirmed bachelor but a couple of years ago had met a rich widow, who had moved to Cape Coral from Boston, and fell in love. The newly acquired wife refused to live at the resort so he had sold it to the young family and now lived in one of those new retirement communities.

Sometimes he would come out on the weekends and guide clients, "just to get away from those damn old people."

Angela was glad they had purchased the resort but now it was a lot more expensive. It seemed every dime they made went back into the resort for repairs and improvements, or to pay off the bank loan on the property. Also it was very hard work especially now that it was theirs. Rico's uncle had always had a couple of local women work for him, cleaning, cooking and doing the rather large amounts of laundry. After they had bought the resort they had decided that Angela would take over these chores to save money. Rico and the boys helped her a lot but the majority of the work fell on her shoulders. She also felt lonely for her sister and mother. Her sister and husband visited at least once a year. Her sister's husband loved to fish and they would come for a week at times. Her mother and father were retired now and talked about moving to Florida, but really they were entrenched in New Jersey, having friends and grandchildren to occupy their time. Also her father liked to go to the office every so often "to keep his hand in the business."

Angela's brother now ran the company and it was flourishing in the post-war economy. Her sister had one child, a little girl who was almost ten now. Angela really loved her little niece, and always looked forward to her coming and when she left there was an empty spot in Angela's heart. Angela wanted her own little girl but she knew the time was not right now what with the resort taking all her time. Also she knew that boys were in her future, that if she had another child it would be a boy.

When Angela first saw Klaus it was at the lunch she had served the first day he had arrived. Angela never much noticed the clients; they could get as high as six or eight a week during the best fishing months.

But Klaus was different; he was a presence, he seemed to fill the room. Angela could feel his eyes on her from the first moment that he had seen her. She was used to men looking at her, from the time that she started to blossom around the age of fourteen until now men's eyes always seemed to follow her. Mostly she was indifferent, but something about this man's attention made a small chill run up her spine.

Now as she made lunch he watched her and she chatted with him. She found out about his wife and daughters and that he lived in West Berlin, though "he spent almost more time in Frankfurt and Bonn as Berlin nowadays."

She asked him about the Berlin blockade that had taken place a few years before. He told her about the brave Americans that had supplied all their needs by flying food and supplies to the beleaguered city. That was when he had met and started doing business with the man whom he had accompanied on this fishing trip.

Klaus smiled at her and told her the other man was, "a Jew and the head of a very powerful private Jewish bank with headquarters in New York."

Angela looked at him with curiosity. "I thought Germans were taught to hate Jews," she exclaimed with candor.

"That is true, but only for a short time in our history. I went to school with and counted many Jews as my friends before the war," he said. "But I am afraid that almost all those people are gone. They either died in the camps or have immigrated to other countries," he said shaking his head. "Their gain and our loss I'm afraid."

Angela stared at this curious man; he seemed to be introspective and gentle though he was big and stern looking.

He must have been beautiful as a boy, now he was a bit thick in the middle and showed his age, she mused. *But still handsome and powerful.* After lunch she asked Dominic, "to take his boat and net and go catch her some shrimp for dinner."

When the boy had left Klaus asked Angela how long it would take him to catch the shrimp. "It will take him about two hours. We should have fresh shrimp for dinner," she said.

Deftly Klaus moved the conversation around to Angela. She told him about her family. "My parents came from Hungary but I was born in New Jersey. I have a brother and sister both married with children." Then what Klaus was waiting for. "We own this resort but are in debt and every dollar goes into making it better and pay off the mortgage." She was obviously worried about the finances which left her vulnerable. Klaus changed his tact. His voice became softer, more intimate. She started to tell him her most heartfelt fears and ambitions. How she got lonely and wished for a daughter, how hard the work was; she told him things she would never tell Rico, her mother or her sister.

He sprung the trap. As she sat at the table he took her hand in his and gently squeezed it. "I know, my dear, how vorried you are I vould like to help you. I will give you one thousand dollars to allow me to make love to you."

Angela was stunned. "One thousand dollars, one thousand dollars, for me?"

She was looking into his eyes mesmerized, almost in a trance. With her hand still in his he stood up and led her quietly down the hall to his bedroom. Softly he closed the door behind them. Deftly he unbuttoned her dress, pulling it off her shoulders, he let it drop to the floor. She had had no underwear on under her dress and stood before him naked. He sucked in his breath. She must be in her mid-thirties with two children, yet she had the figure of a twenty-year-old girl.

Then he found and pulled the pins that held her hair in a roll; her

164

auburn hair cascaded down to almost the middle of her back. He ran his fingers through its soft tresses. He led her to the bed and she obediently lay down. He started to undress and she never took her eyes off him.

Angela felt like she was in a dream; here she lay naked on the bed while a man that wasn't her husband, and that she didn't even know, undressed before her eyes. She had never seen a naked man other than her husband; she was a virgin up until about six weeks before their wedding when finally she had given in to a pleading Rico. Now she noticed how different they were. Klaus was wide shouldered and thick through his middle; his body was plump and white, except where the sun had turned him red. His skin seemed loose; he had breasts that hung down slightly. His weight must be twice that of her husband.

Rico was whipcord lean, tanned, his skin stretched over muscles grown hard from constant physical labor. Rico didn't have much body hair, just a little in his armpits and crotch. This man who now was climbing into bed with her was covered in a golden mass of hair on his chest, shoulders and stomach. She lay quite still as he started to touch her body. She closed her eyes; she could feel his weight on her, his body hair scratched her skin and tickled her nipples. She would let him make love to her, collect her money and go.

Klaus started to run his hand over her breasts and belly; she had skin like silk, her nipples a deep red. She lay rigid under his touch, but he was a man with much experience. He knew where to touch a woman, and soon she was responding to that touch. He rolled over on her, spreading her legs with gentle hands. Now she was breathing quicker; her nipples had hardened. He kissed them as he positioned himself and heard her gasp as he entered her. Now that his face was close to hers he noticed for the first time her almond shaped eyes. He kissed the lids and she opened them and looked into his face.

The jolt rattled him. Her eyes almost glowed; the pupils were such a light blue they were almost white, the eyes of the female wolf. Klaus would remember those eyes for the rest of his life. He would live thirty-two more years; on the day he died the last earthly thing he saw before his mind went dark were those eyes looking up into his.

When they were finished Klaus rolled off her, got out of bed and went for his wallet. She got off the bed and slipped on her dress. Klaus came to her and counted out twelve one hundred dollar bills into her hand. He smiled at her and kissed her lightly on the lips. She went out into the kitchen to her money can.

It was on the top shelf above the refrigerator; she kept any tips the clients gave her there and now as she added Klaus's money it was full.

Angela then went into her bedroom, she removed her dress and stood naked before her mirror. She looked at her body—had it changed? It seemed to her it must have changed because in less than one hour she had become both an adulteress and a whore. She had always thought she would feel terrible or at least guilty if ever she broke one of the Ten Commandments or her marriage vows. Now as she looked at herself she felt only satisfaction. Satisfied that all that money was in her savings can and that she was desirable enough for a man of Klaus's importance to want to have sex with her.

Angela knew she would have to go to confession. She didn't want to go to hell, so in a few days she would travel into Fort Myers to a church where the priest didn't know her. She also couldn't leave that much money in her tip can—she would take that money and deposit it in a new bank account only she would know about. She stroked her belly, she wondered if he had made her pregnant. If he had tonight, she would make it Rico's baby. Rico always told her that she made him glad he was a man. Well, tonight she would make him very, very glad that he was a man.

She smiled to herself as she went into their bathroom to wash.

Nine months and two days later Angela would give birth to a little girl; she had eyes like her mother, white skin and red gold hair.

But what of Rico? He had said many times that they shouldn't have another baby just yet. When Angela announced to him six weeks later that she was pregnant he took it well, if not with much enthusiasm. However when he first held his new daughter he looked into her face and beheld the most beautiful and delicate creature that god had ever placed on this earth. His heart filled with love until it almost burst; she was his princess, his one reason for living now. Rico would outlive his wife and one son, and would not pass away until his ninety-sixth year. The reason he lived such a long life was because of an over-weaning love for his daughter; for another man's child.

Dominic didn't want to leave his mother alone with this large white man. He didn't know why but he didn't trust him, and felt uneasy when he was present. However, his mother had insisted that he get some shrimp for dinner and reluctantly he had gotten out his net and taking his small runabout went over to the next island where the shrimp were most abundant. Papa had always cautioned him about never leaving the dock without checking his boat gas. Today though his mind was full of other things and he had forgotten that task. This day he was lucky; he anchored and dipped in his net. The tide was running in off the Gulf and on the second dip of his net he filled it with large white shrimp. Very quickly he filled his gunnysack and with relief

166

started his motor and headed back home. As he rounded the point of their island his motor sputtered and died.

Once again the luck ran Dominic's way on this momentous day in his young life, because the tide was running in toward his dock. He took out his oars and rowed home. Had the tide been running out he could have been easily been swept away from home out into the gulf. As it was he arrived silently at the dock, and taking his gunnysack of shrimp walked quickly up to the landing before the screened-in porch that was the entrance to their home.

The porch was large; this is where they kept all the equipment they used for their guests. Life jackets, fishing poles, foul weather suits, tackle boxes and many bits and pieces used for the boats. There were two screened doors; the first one let you into the porch and the other led into the large kitchen dining room where everyone ate and lingered after the fishing day was done. Both these doors were on quite heavy springs, which had a tendency to slam the door tight after someone had passed through it. This slamming was heard all over the house and heralded the entrance of anyone, "bang," for the porch and "bang, bang" for the kitchen.

He stood before the first screened door; something was not right. His young sensitive nervous system sensed that something was different, a tension in the air. Slowly he opened the screened door and stepped into the porch. He was dragging his gunnysack and it was still in the doorway when the spring closed the first screened door. The door slammed up against the gunnysack filled with shrimp and no sound was made as it closed. It was now just after two o'clock and the sun coming in from the back of the house left the screened-in porch dark.

Dominic could see down the hallway to the rear of the house very well. As he stood there he thought he heard his mother cry out. He didn't move; his ears and senses at the ready. How long did he stand there not moving, eight maybe ten minutes? Then his mother came out of the guest bedroom; she wasn't like she always was. First her hair was loose and hanging down her back, Dominic had never seen his mother's hair down during the day, only at night when she was going to bed. She walked toward him, something was in her hand. She climbed up on a chair and placed that something in the can she used for tips. Climbing down off the chair he noticed the front of her dress was open almost all the way down; he saw her cleavage then her breast was exposed to him as she moved the chair back to the table. Never glancing his way she went back down the hall and into the bedroom she shared with his father.

He stood rigid in the gloom of the porch. A few more minutes went

167

by and the large white man came out of the guestroom. He moved quickly across the hall into the guest bathroom and closed the door. Dominic saw that he was naked. He didn't move until he heard the water for his mother's bath stop and saw the large white man move back across the hall to his bedroom. Then putting the gunnysack of shrimp over his shoulder he took a deep breath, pushed through the second screen door which banged loudly as it closed, and yelled out, "Mom, I'm home."

Dominic didn't know what the large white man and his mother had been doing, but it bothered him for a long time. He was worried he could have hurt her and he almost said something to his dad about it but didn't because his mother didn't seem any different. After a few years the memory slipped into his subconscience and he thought no more about it until the week of his eighteenth birthday.

His parents had left him alone at home for the weekend while they and his siblings were away in Tampa. His girl friend Mary Rae Luce had told her parents that she was spending the weekend at a sleepover. He had picked her up in his dad's boat and brought her to the vacant fishing camp.

All day they had kissed and petted. They had gone farther than they had ever gone before. Dominic had unbuttoned and removed her blouse, she had taken off his shirt. Suddenly with one quick movement she leaned forward and unhooked her bra. There they were both naked from the waist up. They now had gone too far to turn back.

Dominic took her to the guest bedroom and there they fumbled around until nature took its course and they both lost their virginity. They lay in each other's arms for some while until Dominic had to go pee really badly.

He got out of bed, still naked, and ran to the guest bathroom. As he crossed the hall he suddenly knew what his mother and the large white man had done on that afternoon seven years before.

It was like a punch in the stomach, for awhile he couldn't breathe. He was shaking too much to pee standing up so he sat on the toilet. By the time Mary Rae came into the bathroom he had regained his composure somewhat.

Once again he kept his secret to himself, but his relationship to his mother altered. He never loved her after that revelation.

After graduating from high school he went to Everglades Community College for a year; then he just up and joined the Army. He just had to get away from his mother and from Florida. That is why when he was discharged from Fort Ord, California he chose not to go home but headed north into Oregon to seek his fortune.

So now we have all the pieces in place to continue our little story.

When Katie looked into Dominic's eyes that day she had the same reaction that Klaus had when he looked into Angela's. What is the power over the opposite sex that these white-blue, almond-shaped eyes have? Is it just the power of the unexpected, or maybe once long ago an ancestor on a raiding party had entered the valley of the Tisza and looked into the same eyes. The shock having been imprinted on his genes for all his generations to come. Or maybe is it just looking into eyes that are two thousand years old; the eyes of a little slave girl from Thrace.

Book Two

Book Two

15

Chinook:

I am the spirit of the great western wind and I have always been here. I have moved across and seen the earth in its many forms. But I was not named until man had reached a point in his evolution to be given a conscience and a soul. Primitive man looked to the heavens and earth and gave name to gods and spirits to explain his environment, the first animal to do so. Primitive man didn't question his reason for being alive; his gods had made him and willed his life. He knew his place in the tribe or group, and those who didn't know that place were rejected and soon died. So he conformed, for to do so allowed him the best chance to breed and pass on his genes. The mandate to breed is the strongest emotion living organisms have. Men and women fight wars, kill and risk their lives to copulate and bear their young. One tribe attacks another for their women, for the chance to refresh and spread their seed throughout the world.

First came the family group, then the farm, then the village and the city. Laws that were instinctive were written down later to guide what they call civilization. These laws at their most basic protect man's right to spread his genes, ergo: do not commit adultery, do not covet another man's wife, do not kill. Yet civilized men and women circumvent these laws with regularity; the power to breed is so great. I have seen this situation millions of times as I blow over humankind, so why, you say, do I choose these particular four young people at this time of history? Because, of my audience. You understand them and their period, and also because it is a time of great change for the western part of the United States.

The Sunday dinner with the two young couples had been a success. Dominic, kind of the outsider, fit in well with the other three who had known each other all their lives. The girls had pumped Dominic about his childhood and his family back in Florida. He seemed like a nice and normal guy to the girls; anyone with a father, mother, brother and sister sounded normal to them.

After their guests had left Jimmy had helped Katie clean the house, then they went to bed because Jimmy was leaving at five A.M. the next morning and wouldn't be back for two weeks.

Jimmy asked Katie for sex and she let him make love to her, because the day had gone well and she felt relaxed, happy and proud that her DINNER had gone so well.

When Katie awoke the next morning Jimmy was long gone. She had very little to do that day, so she curled up in bed and thought in depth of the day before. Actually she thought about Dominic mostly. He was extremely beautiful; handsome was not quite a strong enough word. She closed her eyes and her heart raced when she remembered his eyes turning on her. Katie felt something she had never felt before, and it bothered her a bit.

Well I am only happy for Becky, she thought. *Now we must think of a way to get Dom to put a ring on her finger. I will feel better when Becky is married and out of competition. I remember when Becky offered herself to Jimmy and it would be better if she were married.* She resolved to call Becky that night to map out an attack plan. "Poor Dom," she laughed to herself, "he has no chance with two scheming females planning his future."

That evening Katie had just finished a light supper when the phone rang; it was Becky. Katie had been talking to her mother while she had been eating. Her mother had been very interested how the dinner went and what kind of a chap Becky's new boyfriend was.

"Katie my darling," Becky gushed over the phone, "I want to thank you for that lovely day, yesterday. You are, my dear, an excellent cook."

"Oh thank you, my precious," Katie warbled back, "but cook smook, tell me if Dom had a good time, and if we got him pointed in the right direction, namely toward the altar."

"Too early to tell, my pet, but he said he had an excellent time and the best time to attack a man is when his stomach is full of delicious food, don't you agree, my love?"

"Oh I do agree, my dearest, they are basic animals, men are, lots of food and lots of sex seems to be all they need to be happy."

"Why Mrs. Burns, how you talk. Quite shocking the conversations one hears on the telephone these days," Becky giggled.

"But Becky, my dear, we need lunch, shopping and talking, maybe this Saturday?"

"Let me call you later in the week, my love," said Becky. "I hate to burden Bessie with Sonny too much. She is a darling but she still gets tired easily, and Sonny is a bit of a handful for her."

"Oh poor thing," Katie sympathized, "I thought she was her old self again."

"She is so much better," said Becky, "but I don't like to push her too much, so I'll call you say Thursday."

"Ok, dearest, talk to you on Thursday then," said Katie and hung up.

When April had hung up the phone after talking to Katie she felt better than she had for some time about her daughter. Katie had sounded like her old self just now and it had been awhile since that had happened. April was worried about Katie, she suspected that she wasn't very happy with her life, and she also suspected that the problem was the lack of a baby. April knew that Katie wanted to be pregnant and felt she was not providing a family for Jimmy. April had broached the subject about a month ago, and suggested Katie go to Salem to a doctor, maybe he could find the problem. But Katie didn't want to talk about it at that time. She had confided, to April, since then that maybe she was being selfish that Jimmy seemed perfectly happy without children. It pained April to see her daughter unhappy, and now thrilled her to hear an obvious change in her. Then April's heart gave a little jump. *Maybe Katie thinks she is pregnant,* she thought to herself, *Well, well, I had better stay alert, maybe I will be a grandmother yet.*

*   *   *

Katie went to bed early as she often did when Jimmy wasn't home. But this time she didn't think about Jimmy, her parents, the latest *Flame* novel, Becky or of anything or anyone but Dom. He filled her head. She tried to get rid of him by saying her prayers but he was there still. It was his eyes, they seemed to be looking at her in the dark, and it was the way a small smile had swept his lips when their eyes met. She didn't want to admit it right now but she was attracted to him more than any man, including Jimmy, in her life.

She shook her head. *I am married, he is for Becky.* She wondered if she had committed a sin by thinking of him in any other way than a friend. She said to herself, "as soon as Becky and Dom get engaged I will feel just more friendly to him I am sure." With that thought she fell into a restless sleep.

Becky was lying in her bed looking up to the ceiling in her room. She felt so grateful to Katie for providing a nice atmosphere for Dom and herself to get more acquainted. It helped for Dom to see a couple like Katie and Jimmy so obviously in love and happy; she hoped he would want that for them.

She sighed. *Still the battle was young,* she thought. It is just that Dom seemed the man of her dreams, he was so good looking and he had a good job that would grow and soon they could be rich. Well time would tell and she fell asleep with uncertainty etched on her brow.

Dominic Stanza lay in his motel room bed in Coos Bay. He had just brought a load of canned vegetables to the Safeway and Food Mart stores in the small coastal town. His mind was filled with an image of Katie Burns. Damn, he envied that Jimmy guy, maybe he will get killed in a wreck and Katie would be a lonely young widow. Hot damn, what a babe she is. I wonder what it would be like to have her naked in bed now. He went into the bathroom and masturbated. *Maybe,* he thought, *that might get her out of his mind long enough to allow him to go to sleep.*

Jimmy had driven all day. They had stopped in Ontario, Oregon for dinner; now he lay in the sleeper of the truck as Joe drove them over the Snake River Bridge into Idaho. What a great three days he had at home this time. Katie had seemed very happy about the dinner with Dominic and Becky. He seemed like a good enough guy. Maybe they would become buddies; they seemed to like about the same stuff. Katie had let him make love to her twice in three days. It had been sometime since that had happened, and his heart filled with love for her. He loved her so much that he couldn't fathom what life would be without her. He fell asleep as the big truck rolled through Idaho on the way to its final destination, the Red Oak Market's distribution warehouse in Kansas City.

Katie called Becky on Thursday night. Becky had good news, Dom had come into the office as soon as he got back from his last trip and asked her out for Saturday night.

"I am sorry about our shopping trip on Saturday but I had better stay home and get ready for this date. I do want to impress him."

"Oh darling," Katie remonstrated her, "a date with your Mr. Dreamboat is more important than a shopping trip. I'll call you, or you call me, next week if you don't mind, if you want to rehash anything that is," Katie said to her.

"Hopefully there will be things to talk about, fingers crossed," Becky retorted.

Katie went to her parents' house after Mass on Sunday for the day.

Just after lunch Jimmy called. Her father had picked up the phone

176

in the living room when it rang and for about five minutes they could hear him commiserating with someone.

"I hope it is not a patient needing him," said April. "He has had a rough week and he needs to rest at least one day."

In a few minutes he came into the kitchen where the ladies were cleaning up after Sunday lunch. "It's your husband sweetheart," he said to Katie. "He is not going to be home by next weekend. A brake locked up on their trailer and burnt up an axle, they won't be back on the road until Wednesday at least."

"Oh dearest," said Katie into the phone, "are you and Joe ok?"

"Oh, ok sweetheart, we will be waiting for you, yes, uh huh, well drive carefully, we will see you hopefully on Monday then."

Katie stayed until after supper and started home about eight.

After she had left John said to April, "Katie seemed as jumpy as a cat today, something wrong?"

"Well darling, it's girl stuff you probably wouldn't understand."

"Try me," said John.

"Well you know Becky Anderson, she has a new boyfriend and last night was a big date for her, and well Katie just is anxious for Becky."

John got sort of a blank look on his face. "Anxious?"

"Yes darling, you know she would like to see Becky married and settled and happy and she just wants this to work out for her."

"I guess you're right honey, I really don't understand."

"Then of course," she continued, "there was this thing today about Jimmy and the truck, she worries about him being on the road so much."

John brightened. "Oh yes, I understand that, ok."

Katie's stomach had been in knots since yesterday; she was kind of glad to get away from Mother and Father today, she had to think this thing through. Was she really anxious for Becky, or was she jealous of her?

"No, stop it," she argued with herself, "I just want Becky to be happy that is all."

Becky didn't call. By Wednesday night Katie could not stand it anymore.

Becky answered the phone but obviously was distracted and couldn't talk. "Sonny is being a little monster tonight."

"Oh darling pet," Katie cooed, "Jimmy won't be home until Monday at the earliest so let's plan lunch and shopping on Saturday." Becky gave an ok to that and Katie hung up.

Darn, darn, darn, Katie thought, *how am I going to wait until Saturday?*

Katie was early at Bessie's house on Saturday morning; she played with Sonny and chatted with Bessie as Becky finished dressing.

Soon the two friends were settled into the Chevy Impala and on their way to Salem, lunch and girl talk.

Katie was almost bursting inside. *What is wrong with me?* she thought to herself.

* * *

The Entree Cafeteria, a large loud, and inexpensive restaurant, was situated exactly halfway between the State Capitol buildings and the shopping district. It was always full at lunch especially during the week; the daily special was filling, good and cheap. It was a very good place to meet for business or love, no one ever gossiped about who had lunch with whom because it was not a very intimate setting.

After two hours of shopping the ladies went there for food but more important for a chat, for it was certain they would not be overheard in that din.

As soon as they were seated Katie gushed breathlessly, "So tell me, darling, all about it, was it fun?"

Becky smiled. "Yes, it was fun. We went out to the Steak House, then we went to the Slayton Movie Theater. There was this science fiction thing on Dom wanted to see."

Katie wrinkled her nose. "Oh dear, not terribly romantic."

"No," said Becky, "but it got romantic later."

"Well go on, don't let me twist in the wind."

"Well, after the movie, we walked to the Ice Cream Palace and had a dish of ice cream each, and he asked me to come over to his house."

Katie's eyebrows shot up slightly. "Did you go?"

"Oh yes, I had to see how and where he lived. He has a small one bedroom house on a side street over by the Cannery. I must say he must be a good housekeeper because it was immaculate.

"I mentioned to him that he was a better housekeeper than I was. He said it was because of the Army, everything must be kept squared away. I believe that is the way he said it."

"Did he kiss you?" Katie asked.

"Oh yes, as soon as we got our coats off he took me in his arms and started to kiss me," Becky sighed. "I have to admit it has been a long time since I was kissed like that and it felt good."

Katie started to feel her backbone stiffen; she wasn't sure she wanted to hear the rest of the story, but it was too late to turn back now.

"After he kissed me for awhile he asked me if I would like to go to bed with him. I just nodded and he scooped me up in his arms like I was a twig, he is very strong."

Inadvertently Katie's mouth fell open. "Honey, on your first date?"

"It was our third date," Becky said defensively. "First we had a hamburger and a beer one night, after work, just after we first met. He was sweet. Then Sunday dinner at your house last week, and then this date, so that was three."

Katie's face sort of crumpled, so Becky moved on quickly.

"Well he is as beautiful with his clothes off as he is with them on. He was very gentle with me, and," she looked down into her plate and whispered, "he is huge."

"Well dear," said Katie, "I know he is taller than Jimmy but I wouldn't say he was huge."

"No no, I mean down there, you know," Becky pointed to her lap.

Katie's face flushed red. "Oh you mean, oh I see, gosh!"

"I always thought all men were about the same," said Becky, "course I have only seen two men naked, Ralph and Jim . . . oops."

Becky glanced up at Katie's face; her color was now a deeper red and her face strained.

"Hey, maybe I ought to explain. When Jimmy and I were going together in high school one Sunday afternoon his parents and sister went to his Aunt's for the day and Jimmy had to do the chores.

"We went over to the farm early just to kiss. We went up to his room and we took each other's clothes off but we never had sex, believe me. Jimmy and I have never had sex in our lives together. We were much too scared of getting pregnant when we were young. I was a virgin for Ralph.

"After he came back from the Air Force he fell in love with you and I never had a chance." She reached across the table and took Katie's hand. Katie relaxed a little, her face less red.

"But darling," Katie blurted, "what about pregnancy now. Surely you don't need another child."

Becky withdrew her hand and looked down into her plate, her lips slightly pursed. "Well he didn't like it but I made him wear a rubber."

Katie's face was a perfect blank. "A what?"

Becky looked up. "You know, a prophylactic, a condom."

Katie slowly shook her head, the blank look still on her face.

"Well it is a sheath that goes over the man's thing, you know, it stops him from ejaculating into you and therefore keeps you from getting pregnant."

"He said they hurt him, that they were too small. I had brought one

179

in my purse, a girl can't be too careful these days, so he used it. I am glad he did because he is a wonderful lover and it has been a long time since a man has made love to me."

At that they left the restaurant and as Katie had had enough shopping and enough talking they went straight home.

After Katie arrived home she made herself a cup of coffee and sat at the kitchen table. She had hated mess all her life and sex with Dominic sounded like mess to her. At that moment she was glad she was married to Jimmy and she even felt a spark of love in her bosom for him and the easy life he provided for her.

As Becky lay in her bed that night she regretted having told Katie about her and Jimmy. Of course she had not told her everything. She also was sorry she told her the truth about her date. She knew Katie looked at sex differently than she did; she was much more romantic, much more prudish.

Of course Katie was married to a wonderful man who loved her. She didn't have to scrounge for love and warmth and a husband like Becky did. Things had changed in the dating scene, especially for a woman who already had a child. Becky didn't know if she loved Dom but she sure wanted to land him for a husband and she would do whatever it took to do that. Everything anyway except get pregnant, until that ring was on her finger. She knew Dom didn't like to use a rubber but she also knew men and they would almost do anything to have sex with a beautiful woman, and she was she knew a beautiful woman.

She also knew that she had been mean to Katie. Anyway tomorrow she would call and sooth her and suggest they all go out to dinner together.

Katie lay in her bed, thinking about Jimmy, wishing he would hurry home. Mostly she was glad that Jimmy was gone a lot; she didn't have to turn him down for sex as often.

But now she needed him. She wanted him to hold her and remind her that her world wasn't like Becky's world. She fell asleep with a tear of self-pity trickling down her cheek.

*   *   *

Sunday afternoon Becky called Katie. "Darling, any word from Jimmy yet?"

"Yes, I heard from him after I got home from Mass this morning. He will be home tomorrow evening for certain. It was all a big mess with the parts they needed but finally everything came in and the

180

chaps at the garage in Kansas City worked late on Friday night to get it done.

"They drove to the meat place, they are bringing back Kansas City steaks and ribs, the guys there loaded them up on Saturday morning and they left for home as soon as they were done."

"Oh darling, I am so glad," Becky sympathized. "Maybe Saturday night the four of us ought to go out for one of those steaks."

"Oh, ok." Katie didn't sound very enthusiastic. "I don't know if Jimmy will be home."

"Well if he is, darling, it would be a lot of fun," Becky plowed on.

"Ok I will ask him when he gets home, and I'll let you know later," Katie whimpered.

After Becky had hung up she shook her head. *I hope I've not ruined our friendship. I have got to be careful not to burst Katie's romantic bubble,* she thought to herself.

Jimmy drove his pickup into the new double garage they had built about a year earlier, and had no sooner shut the big double doors and turned around than Katie was in his arms. She turned up her face to his for a kiss and he felt the tears on her face and tasted them on her lips.

"Baby, what's wrong?" he said wiping away the tears from her cheeks with his fingertips.

"I am just so glad you're home, darling, I was so worried."

"Boy, I am glad I am home too, baby, I am beat, it has been a long two weeks, too long without you, that is for certain."

Katie sniffed, wiping her eyes with her hankie. She smiled. Jimmy did love her and did miss her, no matter how cruel she was to him sometimes. She had dinner ready for him and he tucked into it like a logger. After dinner Jimmy sat in the living room reading the newspapers while she cleaned the kitchen. When she was done cleaning she sat beside him and snuggled under his arm.

"Thank you darling," she cooed into his ear.

Jimmy kissed the end of her nose. "Thanks for what?"

"Thank you for marrying me and taking me out of the dating mess."

"The pleasure was all mine, my love, but what brought this on?"

"Just Becky and Dom," she said.

"Ah, is there trouble between them?" he asked her.

"No, not trouble. I am just glad I have you."

"Believe me, baby, not nearly as glad as I am that I have you."

She stood up and taking his hand pulled him up. "Come on," she said, "let's go to bed."

When Katie let Jimmy make love to her normally, she always lay quietly with her arms at her side or her fingertips touching his back, her eyes closed and her face turned slightly away from him, while he did all the physical work. This night though while she still lay quietly her hands caressed his face, rumpled his hair, and she kissed his cheek and lips as he made love to her.

Jimmy thought he had died and went to heaven. Secretly he had always wished that Katie would show more passion while they made love, that she wouldn't act like he was an inconvenience to be dealt with. He had come to accept the way she was. She was so extremely beautiful and so soft and warm, that he was just glad she let him make love to her at all. When Jimmy was finished he rolled off her and almost instantly fell asleep while she went to have her bath.

She lay in the bath, the hot water up to her neck, and thought that this was all she wanted out of sex—quick and easy, not nasty and horrible like Dom and Becky. It was nice to see Jimmy enjoy it but she didn't really enjoy it herself, she sighed. *I guess we are well matched, Jimmy and I.*

Jimmy and Joe were given the week off and didn't have to leave again until Sunday morning.

Katie called Becky and said that they would be glad to go out on Saturday night with her and Dom.

Jimmy and Katie picked up the other young couple at six on Saturday evening. Katie made sure they sat as couples, Dom and Becky in the back and her and Jimmy in the front.

They went to a country and western bar and restaurant called The Corral in Salem that had a reputation for big juicy steaks. Katie avoided looking directly into Dom's eyes, though he seemed less edgy than the last time they were all together. After they were done with dinner they went into the bar to dance to a local live band, and to have a drink. Dom asked Katie to dance and as they circled the floor they chatted quite naturally and when he looked into her face his glance didn't undress her like it had done before. She started to relax and really had a good time after that.

Jimmy danced with Becky; it was the first time in years that he had touched her. She fit into his arms so well and she pushed her lower body against him. A little flash of the old feelings ran through his chest just for a second. They didn't talk much; Becky just hummed along with the popular song that the band was playing.

They were home by midnight; all were slightly tipsy and giggly and they made a date for two weeks later to do it again.

Becky invited Dom up to her room but pleaded for him to be extra quiet. He grumbled a bit when she made him put on a rubber. She teased him a bit, "use one or get none," she whispered in his ear. She explained that she would soon have some of the new birth control pills that everyone was talking about. Then he wouldn't have to use that "damn thing" as he called it, ever again, that calmed him down a lot. Becky didn't tell him that she would have let him do it anyway if he had refused to use it, because she had really needed him that night.

When Jimmy and Katie reached home they stood in the living room for awhile and embraced each other.

"You have a good time, baby?" Jimmy asked her.

"Oh yes, it was fun, didn't you think so, darling?"

"Oh yeah, I thought that joke Dom told was really funny!"

"Umm, well it was a little rude, but Dom was a little tipsy so I guess I won't hold it against him."

"Baby, do you think we could have a little love tonight?"

Katie gave a little fake hiccup. "Oh sir," she batted her eyelashes.

Quickly Jimmy led her to their bedroom. After they were finished Jimmy smiled to himself. "This has been the best week in my life."

The two weeks went by quickly and soon the appointed Saturday night date was upon them. This time Jimmy and Katie picked Becky up at home alone. As they were going to do dinner in Slayton then go on to a dance hall called the Armsville Pavilion they would pick Dom up at his house. This dance hall was located in a small country town just a few miles from Slayton.

They had hamburgers at the Slayton Cafe and then about eight o'clock arrived at the dance hall. They followed the other cars into a grass field next to the Pavilion and parked. The Armsville Pavilion was, in truth, an old large hay storage barn that had been "gussied up." There were plenty of tables, a large dance floor and a bench that ran around the outside wall where singles would sit. At the end of the dance floor was a raised platform where the band played. Tonight that band was "Rusty and his Cascade Range Riders." They played popular dance music, some c&w and some rock and roll. A cover charge of two dollars a head was taken at the door. No alcohol was served in the hall, if you wanted a drink you went out to your car where the beer was kept in the cooler or the bottle was stashed. The crowd was mostly local, with the exception of a group of college kids from Salem. Farmers, town people, some loggers, mill workers and older high school kids from surrounding towns made up the dancers.

The May evening was warm and the place was packed; soon the sweat was running down the backs of the men and dewing on the cheeks, and upper lips, of the ladies. The two young couples danced for the first hour almost constantly. They switched back and forth every few dances so Jimmy and Katie danced with Becky and Dom almost as much as they danced together. Katie was warming to Dom more and more, he was a gentleman, handled Katie gently and was a very good dancer.

Jimmy and Becky danced some slow dances. Becky cuddled in his arms and pressed her whole body against him. Slowly she moved with the music and smiled at him when she felt a response from down below.

Dom had brought a bottle of bourbon and a couple of times the men slipped out for a quick sip when the women went to the bathroom.

Katie didn't care for the smell of whiskey on Jimmy's breath, but Dom kept his head back so as not to breathe in her face when they danced.

Becky on the other hand pushed her nose up to Jimmy's nose and sniffed, "seems the boys have been naughty while the girls were having a pee," she said smiling at Jimmy. They left at eleven, bodies tired and aching. Jimmy went out to the Chevy, opened the passenger side door and held the front seat forward so there would be easy entry to the rear seat. The first on the scene was Katie.

"Oh," she said, "I'll get in the back with Becky," and in she went.

The next on the scene was Dom. Before Jimmy could speak he said, "thanks," to Jimmy and popped into the back seat. Becky arrived just then and popping her head into the car said, "Hey, the back is filled. Oh well, I'll sit up here with Jimmy and tell him how to drive."

For just a second Katie was frozen, but Dom turned his beautiful eyes on her and smiled. "Seems you are trapped back here with me." His voice was light and not in any way suggesting so Katie relaxed and actually started to enjoy being back there with him. Once on the way into Slayton Jimmy took a corner too fast and Katie slid up against him, their legs touched for a second. Katie felt a warm blush come over her from her head to her toes. They stopped at the Slayton Ice Cream Palace for milk shakes and then they dropped both Becky and Dom off at his house.

"Dom will take me home later," she informed Jimmy and Katie. "Thank you so much for a great evening," she said, and they turned and walked up to Dom's door.

On the drive home Katie was very quiet. Jimmy glanced at her. "Penny for your thoughts," he said.

"Oh it's nothing, darling, I just think Becky jumped into his bed rather quickly that is all."

"Oh, are they doing it?" Jimmy inquired.

"Unfortunately yes, anyway she said they are."

"Ah, well I guess they are adults, but I must admit it did rather take me back when she said Dom would bring her home," Jimmy mused, and they talked no more about it that night.

It was ten o'clock at night, Mountain Time, and the big rig was heading down highway U.S. 60 toward Phoenix. Jimmy was driving and he could see a faint glow in the East that would be the lights of the city. They were on their way this time to Tucson with a truck and trailer filled with frozen berries.

The trips they made to Arizona were becoming his favorite ride. He found that he liked the desert; the stark landscape, the warm evenings, the bright moon and stars in the heavens, the wide open spaces where it seemed you could see a hundred miles, and especially the sunsets. The sunsets were like nothing he had ever encountered in his life; yellow, orange, red, and blue then black. The whole of the horizon on fire to the west, and behind you the black of the desert night.

Within an hour he was past Del Webb's Sun City, a new small city that was devoted to old retired people. *Who knows, maybe some day in the far, distant future Katie and I will retire there,* Jimmy thought to himself.

In another four hours he was at Florence Junction leaving highway 60 he picked up state highway 79 and he turned south toward Tucson.

They had left Slayton at six A.M. on Monday morning; now it was just past two A.M. on Thursday morning and his mind still was bothered by the happenings on Saturday night. He felt confused. Becky had almost raped him on the dance floor Saturday night; she had even nibbled his ear. Yet when he and his wife danced Katie kept an inch between them, afraid he presumed not to be too brazen in public.

"Damn, life and women are funny," he said to himself quietly. He wondered if he would ever understand them.

It was nine P.M. on Wednesday evening. Becky sat at the table alone. She had just gotten Sonny down and to sleep and she was exhausted.

It seemed lately that Sonny was trying every unreasonable tactic to stay up later. Of course when she let him stay up maybe an hour past his normal bedtime he was a bear and a handful to Bessie, whose job it was to get him off to school in the morning.

Her mind turned to lighter thoughts. She smiled to herself. "I was such a bitch Saturday night to Jimmy. I probably have his head so screwed up now he doesn't know which way to turn." She knew she had given him almost a direct invitation for sex with her. Snuggling in his arms, full body contact and the best part, the chewing on and blowing into his ear. She wondered why she did that, probably as a direct reaction to all the grief she was getting from Dom on the contraceptive thing. She had started taking the pill almost two weeks before just after her last period. They had made her miserable, stomach cramps and vomiting. She called the doctor and he had put her on a lighter dosage. It was somewhat better, but he had strongly suggested she take them until at least her next period before she had unprotected sex. Hopefully by then all her eggs would be flushed out. Of course Dom didn't understand; for a big guy he sure could whine a lot. If only he wasn't so beautiful and so eligible. Still sometimes she wished she would have taken Jimmy when he offered himself, her life would be so less complicated.

Dom had just returned home from a trip to Yakima, Washington. He had dropped off a load of canned beans and peas, and picked up a load of applesauce. He went straight to bed and lay there not being able to fall asleep right away. Becky filled his thoughts as she almost always did now, except when he was thinking about ways to get into Katie's pants. Becky was being a bitch about the rubber thing. She knew he hated them but was making him wear them because she was afraid of getting pregnant, or so she said. He had explained he had never made any girl pregnant in his life, that he was probably sterile. He missed Mary Rae, his first love. He closed his eyes and pictured her naked; those huge tits, he sighed. He had never made her pregnant. Of course he hadn't been in basic training for hardly more than a month when he got the "Dear John" letter. She was marrying the local owner of the Chevrolet dealership in Ft. Myers.

Chinook:

Doug Johnson, the owner of Doug Johnson's Chevrolet, had been divorced about six months when he met the daughter of one of his mechanics at the annual company barbecue. He was thirty-eight, she was twenty and she was a knockout. He had been happily married until a year ago when one day at lunch he came home to surprise his wife for a quickie and found her in bed with the pool boy, Juan. He was on his back, his hands under his head with a very satisfied look on his face. Doug's wife was kneeled between Juan's legs doing what she had told Doug she would never do to him, because it was yucky. Well damn, if she had just been screwing Juan he might have forgiven her but not a blow-job; that was too much. So needless to say he dumped both his pool cleaning contract and his wife. He had asked her why she was doing to Juan what she wouldn't do to her own husband.

She laughed at him, shrugged her shoulders and said, "Because he was so damn good-lookin', and it seemed like a good idea at the time."

Oh well, Doug always did like big tits and his ex-wife had small ones so he set out to find a girl with a large set and there was Mary Rae. She was an easy conquest and when he took off her bra ol' Doug was hooked. A week after they met they flew to Las Vegas and were married on the strip in the "Chapel of Forever." Doug got his big tits and Mary Rae got a new Chevrolet convertible to drive every six months; it was a marriage made in heaven. Mary Rae presented him with a daughter one week less than eight months after they were married. At first Doug was a little mad; his bride was obviously pregnant when they had gotten married, but what the heck, he reasoned he needed a family for his TV ads and now he had one, so it worked out.

After Dom had been at Fort Ord for about a year he went to a Thursday "dime a shot night" at the NCO club. Generally Thursday night had been slow at the NCO club so they opened it up for all the soldiers for beers and shots for only a dime. With the young men came young women, both WAC's and civilians and soon a live band was hired for dancing. When Dom walked into the club he stood scanning the tables for unattached women. He saw a table of four older looking women over in the corner, one of them met his eye. He turned and went to the bar for a drink and when he returned she was still looking in his direction. She was good looking so after a few minutes of checking for younger babes—there were none available—he moseyed over to their table and asked the one who had been looking at him for a dance. Her name was Gloria and she and her lady friends were the wives of NCO's. They were out for a girl's night out while their husbands were home watching the kids. The other ladies danced with a mixture of the soldiers or each other. Dom and Gloria danced every dance together and with every drink Gloria moved closer to him and on the last dance of the night with her body pressing close to his he kissed her. The moment his lips touched Gloria's her tongue flew into his mouth, when they finished with the kiss they were both a bit breathless. He asked her to come again next week and she said she would, and so it started. The next week they slipped out halfway through the dance and sat in the back seat of her car where they got to know each other better physically. As they kissed Dom explored Gloria's body with his free hand; she was the first mature woman he had touched like this. She let him touch her belly; it was kind of flabby, not smooth and hard like Mary Rae's. He touched her breasts and they kind of hung and were soft, not at all like Mary Rae's, which while large stood firm. When he tried to slip his hand between her legs she stopped him; instead she unzipped his fly and put her hand in his jeans but not in his shorts. She gasped when she touched him.

Gloria was thirty-two years old. She had been married ten years and had two kids, both boys eight and seven. She had the seven-year itch bad. It is not that she didn't love her husband, or would ever leave him, she just wanted to know what else was out there. On their third date she found out, there in the front seat of her Buick. Dom had never known women could react to sex like Gloria did. She was a handful and when she climaxed she stopped breathing and arched her back, he was afraid he had killed her.

For three months, almost every Thursday night, they met but never made love in the car again. They found a cheap motel off base on Route 68. Dom would meet her at the NCO club and she would hunker down in the back seat, as he would drive off base. They would spend an hour to an hour and a half in the hotel and return to base the same as they left. Her lady friends knew what was going on and covered for her. Actually they were jealous of her and wished they had the guts to find some guy like Dom to screw them. Then one night, three months later, he showed up at the club and Gloria wasn't with her friends. Dom asked them where she was.

"Oh, she told me to tell you that she couldn't get away this week but she would be here next week," the one named Suzy told him.

"Wouldn't her husband let her out?" Dom asked Suzy.

"No, I believe she said she was sick and had been throwing up for a couple of days."

The next Thursday she wasn't there again, but when Dom questioned her friends they stared at him hard for a few minutes. The one named Joan finally spoke.

"She won't be coming again."

"Why," Dom asked, "there has to be a reason?" Again the hard stares.

"Look," the one named Fran said, "we don't know, just go and leave us alone."

Dejectedly Dom walked over to the bar and got a drink. He found an empty table and was crying into his beer when he felt someone touch his arm. It was the one named Suzy, "Look honey," she said, "Gloria is pregnant and can't come again, ok?"

"Thanks," he said to Suzy. "I thought maybe it was something I did." He felt better instantly.

Suzy stood there for a few seconds looking at him funny like, then she shook her head and walked away.

Eight months later Dom had almost forgotten Gloria when one day he was walking to the Base Exchange. A Buick pulled up to the curb in front of him. A short man with big shoulders and arms got out of the driver's side of the car. He walked around to the passenger side and opened the back door. Two young boys jumped out of the car and stood there while the man opened the front passenger door. He reached in the car and gently helped out his very pregnant wife. While he went to park the car the boys led her to the entrance. She never saw him but he recognized Gloria instantly; he almost went up to her as she stood inside the entrance waiting for her husband but he decided at the last second not to. He watched them from a distance while they shopped. She would tell the man and boys what she wanted and they would get it for her and put it in the cart. In a few minutes he turned and walked away. He never saw her again.

Frank Godson was a partner in the accounting firm of Clyde, Hobson, Densmire, Densmire, and Godson. One of the most respected firms in the city, they had an office in the new Transamerica tower overlooking the Golden Gate Bridge and San Francisco Bay. At forty years of age Frank was already a very rich man. He had a pretty wife, two lovely teenaged daughters and a beautifully restored Victorian home out in the "Aves" just a few blocks off Golden Gate Park. Although Frank had reached material wealth he was restless.

What is wrong with me, he often thought to himself. *Most men would kill for what I have.* But still he sensed that something was missing from his life.

One morning he came to work and to his chagrin found that his secretary, the rock of his business life, had been rushed to the hospital the night before with an attack of acute appendicitis. She was ok but would be missing for a month, in convalescence from her operation. Frank needed someone to anchor his office so a temporary secretary was acquired from TempEx, a company that had a good reputation for providing temporary help to the San Francisco business community. The next morning as Frank entered his outer office he found out what was missing in his life, Cindy Blank. Five foot two, chestnut hair, star-

189

tling deep blue eyes, a figure like the Venus de Milo, and all packaged in a rose-colored business suit. Frank fell in love that instant, and by the time his regular secretary returned had been sleeping with his true love for two weeks.

The conquest of Miss Blank was a piece of cake. As soon as Frank got up the nerve to ask her out for lunch, he took her to the Sir Francis Drake Hotel; she was the dessert. Actually it was her suggestion that they might dally in one of the hotels rooms for the afternoon. Frank no longer felt restless, now his life was complete. When Frank's secretary returned he had to do something about Cindy; he sure couldn't let her go.

When Frank breached the question to her at their last rendezvous before he terminated her TempEx contract she lay in his arms weeping.

"Oh, daddy darling, you can't send me away, I need you so." Frank agreed. Her perfect naked body was pressing against his and he would have done anything to keep her, but he couldn't think of a way just now.

Then it was Cindy who made a suggestion. "Daddy, maybe you could put me full time on the payroll as your personal assistant except I wouldn't be coming to the office. I would wait for you every day in my apartment. You could come to me whenever you wanted."

Yes, he thought, *I could do that. I have my own budget. I can hire whom I want! Of course I would have to be discreet. Alison or the girls can't ever find out or I would be dead, umm well I will look into it.*

Drying Cindy's tears with the corner of the bedsheet he said, "Ok Dolly-baby, I will make it happen, I could never live without you." Frank got something extra from Dolly-baby that afternoon, something Alison always refused to do. The next three months went along very well. Frank was in heaven. Cindy's apartment was only a ten minute cable car ride away and he spent almost every lunch there.

It was perfect. Cindy didn't demand any of his time. He spent evenings, weekends and holidays with his family, and blissful lunches with Dolly-baby. Of course there was one little hitch at first. Dolly-baby had demanded double what he had been paying TempEx for her salary. She claimed, when he balked, that she needed more money to keep her person and apartment in perfect condition for him. Well he found a way to hide it in his budget so it worked out but he, just for a flash, saw a ruthless side of Dolly-baby he didn't know existed. He thought it might be better never to cross her. There was another small problem that he didn't like; there were telltale signs of another male in her apartment. Cindy assured him that it was just her artist brother who stayed with her at times when he was down and out, which was most of the time.

"There is not another man could make love to me like my Daddy," she cooed to him.

Well how can a guy fight that?

It hit the fan three months and four days into Frank's perfect life. He came home to an empty house and a terse note, which was still damp with tears.

It read, "If you want that slut more than you want your family, then your family doesn't want you anymore. You will find your children and WIFE in Monterey, at Mom and Dad's if you ever come to your senses."

Frank was devastated—how did she find out, he took such pains to keep it a secret. He sat and pondered who might have been a traitor to him. His secretary. He knew she suspected what was going on. She had questioned him about the irregularities in his budget. The busybody partners' wives; there were whispers going around the office about him and they had obviously picked up on them. As he sat and pondered and thought about revenge, he would have been surprised who actually done him in.

He would be stunned to know that just two weeks before Alison, at home, answered a phone call that was from obviously a young female. The voice, calling herself "a friend," wouldn't give her name. Instead she gave Alison an address to an apartment building in the city. The voice told her that her husband was having an affair with a woman in a room in that building.

Alison at first would not believe it; her Frank was not that type of man. She knew Frank loved her and the children; she would have almost believed that he would cheat at accounting before he cheated on her. Just to ease her mind though Alison arranged a lunch date with Rachel Densmire, a senior partner's wife.

Rachel was a very astute woman; she knew all the latest gossip that enveloped the office and Alison was sure would debunk this vicious lie. Deftly, as they ate, Alison moved Rachel to the subject of scandal in the office.

"Well, my dear, it seems Roger Hobson's secretary, Mary Osborn, is having a cheating husband problem and has given him the ultimatum—give up the harlot or give up his marriage."

"Oh dear, poor thing," Alison pitied. "I am so glad that my Frank would never do that to me."

Alison couldn't breathe for a few seconds; it was like someone had

191

hit her in the chest. With horror she saw the look that flashed over Rachel's face just for a split second, and she knew the truth.

"Oh you are my dear, you are so lucky your Frank does love you," the older lady lied. Alison went home and cried until the children came home from school. She pulled herself together and decided she had to ascertain the real truth. She cut Frank off from all affection; he didn't seem to notice.

The morning she left him Alison took the bus downtown and found the address on an older building. She settled herself in the window of a coffee shop across from it; she didn't have to wait long. Around the corner walked Frank, she almost didn't know him. He looked like he had lost twenty years, more like the boy she had fallen in love with those many years before. He was smiling and in his step was the skip of youth. He entered the building and in five minutes came out again, a girl almost half his age on his arm. They walked arm-in-arm across the street toward her. She was so stunned she didn't try to cover her face.

The girl was young and beautiful; she felt suddenly old and plain. The happy couple turned and walked up the street. The girl tugged on Frank's arm to stop him. When he looked at her she jumped into his arms and gave him a long kiss right there on the street. The thought flashed through Alison's brain, *My lord, Frank is doing to her what he does to me.* She felt her stomach heave and almost threw up on the table.

As soon as they were out of sight she caught a taxi home and started to pack and she called her mother. When her daughters arrived home she loaded them into her car, with much protesting on their part, and headed for Monterey.

Frank lay in bed, and the bed was empty except for him. He reached over to the phone and called Cindy; a man answered. Must be the brother; he asked for her.

Within a second Cindy was on the phone. He told her that his wife had left him.

"Are you all alone, Daddy?" she asked him.

"Yes I am all alone," he whined.

"I'm coming to you, Daddy. I'll be there as soon as I can!"

When Cindy hung up she turned to the man standing there smiled and said, "Well we have a new home, help me pack." Two hours later the bell rang and when Frank answered his front door there stood Cindy surrounded by four suitcases. She leaped into his arms, kissed him passionately and asked Frank to bring in her bags.

"Are you moving in?" Frank asked.

"Yes Daddy. I will not leave you alone."

Frank seemed a little nervous. "I thought we would keep on just as we were."

"Oh Daddy, just come to bed now and let me make you forget all about her, then we will discuss it tomorrow." Cindy did make Frank forget for awhile that night.

He left her sleeping in the morning and when he returned home from work that evening she was all moved in. Her underwear was in the drawers that Alison used for her underwear, and Alison's walk-in closet now contained Cindy's clothes and shoes. Anything that Alison had used and had left behind now was packed in boxes and in the basement or was in the trash.

Cindy Blank was there to stay.

When Frank walked into the house Cindy jumped into his arms, he kissed her, the house smelled of cooking dinner. Cindy sat him down and put on his slippers and brought him a whisky and soda just the way he liked it.

He liked it with a twist of lemon peel. After dinner they sat on the sofa and she cuddled under his arm. She took his hand and placed it in her blouse; she didn't have a bra on and he could feel her nipple hardening under his palm.

Frank thought, *this isn't so bad,*, but way down deep inside he was racked with guilt.

The next night was the same scenario but this time Cindy laid her head against his shoulder and said, "Daddy, have you liked the dinners you've eaten the last two nights?"

"Yes," he said. "I didn't realize you were such a good cook."

Cindy sat up and looked him in the eye. "I don't cook at all, Daddy, that was my brother. He is fantastic in the kitchen, and umm Daddy he needs a job."

Frank's eyes flew open. "Your brother is in the house, in this house now?"

"Yes Daddy, he needs a job and we need a cook and housekeeper. Please, Daddy, let him stay please."

Frank was about to say no when Cindy continued. "There is plenty of room here, Daddy, and he won't be underfoot. He will stay out of our way. The only time you will see him is when he is serving or cooking."

Frank looked at her. "Can I meet him now before I decide?"

"I'll get him." She walked back to the rear of the house to what was once a housekeeper's room, and now served as a guest bedroom. She brought him out. He looked nothing like Cindy; there seemed to be no family resemblance at all.

"Daddy, this is Rodney, my brother." Frank stood up and shook his

193

hand. He was a big boy, six foot two or three, blond, body like a weightlifter and an absolutely blank face, like he had no personality at all. When Frank shook his hand Rodney sort of grunted and looked at him with blank blue eyes.

"Ok Rodney, you can go back to your room now," Cindy said. With that Rodney turned and ambled to his room. "See, Daddy, he won't be in the way and he is a good cook, you said so yourself."

"Ok Dolly-baby, we can keep him."

"Oh thank you, Daddy, and because he lives here you can pay him only half of my wages."

Frank's eyes flew open again, but before he could say anything her lips were on his and her sweet little tongue was in his mouth.

You know, he thought to himself, *this is why I like Dolly-baby so much. Alison would never do anything as intimate as putting her tongue in my mouth. Alison would never put my hand on her naked breast or for that matter give me a blow-job.* So with those thoughts Frank wet his bed, and would now have to sleep in it.

Alison informed her parents that her marriage was over. She moved into her old room and put the girls in the room her brothers had shared when they were boys.

Frank called about a week after they left. He talked to her mother and to his daughters but she refused to talk to him. He asked her mother for her bank account number and told her he would have two hundred dollars a week transferred to her account for the upkeep of his family.

Alison refused to touch what she called, "his guilt money," but her parents were very happy to get it as they had just retired and three extra mouths to feed were a burden on them financially.

In about a month Alison started as a bartender trainee at a restaurant on cannery row. Three months later she was a full-fledged bartender and was working the Friday night shift when a tall good-looking boy entered the lounge and sat in the seat at the far end of the bar. He seemed very young to her so she asked him for his I.D.; he was twenty-three. He had the most beautiful eyes she had ever seen. She set him up with a beer and moved to help the waiters coming in to pick up drinks for their tables, but she kept her eyes on him.

Alison had always considered herself an ordinary, plain girl. She had been tall and slender since her teenage years; some people said painfully skinny. Growing up she had been rather boyish; she didn't blossom really until she was sixteen when she finally got a figure, but her breasts were small and as she always complained, "I don't have a

194

butt." Her face, below a shock of red hair, was rather flat. She had a handful of freckles scattered across her nose, and she tended to blush easily so her face was red much of the time also. Her one redeeming feature was a pair of sea green eyes. By the time she had met Frank, at the age of twenty-two, she had learned to cover most of her flaws with make-up. Frank, then twenty-four, fell head over heels in love with this sweet, kind, shy girl with the beautiful sea green eyes. They married one year later; nine months two weeks after they married Alison had their first child, and then exactly one year one day later they had their second daughter. They were a very happy family most suited to each other. Alison, though not a very passionate person, usually gave Frank sex on demand as long as it was not "weird stuff." Frank seemed happy with his lot; his wife, while not sexy, never ever looked at another man.

Dom nursed the beer the lady bartender had served him. He watched her out of the corner of his eye; she wasn't beautiful but she was striking. Since he had had his affair with Gloria he had yearned to replace her; he had many choices of girls his own age but Gloria had spoiled him. She had been so easy to have sex with and she never expected anything beyond just that, "sex from him." Gloria was the first mature woman he had made love to; he loved her, missed her terribly and wished her husband had not made her pregnant just when they were going so good.

Alison, whenever she had a break, paid special attention to the young man. She found excuses to refresh his beer, wipe the bar and ordered him a burger and fries when he was ready to eat.

He was very friendly to her, had a very nice smile, and was dead handsome.

After he had finished his meal Dom sat sipping his beer and his mind moved back to one night, over a year ago now, the second night Gloria and he had spent in the motel. After a quick kiss he started to undress Gloria. He loved to undress her watching as her body was revealed bit by bit.

Soon he had all her clothes off except her panties; as he reached for them she stopped his hand.

"Not those tonight, lover."

"Why not," he said bewildered.

"I am afraid that I am in the last days of my period and it wouldn't be very nice for you and there is something already in there."

"Damn," he said. "So the evening is lost, no fair I really wanted you."

She smiled at his disappointed little boy face, then she slowly raised her right hand and with the tips of her fingers gently moved a curl of hair off his forehead. Her face became softer and as she moved her right hand down to his cheek she raised her left hand to place it on his other cheek.

Her eyes became pools of liquid. "Baby, you are one of God's most gorgeous creations," and she stood on her tiptoes and kissed the tip of his nose.

"But you are a bit of a bull in my china shop."

With that the old Gloria was back. "You know, lover, there is more to me than just what is between my legs. If we are going to have a long-term affair there are some things I would like to show you.

"Now, lover, it's my turn to undress you," and she unbuckled his belt. When he was naked she came into his arms, lifting her mouth to his. She started to kiss him, she slipped her tongue into his mouth and with its tip caressed his lips and then the tip of his tongue. In a little while she pulled back her tongue and whispered, "Now, lover, do the same to me."

Just like she did he ran the tip of his tongue over her lips and just inside her lips. He then pushed it further and fully into her mouth; she pulled her head back.

"No, lover, that is too much, just put the tip on the tip of my tongue." Then she gently nibbled and sucked on the tip of his tongue tickling it with the tip of her tongue. In a few minutes she led him to the bed and lay down beside him and kissed him some more.

So Gloria taught Dom the techniques that would turn him into a competent and thoughtful lover. It would serve him well in the coming years.

He was really enjoying himself when after a while she gently said, "Well done, lover, now it is time for your reward." When she had finished with his reward and he had opened his eyes she was looking at him with a smile playing around her lips. "Did you enjoy that lover?"

"Oh yes," he gasped.

"Was that your first?" she asked him.

He nodded his head in the affirmative. "Uh-huh."

"Well, maybe we can do it again sometime," she laughed.

"Maybe?"

"But baby, that is better than the other way. Can't we do that all the time?"

She looked at him. "When Ed and I were first married we were poor. We didn't think we could afford a child until Ed had gotten another stripe. Also we both hated condoms so this is all we did for a while. It is a lot of fun but after a time we started getting on each other's nerves and we both really missed regular sex. You know it is the way Mother Nature intended men and women to mate. So we started doing regular sex with stuff like we just did only once in a while, and we have lived happily ever after."

Dom looked at her. "Does Ed know about us?" he asked.

"Of course he doesn't, lover. He would probably kill us both if he knew. Lover, what we do together has nothing to do with Ed or what I feel about him, or our children. This is between you and me period. I fell in love with you the first time I saw you and when we first danced I knew I wanted you, that I wanted you inside me as soon as possible. I don't know why, I have never wanted another man except Ed until you, and now I want you as long as we can manage it. Ok?"

Dom smiled at her. "It is ok with me!"

"A penny for your thoughts," Alison said. Dom jerked himself back to the present and looked into her sea green eyes.

"I was just working up the nerve to ask you out after you get off work."

"Well," said Alison, "I don't get off until 11:30. Would that be too late?"

"No," said Dom smiling, "that would be fine."

"Well," said Alison, "can I get back to you in about half an hour?"

"Sure, I'll be right here," he said.

Alison called her mother from the supply room as soon as she had a minute. "Mom, I am not coming home tonight, so don't worry. The reason? Well they asked me to stay tonight and help clean, then start early tomorrow for lunch. They want the bar open early for Saturday lunch. Where will I be staying? Well one of the waitresses here has a house just a couple of blocks away and she offered me her hide-a-bed. Yes Mom, hopefully I can do this every weekend, I could use the extra money. Yes I will take care, Mom, it is ok darling, don't worry."

Ok, thought Alison, *that is out of the way.* She walked up to Dom. "'I accept your lovely invitation for a date if the offer is still open?"

"The offer is still open." He held out his hand, "My name is Dominic!"

"I know," she said. "I saw your I.D., remember?"

Dom nodded his head in assent.

She took his hand. "My name is Alison, so very nice to meet you," she replied formally while looking into those beautiful almond-shaped blue-white eyes. She felt a shiver run down her backbone and a tightening of her stomach muscles.

It was a good thing that the number of drink orders had slackened, because after she had accepted his offer Alison couldn't concentrate at all. Finally at eleven the last customers had left the restaurant. She cleaned up getting everything in place for tomorrow. At eleven-thirty sharp Alison and Dom left by the employee entrance. They stood in the parking lot behind her car. "Where do you want to go?" she inquired.

"I don't know. I was hoping you knew about this area. I am afraid I know very little of Monterey night life."

"There is an older motel at the beginning of the dock, shall we get a room?" Alison was stunned. Was that her voice that just said that? Plain little Alison, the shy one, who could never ask a boy out to a movie? Now she was offering to go to a motel room with one she had known only three hours?

Her mind was whirling, she didn't feel like she was in her own body. She couldn't keep her mouth shut. "I have almost one hundred dollars in tips. I'll pay for the room."

"That would be very nice," Dom smiled down at her. "Shall we walk or take the car?"

"Oh let's walk. It is only two blocks at the most."

The cool fog off the water brushed Alison's cheek but it did little to calm the heat in her brain.

I wonder, she thought to herself, *just at what moment tonight had I made up my mind that I was spending the night with this boy?*

They walked into the hotel lobby. Alison boldly walked up to the desk while Dom stayed back. She registered them in as Mr. and Mrs. Rogers. The clerk raised one eyebrow slightly, but lowered it again when she gave him forty-five dollars in cash for the night. Taking the key Alison took Dom's hand and they walked to their room. Upon entering the door Alison took off her coat and threw it onto the only chair in the room; she turned and started to unbutton his shirt. Soon with his help he stood before her naked. The only other man Alison had seen naked was Frank; the difference between their bodies couldn't have been greater. Frank had never been an athlete. He, even when they were first married, had a small potbelly, and a bad case of acne when he was a teenager had left his skin pocked and slightly scarred. He had little muscle tone in his arms and legs. Frank's shoulders, chest and stomach were covered with hair and his skin had a pale cast to it. Alison reached out her hand to touch Dom's honey-colored skin, but just then the bold confidence that had led her to this moment failed her. Her slightly trembling hand stopped just a few inches short of Dom's body.

Dom smiled at her and reaching out his hand took hers and placed her palm on his chest. She stood rooted; slowly he moved her hand down toward his cock. *His skin is so soft, warm and smooth,* she thought.

She was looking into his face when her fingers first touched the head of his penis. An electric shock ran through her body and she jerked her hand back from him. Involuntarily she stared down at the object she had touched, she gasped slightly. Frank's thing was covered with skin but this one wasn't. The head was red and it stood atop a large and ridged shaft; it reminded her of a picture she had seen once of a King Cobra poised to strike.

Dom started to undo the buttons on her blouse and soon too she was naked. When he had discarded the last of her clothes he took her in his arms and started to kiss her; she felt warm and safe there in his arms.

Dom used all the techniques that Gloria had taught him on Alison that night and for the first time in her life she had reached a climax. Alison fell in love and not just any love, but a love she thought only resided in fairy tales.

She realized then that she had never loved Frank, that her life except for her children had been an emotional blank. She surrendered, she succumbed to love, she felt sixteen again, her world turned golden and her emotions were held on her sleeve like a young girl.

The next weekend was the same as the first except Alison did something to Dom that she had sworn never to do and had refused to do to Frank, no matter how many times he asked her, for as long as they had been married. She found it to her liking; because Dom had liked it very much, she found anything that delighted him, delighted her.

The third Friday night, Dom had been held up on duty longer than he had expected, a rush part for a tank had to be delivered. At 10:30 one of the waitresses came into the bar with a drink request from a customer and found Alison gone. She called her name, walked around the bar and finally went into the supply room where she found Alison in tears and near hysteria.

"Darling, what's wrong?" the waitress blurted.

"He, he didn't come, he, he isn't here," Alison sobbed.

"Darling, he is here. Just when I came back looking for you I saw him walk through the door."

Alison ran out the door of the supply room, round the bar and launched herself into Dom's arms clinging to him and sobbing into his chest. "Baby, what's wrong?" he whispered into her ear.

"I, I, I, didn't think you were coming, I, I, thought I would never see you again."

199

"Oh baby I am so sorry. I should have called. I was held up on Base for awhile." He turned her face up to his and started kissing her swollen eyes. "You'll never get rid of me, soon you will tire of me but I'll still be around making a pest of myself."

She gave him a small smile and had a small hiccup; he gave her his hankie to blow her nose and in a few minutes she went back to work. He glanced over to the waitress who was patiently awaiting her customer's drink. The waitress rolled her eyes up and shook her head. Dom just gave her a smile.

Frank was living the perfect life. He had lost almost twenty pounds, and felt years younger. His house had never looked better. Alison was a so-so housekeeper; their house had always been reasonably clean, now it was immaculate. Dolly-baby and he had just returned from a perfect week in Acapulco, Mexico.

The house had been transformed. The white carpeting in the living room that had always looked a bit dingy now shown white like a mountain snowdrift. As his eyes moved around the room he noticed that the walls were painted a lighter cream color. Newly installed over the fireplace was a large painting of a girl sitting on a riverbank in a white summer dress; it seemed to tie the whole room together. The cobweb was gone from the high corner of the kitchen and a new black cooking range stood where the old white one had been. The master bedroom, which had always smelled a little like unwashed feet, had had the carpets shampooed and air-fresheners installed around the room.

A light refreshing supper had been laid out in the dining room and when they were done eating and returned to the bedroom their bags had been unpacked and the bed turned down.

There permeated throughout the house a quiet so deep that little birds chirping in the garden could be heard in the bedroom; no stereo, no television, no loud teen voices to quell the perfect peace.

His clothes were always immaculate; now he never stopped by the dry cleaners or the laundry. The food served in his home was delicious, always fresh and expertly prepared. He never had to stop at the grocery store on his way home these days. His automobile had been serviced, washed and waxed; it hadn't run so smoothly since it was new.

The sex, yes the sex was endless. He had surprised even himself with his stamina; he had never realized his capacity for pleasure of all kinds. Dolly-baby was always there and never said no to anything. It was the perfect life but was Frank happy? Actually he felt hollow; all the stuff he had now was wonderful but somehow it was just surface. It was mechanical; it just didn't feel like love. Of course it wasn't love, in fact it was very superficial and very expensive. Just before they left for Mexico Dolly-baby had talked him into doubling both her and her brother's wages.

As an accountant money was important to Frank and he was going through a lot of it right now, not saving anything. But he couldn't say no to her, and she knew which buttons to push to expedite his saying yes.

He missed his children and his wife; well not, so much Alison herself. He didn't love Alison anymore but he cared for her and the family life they had had before his perfect life started. He supposed if he could have his daughters, Dolly-baby, and the cost of all this was lowered somewhat he could be extremely happy. But, of course, no man has it all as Frank would soon discover.

Almost six months to the day that he had first bedded Cindy he walked out of his house to the bus stop. It was a beautiful San Francisco morning. A fresh breeze blew off the Pacific Ocean with a scent of the neighborhood, fresh cut grass, flowers and pine trees mingled in the tang of salt air. The sky was that sparkling blue that only seaside cities have. Clumps of white clouds scurried across the sky and the bright sun glinted off windows and passing cars. Frank stood at his bus stop drinking in the beauty of the morning at peace with the world.

Then it hit him. "Damn I left my briefcase in the bedroom!" He looked at his watch. "Five minutes until the bus comes, I can just make it if I run!" Down the street through the front yard, key in the front door, down the hall up the stairs into his bedroom where he stopped stark still, his mouth flying open.

There lay Cindy on her back naked, her knees up and spread wide, her head turned to one side, her eyes closed. A moan of ecstasy came from her parted lips. Between her legs, fucking her, was her brother. Rodney glanced up into the mirror that was on the wall at the head of the bed. He saw Frank standing there rigid with surprise. Rodney's facial expression never altered, his thrusting into Cindy never faltered but his eyes didn't leave Frank's face after that. Even when Cindy let out a sigh and her body bucked in climax did his eyes leave Frank. After a few seconds Cindy was spent, her body collapsed in exhaustion. Rodney removed his cock from her and climbed off the bed. He stood between Frank and Cindy, his expression never changing. Slowly Cindy opened her eyes and saw him.

Just for a second Frank saw panic in her eyes, then calm flooded across her face again.

For the first time Rodney's eyes flicked off Frank toward Cindy's face. "You can go," she ordered Rodney. He hesitated. "Go on, Rodney, it is ok," she said to him. Rodney brushed by Frank with a threatening glance and left the room.

She reached up to the headboard, extracted two tissues from the box there and wiped herself between her legs.

Frank got his tongue back just then. "You, you let your brother fuck you?" he stammered.

Cindy glanced at his stricken face and sat up on the bed. "He is not my brother, Daddy he is my husband!"

"Your husband, husband?" Frank mouthed the words like he was spitting rotten food out of his mouth.

Cindy got out of bed and stood before him; he saw just a slight look of fear pass over her face.

"Yes, Daddy, we have been married five years. You know we do this every morning after you go to work."

Slowly Frank let that sink in. "So you're an adulteress and a whore?" he sneered at her.

"I am not either one, Daddy, I am a businesswoman. Rodney and I have this business which is very lucrative, and we are very good at, I might add."

"You mean there have been other guys like me?"

"Well not exactly like you, Daddy, most of the time Rodney and I are kept in a separate house. This is a first time we have supplanted a wife. Most of our customers are much richer than you. The last one gave us a very large house; limousine and chauffeur, plus lots more money. Rodney didn't want to take you on, he thought we could do much better than you, like our last client, but I thought you were sweet and it was fun fucking you."

Frank looked at her. "Who was your last client?" he demanded.

"I don't want to say his name because he was a very prominent man in this city," she answered. "But unfortunately he died rather suddenly last year. It was awful, he was such a wonderful man."

"We had to leave the house quickly because his wife and family didn't know about the house we lived in, or of us. When we made love he used to call me his perfect warm baby. I guess his wife was a cold grasping bitch!"

Frank's mouth dropped open. "Jack Brainwater, my gosh! I remember the questions in the *Examiner* about his secret life once the unknown house turned up in the will, the speculation in the city was rampant. I agree about his wife. I met her once. She could suck the warmth out of a room just by entering it. Everyone said you never wanted to get on her bad side if you wanted to live in San Francisco."

After a few minutes Cindy broke the silence. "What about us, Daddy, I want to go on like we were before. What you saw shouldn't change our business deal. I promise, Daddy, that I will never have sex with Rodney in our bed again."

Frank was brought back to the present with a jerk. "No Cindy, I couldn't go on with you, you two will have to leave."

Cindy's expression changed instantly. Looking at him coldly she said, "Are you sure, Daddy, is this really what you want? We were very good together!"

Oh damn, she was so beautiful, so perfect he almost changed his mind. But Frank had just a touch of morals left. "No, you must both go and go today!"

"Ok Daddy, if that is what you want. We will start to pack immediately, but you must have a cashiers check for twenty-five thousand dollars made out to me and in my hand by noon."

"What, you crazy bitch?" Frank bellowed. "Twenty-five thousand, you must be out of your fucking mind."

Frank saw a movement in the mirror. Rodney had stepped into the doorway of the bedroom, his face blank but his body ready to spring.

"I am sorry, Daddy, but you leave me no choice. I know you have an account that has fifty thousand in it and I could ask for the whole thing but we don't want to be greedy."

"Why in the world would I give you that much money?" Frank asked calmer now.

"Because otherwise we will ruin you forever. We have photos of you and me in every sexual position, and we have documents about how you have been paying us that I believe the IRS and your partners would love to see. We have the addresses of everyone in your family and your wife's family and your partners, also your largest clients. They would all receive packets of pictures, of you and I. Do you want that to happen?"

"It is called blackmail, missy, and that would get you a long time behind bars," Frank retorted, a small bitter smile stealing over his lips.

"That is true, Daddy, we both might get five to ten years but you would be ruined forever, forever, Daddy," she said. "Twenty-five thousand is not much to ask for in this circumstance, don't you agree, Daddy?"

Frank was beaten. "Ok, ok, I'll get you the money, just get out," he said and turning on his heel stalked out of the house.

For the next couple of weeks Frank was miserable, he was a beaten man. A few days after the Blanks had left the bills for the cleaning, the painting of the house, the new appliances and the art arrived.

The total bill for the six months of his perfect life came to just over sixty thousand, because he paid back to his company all the wages he had paid to Cindy and Rodney. Frank went into a depression, he was racked with guilt and filled with self-loathing.

"I had everything and I threw it all away for that little whore, why, why did I do that." He cried himself to sleep at night, was lethargic during the day; almost comatose at work.

Finally one of the senior partners called him into his office. "Frank, you have to do something about yourself. The office has come to a standstill because of you, your customers are complaining. We feel you are on the road to personal destruction, maybe even suicide unless you get some help. I will give you a name of a psychiatrist and you must use him or we will be forced to rescind your partnership. Also, Frank, you are, as of now, on a month of medical leave. Please gather your personal things and go home."

The shock of being sent home like a schoolboy helped snap Frank out of his depression. For two days he sat at home and finally he made a decision; he was going to Monterey, and he wouldn't return until he had his family with him.

Alison had known for almost a month that she was pregnant. For the first two weeks after she discovered her condition she had been on an emotional roller coaster ride. First incredulity, than unrestrained happiness, fear, euphoria, terror, calm consideration, hopelessness, and elation. All this was lubricated by days of sunny smiles or buckets of tears. Her parents and her daughters waited on pins and needles each morning to find which Alison got out of bed; it was terribly hard on everyone.

But, somewhere in all that mess something happened to Alison; she matured. For thirty-eight years she had been rather a self-centered princess. Now she had become a grown woman and had made her decision; she would keep her baby and never tell Dom that she carried his child. She knew she would never be able to keep Dom, their ages were too disparate. While she loved him with every molecule in her body, to him she was just something to have sex with until another came along. It was a painful revelation but she knew it to be true. She would stay with him until she started to show, then she would break it off.

Now it was enough for her to think of ways to tell him; she concocted long sweet painful letters in her mind telling him it had come to an end. She imagined tear-filled good-bye's, long last kisses while he begged her to stay, entreating her for the reason she was leaving him.

It never came to anything that romantic. When she got home that Sunday night, flushed and satisfied after spending two whole nights in Dom's arms, she discovered Frank sitting in her parents' living room.

Cuddled under each arm was a daughter; she knew how desperately the girls missed their father. They had only known that mama was mad at papa but they never knew why, or wanted to know why. She could see how happy they were, how they clung to him now, and her fury at seeing him was tempered by their obvious joy.

Alison tried not to glare at Frank while the girls were up, but finally around midnight she ordered them to bed stating, "school will be coming quickly and you both know how grumpy you are if you don't get enough sleep."

"Mama, please, we haven't seen Papa for so long, just a little while longer," they pleaded.

"Go on girls," Frank said. "You can see Papa tomorrow night. I will take you both out to dinner."

Squealing "oh Papa will you," they both trooped off to bed.

Alison's parents had gone to bed an hour before so they were alone.

"Ok, Frank, what's going on, why are you here. Your little whore kick you out?"

"No I kicked her out," Frank hung his head not knowing how to proceed. Finally he just blurted out, "Alison, I am so sorry, I don't know what had gotten in to me, but, but I have come to ask you to forgive me, darling." Frank slipped off the couch on to his knees. "Please, please forgive me and come back to me."

Alison hissed, "Get off your knees, you bastard, why would I forgive you. I can barely stand to look at you now."

"Please, darling, I will give you anything, anything you want, I promise I will never cheat on you again."

Alison sneered at him. "I believe you already promised me that once. I believe it was called your wedding vows to me. That didn't stop you this time. Will this promise now stop you next time?"

Frank saw now that it would be a long hard battle to get Alison back and in fact it did take almost two weeks.

Alison left for her job on Friday afternoon and didn't return until Sunday evening as usual. She had a very satisfying weekend with Dom; the sex was particularly intense and loving for her.

She didn't mention Frank because she didn't want to ruin even a second of the time that they had together. Frank had spent the weekend with the girls; the three of them had had a great time. When she arrived home on Sunday evening, after the girls had gone to bed, she walked with Frank, on his invitation, down to the neighborhood strip mall that had a small bar. Alison was, after her satisfying weekend, emotionally drained. She was being almost civil to him, but she had not decided that she would come home with him. At this time she felt revulsion for him but she knew she needed a stable home for her new baby. Nothing was resolved that night of course but Frank felt he had made progress.

The next two days were agony for Alison; she knew she had to decide one way or the other soon. The thought of giving up Dom almost made her physically sick but the worst part of this whole equation was the thought of letting Frank back inside her body. She knew if she went home with Frank, he would want sex again as if nothing had happened. Of course something had happened—she had fallen in love with another man and the fruit of that love was growing safely deep in her womb. How long could she keep Dom interested in her, three months, five months? The three, four or five months of Dom would be superior to forty more years of Frank, this much she knew. But it wasn't only her, it was also the girls who worshiped their father and the new baby, who deserved a much better home than she, as a single mother, could provide. Finally she decided on a course that would take the actual decision, which she was powerless to make, out of her hands.

After dinner on Tuesday she called Frank's hotel room and told him that she would meet him by the Surfs Edge motel, out on Beach Loop road in Pacific Grove, at midnight. When she entered the parking lot she saw the Buick already there; her headlights illuminated, just for a second, Frank's face as she turned into an empty spot. She didn't go over to his car; instead she walked quickly across the parking lot and down the steps onto the beach.

It was a surreal night; a full silver moon hung in the cloudless sky turning the night into ghostly twilight. Just off the beach lurked a gossamer white bank of fog; it moved silently toward the land like a great silvery white bird.

If Alison had not been totally immersed in her own self she would have noticed the small hermit crabs scuttling in terror out of her path. One small crab didn't make it and Alisons heel drove it into the sand, to die, its borrowed shell crushed. As she walked unhurriedly along the surf line, Frank caught up to her and touched her arm. She turned to look at him, his face shown silver on the side to the moon, shaded on the other. She hit the shaded side with her open palm as hard as she could. The crack of palm to face echoed like a pistol shot down the beach and

Frank caught totally unprepared staggered back. He put his hand to his blistering face and said, "Why the hell did you do that for?"

"You son of a-bitch, Frank, you bastard. I was happy. We had a good life. Why did you have to fuck that little whore?"

At that point Frank didn't know which surprised him more, the slap or Alison's mouth. His old Alison would have never used profanity of any kind.

Gaping at her he said sarcastically, "Working in that bar taught you to be a sailor it seems."

"Don't try to change the subject, you shit, just tell me why. Did I do something, or better yet, did you think I did something to deserve this treatment?"

Frank hung his head under the barrage and said nothing.

"You know you humiliated me before all our friends and family." The tears started to run down her face. "Didn't you care how I would feel, didn't you think about our daughters?" Frank lifted tear-filled eyes up to her face; he started to say something, but Alison cut him short. "I'm pregnant."

Her words struck like a knife into his heart. "Oh baby, I, I didn't know, my word had I known I would have never started this thing."

Alison pulled herself up to her full height and sneered, "It is not yours, Frank. You see I can do the same things you can." With those words she saw his face contort, the corner of his mouth twisted and drooped, he looked at her with eyes full of disbelief.

"Not mine," he choked. "You are pregnant with another man's baby?"

"How does it feel, Frank does it hurt? Well it didn't hurt me, I enjoyed every second of it."

She didn't see his fist coming until it hit the side of her face next to her eye. A flash of pain and she was laying back in the sand. Just then a wave broke on her head and she sat up sputtering; her head still spinning.

Frank reached down, grabbed her by her arms and roughly pulled her up. "You will get an abortion, you ain't keeping this baby!"

She jerked away and started crying. "Yes I am, Frank. I am not letting this baby go," she sobbed. Alison turned and started to stagger back down the beach toward her car, holding the side of her head. Frank ran after her, turning her to face him. She screamed, "Don't hit me, let me go," and tried to jerk her arms out of his grasp.

"I'm not going to hit you."

Alison spit into his face and he loosened his grip just a bit. She jerked one arm loose but he held on to her other and pulled her into his arms. They stood there both defeated, the tears of self-pity, hurt and physical pain pouring down their faces. Her arms were pinned to her side by Frank's arms around her waist.

"Baby, I am so sorry. I, I don't know what came over me. Please, please forgive me!"

"If you want me, Frank, you have to take me with this baby. I will not add to my shame by getting rid of it!"

He started to kiss her slowly. At first she turned her head away but it hurt to do that, so she let him kiss her. First her eyes, then her brow, then her face, finally her lips. Slowly she let her lips go soft and in that second Alison returned to her husband.

The next morning Alison woke up in her bed. Her head ached something awful. She got slowly out of bed and crossed gingerly to the mirror in her bedroom.

Looking into the mirror she gasped; her left eye was almost swollen shut. Her eye socket and cheek were black and yellow tinged; she looked like she had been in a knockdown brawl. She applied a lot of makeup and she looked almost normal. After she explained to her mother and father that she had walked into a revolving door, she sat down to write a good-bye letter to Dom.

After lunch she went to the restaurant, walked into her boss's office, and resigned. He was not very happy. "Well I hope I can get Margo to work the weekend, because otherwise I am stuck for a bartender."

Alison and her boss walked out to the bar to talk to Margo who worked Monday through Thursday.

"Oh yes," Margo said. "I can work this weekend because my husband and his buddies are going on their annual fishing trip to Nevada and won't be home until late Sunday night. In fact I prefer to work rather than just sitting home by myself."

Alison then profusely thanked her boss for originally having confidence in her by giving her a job.

After he had returned to his office she turned to Margo, opened her purse and took out a letter. "Could you give this letter to someone for me?"

Margo took the letter. "Oh is it for your boyfriend, the one everyone is talking about?"

"Yes, he always comes into the bar Friday nights and sits there at the end," Alison pointed to Dom's usual chair. "And his name is Dominic."

"Sure I'll give it to him."

"Thank you, Margo, please don't forget, this is really important to me," begged Alison.

When Dom walked into the bar Friday night he looked around for Alison. He didn't see her, so he walked over to his usual place and sat down. In a couple of minutes a woman walked out from the storage room and moved behind the bar to help the waiters waiting to collect drinks.

Dom looked her over. *Umm looks good, prettier, younger and definitely bigger tits than Alison,* he thought.

He saw her glance over toward him, saw her eyebrows move up slightly. In about five minutes she moved down the bar and came to a stop in front of Dom.

"Could I get you something to drink, sir?" she said as she wiped the bar in front of him.

"Yah I'll have a beer," he said smiling at her. As she walked over to get his beer he also noted she had a very nice little ass.

As she served him the beer she looked into his eyes and said, "Your name wouldn't happen to be Dominic would it?"

"Yeah it is," he said expecting her to say that Alison was sick or something.

"Well here I have a letter from Alison for you," she said as she handed him a small pink envelope.

Now it was Dom's turn to raise his eyebrows. He read, "My Dearest Darling Dom, I am afraid my love that I won't be able to see you again. I am going back to my husband for my children's sake. I want you to know that I didn't take this decision lightly and that I will love you until the minute of my death. Please don't think harshly of me Darling, and don't forget me as I shall never forget you. Every second that I have left on this earth I will long to be in your arms. Good-bye my Darling I shall love you forever, Alison."

Margo walked over to Dom about ten minutes later to refresh his beer. "Good news or bad news," she said smiling at him.

He handed her the pieces of the letter that he had ripped up. "Could you toss this in the trash," he said to her.

"Sure hon. You want another beer, or do you want to talk, or both?"

Dom shrugged. "She went back to her husband, no big deal. It was fun while it lasted," he said.

Margo looked at him. "So that means you're without a date this weekend. My husband is gone for the weekend, so I am free."

Dom smiled at her. "Would you like to go out tonight?"

She smiled back at him and batted her eyelashes "I don't get off until 11:30 tonight. Is that alright?"

Dom laughed. "That is fine with me."

Seven months two weeks later Alison gave birth to a beautiful little boy. He had honey-colored skin, red hair like his mother, and almond eyes that were such a light blue that they were almost white. Alison took her newborn baby into her arms and put him to her breast. As he suckled she lovingly stroked his face and head with her fingertips. She smiled to herself; her Dom had come back to her.

Jimmy had left early that morning so Katie slept in a bit. When she finally got up she felt tired—her mind filled with Dom, the back seat and the chance touch of their legs. She made herself a pot of coffee. As it percolated she looked out the kitchen window. She saw the mailman's car moving down the road toward the neighbors, that meant that he had already delivered her mail. She pulled a wooly cap over her uncombed hair and slipped into her winter coat, it covered her nightgown sufficiently. She drove her car down to the mailbox and retrieved the mail from it. Back in her kitchen sipping her coffee she sorted through the mail and with satisfaction noticed her *Woman's World* magazine had arrived.

Woman's World's most favorite author was of course Susan Pink, that unstoppable producer of romance novels. Whenever Miss Pink turned out a new novel *Woman's World* would gleefully be the first magazine to critique every nuance to their eager readers.

"This new book, my dears," the magazine critic gushed, "is so different from the romantic haven that Miss Pink normally leads us into, that it beggars the mind to believe that someone else has taken over our favorite author's body. This is not romance, no, no my dears this is woman exploited, used for political purpose; i.e. betrothed at the age of nine, raped, scorned, jailed, and stripped of her inheritance. This poor girl, Alais Capet, a Princess of France, was born in a time, the 12th century, when women were considered property to be used to bolster her father's, husband's or brother's standing in the world or to add to his possessions or profit. And my dears, what gives one pause is this is a true story, could it happen again?

"Her father was King Louie VII of France and her mother the Princess Constance of Spain, who promptly died after giving birth to Alais. Most people of the time believed she died from embarrassment for not giving Louie and France a male heir. As the court Scribe wrote, having seen that her babe was a girl she closed her eyes and passed from this world; but it is more likely she died from childbed fever. As stated before at the age of nine Alais was given as a fiancée to Prince Richard Plantagenet, one day to be King Richard the Lion Heart, of England, who was twelve. King Louis VII of France wanted peace with England and to reattach to his court the Duchy of Aquitaine and county of Poitou, which he had lost when he divorced Eleanor of Aquitaine. Henry Plantagenet, that is King Henry II of England, who was Eleanor's second husband and father to Richard, wanted the strategic County of Berri which came with this Princess as her dowry, to add to his Kingdom, hence the book's name *Flame over Poitou*. Well my dears, this story has tugged at my heart and I could go on forever about it, however I will leave it to you to rush down to your local book shop, post haste, to purchase it. I give it a definite buy and read, if for nothing else to prove to each and everyone of us, the female half of the population, just how far we have come and where with careful vigilance we must never return."

Katie's day to shop was Thursday so she went to Salem and finding a parking place on Main street, quickly took it. After she parked she strolled down the block causally window shopping, the shop just before the Mode-O-Day clothing store was called "Pierre de Paris."

Chinook:

On September the twenty-first 1944 four transport planes from England landed at Le Bourget aerodrome six miles northeast of Paris, France. The runway they landed on was the one used exactly seventeen years four months earlier by Charles Lindbergh at the end of his famous solo Trans-Atlantic flight from New York. On board the lead plane sat Sergeant Peter Jones, NCO, United States Army Air Force, from Portland, Oregon. Less than one month earlier the Free French Armored division had liberated Paris from the German army command in that city.

The planes taxied up to empty hangars and as soon as they stopped Sergeant Jones ordered his men to start unloading the planes and to start setting up a supply base. Within a few days many more supply transports started arriving, quickly filling the hangars.

These hangars would be the supply depot for the Allied forces attacking the Germans as they pulled out of France into the Low Countries and on to Germany herself. Every few minutes planes left Le Bourget for the front taking needed supplies: medical surgical, food, clothing, weapons and ammunition to the troops.

On the few days he had off Sergeant Jones would take the train into Paris itself, to spend the day. The young, beautiful, French women he would see and meet fascinated him. How different they were from the girls at home. How even during the middle of a World War they seemed to wear the most fashionable and stylish clothes he had ever seen. Their clothes enhanced their figures, clothes that moved when they moved, clothes that emphasized their bodies not just covering them.

Peter was wandering around Place-Clichy one afternoon waiting for a girl he had met to finish work, when he stumbled onto a small shop that would change his life forever. It was a lingerie shop, selling what he and his family would call ladies unmentionables. Peter had a mother and two sisters and he had seen women's underwear hanging out on the clothesline drying on laundry day many times, but never underwear like this. Frilly corsets cut away in the crouch to allow a lover access without having to remove the garment. Gossamer panties that left nothing to the imagination and bras with a hole cut at the end of the cup so a lady's nipples would stick through. After his new girlfriend, Nicole, had finished work he casually led her by the shop and made a little comment to her about it. She gave him a big smile and soon they were both in the shop buying everything in Nicole's size. They took it to a hotel room. Nicole stayed with her only living relative, an aunt; both parents and a brother died during the war.

She modeled all the lingerie for him. Nicole was, a few months later, a war bride. She went with her new husband, at the end of the war, back to Portland and helped him open his first lingerie shop. Now the "Pierre de Paris" store chain consisted of about twenty stores in Northern California, Oregon, Idaho and Washington. They specialized in sexy revealing underwear and nylon net lingerie, with fake and real fur around the arms, wrists or necks and the hems of the see-through nightwear. Their customers were mainly working class and middle class husbands, who out of desperation to buy a present for their wives for that special occasion, would rush in and overpay for sexy underwear. Also wives, who after a few years of marriage and a couple of kids, were looking to once again capture their husbands' interest.

Peter and Nicole were rich now. They traveled to L.A., New York and sometimes back to Paris to buy special things for special customers, and merchandise lines for their stores. So it happened on a buying trip to New York that Peter stumbled onto a lot of two thousand peignoir sets in the finest Chinese silk. As the original buyer had gone broke these sets were going at almost cost and he bought the entire lot.

Katie never usually even glanced into the windows of this shop; she considered the merchandise of these stores to be tacky and vulgar. Today, though, out of the corner of her eye, Katie caught the flash of shimmering white. She turned to look into the window and there on a chesty mannekin hung a long flowing negligee of pure white shimmering silk. The "V" top showed just enough cleavage, around it and the sleeves were embroidered exquisite small yellow roses that were almost the perfect match for her hair. The shimmering silk let her see the outlines of the mannekin's breasts, legs and torso as if looking through a luminous fog.

Katie sucked in her breath; there hanging in the window of Pierre de Paris was the self-same negligee, as described by Susan Pink, worn by Elizabeth Woodville as she lay in her bed awaiting her new husband Edward IV, to come to her on her wedding night. This book *Flame Over York,* was probably Katie's favorite, she had read it many times.

Chinook:

Ms. Susan Pink, author of the famous *Flame* books, took her position as the world's leading romance novelist very seriously. She knew that millions of adolescent girls and young women read her books and she tried to make sure that "nice girls" won the hearts of the men they loved. She tried to emphasize that by not having her heroine giving herself cheaply to any man whom professed love. In her novels every nice girl had a better chance of success and happiness. Therefore *Flame over York* was an easy book to write because her heroine Elizabeth Woodville was a real life testament to that philosophy.

Lady Elizabeth Woodville was a commoner and a widow with two children when Edward IV met her. She was considered one of the most beautiful women in England, with her silver blonde hair and sea green eyes. Edward IV was a man of prodigious sexual appetite. Dominic Mancini, a foreigner who visited England during Edward IV's reign wrote that "he pursued with no discrimination the married and the unmarried, the noble and lowly." When he met Elizabeth in 1464 he tried to talk her into bed, like he had so many other women, but she refused to give herself to him until he out of frustration married her. Because of this intelligence and determination Elizabeth, instead of being lost to history as just another royal concubine, became a queen of England and the mother of Elizabeth of York. Elizabeth of York married Henry VII, she in turn became the mother of Henry VIII. Also grandmother of Edward VI, Mary I and that greatest of English monarchs, Elizabeth I. Her prudence and morality allowed Elizabeth Woodville to add her name and blood to England's history, and that was her reward.

Whether that thought or another passed through Katie's head we shall never know. Within a few seconds she realized she was staring, quickly glancing around to see if anyone she knew noticed her fascination. She hurried on to the Downtown bookstore.

Katie noticed only three books of *Flame over Poitou* were left on the sale table. A handwritten sign stated, "Due to worldwide demand these are the last of Ms. Pink's latest novel we will receive for some time. Customers are encouraged to submit their names to the store's order desk to insure they will not be disappointed at the next printing. Thank you." Katie thanked her lucky stars that she had been in time; she would have been distraught if she would have missed the first printing.

That night after she had eaten a small supper she curled up on her sofa and, thanking heaven that Jimmy was not around to distract her, started to read.

Chinook:

Katie was not a stupid person, however her intelligence was of an emotional nature rather than intellectual. She was provincial as she had little experience outside her small world of family and Low Sky. She had turned down the offer of University and higher education that her parents had offered, because she was, quite frankly, shy and afraid of leaving that small world she was comfortable in. Therefore as she read the story of Alais Capet, a poor unfortunate pawn of the feudal world of the twelfth century, Katie's resentment of Alais's treatment was more intense as she turned each page.

The first chapter of the book started at the betrothal of Alais to Prince Richard of England, Duke of Aquitaine and Count of Poitou. The ceremony took place at Montmirail Cathedral, in France, at Epiphany January 6, 1169. Alais, dressed in emerald green, moved up the center aisle with her nurse toward the altar where a group of men stood. As she drew near the men she saw for the first time the boy she would be betrothed to for almost half her life yet was never to marry. Prince Richard, one day to be the Coeur de Lyon, the Lion Heart of England, cast her an uninterested glance.

He at the age of twelve was already on his way to becoming a man. His arms long and strong, chest deepening, his red gold hair shining down to his shoulders, and his eyes the color of the sky. Even at the young age of nine Alais fell in love with him. The time passed quickly as Katie turned page after page of her book. Eleanor of Aquitaine, now also Queen Eleanor of England, took control of Alais and took her to Poitiers in Poitou, Eleanor's home city and capital of the Duchy of Aquitaine. There, while Henry the Second was off defending his kingdom, Eleanor held a scandalous court of poetry and love. For three years the rumors flew to the ears of the King of the scandals breeding in that court. Eleanor and her court dressed and loved lavishly, prompting the famous Abbe Bernard (soon to be Saint Bernard) to say, "from the Devil they came, to the devil they will go."

All of her court except Alais—she was cosseted and guarded so no one would ever touch, or for that matter even see, the bride to be of Eleanor's golden boy, her bright and rising son Richard. Finally King Henry had had enough and he came to Poiters to end this debauched court.

He removed from Poitiers Eleanor, their children, Alais and her nurse and transported them across the channel to a damp cold palace called the tower of Salisbury. The rest of the court scattered in fear of their lives, for the king was very angered. Eleanor and Alais would be held there; Alais captive for eight years, Eleanor until the king died in 1189. In 1180 Alais was twenty years old; while not a beauty she was comely, with large brown eyes, dark hair and a fair figure.

Henry's mistress, the daughter of an Earl, had just died in childbirth and he was very low, as he loved her very much. His rebellious sons were causing him much trouble on the mainland as they had allied with Phillip the new King of France, a shrewd and ambitious young man, far different than his father Louis. Phillip had petitioned Richard to marry Alais, but he demurred. He asked Henry to return his sister to the court of France as Richard would not marry her at this time. Henry demurred; the county of Berri was just too important.

Henry hatched a plan; he would take Alais to bed and divorce Eleanor, he would then disown his sons. Alais would by then have produced him another son and he would bring him up to be the next King of England. He petitioned the Pope in Rome to divorce Eleanor. He removed Alais from Salisbury and against her will bedded her, and she was soon with child.

In 1180 Henry was forty-five years old, while still handsome and strong, to Alais he was an old man, his hair graying, his face deeply lined, his hands hard and rough. He was her liege lord, her King and she had to submit to him which she did, but with a breaking heart and with fear of her soul because she was not his wife.

In the summer of 1181 Alais presented Henry a son. But just a few months later the Petition for his divorce of Eleanor, to the Holy See, came back denied. Henry then changed his tactics. He imprisoned

215

Alais and her son in his castle at Angers, where some weeks later their son died in infancy. Then he took up as his heir his youngest son by Eleanor, Prince John Lackland, and disowned Richard. When the news reached Eleanor of this proclamation she was furious but unable to do anything from her prison but fume and scheme.

It was now about one A.M. in the morning. Katie was tired, her eyelids hung heavy but she would not, could not put down her book. Katie had very rarely stayed up past ten o'clock in her entire life. She had always slept deeply and serenely waking at eight o'clock or later the next morning. Sleep deprived, her brain started to deviate away from its normal path. The caricatures in the book now morphed into the personalities present in her life. King Henry became Jimmy, Prince Richard became Dominic, Becky became Eleanor of Aquitaine, and her mother became Alais's trusty old nurse. Katie became the personification of Alais, of course.

Chinook:

When Henry imprisoned Alais at Angers she was relieved she would no longer be the concubine of the King and she could begin her long penance.

As was the custom in medieval times, ladies of better birth had personal confessors. Henry allowed Alais her own confessor and Alais made use of him to rid her soul of the sin of intercourse and childbirth which was "without benefit of clergy."

Another custom of that time for rich women was to wet nurse out your baby, the other woman being generally of low birth and in need of the income.

But Alais was stricken and in such need of comfort that she fed her own child, much to the scandal of the castle and city. Alais was starting to gain a small modicum of happiness when once again her world was ripped apart by the sudden death of her baby. The death of children in medieval times was common, fully one half of children born alive died within the first few years. Nonetheless Alais was devastated unto death herself. Slowly her old Nurse brought her back to the land of the living and Alais was after awhile able to function again. One year later on the anniversary of her baby's death, a small epidemic, of what was known in medieval time as the bloody flux, took her old Nurse. Now for the first time in her life Alais was truly alone, her old Nurse was the only mother she had ever known. God, Alais felt, had abandoned her because of her sins.

It was 1:30 A.M. When Katie reached the part in the book where the old Nurse died she lay down her book, and she hung her head and wept for Alais and herself.

Chinook:

When she had recovered a little from her grief Alais petitioned her brother to persuade the Plantagenets to release her to her brother's care. They refused. In 1189 the old King died. Eleanor was set free and once again Alais asked her brother to be released to his care.

Phillip was on crusade along with Richard. They were in Sicily on the way to the Holy Land, when he received Alais's letter. Phillip demanded Richard marry Alais, "let the King of the English know if he puts aside my sister Alais and marries another woman, I will be his enemy as long as I shall live!"

Richard, to save his honor, exclaimed that Alais had been the mistress of his father King Henry and had bore him a child; that was the reason he had forbore to marry her. This was common knowledge in France but had never been aired in public before. Phillip therefore acquiesced and waited until another chance to restore his sister to him presented itself.

In the year 1199 King Richard was killed, with an arrow in his neck, at the siege of Chalus. As Richard died without an heir the Crown of England was bestowed on his younger brother John. Legend aside Richard never spent any time in England except a few months as a teenager. John however became a true English King; he cared little for his French lands. He had little use of Alais and the county of Berri. After her golden son died Eleanor retired to a convent to live out the rest of her days where she died in 1202 at the age of eighty-two. Alais was released to her family at the age of thirty-seven. Phillip promptly married her to Count Guillaume de Ponthieu, his vassal. It was a political marriage but at last she was properly married and got an honorable name of her own. (She died three years later at the age of forty during the birth of her third child.)

At 2:30 A.M. Katie finished her book and she went gladly to bed. But in her brain a thought was installed and Katie, though not knowing it now, was a different person than she was only a few hours before when she first picked up *Flame over Poitou.*

Katie awoke the next morning just after noon; she was still groggy from her reading ordeal of the night before. She lay in bed and ran the story over in her head once again. She got up finally and that evening called Becky at home to ask her if she would like a shopping trip to Salem on Saturday.

Becky said that was just the thing she needed as her week, so far, had been rather hectic. Becky's life had become more complicated since Dom had entered it. Katie was her best friend and she quite frankly needed to have someone to talk to. So at ten A.M. Saturday morning Katie picked her up and they headed to Salem. When Katie drove down Main she noticed a parking space just in front of Pierre de Paris, but she didn't stop there. Instead she continued west for another block and pulled up at the main entrance to Frederick's department store.

"Honey," she said to Becky, "I will drop you off and go back and get that parking spot I missed."

"Oh, I can come with you, I mean I can walk a few blocks," Becky explained.

"Well sweetie, I was thinking that you could grab us a good seat in the restaurant. I believe there is to be a fashion show during lunch. I will be just a few minutes."

Becky shrugged, "ok," and got out of the car. She took the elevator to the fourth floor restaurant. She chose a table by the window that looked out over Main. The Maitre d' confirmed the fashion show and left her menus with a promise she would bring Katie over as soon as she came up. Becky fingered the menu idly and glanced down to the street. She saw Katie's car pull into the parking space they had passed and watched as Katie got out and disappeared onto the sidewalk. She waited to see her move through the crosswalk, as that would be the next place she would come into view. In a few minutes she started to watch closer because Katie didn't appear.

Maybe she had missed her, she is probably in the elevator by now, she thought. Five minutes passed, no Katie. Ten minutes passed then she saw her walking back to her car. Becky watched as Katie hesitated beside her car and look both ways before moving to the rear and opening the trunk quickly sliding a package into it. She caught a glimpse of a rose pink sack as the package disappeared into the dark of Katie's car's trunk. *Oh,* Becky thought, *that pink sack could only come from one place, the Pierre de Paris shop.*

"How sweet," Becky smiled to herself, "she bought something sexy to wear for Jimmy and was too shy to tell me about it. Well I won't say anything, I don't want to embarrass her."

Chinook:

When Katie parked she got out of her car and quickly glanced toward Frederick's. No sign of Becky; she quickly moved to the entrance of the Pierre de Paris shop. Another glance confirmed that no one she knew was in sight.

Quickly Katie moved to the counter.

"May I help you, madam", intoned a rather stuffy older woman with a funny, almost English accent.

"Yes I would like that negligee in a size six," Katie said pointing to the mannekin.

"They only come in petit, small, medium and large, Madam," cooed the stuffy woman. "I believe you would take a small. Humm except for your bust, but they are cut a bit full through the chest so I believe you would be ok there. Would you like to try one on, Madam?"

"No, I am in a hurry, someone is waiting for me. I'll try it on at home."

"Very well, Madam, just remember we can't take back lingerie once it has been worn."

"I understand, please hurry," pleaded Katie. She reversed her footsteps and sighed a sigh of relief once the package was safely concealed in her trunk.

While waiting for the traffic light to cross the crosswalk to the department store she had buyer's remorse. *Why did I buy that,* she thought to herself, she mentally shrugged, *I'll wear it for Jimmy someday maybe.* But in reality she knew that "someday" would never come.

They ate their ladies lunch and as they did models passed by their table; if any lady showed an interest the model would stop and give out any information the customer needed such as designer or cost of the garment. They were having great fun commenting to one another on each piece.

"My word, what an awful color," Becky whispered behind her hand to Katie.

"Oh," countered Katie. "I kind of liked it."

"Oh I meant for me," Becky quickly followed.

Finally the last model passed by and the girls turned to girl talk. "I got a little dirt to pitch, honey," Becky lowered her voice.

"Remember Asia Kirk, now of course Brown?"

"Oh yes, the most beautiful girl in school. How could anyone help but remember her?"

"Well the word around is that Bob has left her," Becky's eyebrows raised slightly as she imparted this gossip.

"Oh dear poor Asia, how could Bob leave her, she is so beautiful," said Katie, a look of sadness coming over her face.

Becky's eyes searched Katie's face; sometimes she wondered if Katie was for real. "Well honey, she was always a shrew, you know. It was always better to face her or she would bite you in the back and because of that she never really had any close friends."

"Yes, I know she was like that but I always wanted to look like her," Katie said.

"You wanted to look like her, you thought she was really that beautiful?" Becky was astonished.

"Yes, those long legs, that long dark hair, the big brown eyes," Katie sighed.

"Darling, she was striking maybe, she had a figure like a stick, no butt and those small pancake breasts, compared to you she was an ugly witch."

"For some reason she hated me," Katie noted. "She used to stare at me after gym like I was a poisoned toad or something."

"She didn't hate you, darling, she was dammed jealous of you. Remember that time I told you about that awful thing that one of the girls said about you, well that was her. After you had left the dressing room one afternoon she looked at us girls and said why does she have them and I have these. Well we all looked at her and I said what are you talking about? She said tits, why can't I have her tits and she have mine, she is never going to use them anyway."

Becky saw Katie's face tighten and redden. "That was her, she really said that?"

"Yes, I am afraid so darling," Becky's voice softened.

She had never seen Katie so mad, not even that time she had made that one last pass at Jimmy, that afternoon when they were cleaning out her garage.

Katie had informed her, the next day, that Jimmy was no longer available. Katie's eyes were all ice and she was very calm that time; this time she was red-faced, indignant, and spluttering.

"How could she, how could she say that?" she raged through clenched teeth. "Did she think I would never have a boyfriend, a husband or a baby, or that—or that . . ." Katie couldn't finish her thought.

"Darling, don't you realize that you were the most beautiful girl in school? We all envied you your figure, your hair and your beautiful blue eyes. None of us shall ever know what thoughts were in Asia's empty head, she probably just said it to draw attention to herself. She always wanted to be the center of everything. Jane, the girl at work who knows her, said she treated Bob like dirt, and I guess he just couldn't take it anymore."

Chinook:

Becky was taken aback by Katie's anger and she quickly changed the subject to the fashion show they had just seen. Within a few minutes Katie returned to her old shy quiet self but another prop had been pulled out from under Katie's idea of how the world worked. The revelation by Becky that all the girls envied her beauty settled into Katie's consciousness; she was surprised and secretly pleased.

She always thought she was too fat and dumpy, that her breasts were too big for her body, that all the girls didn't like her. She always thought she had a funny shape. Slowly the old naive Katie was being replaced by the Katie that was to come.

The four friends became closer. Dom almost never drove on weekends, so whenever Jimmy was home they were together at least one day, or had a double date one evening. Katie watched Dom's eyes when they were together and she noticed the hunger in them whenever his look swept her. One evening as they were being led to their seats while at a restaurant, Katie who had walked ahead of Dom glanced into a mirror that they were passing. Dom, two steps behind her, had his eyes on her rear and the look in them made a little chill run up her spine. The Katie of old would have been mortified and embarrassed, but since Becky's revelation to her she did something that would have been impossible just a couple of months ago, she started to sway her bottom just a bit more in a sexy fashion. *Take that big boy, there's plenty more where that came from,* she thought.

April came around and with it the opening of trout fishing season. Jimmy had invited Dom to go with him and the two set off to the Crabtree River at daybreak. Dom had never fished for trout or fished a stream before. Jimmy showed him how to thread a worm on a hook and cast it into the current so the line with the bait would cross a hole that Jimmy said would contain a trout. On Dom's second cast just as the bait dropped into a slack water at the tail of a riffle the pole was almost jerked from his hand. He raised the tip of the rod smartly and felt the

221

weight of a fish. Keeping his rod tip high the trout jumped. The beautiful sixteen-inch stream bred rainbow arched its back in the morning light, the sun glinting off its green back and pink slashed sides. In a few short minutes Dom glided his first trout into the net Jimmy had loaned him and marveled at this beautiful creature. He quickly killed the trout and put it into his sack. Glancing down the river he saw Jimmy's pole bent as he fought his first trout of the season.

Becky arrived at the farm at around noon and she started helping Katie fix the salads and other things that they would eat with the fresh trout the boys would bring back if they were lucky. If they weren't lucky there was a cold ham sliced and waiting in the refrigerator. At one o'clock Jimmy's truck pulled up to the back door of the house and they brought in their catch. Each had five beautiful rainbows all about the size of the first one Dom had caught. As Jimmy cleaned and filleted the fish Katie put Dom in charge of heating the bacon grease while she made up the flour and spice batter. The recipe handed down to her from her grandmother.

Becky set the table and seated Sonny while Katie dipped the trout in the batter and placed it into the bubbling bacon grease. As she did so she innocently brushed her breast against Dom's elbow. She felt an electric shock surge through her body and both her nipples became hard instantly. She didn't dare look up at Dom but she could feel his glance. Within minutes the fresh trout was cooked and the friends all sat down to the table to eat one of nature's most delectable treats, fresh caught wild trout. Not one person living in the world's most sophisticated cities, eating at the most wonderful restaurants ever ate anything this delicious.

Chinook:

That night when Jimmy was asleep Katie had time to consider Dom's touch on her breast. Did she brush against him on purpose. She felt a little lightheaded; where was she going with this?

She finally convinced herself "NOWHERE," it was just an accident, it meant nothing, especially to Dom.

Before Dom fell asleep he lay thinking of the day. *How different trout fishing in a stream was from the kind of fishing he was used to, and how wonderful the cooked trout had tasted.* His mind turned to the brush of Katie's breast against his elbow. *She hadn't jerked away, he had felt her nipple harden.* He smiled to himself.

She was to him the perfect woman. She was beautiful, shy and an excellent cook. Dom had found over the years that he much preferred married woman. They were mature, knew what they wanted and very eager to have what he could give them. But here was the problem; he had never met, let alone was a friend to, the husbands of the married women he had bedded. Jimmy was a good guy; they were probably as good friends as any he had had over his life. However he wanted Katie and friendship would naturally take a back seat if he ever had a chance to fuck her.

Was that the reason the large white man did that to his mother? He could never bring himself to imagine the large white German's cock in his mother, of his laying on her and rutting into her! The knot that hit his stomach whenever he thought of that afternoon came back hard just now. He had managed to put it behind him while he was in the Army, but just lately he had been thinking more about it. Also the dream had come back; it always started with his mother walking down a long corridor with the sun behind her. Her dress was open and he could see one of her breasts. She would never look at him but would turn and walk back down the hall and into her bedroom. Then the large white man would enter the hall naked. He would turn and look at Dom, his eyes boring into Dom's. Dom could see his huge stomach covered with hair and his long white penis hanging down. Slowly he would walk toward the porch where Dom stood cowering, closer, closer, Dom wanting to run but being frozen in his tracks. Then Dom would awaken covered in sweat and trembling. Son of a bitch, he hated that damn dream but he just couldn't shake it. He, just lately, found himself putting off going to sleep just to avoid having the dream. But tonight he was extremely tired. He had been up very early to go fishing. He fell asleep quickly and the bad dream didn't return this night; instead he dreamed of taking off Katie's clothes only to find Gloria's body under Katie's garments.

The month of May, after a first week of steady warm rain, broke into a warm glorious early summer. Wild flowers covered pastures, fields and mountainsides. Gardens filled with tulips, jonquils and other spring flowers burst into color everywhere. After a long gray winter and wetter than average spring the warm days and blue sky were a godsend.

A few of the warehouse employees had been planning a barbecue on Memorial Day.

Slowly the plans grew as more people heard about the outing and finally they asked the drivers and the girls in the new dispatch office located in the warehouse area to join. Joe and Barbara offered to hold the barbecue at their farm because they were the only couple who had a lawn big enough to handle the almost sixty people who would come. Joe also had had a new barn built last year so if for some reason the weather didn't cooperate they would all fit into the barn.

Since the fishing day Jimmy had been very busy; he had hardly been home at all. Katie, Dom and Becky had gone out one Saturday evening for dinner. Katie had sat on one side of the table and the couple had sat on the other. After they sat down Katie had moved her left leg toward Dom. Within a few seconds she felt his leg against hers and they sat that way all through dinner. Slowly he had moved his foot along her instep, then up the calf of her leg. She liked that very much; later as she thought about it she was so surprised that she could do that with Becky right there and not be embarrassed.

I am becoming a brazen hussy, she thought, but she really didn't believe that it was anything more than just harmless fun they were having.

The sun on Memorial Day rose in a clear blue sky. Soft, middle of the summer, breezes flitted and ebbed and the temperature would be over eighty by noon.

Jimmy and Katie arrived at the Wallis farm at 10 A.M. to help Joe and Barbara set up for the barbecue. They both had on shorts, Katie a light sleeveless blouse that showed her chest off nicely. The men did the heavy work; they set up the big cooker Joe had made. He had cut a steel barrel lengthways, welded legs on to it and fashioned a square of steel mesh to sit on top. They loaded two sacks of charcoal into the barrel ready to light. Next they unloaded the tables from the back of Jimmy's pickup that he had picked up from the cafeteria at work, and set them up in rows.

Katie had joined Barbara in her kitchen and started helping her wrap baking potatoes with foil. At 11:30 the butcher's truck arrived with steaks and hamburgers and they packed the packages with ice to keep the meat cool. The men then lighted the charcoal, grabbed two cold beers and sat watching the fire burn down to glowing coals.

After the coals turned red they lifted the wire mesh and placed the potatoes on the coals. Soon the families started to arrive. Katie watched for Becky and Dom to arrive; when they did Sonny ran off to play with the other children and the girls sat down together in a couple of lawn chairs Becky had brought. Dom grabbed a cold beer and walked over to where Jimmy and Joe sat. Jimmy rousted himself because he had volunteered to be cook for the day; he started to place the steaks, hamburgers and buns on the grill. Dom asked Joe where their bathroom was and started toward the house to find it. Halfway across the lawn he caught Katie's eye; she watched him as he walked around the corner of the house toward the stairs leading to the bathroom on the main floor. In a few minutes a little girl ran up to Becky, "Mrs. Skinner, Sonny fell and hit his head." Becky jumped up and followed the little girl. Katie waited a few more minutes, then started to follow the path Dom had used around the corner of the house. She started to climb the steps when Dom walked out through the screen door of the porch and started down the steps. They met halfway. Dom leaned against the outside wall of the house with his left shoulder, Katie followed his lead and leaned against the wall with her right shoulder. They were alone as everyone was around the other side of the house.

"Hi," he said smiling at her, glancing down at her front, "you are looking very good today!"

She smiled back. "I might say the same about you," she said.

Impulsively he put out his left hand and cupped her right breast with it. Katie stiffened slightly when he touched her and he thought just for a second he had gone too far. Then she leaned forward slightly pushing her breast into his hand. They stood there looking into one another's eyes not saying a word.

Jimmy back at the grill asked Barbara if she knew where the season salt shaker was.

"Oh yes," she said after a moment. "Left it on the kitchen table. I'll run and get it for you."

"No Barb, that is alright, I'll get it. I have a few minutes until the steaks are ready."

He laid down the fork he had in his left hand but for some reason kept the long handled knife he had in his right hand. He trotted around the corner of the house, his head down as he headed for the stairs.

Katie felt Dom's hand quickly drop from her breast, and saw the color leave his face. Just then she heard a footstep on the first step of the stairs they were standing on. She turned and looked, her heart almost stopped because up the stairs ran Jimmy with a knife in his hand.

Chinook:

Guilt: that many headed monster that so racks the human consciousness and unconsciousness along with its subplots, embarrassment, fear, anguish, regret, envy, hate and longing. The mish-mash of human emotions that can destroy lives, end promise and seal dooms.

When Jimmy passed by his wife and friend on the steps he smiled at them and said, "Hi guys." In response to his greeting he saw eyes and faces filled by embarrassment and anguish from Katie, fear and envy from Dom. He didn't stop, but those reactions were recorded in his memory. He had never seen a man look at him with fear before so at first he didn't recognize the emotion; he also couldn't feature a situation where his presence would elicit such an emotion.

When Jimmy returned seconds later, season salt in hand, to the stairs, both his wife and friend would be gone, but he felt a strange tension still hovering in the air. He also didn't see the inquiring glances that were shot between that selfsame couple and his back all afternoon.

Katie decided that maybe her flirting—she persuaded herself that was all it was—had better be cooled. So she avoided any contact with Dom and Becky for almost two months. Becky was rather hurt that Katie had always been busy each time she called and suggested an outing. She decided to give it one more shot the second week in July.

"Darling, hi, it's Becs."

"Oh hi sweetie, how you doin'?"

"Fine, precious, and you?"

"Oh fine, just a bit lonely. Jimmy has been gone almost constantly since the barbecue."

"Yeah same here. Dom has been working a lot too. So I was kind of hoping we might take a picnic up to Dutchman's maybe next weekend, swim and bag some sun on the beach."

"Sounds divine. Hold on. I think Jimmy will be home all of next weekend. Yeah, he arrives Friday night so maybe Saturday we can go up, take the tent and camp until Sunday. That would be fun."

"Great, sweetie. We haven't been up there since last summer and I love Dutchman's."

Chinook:

In the early summer of 1874 a large man with a backpack slung over one shoulder and his hand holding the arm of a short stout woman climbed over a rise and looked down on his homestead. A month before he had paid ten dollars to the state land office in Portland for the deed to two sections, 1280 acres of land sight unseen. The only description was "mountainous land with large trees and frontage on a good lake, with plenty of fish." The only restrictions were he must build a cabin, or improve the land within one year.

Twenty years before when he was only nineteen he left his native Ontario, Canada to join the U.S. Calvary. They were paying twenty

226

dollars to join, to go fight the Indians out west. He had fought in the Shoshone and Modoc wars. Once the Modoc were installed on the reservation he left the Calvary, took his mustering out money to Portland to see if he could buy a homestead. He guessed the land he bought would not be good for farming. However this was largest acreage he could get for ten dollars.

His name was Hans Holland; his father was English, his mother German. He was the couple's only living child; the first three were stillborn. His father died when he was five. Because his mother raised him he spoke English with a thick German accent. Therefore almost all his life he was called Dutchman.

Dutchman had been sleeping with a seventeen-year-old prostitute since he had been in Portland. She was not beautiful by any means but she was strong. When he had sex with her she would wrap her strong legs and arms around him and he liked that. He offered her his hand in marriage if she would come with him to clear his land, she accepted. Together they hacked a horse trail from the wagon road, which ran between Low Sky and Mill City, to their land ten miles up the mountain. They built a cabin together, living off the game he shot and the beautiful large native rainbow trout that filled the lake. At the western end of the property an enormous flat granite slab of rock stuck out over a cliff. From this rock you could see the whole of the valley stretched before you. In later years Hans and his wife would decorate a conical fir tree that grew on one area of the rock at Christmas time, hence the name Christmas Tree Point was born.

At Christmas Tree Point Hans and his wife built a guest lodge; people would come for the fishing and to swim in the clear cold lake. Hans and his wife were childless; neither one had living family so when Mrs. Holland died in 1945 she bequeathed the whole of their land for a state park. Soon after the State of Oregon received the land they sold the lodge and the surrounding ten acres, including the large flat granite slab of rock to a private party with the stipulation that the lodge be expanded. So it was, the lodge besides having more rooms and an adjacent small camp grounds now includes an upscale restaurant with adjacent bar and night club. These facilities are used by the locals, and people from as far away as Salem for special occasions. From the restaurant and nightclub you can walk out on a deck that runs out over the old slab of rock and look down at the valley below you.

Every year at Christmas the conical fir-tree is decorated; it has become a tradition. Dutchman Lake State Park is the jewel of the Cascades. The entire lake winds through the mountains for almost twenty-five miles. The water is crystal clear, rocks and old logs can be

227

seen on the bottom 100 feet down. Over the millenniums the blowing wind has created a large crescent beach, now named Old Sand Harbor Beach, at the western end of the lake less than half a mile from the Christmas Tree Point Lodge. The beach stretches about a mile. Behind the beach is an area of large evergreen trees; scattered throughout the trees are parking lots. There are toilets with dressing rooms, grills for barbecuing and picnic tables for the visitors that throng the beach area in the summer. On the far left of the beach along a mountain there is a boat launch and parking for cars and trucks with boat trailers. On the far right of the beach at the end of the access road is a large meadow; interspersed across this meadow are old lava flows that are now just piles of rocks. A good place for people to go for a walk, or to sit among the rocks if they want some privacy from the crowds at the beach.

When Jimmy arrived home early on Friday afternoon, Katie told him about the camping trip planned for the weekend.

So instead of the yard work he had planned he loaded up their tent in his pickup and pulled his boat from the shed where it had been stored all winter. He readied his fishing equipment and stored it in the boat, gassed up the boat tanks and started the motor. To his relief it ran like a top.

After dinner they went to bed early, for Dom was scheduled to be at the farm at 6 A.M. the next morning. When they got to bed Jimmy rolled over to his wife; she was willing and seemed in a good mood, much to his relief, and after making love to her he fell into a deep sleep.

At 5 A.M. Jimmy was up. Katie had made egg sandwiches the night before. He filled a thermos with hot coffee and was climbing into his pickup when Dom, in his red truck, pulled into the farmyard. Dom quickly climbed into the cab with Jimmy and they set off to claim their campsite for the weekend. By 7 A.M. they had chosen their site and unloaded the tent. Next they went into the park and launched the boat; already the dock was filling up and they got one of the last berths for the weekend. They went back to the campground and set up the tent; by 8:30 they were done and gratefully sat at the picnic table at their campsite and wolfed down the sandwiches and coffee. Jimmy strolled down to the lodge and called Katie to tell her the campsite number. The two boys then walked down the trail through the woods to the boat to get in a bit of fishing before the girls arrived at about noon. They had motored down the lake and found a secluded cove; there they let the boat drift and cast nymphs on sinking tip lines into the rocks along the edge of the lake. By 11:00 they had caught enough trout for lunch and now were just sitting in the boat enjoying the calm and cool morning.

228

After about ten minutes of quiet drifting Dom looked at Jimmy. "I hear you long-distance guys get a lot on your layovers."

Jimmy glanced at him with a puzzled look. "A lot of what?"

"You know, pussy," Dom smiled at him.

"Some may," Jimmy retorted. "I don't, I am married, and I don't cheat on my wife."

"Really," Dom smirked, "you're stupid man. It has been my experience that wives cheat on their husbands all the time and believe me your wife will do the same someday."

Jimmy stared at Dom for a few seconds. "Well I know my wife. She would never cheat on me. I would bet my life on her."

Dom was about to make a cynical reply when he glanced at Jimmy's face; his face was calm and his eyes had a cold look in them. "If I ever caught anyone in bed with Katie I would kill them."

A small chill went down Dom's backbone. He would have to be careful what he said around Jimmy!

Dom had thought that with the large amount of time Jimmy spent away from his wife he would have, at least, one woman out there that he was screwing.

In a few minutes Jimmy turned, reached for and pulled the cord, started the motor and they went back to the dock in silence.

Katie got up at 9:00 A.M. She had most of the things they would need to eat for the weekend already in the freezer and refrigerator. She packed up the food she would be taking in coolers and covered them with ice. She got out sleeping bags and blow up mattresses for her and Jimmy and stacked them up with the coolers. Becky would be bringing the beer, pop, chips, condiments and charcoal. Katie then went to take a bath. She had taken a long bath after Jimmy had had sex with her last night as she normally did. But she felt the need to take another this morning, as she wouldn't have one at the campgrounds. After her bath she went to her secret storage box where she kept her things that were not for Jimmy to see, and took out a new bra and panties. The bra was the kind that push up her breasts and exposed a deep cleavage. The panties were cut high on the thigh and very low on her tummy, just barely covering the mound of hair on her crotch. She looked at herself in the mirror. The underwear shaped her well; it was very sexy.

"Why," she wondered to herself, "was she wearing this on a camping trip?" but she didn't remove them. Instead, she put on some long shorts and a thick blouse to cover her secret well.

Becky arrived in her car.

When the girls and Sonny reached the campsite the guys had the trout cleaned and ready to cook. Quickly Katie got out her frying pan, bacon grease, and flour and dredged the trout while Jimmy started the charcoal fire. In forty-five minutes they were sitting down to fresh fried trout and salad. As Katie cooked Dom and Becky unloaded the car and set up the camp.

After lunch Dom, Becky and Sonny put on their swimming suits and went to the beach to swim. Jimmy and Katie walked along with them as far as the beach then walked along the beach toward the meadow a mile away. They walked through the meadow, which was still soft and slightly muddy from the melted snow that had covered it less than two months before. Katie noted the piles of old lava as they passed. Finally they turned to retrace their route back to the beach and Dom and Becky. When they arrived they saw Dom sitting at the water's edge watching Sonny as he splashed about in the lake; Becky was laid out on her tummy on a towel, the backstrap on her bikini undone.

Jimmy looked at Becky, and found it very hard to pull his eyes away from her bare back. Katie walked down to the lake and stooping down cupped her hand and threw water on Dom and Sonny. They in turn started splashing Katie who screamed. Becky sat up, turning as she did so to look at the melee. For just one second before Becky grabbed the strap the top of her bikini fell open and Jimmy had a view of her breast and nipple. The old feelings that he had always had for Becky surged through him; just in that moment he felt regret, then tearing his eyes away, he turned his attention to the water fight going on a few feet away.

They ate hot dogs and hamburgers cooked on their grill that night and sat toasting marshmallows over the coals until Sonny fell asleep. They all turned in to their respective sleeping bags in the tent. Becky on the far right, then Sonny between her and Dom, Katie and finally Jimmy on the left.

Dom lay there not sleeping but hearing first Becky breathing deeply and then Jimmy started snoring softly. He glanced at Katie; she was laying on her back, her eyes closed but he couldn't tell if she was asleep or not. He started having a fantasy about her, he could see himself reaching his hand into Katie's sleeping bag feeling her warm breast cupped in his hand. In his mind she looked at him and beckoned him into her sleeping bag.

With five people in the tent it soon became stuffy and Dom felt perspiration forming on his lip and forehead. Just as his fantasy had him climbing into Katie's sleeping bag Katie suddenly sat up and took off her blouse. It made him jump just a bit, but he was soon distracted by Katie's bra just inches from his nose. Her full breasts and cleavage, just for a second, grabbed all his attention. Abruptly she lay down again cuddled down in her sleeping bag and fell asleep; she never even noticed him watching her.

In the morning Dom woke up to an empty tent. He crawled out of his sleeping bag, pulled on his sneakers and opened the tent flap. Everyone but Becky was gone. He grabbed a coffee cup, filled it from the pot on the grill and sat at the table across from Becky.

"Hi gorgeous, slept well it seems." She ran her foot up the inside of his leg and smiled at him.

"Yah, babe, I did. Where is everyone?"

"Well Jimmy and Sonny went fishing about an hour ago, Katie is taking a pee and washing her face, and I am about to make you some breakfast if you want."

All of a sudden he felt starved. "Yes, I am famished, how about some eggs."

"Coming up. What's our plans for the day?"

"Let's go out into the woods and fuck."

Becky put her fingers over her mouth in mock horror. "Oh you naughty boy." She glanced at him and said sarcastically, "You always say the sweetest things." She looked up. "I think we should cool the language. I see sweet little Katie coming our way. We don't want to shock her."

Dom smirked to himself. "Sweet, huh."

While Dom ate his breakfast the girls cleaned up the camp and when they were done the three walked to the docks to see if Jimmy and Sonny were back. The three sat on the dock dipping their feet into the water and chatting when they saw Jimmy's boat round the point and head for the dock.

Becky stood up; she shielded her eyes with her hand from the glare off the water and watched the boat advancing toward them. Sonny was sitting in the middle seat, wrapped in an orange life jacket, holding on for dear life as the boat sped along, a big smile on his face. For just a second Becky felt a small pang; that could be her husband with her son. But the feeling passed because Sonny, seeing her, started to yell at the top of his voice.

"Mommy, Mommy, I caught a fish, I caught a fish!"

The boat pulled up to the dock and Jimmy secured the boat to the turn buckle with a rope. He picked Sonny up and handed him into his mother's arms.

"Show her, Uncle Jimmy, show her." He wriggled free of Becky's hug and taking the stringer from Jimmy and held up his ten-inch trout with pride to his mother.

"Oh sweetheart, how wonderful. Did he fight hard?"

"Yes he jumped and Uncle Jimmy had to put him in the net, but I couldn't take him off the hook 'cause he was slippery."

Everyone gathered around admiring the fish; the little boy beaming in their midst.

Becky glanced at Jimmy. *He would make a wonderful father* she thought to herself. *He would have made Sonny a wonderful father if she hadn't been so pig headed.* She often wondered why Katie wasn't pregnant yet; she knew she longed for a child. Oh well, it wasn't her business.

The blissful morning wound down, and soon it was lunchtime. Katie cooked Sonny's trout but he wouldn't taste it. "I won't like it," he announced. "I am just the catcher not the eater."

After lunch it was time to start cleaning up the camp and taking down and packing up the tent. The men went down to the lake loaded the boat on the trailer and pulled it back to the campsite. With all of them working everything was in the vehicles by three o'clock and they were ready to head for home. When Katie got into the pickup cab next to Jimmy she sighed.

"What's wrong, honey?" he said.

"Oh it has been such a great weekend, I don't want to go home yet!"

"Ok, where shall we go then?"

"Lets' go back to that meadow we walked up to yesterday. Ask Dom and Becky to come too."

Jimmy rolled down his window and motioned Dom to do the same. "Katie doesn't want to go home yet. We're going over to the meadow for awhile. Want to come along?"

"Sure lead the way!"

Dom smiled to himself. When they were alone for a few minutes that morning Katie had mentioned the meadow and had given him a look. "It's rather a romantic spot," she had said. "A good place for two people to be alone."

This is getting more interesting all the time, he thought.

"This looks like a good spot," Katie said, and Jimmy pulled over to the shoulder of the road and parked. Katie slipped out of the pickup; there was a tension in the air, Jimmy could feel it. Jimmy got out of the truck and walked around the back. When he looked up Katie had already removed her shoes and had started across the meadow in her bare feet. Katie had stepped on the grass of the meadow and found that it was quite wet underneath, so she had slipped off her white tennis shoes and had started to walk through the damp grass toward a large lava remnant that was shaped like a sofa. Facing the road the remnant had a shelf about four feet above the meadow and then behind the shelf a wall went up to over ten feet.

Jimmy glanced at the rock. *What was she heading for that for?* he thought. *There could be a snake in those rocks!*

Jimmy had on flip-flops and started to walk slowly after Katie just in case she did encounter a snake; this part of the meadow seemed quite muddy. Sonny had picked up a small stone by the road's edge and had thrown it into the meadow. Then he started to go after it. Katie had reached the lava remnant and had gingerly climbed up onto the shelf and sat on a broken rock along the wall.

Dom and Becky had been leaning against the car. Dom watched Katie and this tableau enfolding with interest and Becky with her arms folded below her breasts watched Sonny going after his rock.

Suddenly the little boy stopped. "Snake Mommy," he called. Becky's heart froze in her chest. "Jimmy," she called. "Sonny sees a snake!"

Jimmy, who was almost at the rock, turned and saw the little boy frozen half way up the meadow. "Don't move, Sonny," he yelled. "I'm coming." Quickly Jimmy went to Sonny who hadn't moved an inch; he stopped a few feet away to see what kind of snake it was. Rattlesnakes were rare in that part of the state but not unheard of. He soon saw that it was just a grass snake of some kind; a big one but harmless. Slowly he leaned over and slipping his hands beneath Sonny's arms lifted him out of the path of the snake. The snake, relieved that the danger was gone, quickly slithered away. Jimmy carried Sonny back to the car, the little boy had been quite scared and was shaking a little. Jimmy handed the little boy into his mother's arms and turned to see Dom almost to the lava remnant that Katie sat on. He must have started toward Katie as Jimmy was bringing Sonny back to the car. Dom climbed up on the shelf, proceeded to the wall and climbed it looking over. He then walked back to Katie; Becky had put Sonny on the hood of the car, and was cleaning the mud off his shoes. All the while keeping an eye cocked toward Katie and Dom. Jimmy leaned against the car and was watching his wife and Dom. Becky said, "What do you think they plan on doing?"

"I don't know," Jimmy said, but he didn't like this one bit. He felt jealousy welling up in his chest, and he remembered what Dom had said in the boat about Katie one day having an affair. They saw them talking to each other but couldn't hear the words.

Then Becky and Jimmy saw Dom's mouth form the words, "Do you think they'll go?"

Katie's mouth then formed the words, "I don't know."

Becky looked at Jimmy slightly aghast. "I think they want us to go."

"So it seems, but everyone doesn't always get exactly what they want!" For awhile Katie and Dom stayed on the rock, when they saw that Jimmy and Becky were not leaving slowly Katie got up and started back to the cars. In a minute Dom casually started back also.

Katie cleaned off her feet, put on her shoes and climbed into the pickup. She sat on her side of the seat sullenly not looking at Jimmy as they drove home.

Finally Jimmy said, "What did Dom say to you when you were out on the rock?"

Katie never glancing at him replied with the first lie she had ever told him, "He said how beautiful it was out there." Jimmy never contradicted her, or asked her anymore but he kept that incident in his heart all the rest of his life.

Years later, thinking back, he wished he had taken Becky and Sonny home and left them both there on that rock and had called it quits. If he would have the pain might had been less in his life.

*   *   *

The rest of the summer slid by quickly and soon it was September. Jimmy was rarely home after the weekend at the lake. As the reports spread thoughout the midwest and East of the quality of canned and frozen fruits and vegetables produced by the Slayton Canning Company demand rose sharply. Soon companies sent their own brand labels to be affixed to the cans and boxes of the food, and ordered large amounts to be delivered to their warehouses for distribution to customers.

Jimmy and Joe were traveling to Wisconsin, Illinois, Indiana, Michigan and Ohio, now on a regular basis.

Katie hadn't seen Dom since the lake weekend. Every Saturday, though, Becky and her went shopping in either Salem or Portland. Becky had never mentioned the incident at the lake and Katie was grateful, but at the same time she hadn't invited Katie to go out with them again either.

Katie had been very disappointed that Becky and Jimmy had not left her and Dom at the lake together. She felt very confident that they could have handled it.

"What were they afraid of, that she would kiss Dom?"

That might have happened, of course. Katie longed to be in his arms and to be kissed by him. *Would that have been such a tragedy?*

Were they afraid that I and Dom would have had sex? At that thought Katie felt her stomach muscles contract and her heart give a little flutter. *Never could that happen, that would be adultery, I would never do that.*

One morning in the third week of September the phone rang just as Katie had finished canning a bushel of peaches. Katie walked into the dining room, where the phone was, and answered it.

A voice with a funny accent said, "Hello, can I speak to Mrs. Jimmy Burns please?" The voice pronounced her name Mis Jimmy Buans.

"This is she," said Katie into the receiver.

"Hello Mis Buans," the voice with the funny accent said, "my name is Petea Solano callin' you from Boston, Massachusetts, how are you this afternoon?"

"I am fine, thank you," replied Katie wondering what this was all about.

"Mis Buans, I repaesent an oaganization called the Brotheahood of Taruckas, have you heard of us, Mis Buans?"

"I am afraid I don't understand, what was that organization again?"

"Let me put it like this, Mis Buans," said the voice not quite so friendly now, we are a union of taruck dariveas. You know what youah husband does, he darives a taruck!"

The light came on. "Oh you mean the Truck Drivers Union, oh yes I have heard of your organization," then with note of caution in her voice, "what can I do for you?"

"Mis Buans, how would youah like youah husband to bring home twice the wages he does now, wouldn't that be wonderful, Mis Buans?"

"Yes, I suppose that would be fine," Katie was confused, she was probably the richest person she knew; Jimmy already made more money than her father.

"Not only that, Mis Buans," the funny voice went on, "but youah husband would be cavaed by a free medical policy!"

"Oh well," said Katie, "my father is a medical doctor, we don't have to worry about that."

"Ok Mis Buans," the funny voice was getting more irritated, "but othea people do and our Union cavas everyone that belongs to it."

"Plus, Mis Buans, he would have a good retiaement when he gets too old to woak, do you undeastand, Mis Buans?"

"Yes, I understand," said Katie meekly.

The voice became friendly again. "Ok, Mis Buans, all we would like you to do is mention this to youah husband and think what you Mis

235

Buans and Mista Buans could do with double the wages he makes now, will you do this for me?"

"Yes, I will mention it to him."

"Thank you, Mis Buans, thank you, now you have a nice day now, good-bye."

"Good-bye," Katie said hanging up the phone, her head swirling.

Chinook:

The International Brotherhood of Truck Drivers, Warehousemen and Machine Operators, known as The Truckers, was born in Boston in the 1870's. Ten years after the start of the Civil War large industrialists in the Boston area thought they were paying too much for the transportation of their manufactured goods. So they held secret meetings to discuss what they might do. They knew they all had to stick together and they decided that they would arbitrarily lower the wages by half for the men who drove, loaded and unloaded their wagons. It was a very bad idea; within a few days of implementation of this new pay policy men started dying, factories caught on fire and burnt to the ground; riot was the rule of the streets.

The city that spawned the Colonies revolution against the King of England also helped spawn the labor movement. The Boston police force protected the factories as best they could. Finally out of fear and frustration one afternoon they shot into a surging crowd of men and fifteen of the workers lay dead on the cold ground. The city then exploded into total lawlessness.

The Boston Post's headlines called it "The Boston Massacre II," and finally the federal government sent in the army to quell the anarchy. The politicians in the State Legislature argued for the laborers; and the first protections for working men, women and children became law.

The movement quickly spread to New York, Philadelphia, Baltimore and Chicago. Soon the organization that was to become the Truckers Union began to wield a magnitude of power unknown just a few years before.

In 1947 the Federal Government passed the Labor-Management Relations Act and The Truckers became the most powerful union in the United States and Canada. They were a law unto themselves. Politicians, state and federal, lawyers, and judges were in their pockets. When they called a strike no one dared to defy them; those who did were cowed into capitulation, badly beaten or found dead. No matter

236

the type of crime committed the fact that not one union person was ever brought to justice always played in the minds of those who would object. The large cities of the west like Portland, Seattle, San Francisco, and Los Angeles had been unionized since the turn of the century. But the unions were not much represented in the rural west where most of the canneries were located.

As the food products of the Slayton Canning Company appeared in the east hungry eyes turned west and soon it was found that the loyal workers of the Slayton Canning Company were without union representation. First a lawyer representing the Truckers was sent to a meeting of the owner's board. The lawyer presented his case; if the board was to choose the Truckers as their employees representative a lot of work could be saved for the company. True, the wages would go up and the shifts would be changed from two twelve-hour shifts to three eight-hour shifts. That would mean hiring one third more people but the productivity would increase three fold. The union would, through charging their workers dues, pay for hospitalization and retirement. All this would guarantee happy loyal workers and the company would actually make more money than they were now. The board, seeing a loss of their power and crippling strikes in the future, rejected this presentation out of hand. The lawyer humbly left the building; the board thought that was the end of it. Exactly one week later the manager of the cannery received a friendly call from a man with a thick Boston accent, just to "update the Manaja." Trucker Union members made the cans and boxes, and also delivered them, and these were the finished goods the cannery needed to stay in business. The threat was veiled and delivered in a friendly way, as information from one businessman to another; the board ignored this veiled threat. The Union had the front door closed in their face but they had entered the back door many times before and now proceeded to do so. The law provided ways to inform employees about the advantages of joining a union. That was the call that Katie received, as did many spouses of the more influential workers. The union rented a small office just a block from the cannery. This office carried pamphlets and dispensed advice on how to start a Union shop at your workplace. Also just off cannery property an informational picket was set up so cannery workers could talk to them during their lunch hour or when going home. The Cannery Board asked the manager to have the police remove this picket. The local police chief checked out the pickets and checked with the attorney general in Salem. The attorney general gave his advice that as long as the pickets stayed off of the cannery property and didn't hinder or harass people walking or the movement of traffic they had every right to be there.

The chief of police had a meeting with the board and told them he was sorry that the union had a right to be there as long as they stayed off cannery property and followed the rules of the community. So it started, and though the board didn't know it yet, in the long run the union would win.

When Jimmy and Joe returned home their wives informed them of the phone calls. Jimmy called Joe at home and they talked about what was going on. They decided that neither would form an opinion until they had more information. Dom on the other hand had already made his decision and in fact had become a union mole in the workplace. The union official in the area schooled him in subtle ways to push the Union when around his co-workers and to counter negative information other workers might bring up about a union. The union official also asked him to gather the names of the people who might be arguing strongly against having union representation. That way the union could give them more information to maybe "change their minds."

When Jimmy and Joe returned in October from a long trip the warehouse was abuzz with talk of the union. That was the only subject that seemed to be on everyone's lips.

The board was so adamantly opposed to the union that the word came down that anyone talking up the union on company time would be instantly terminated. Jerry Samson, one of the largest farmers on the board, had his barn torched that night. The barn was a total loss but he had saved his horses and cows before it collapsed. Things were getting nasty; two line managers who were against the union were beaten up by unknown assailants as they walked from the bar to their car the next night. There were no suspects and no one was arrested for these two incidents. Jimmy and Joe gladly left for California and Arizona the next morning; they would be gone ten days. While they were gone the local Chief of Police called Salem for help and the State Highway Patrol moved eight troopers into Slayton and things calmed down for awhile.

When Jimmy and Joe arrived back from Arizona they parked their truck and entered the warehouse office to hand in their trip tickets. There they were informed, on strictest confidentiality, that in about two hours a union question and answer session was going to be held in the town hall. The two men decided to go so they went down to the cafe for a couple of hamburgers and arrived in plenty of time at the town hall to get good seats. Jimmy noticed the place filling rapidly and soon the rule was standing room only. The crowd was tense; a low murmur filled the room. Just before the start three men walked onto the stage and sat in folding chairs provided for them. One was big and burly with black curly hair and swarthy skin. One looked fairly normal and he smiled as he talked to a greasy haired tall guy with buckteeth who wore a red and white striped sports coat and wrinkled red slacks. After a few minutes the fairly normal guy stood up and walked to the microphone on the stage, a hush fell over the crowd.

"Good evening, ladies and gentlemen," the fairly normal guy said, "my name is Stan Gets." He smiled down on the crowd. "No I am not any relation to the famous jazz player," he explained. "I'm always asked that," he beamed at the crowd. "I am the Oregon State representative of the International Brotherhood of Truck Drivers, Warehousemen and Machine Operators Union. Quite a mouthful huh. So we're generally known as The Truckers."

"We are here tonight to answer any questions you all might have about our union and how we might fit unto your future. On my right," he said indicating the big man with the black curly hair, "is a man from our main affiliate in Boston. May I introduce Rocko Spinelly."

The big man stood up. He had a black suit on and Jimmy noticed a bulge under his left arm. *I bet that guy is packing a gun,* he thought.

The big man sat down.

"On my left is the head of our Kansas City, Missouri affiliate Jed Piker." Jed stood up. "Jed is also in charge of all the Western affiliates." Jed sat back down. "I know that the rumors have been flying about this meeting and I wish to assure you that this session is just about how we, as the Truckers, can make life better for you and your families." Stan Gets talked in a pleasant soothing voice for twenty minutes on the advantages of a work force being represented by the union. The crowed relaxed and a few started to dose off under the pleasantly softly controlled voice of Mr. Gets. At the end of his speech he asked for questions; there were a few general inquires on the subjects of medical coverage, retirements and work environment, all very boring to most of the men seated in the hall.

Then Jed Piker stood up. He glanced around the crowded room, his face slack but his eyes ablaze. Then he spoke and all those that had dozed off woke up instantly.

"Let me tell you what I love about the Truckers." His voice a nasal twang that seemed to bore into your brain. "They protect me and my job, unconditionally! Once you're a Trucker you're always a Trucker. We are a kick ass organization that takes no shit from anybody. You got a problem with some management kiss ass boss, you come to your union rep and the problem goes away, or your boss goes away." He glared around the room; a weasel smile forming on his lips. "You know

239

what I mean?" Everyone at the meeting knew exactly what Jed meant. Some of the men fidgeted in their chairs.

Jimmy took an instant dislike to Jed; he was the crude, rude type of individual that he heard ran the Truckers in the field.

"Management," Jed spat out the word like he had just learned the drink he had taken was poisonous. "Management is out to get the working man, guys like you and me, dey tink we are shit to be used and then flushed!" He paused for just a second, pleased with the analogy he would store that away in his brain to be used at another time. "Well the Truckers don't allow dat shit to happen, once you are a Trucker, we are all brothers."

"Yah BROTHERS," he emphasized the word. "And BROTHERS don't allow nothing to happen to their other BROTHERS." When he used the word a little spray of saliva shot out of his mouth. Some of the men at the meeting weren't sure they wanted to be brothers with Jed. When he had finished Jed straightened up to his full height, a self-satisfied look on his face.

"If there is any questions I will take dem now!" Jimmy stood up. Jed looked surprised. Not many men questioned him after his speeches.

He pointed to Jimmy. "You sir, you got a question?"

"Yes, I travel back to the midwest a lot. I have heard many people say the Truckers are involved in a lot of beatings and maybe some murders. Can you elaborate on that?"

The whole room went silent. Jimmy noticed Rocko shift in his chair and turn his vile gaze on him, his hand automatically moving inside his left lapel.

Jed just stood there, his mouth open with a look of hatred etched on his face.

Stan Gets stood up and put his hand on Jed's shoulder and said something into his ear. Jed sat down, his eyes never leaving Jimmy's face.

"I am sorry, sir, I don't know your name," Stan said in his mild voice.

"My name is Jimmy Burns," Jimmy said.

"Oh yes, Mister Burns. You are a much respected employee of the cannery. I have heard your name mentioned many times. Mr. Burns, let me assure you that there is no truth to anything like that. The Truckers have many enemies, much brought about by the spirited way we defend our brothers," Mr. Gets smiled a reassuring smile. "The Truckers always work within the law Mr. Burns, always," his eyes moved around the room. "Are there any other questions?" There were none so Stan Gets quickly called the meeting adjourned.

Everyone hurriedly filed out of the hall. Some slapped Jimmy on the back but most brushed by ignoring him, avoiding his look.

When everyone had left the three men on the stage stood in a group talking in low voices. A fourth man came out of curtains behind the stage and spoke to the three men standing there. In a few minutes the fourth man returned to the curtains and slipped out the back of the hall. Dominic Stanza had his orders—Jimmy would be watched like a hawk now that he could be a troublemaker. Everything he would say, every action he would take, would be reported to the Truckers.

During the few days he was home this time he talked to Katie about the dread he felt toward the Truckers. He told her some of the less gruesome stories he had heard of them while traveling back east.

She countered that Becky seemed very enthusiastic about joining them. "Becky told me on our last shopping trip that the union, which she always calls it, would double her pay."

Jimmy frowned. "I thought Becky was management and management can't join the union," he said to Katie.

"I don't know, darling," Katie shrugged. "That is what she said to me."

In actual fact Becky had said that Dom's pay would be doubled, but Katie didn't like to mention anything about Dom to Jimmy. She didn't want to bring up his name just in case Jimmy asked questions about the lake; she preferred he forget about that incident. Katie constantly thought about Dom, even when Jimmy was making love to her; her mind would wander off to Dom and she would wonder what it would be like to have him make love to her. She would close her eyes tight and she wished that it was Dom making love to her. She had, a few times, tried to get Becky to talk about Dom but Becky didn't reveal much anymore about her love life with him. Though Katie didn't know it yet she was falling deeply in love and lust with Dom. She didn't recognize her feelings toward Dom, because she had never been in sexual love before and didn't know its symptoms.

*   *   *

The next Monday Jimmy and Joe left for the east, their truck and trailer filled with frozen packages of berries. In Ohio and West Virginia the Truckers were embroiled in a local dispute with independent owner-operators. It seemed the independents, in these two states, had gotten together and formed a loose organization undercutting the

241

Truckers' haulage rates for small manufactures. They knew better than to undercut rates for large manufacturer's and shipping companies, but thought the Truckers wouldn't notice the small ones; they were wrong, dead wrong! The day Jimmy and Joe arrived in Cincinnati a young independent was shot leaving a small manufacturer in a rural area in Ohio. His truck filled with window clips used to attach window glass to the moving harness in the doors of Ford cars and trucks. The bullet fired from a wooded hill just outside the factory entered the driver side window striking him in the head. He was killed instantly, his trip to Dearborn, Michigan cut short. The highway patrols of both states issued a warning that all truck drivers keep to Federal highways until this killer was brought to justice.

The next day Jimmy and Joe arrived in Charleston, West Virginia to unload the last of their frozen berries before heading to Pittsburgh where the truck and trailer would be filled with a special institutional sized can, not yet available on the West Coast.

That night in West Virginia, a barrel of nails would be dropped off an overpass; the barrel would bounce off the hood of a truck and smash through the windshield killing the owner-driver. The owner-driver, in his mid-thirties, left a wife, three kids and a house that was mortgaged to the hilt to pay for his truck.

The truck, after being hit, left the highway and rolled down into a hollow smashing into the small home of a coal miner. The truck ploughed through the small house killing the coal miner's two children and crippling the miner and his wife. They would both never walk again. No one claimed responsibility for these atrocities. No one would ever be brought to justice but the violence prompted the Federal government to send a mediator to talk to the two sides and the independent owner-drivers would raise their rates back up to the amount charged by the Truckers.

When Jimmy and Joe returned to Slayton it was October already and the cooler nights were quickly getting longer. By the time they had checked in it was 7 P.M. and the dispatcher told them of a get-together at a local tavern for everyone interested in joining the union. They walked down to the tavern, which was packed to overflowing. The crowd parted and let Jimmy and Joe in. They heard a couple of derogatory murmurs as they walked in but ignored them, and leaned against one wall close to the door.

Jimmy noticed one of the new truck drivers talking to a group of the warehousemen and forklift drivers, but he couldn't hear, over the babble, what they were saying. A waitress came to them and got their order for beers and in a minute the new truck driver banged on a table

242

with his fist and shouted for quiet. He started talking slowly about the union and management at the cannery. Slowly he turned the conversation more against management and more pro union. Jimmy didn't really know this new driver but was impressed by how much he knew about the union's benefits and how he handled the crowd. At first he was telling jokes, and everyone relaxed, then he pointed out a few of the management's gaffes of the last few weeks, and played on that theme for a period until everyone became slightly worked up. Next he pointed out how the union would rectify any slight that befell them from middle or upper management. And how once they reported the problem to their local rep it would be taken care of without the employee's further involvement; to the employee's satisfaction.

One by one different men got up to tell him about their frustrations and he would counter with how the union would likely resolve the grievance, as he now called them.

"The union would solve the grievance this way or another grievance another way," he explained.

Finally Jimmy had had enough. When he stood up to speak the entire tavern fell silent. He told them in lurid detail of the murders that had occurred when they were back east.

He finished, "Look I am not telling you guys how to vote but you might like to look into what kind of organization you are getting yourself into."

The silence hung like a fog in the tavern. When he had finished speaking some men glanced at each other nervously and others looked at the floor, not saying anything.

Finally one pro union line formen stood slowly up. "Are you saying this organization is evil?"

"I am just telling you what the union did. You can form your own opinion if it is evil," Jimmy said.

The new driver spoke up. "Just a minute, can you prove the union did any of that stuff. You just said no one was arrested. Those are pretty harsh words against the union if you can't prove it."

A buzz swept the crowd; it was like a dam of tension broke the water spilling over the crowd.

Some guy in the back yelled, "You're against the union but you can't prove anything against them." The murmur increased.

Someone else over by the bar said, "Hey maybe I am wrong but what if we don't agree with the union once were in it, will they kill us?"

"Yah," another yelled, "the union always talks about what they will do for us, what if we have a grievance against them. Will they shoot us too?"

The meeting then fell apart. The new driver couldn't control this new situation. A fight broke out, the cops were called, some men ran for their cars, others for their homes. Jimmy and Joe were swept out the door by the surge of the crowd and they both quickly walked back to their cars they had left in the employee parking lot.

Jimmy or Joe hadn't noticed but in the shadows at the extreme left of the bar sat Dominic Stanza. He hadn't said a word; he kept a low profile, but he noted down the things Jimmy had said and soon he would be on the phone reporting to Stan Gets in Portland.

*   *   *

Jimmy sat in his car for awhile. He saw some men running by and some scrambling for their cars driving off quickly. Within a few minutes the sirens and piercing lights of police cars flashed by on their way to the tavern. But the bedlam was brief and in minutes the streets were empty of people and cars. He drove out of the parking lot and cautiously by the tavern; the police lights still blinked a piercing red and blue but all was quiet. One man he didn't recognize leaned against an outside wall of the tavern, a handkerchief soaked in blood covering his nose. One policeman stood close to him, talking to him. Jimmy turned right onto the Low Sky road and headed home.

Katie sat at her kitchen table tense. Jimmy was due home tonight and she wished he would hurry! Finally about 9:00 P.M. lights passed by the kitchen window and she went to the window. "Thank heavens it was Jimmy's pick-up." In a minute he walked through the door and she came into his arms. This was unusual; for the past six months or so she rarely came to him for a hug. If he came to her she would stand there while he hugged her but would only put her hands on his side.

"Oh Jimmy, I'm so glad you're back," she said.

"What's wrong, babe?" he replied moving back to look into her face.

"I have been getting phone calls some times at night, sometimes during the day, it is awful, and I am very frightened!"

"What kind of calls, babe?"

She looked at him. "Are you hungry?"

He nodded. "I haven't eaten since lunch."

"Want a roast beef sandwich? I also have some coleslaw and I made a cheery pie today."

"Ok, sure I could eat a horse. Now tell me about these phone calls."

As she worked on his meal she started to talk. "Well right after you left last time the man with the funny accent, you know the one who called before telling me about the union? Well he said you were pretty

244

anti-union and to tell you when I talked to you to keep it to yourself. 'Cause others wanted the union, and you were causing dissension and confusing people's minds."

"I wonder how in the hell I could do that. I am gone most of the time?"

"Well that was ok. The next one though was really scary. This really rough sounding man said we know your husband is on the road and we know where you live. This is your last warning. Then he just hung up."

"The cowardly bastards. Why did they call you, I am the one they want." Then he told her about the murders back east and the meeting at the tavern that night. "I am sorry, babe, I had no idea they would attack you."

Katie stood with her back to the sink, her hand gripping the counter so tightly her knuckles were white. "My lord, Jimmy, they might shoot you, they might do anything to you, or to me!"

"Don't worry, babe, they won't hurt us, but if you're scared you might want to move to your mother's for awhile until this all blows over!"

"Jimmy, why are you so against this union? Becky says it will be great for everyone. The wages will go up, they will hire more people from this area, why are you against all that?"

"I don't know. I guess I am just against the whole thought of unions. We never needed them before. What's wrong with a man just raising his family the old fashioned way?"

"Unions are an east coast thing anyway. My Dad never needed them. We are westerners—if we are hungry we go shoot a deer or elk or maybe catch a salmon!"

"Well, Jimmy, maybe those days are over and now we need something more, something to protect us!"

"Well damn it, Katie I am not union and look around at what we got right here. We live pretty damn good." He saw her face crumble. She turned and ran from the room. Instantly he felt sorry. He walked to their bedroom door. He tried it, but it was locked. He could hear her crying in there and he felt foolish and stupid. He had brought his work home and it was going to cost him a night or two in bed with his wife.

"I'm sorry sweetheart," he said. He heard a muffled "go away, and don't come back." Jimmy turned away from the door, went back into the kitchen and finished his meal alone.

Chinook:

Jimmy had told Katie that that they would not hurt him, but he was wrong. After the word reached the union about the fracas at the tavern, they had had enough, a bellyful, of Jimmy Burns. Plans were being made now as to how to take care of this thorn in their side once and for all.

Jimmy awoke the next morning in the guest bedroom upstairs. Forgetting just for a second, he put out his hand to touch his wife but the other side of the bed was empty and cold. Then he remembered and was turning over when he caught the smell of bacon and coffee floating up the stairwell. He jumped out of bed and pulled on his jeans. Katie was at the stove when he walked in. She made a sour glance in his direction. He went over to her and tried to kiss her cheek; all he got was a cold shoulder as she turned her face away from him. He went to the table for his coffee cup, filled it from the coffeepot percolating on the stove and sat down at the table where a plate, knife, and fork were laid out for him. When his eggs and bacon were finished Katie stiffly brought them to him. Placing the food in his plate she turned and walked out of the kitchen without a word. To her retreating back he murmured another apology. "Baby, please forgive me. I am sorry. Of course you are right. I was just tired last night." Katie did not acknowledge his capitulation and walked to their bedroom slamming, then locking, the door. Jimmy sighed, ate his breakfast and when finished walked down the lane to the main road to get the morning paper.

The walk in the cool morning air cleared his mind, it was a beautiful morning. Walking back to the house, he glanced up to the mountains that rose behind the farm. In among the dark firs that covered the mountainside were splashes of intense yellow from the birches in their autumn colors.

Off above the roof of the barn he could see the canyon filled with a white luminescent fog.

This is the most beautiful place on this earth, he thought to himself. He would be the happiest man on earth if it weren't for those few harsh words he had uttered to Katie last night. As he stood there drinking his fill of the beauty of Oregon he decided to climb up into the mountains this morning. He went into the kitchen; Katie was not there and it sounded as if she was running water for her bath. He laid the newspaper on the table and went to his gun closet. He removed his 30-30 Winchester rifle and grabbed a box of ammo. Next he went to the coat closet and put on his red hunting coat and old felt hat. He stepped

246

out side and loaded the magazine of his rifle and levered a shell into the chamber. carefully releasing the hammer he set it on safety. He put the rifle over his shoulder and opening and closing the gate to the corral he headed for the upper pasture and the tree line.

As soon as he cleared the corral and picked up the cattle trail to the pasture he felt the pressure of Katie and their disagreement leave his body. He forgot about everything except the mountain before him and he became serene. As he climbed though the pasture he once again became the Westerner that had always lurked just beneath his consciousness. Beneath that thin film of civilization that he must maintain to keep a job and have a wife.

As he stepped over the fence from the pasture and entered the dark green of the trees, he now became a hunter. His eyes moved constantly looking for the movement that might be game or maybe danger, in the form of a mountain lion or bear.

Now he cared nothing for his job, the union or even Katie, now he was free as no man of the east ever could be.

In about one-quarter mile he came to a clearing; he stopped at the edge of the trees and looked warily into the open clearing. The trees ringed it on three sides but on the north side, where the mountain rose he saw a large patch of blackberry bushes. Just beyond the blackberries the mountain had been clear-cut. He entered the clearing his eyes scanned the mountain behind the berry bushes. The clear-cut must have taken place fifteen or so years ago because the young firs were probably ten to fifteen feet tall now. Bears will come to berry bushes in the fall to fatten up for the winter; he saw none here.

On the right side of the clearing he noticed a path skirting the berry patch leading up out of the clearing; he took the path. Once on the path he realized that it was an old logging road, obviously not maintained for the brush had reclaimed most of it. It was most likely used only during the clear-cut. Now it was a game trail. As the mountain climbed the road hugged its right side; the canyon that could be seen from the barn dropped off to the right. After a hundred yards or so he came to a Y in the trail. The logging road originally carried on around the mountain so this trail to the right was an animal trail that led off down the canyon. He angled to the right and for awhile walked down the animal trail. Soon the trail dropped off quite sharply.

He was not in the shape he had been six years ago. He had developed a definite stomach since his wedding day, and so decided not to drop further down into the canyon. He retraced his steps up the trail toward the logging road. As he walked back up he noticed to his left a huge stump right on the edge of the canyon where it plunged straight

247

down. He hadn't noticed it on the way down for it was concealed by a patch of four or five-foot firs.

He hesitated then moved gingerly toward it. With a lot of caution he climbed onto the stump; it must have been a huge old growth fir because the stump was almost ten feet across. He laid his rifle beside him on the stump and slid forward on his rear until his legs dangled over the edge of the stump. A panorama opened up before him.

On his right he could look down on his farm, less than a mile away. It seemed like, through the clear mountain air, he could almost touch the roof of the barn. Below him the canyon fell away, straight down, to the bottom two hundred feet below him. Dark tall old growth firs reached up from the canyon. One right below his perch ended only thirty to forty feet under him. It made him feel more secure; it seemed like he could just fall on to the tops of the trees and be all right. He looked to his left, he could see the deer trail he had just left angling down the slope into the dark trees. Just as he was looking away he noticed a movement out of the corner of his eye. Jerking his head back he saw a Black Tail Buck rise out of his bed. He had a good rack of horns, probably a four or five point. He mumbled to himself, "Damn, if I had just went along that trail another fifty yards I would have jumped that baby." Deer season was still a week away but no one would have reported a single rifle shot; every farmer kept his freezer full of fresh venison year around anyway. Also the game wardens turned a blind eye to locals who might take a chance deer if they didn't get too greedy. He calculated the shot he had now at about one hundred twenty-five yards.

He thought he had spooked the deer but it wasn't looking at him; it was looking down at the bottom of the trail where it entered the old growth trees. Slowly he raised his rifle and sighted on the exposed right side of the deer's neck. As quietly as he could he cocked the hammer back, his finger tightened on the trigger. With a bound the deer was gone into the brush. Uttering a small curse he took the rifle off his shoulder and released the hammer. Then he saw what spooked the deer in the first place. Up out of the timber came a black bear. As soon as the bear got in the open he stood on his hind legs sniffing the breeze. Jimmy knew he couldn't scent him as the wind, such as it was, was blowing from the bear to him. Still he gripped the rifle just a little tighter; he would just as soon not have to shoot a bear with a 30-30, but of course he would if the bear came at him. The bear dropped to all fours again satisfied that the coast was clear and started to amble up the trail. Jimmy's heart speeded up just a little.

The bear was a beautiful creature; his black glossy coat shone in the sun, the fat rippled just under his coat. Just before he came to the deer bed he stopped at a blackberry bush; his journey complete.

*   *   *

Jimmy relaxed just a little and sat back on the stump; as long as the wind was in his face he knew the bear would never know he was there. Of course if the bear knew he was there he might not charge him, you couldn't predict what might happen with these animals. More than likely the bear would just run away. But you never really knew so he kept his rifle at the ready. It took almost two hours but finally the bear had his fill and ambled back down the trail toward the old growth timber. Jimmy realized then that he had been tensed up for a long time and his muscles ached, and he was getting a headache. He would have liked to go home but he dreaded going back, as Katie was probably still mad at him. So he went up the logging road to see if he could pick up the Buck Deer's trail. So he scouted the mountain until late in the afternoon; he never saw the deer again. Finally he realized he was starving, and as he was leaving tomorrow morning early he needed to pack clean clothes for his trip.

When he walked into the kitchen Katie was cooking dinner; she glanced at him and said, "Where have you been?"

She sounded normal, so he told her about his day, about the deer and bear. As he ate his dinner he said, "Uh honey, I am leaving tomorrow morning."

She looked at him. "Yeah, I know, I washed your dirty clothes and packed you clean ones."

"Thanks, sweetheart, umm do you think . . . ?"

She gave him a small smile. "I suppose we can!"

Chinook:

Katie had been just a little worried all day. "What would happen to her if Jimmy didn't come back like she suggested to him, he was her only source of enough money to live the life style she had become accustomed to!" So she was glad to see him walk through the door. Jimmy was a happy man because he would've hated not having sex for another two weeks.

Joe and Jimmy left the next morning for a trip through the Southwest, first Salt Lake City, then Phoenix then the L.A. area.

They arrived home twelve days later on a showery, very dark Friday night. When they pulled into the warehouse unloading area a truck was already in the loading dock so Joe sat in the truck while Jimmy ran into the dispatch office to see how long it would be before they would be unloaded.

"About thirty to forty-five minutes, Jimmy," Jake Johnson answered from his inter-office.

"Hey, Jake, what's the boss doing here at this late hour?" Jimmy razzed him.

Jake answered in a low voice beckoning Jimmy closer to his office door. "This day has been very busy, lots of trucks in and out, and this damn Union thing has been going on so long everyone is tighter than a bow string!"

"Anything special goin' on, Jake?" Jimmy looked at him hard.

"Nah, nothing special, just constant tension. I'll be glad when it is finally decided."

"Yeah, Buddy, I understand," Jimmy agreed. "Joe is out in the truck, what should I tell him?"

"Tell him to pull your truck over by the fence out of the way and then come into the cafeteria and have something to eat. We'll call you when we are ready for you."

Jimmy walked back to the truck. The rain had picked up and was now being driven by a wind gust. Jimmy put his head down and ran for the truck cab; maybe because of this he never noticed a long black Buick Road-Master sitting with its lights out in a dark part of the truck parking area.

Forty-five minutes later Joe had just finished a cup of coffee and a roast beef sandwich, when Jake walked into the cafeteria. "Ok boys, pull your truck into bay 3, we are ready to unload you."

"I'll go," Jimmy mumbled, his mouth full of sandwich.

"No, no, finish your sandwich, I'll pull it up," Joe said standing up. He walked through the warehouse and out the dispatch door. Pulling his hat down over his eyes to protect them from the rain he made a run for the truck. He was just reaching up to open the door when his arms were pinned to his side by powerful arms.

A voice whispered in his ear, "scab, youse fuckin' scab, dis is what we do to youse fuckin' scabs!"

All his life he would never forget the smell of cigarettes, rotten teeth and stale sweat that filled his nostrils from that fetid body. Another hand clapped over his mouth and nose, and pushed his head against the chest of the thing that held him. He had a vague impression of something moving toward his left eye; he felt pressure on his cornea and than the searing pain exploded through his brain. He wanted to scream from the pain and helplessness he felt, but he couldn't breathe from that hand covering his mouth and nose. Just then a huge fist smashed into his solar plexus; he heard rather than felt his rib break. He was released and he fell face first into a puddle; he was desperately trying to breathe but he had no strength to pull the air into his gasping lungs.

Suddenly he was grasped by the hair and his face was jerked up. The voice said, "Youse scab, youse better keep youse stinkin' mouth closed or we will come for your othea eye."

The men dropped him again and slowly but steadily walked toward the big black Buick. They climbed in the rear seat talking and laughing easily, and the car pulled out into a back street that ran parallel to the main road. About four blocks away the headlights were turned on and the car headed north on state route 214 to Portland. On the south side of Portland, at a town called Canby, the car pulled into a small municipal airstrip. A Cessna parked there started its engines as soon as the pilot saw the Buick pull up to the small terminal. Two very rough looking men piled into the plane and the pilot taxied out and started down the runway. Once up and in contact with Portland tower he turned the nose of his plane south for San Francisco.

Jake never could remember how he got back to the warehouse but he pulled his bruised and battered body up the steps and into the dispatch office. Jimmy sat at a desk about ready to go look for his friend when the door from the outside opened. Joe didn't walk in, he fell in. Jimmy didn't recognize the muddy wet human staring at him with one eye and one hand covering the left side of his face.

The human opened his mouth and said in a gasping whimpering voice, "Jimmy, Jimmy, they took my eye," then he collapsed.

"Joe, my god, Joe. Jake, call the ambulance. Damn it, hurry, call the ambulance!"

It was getting close to midnight and Jimmy paced the hospital waiting room, glancing now and than toward Barbara who had been there about an hour. She was curled up in a chair silently weeping, her silvered hair disheveled, her eyes red.

Finally she looked at Jimmy, "So you really don't know how Joe got hurt?"

"I am not certain, he may have fallen?"

"Well if he had fallen, why did he say to you they took my eye?"

"I don't know, Barb, I don't know what happened." But way down deep in his soul he feared he might know what happened; just now his

251

brain wouldn't let him think of that. Just then a young doctor walked into the waiting area.

"Excuse me," he addressed Barbara, "the nurse tells me you are Mister Wallis' wife?"

Barbara went white. "Doctor, is he dead?"

"No, Mrs. Wallis," he paused for a second. "I would be lying if I told you he was out of the woods. He is a very sick man. They beat him very badly and also he is in shock. We have a surgeon coming from Salem to help me. He will be here in a few minutes. There might be internal bleeding and he has at least one fractured rib."

Once again Barbara burst into tears, her sobs racked her body. "Doctor, someone beat him, not Joe, why Joe?"

"I don't know, Mrs. Wallis, but on the positive side he is in very good physical shape. God willing he will be ok." Barbara started to collapse. Jimmy jumped up to catch her but the doctor had already put his arm around her.

"Mrs. Wallis, come with me, I think your presence will help him." He glanced at Jimmy. "I think you could go home, there is nothing you can do here."

Jimmy felt a touch of guilt because he was relieved to leave. He was just going out the door of the hospital when a car drove up and a man with a large black bag ran up the stairs and into the reception area. He heard the nurse at the desk say, "This way, doctor."

Jimmy arrived home just after one o'clock. Katie was fast asleep. He undressed and slipped into their bed. All sorts of thoughts swirled around in his head but he was so exhausted that within minutes he was fast asleep.

Katie awoke at seven the next morning; the sound of the shower coming from their bathroom. She got up, slipped on her robe and walked sleepily into the steaming room.

"Jimmy?" she inquired trying to repress a yawn.

"Yeah, babe," he answered. "What time did you get home last night. I didn't even hear you come to bed?"

"I got home about one in the morning," he said above the shower's noise.

"Ok then why are you up so early, do you feel alright?"

Jimmy turned off the shower. "No, I don't feel good at all!"

Katie reached out and opened the shower door, the sound of his voice gave her a chill.

"Jimmy, what's wrong, what happened?"

He stood there dripping water, shivering like he was cold.

She grabbed a towel and handed it to him. "What is wrong?"

"It's Joe, Joe, aaah, Joe got beat up badly last night!"

"What, Joe, why?"

"I think it was the union and I think they were after me and got Joe by mistake." Then as he stood there, the towel unused in his hand, the whole story spilled from his trembling lips.

In a few minutes he was done. Katie stood in absolute shock. Finally she said, "My god, Jimmy, they put out his eye and beat him." She fought back nausea, she couldn't let herself be sick.

Two hours later Jimmy and Katie walked up to the hospital reception desk. They had noticed a state patrol cruiser sitting in front of the entrance door and a burly policeman was leaning against a wall next to the desk, his arms crossed. Jimmy noticed his eyes never left them once they had entered the door. Ignoring him Jimmy asked the receptionist about Joe.

"What is your name, sir?" the receptionist said quickly glancing at his face.

"Jimmy Burns. I work with Mr. Wallis. We are driving partners."

"Oh, Mister Burns, these gentlemen are looking for you." She indicated toward the waiting area. Jimmy turned and saw the Slayton Chief of Police and the cannery manager standing there.

He walked over to the two men. "Excuse me, but the nurse said you were looking for me."

They halted their conversation and turned toward him.

The cannery manager said, "Jimmy Burns, this is Chief Thomas. I don't know if you have ever met."

"No I have never met this gentleman," Chief Thomas crooned in his deep voice, "but I am very glad to make your acquaintance, especially at this moment. We were about to send a State Patrol cruiser out to your place because we feel the need to grant you and your lovely wife protection."

"Protection, sir?" Jimmy looked puzzled.

"Why yes, sir, as you an' Mister Wallis is partners we feel they might come after you next."

"After me, I mean why and why did they hurt Joe, he never did anything. The only thing I ever did was tell people about what happened in Ohio."

"Maybe I can shed some light on this subject." The voice behind Jimmy made him jump and turn. Jimmy hadn't noticed the smartly dressed and immaculately groomed man sitting in the corner of the waiting room. Stan Gets stood up and laying down a note pad he had been writing on walked over to the group of three men.

253

"Mister Burns, you are causing consternation in some quarters of the Truckers, and because of this I am afraid your friend had to suffer!"

"My god, Mr. Gets, what did I do. I mean I just pointed out some things I had heard on the radio, at the meetings," Jimmy gasped.

"I am afraid you made yourself a marked man by bringing up the obvious," Mr. Gets retorted. "Listen, Mr. Burns, I am sorry about your partner, things are starting to change in the Truckers but many of the old school people are still in charge. Their days are numbered but in the meantime it would be better if you and your wife maybe took a trip for say a week." By now Katie had sidled up close enough to the group of men to hear what they were saying, her eyes widened with panic.

"Jimmy, let's go now," she interjected.

Chief Thomas crooned in his deep voice, "I think your misses is speaking words of wisdom, Mr. Burns. Don't get me wrong, sir, we have no evidence of danger to you or your lovely wife's person, but just as a caution until we know the lay of the land a bit better, you see!"

"Yes sir, I see," said Jimmy, "we will leave now."

Just as they were turning Stan Gets said, "Mr. Burns, we have a very good union, but we do have to work out some kinks, and don't worry about your partner I will personally see he gets the best of care!"

First they went to Jimmy's parents' farm; they explained the problem to his mom and dad.

Their next stop was Katie's parents' house; April's face went white as she heard the story.

"Oh dear, children, please don't hesitate. If you want I will call Grandpa and Grandma Overmars in Boise to expect you tomorrow."

"Thanks Mother," Katie said coming to her mother's arms. "I think that would be great." She started to weep. April held her close, kissed her forehead and they left. The young couple drove straight home and quickly packed two bags. They drove to Lebanon and picked up highway 20 over the Santiam pass and down to Bend. When they arrived in Bend it was dark and they got a motel room for the night. The next morning they had an early breakfast and by that evening pulled into Katie's grandparents' driveway in Boise. Her frantic grandmother gave them big hugs of relief and made them call both sets of parents before they even unloaded their bags from the car.

They spent a tense week in Boise; Katie only left her grandparents' yard once when she and Jimmy took a walk around the neighborhood Thursday evening.

Katie had been mostly quiet and somber since they had left the hospital that day; Jimmy knew that she blamed him for all this. He remembered the fight they had had about the union and how maybe it would be better to co-operate with them instead of pointing out, to everyone, their faults. Jimmy had tried to make love to her twice since they had left home; for his trouble he had received a curt no and a view of her back. He gave up trying to push her; he tried to remember how terrified she was.

He called the cannery on Friday and the manager had told him that as far as the State Police were concerned he was free to return, and also they needed him to come back to work. So early Saturday morning he left Boise for home. He suggested to Katie that she stay with her grandparents for awhile longer, much to her relief. He would check out the situation at home and when he thought all was safe she could fly home. Without Katie he drove straight through to the farm, stopping only for food and gas. Arriving home just after ten P.M. he loaded his pistol, laying it on the pillow Katie used. The next morning with his loaded pistol in the glove box of his pickup he headed to Slayton and the hospital.

He was admitted to Joe's room after the State Police Officer whose job it was to guard Joe had checked his I.D. and frisked him. Coming into the hospital room where Joe lay took his breath away, Joe looked pitiable laying there, his head swathed in bandages, the solution from a bag dripping into a tube that was attached to a vein in his arm by a needle.

Joe was very happy to see him. "Hey, buddy, how you feeling?" Jimmy inquired grabbing Joe's proffered hand.

"A lot better than last week at this time," Joe winced in pain as Jimmy shook his hand. "Still a little sore as you see!"

"Damn it, Joe, I don't know how to say I'm sorry, man. I would give up my eye to get yours back."

"No, Jimmy, no I . . ." Joe started.

"I swear I'll get those assholes if it is the last thing I do," Jimmy said through gritted teeth.

"No, Jimmy, listen to me. Don't get anybody. It happened, it's over. Don't even think about ruining your life, for this."

"But . . ." Jimmy said.

"Jimmy, this is a godsend for me. Two days ago the Governor of the State and the new head of the Truckers from Boston came to see me. Me, you know? They were both really nice and you know what the head of the Truckers said that if the cannery voted union I would get a full pension as if I had worked for the union forty years. Jimmy, with that pension I don't ever have to leave my farm and Barbara again, Jimmy, that was worth an eye. Jimmy, if you want to help me campaign for the union."

"But, Joe, they said you almost died, that when they hit you in the gut a piece of your rib punctured one of your main blood vessels."

"That is true, Jimmy, but I didn't die, a doctor from Salem saved my life, see?" Joe opened up his hospital gown and Jimmy could see his middle area was covered with a huge bandage.

Jimmy felt lightheaded and he almost fainted. Quickly he sat down in the chair that was beside Joe's bed.

Joe smiled a little. "Hey buddy, you are just a little white. Better put your head between your knees or you'll be in here with me!"

So Jimmy campaigned for the union and when the time came to vote at the end of October he voted for the union. Not because he believed in the union, but because it was his duty to help Joe. Now at the middle of November, the vote ratified and the union in, the cannery settled down just in time for the holiday season. True to the union's word Joe was pensioned off and he retired to his farm.

Chinook:

Three years later almost to the day Jimmy was sitting in his hotel room at the High Desert truck stop just on the outskirts of El Paso, Texas watching the National Evening News. The anchor listening into his earpiece said, "Excuse me, but we are switching to Connie in Boston for this breaking news!"

"Good evening to all you in our audience for this exclusive report. I am standing here on the steps of the Boston Federal Court House where a Grand Jury has just indicted ten of the old leaders of the International Brotherhood of Truck Drivers Warehousemen and Machine Operators; we in the real world know them as the Truckers."

"Excuse me, Connie, what do you mean by the old leaders?" the anchor interrupted.

"Oh sorry, Bryan. About six months ago many of the men who headed up the Council of Brotherhood, that is to say the governing body of the Truckers, were voted out by the rank and file. The word coming down then was the Truckers were changing the way they did business."

"Just one minute, Connie, some news related to this story is just coming into us. Excuse us, folks, as we switch to John in Kansas City. John, John you're on."

The television erupted into chaos, people were cursing, yelling and

256

milling around. "Thank you, Bryan, we are coming to you from the Western headquarters of the Truckers in Kansas City." John was yelling into the microphone trying to report over the considerable din. "Federal Marshals have just arrested some officials from the Western division office of the Truckers; they are bringing them out now."

Jimmy's jaw dropped and his eyes widened as he recognized two of the men in handcuffs being literally dragged out the front door of the Truckers building.

"Holy cow, that is Rocko Spinelly." The big man, his hands cuffed behind his back, his face distorted in rage, had a Federal Marshal on each arm. Then all hell broke loose and out the door in the same situation came Jed Piker, except Jed was being bodily carried. Jimmy watched in fascination—Jed's eyes were bulging, his mouth open and a spray of saliva was emitting from his mouth as he hurled the most vulgar oaths toward his captors.

My gosh, thought Jimmy, *he has the same clothes on he had in the meeting that night.*

The news report then switched to Dallas, to LA, to Miami, where the same things were happening at the same time.

"Back to Bryan at News Central," a voice said.

"Well folks you have seen exclusively on our network the arrests of men around the country affiliated with the Truckers. Now back to Connie at the Truckers headquarters in Boston."

"Thank you, Bryan. We have with us tonight four FBI undercover agents that infiltrated the Truckers twenty years ago and worked their way up into the higher echelons of the old Trucker hierarchy."

"We start with Mister Stanley Gets who started out as an office worker and at this time is the head of one of the Western state's offices. Mr. Gets, your story is fascinating and we will have a special report tomorrow night on the exploits of all you gentlemen. For now, though, can you fill us in on the charges brought on the governing bodies members."

"Yes, Miss Channing, the main charges are racketeering and extortion . . ."

Jimmy picked up the telephone and called Katie. "Sweetheart, be sure you watch the National News tonight . . ." When he was done talking to Katie he called Joe and Barbara and told them the same thing; then with a smile on his face and a light feeling in his heart he went down to the restaurant for dinner.

When the trials of the arrested and indicted ex-trucker officials took place a year later, almost all were found innocent. It had turned out some of the evidence gathered by the Federal Government was obtained improperly, and that cast the rest of the evidence suspect. The ex-trucker's lawyers had a field day against the government lawyers. Finally a federal judge threw out the evidence and voided the trials remaining; the government decided not to appeal.

Katie returned home two weeks later when the vote was assured to go the union's way. She flew from Boise to Portland; as this was the first time she had ever flown she was fascinated by the whole experience. She babbled to April, "Oh mother, it is so fantastic, you can see the whole country and the mountains that look so tall on the ground look really small from the air. The trip that takes almost one and a half days in our car, only takes one hour in a plane. It's wonderful!"

Jimmy didn't see Katie for almost a month after he left her in Boise, for when she arrived home he was on a trip to the midwest with his new partner. The day after Katie arrived home she called up Becky and arranged a lunch and shopping trip for Saturday morning. During lunch Becky brought her up to date on all the gossip.

Jimmy had called Katie in Boise a few days after returning home but she was still very angry with him, and quite honestly she took up the short time of their phone call venting her grievances to him. She had pointed out quite distinctly to him how his obstinate attitude had caused the problems everyone was now facing.

When she was finished he had simply said, "I am sorry," and hung up. He didn't call her again while she was in Boise. In fact she came home because Becky had called April and she in turn had called her daughter and gave the all-clear signal.

Katie now was confiding in Becky that her marriage to Jimmy was at a very low point, and that she was infuriated with him. Becky listened calmly letting her friend vent, and afterwards Katie felt better and not so cross. Becky told Katie that they had offered Dom the promotion to Jimmy's driving partner but he turned it down.

Becky said, "I am so glad that Dom turned that job with Jimmy down. I don't know how you and Jimmy stand being apart so much."

Katie just shrugged. "Well, you know, it has always been that way. . . ."

"Well Dom was so sweet, he said the two days away from me each week was already too much," Becky gushed.

Chinook:

In actual fact Dom had his life set up just as he wanted it. One week he would deliver to the southern Oregon coast, spending the night in a motel in Coos Bay. He had one of the Safeway checkers, a very cute buxom little number, whom he would spend the night with. The next week was the run to the east side of the Cascade Mountains and he would overnight in Klamath Falls. The wife of the owner of the regional distribution warehouse, who was also his office manager, quickly had gotten Dom in bed. She was pretty, forty-five and had three children in their late teens and early twenties, who no longer needed her. Her husband would rather be with his buddies fishing and hunting than with her and she was lonely and starved for affection. When she first saw Dom she fell deeply in lust. He was not much older than her oldest son, but her inhibitions deserted her because he was so damn good looking and she was so in need of affection. She had originally come to his motel room one night with the excuse of taking him out to dinner and showing him the area. She was alone that night and in need of company. But they never left his motel room; she was so happy that a woman her age could seduce a boy. No, he was actually a man, almost half her age; it did wonders for her ego. Dom let her think she seduced him, but in reality he much preferred middle-aged women. *She reminded him of Gloria, in a way,* he thought. She surprised him; he had never known a more passionate woman, or one that wanted to please him more.

Then when he got home there was always Becky, so his life was full. Well maybe not as full with Becky as he would hope. Other women gave themselves to him freely, but Becky had an agenda, and that agenda was marriage. But he didn't want to marry Becky, would never marry Becky. He would never marry anyone, because he would be trapped just as he perceived his father was trapped with an unfaithful wife. Of course he would never tell Becky, or anyone, that. One other reason he didn't want to go driving with Jimmy is because he wanted to seduce Katie. He knew that it was just a matter of time, and of course he would never be able to do that if he was with her husband all the time. Once he had his mind straight about his mother he would return to Florida; he would be there now if he hadn't witnessed her infidelity.

Becky also told Katie about the upcoming drivers, warehouse, dispatch and office Christmas party. She confided in Katie that the office people always elected to join the drivers at the company parties because the cannery people were such duds. She gushed that the party this year would be held at the Christmas Tree Point Inn. "Do you think, darling, that it would be too early to shop for our Christmas party dresses now?"

"Oh precious, I think not," Katie replied. "In fact, my Cherie I believe Frederick's has a sale on just this minute!" They looked at each other and giggled, and off they went to buy their drop-dead dresses.

The girls chose their dresses well, to suit not only their personal taste but also, more importantly, to frame their individual assets. Katie chose a satin royal blue dress with a plunging neckline that showed off her ample cleavage. Becky chose a high necked red sequined dress that complimented her coloring perfectly; she added a fake cream colored pearl necklace with a sparkling rhinestone in the shape of a heart to lay at the base of her throat. Two beautiful woman with the same agenda of conquering the same man.

Chinook:

After her lunch with Becky, and with her new dress and all the accessories bought and stored in her closet ready for the big night, Katie's attitude toward Jimmy had changed. In her mind she forgave him for being such a bastard, a new word to describe Jimmy that six months earlier she would had never considered using.

Of course she only used it in her mind to justify her new attitude toward Jimmy, "the bastard," she would never voice it; much too tacky and embarrassing. Nice girls didn't say things like that and if she was anything she was a nice, well brought up, girl.

Jimmy returned home with trepidation, not knowing what kind of reception he would receive. To his amazement and joy Boise wasn't mentioned; in fact Katie was quite warm, and seemed glad to see him home. Each time he asked her for sex she obliged him. So he meekly went with her to buy a new suit, shirt and tie in Salem, and promised that he wouldn't be on the road the weekend of the Christmas party. You see Katie needed a date to go to the party; she could never go by herself. Without Jimmy she would miss it and death would be preferable to that.

A month passed and Saturday before Christmas arrived. Jimmy had taken the week between the party and Christmas off. Jake Johnson had wanted him to fly to Phoenix to pick up a repaired truck that had broken down there almost a month earlier. But he told Jake that if he missed the party his wife would divorce him. So Jake had given him the week before Christmas off, even though the company needed the truck desperately. Jake could never chance losing Jimmy; he was his best and most reliable driver, ever willing to sacrifice his personal life to help the company. However, early on December 26th, Jimmy would fly from Portland to Phoenix to pick up the repaired tractor. Jimmy accepted that compromise willingly.

Katie spent the day after breakfast getting ready. Once the breakfast dishes were done she disappeared into their bed and bathrooms and when she came out to make lunch her hair was up in curlers and some kind of white stuff was all over her face.

"Be sure and eat a good lunch," she told him, "dinner won't be until eight tonight!" Jimmy didn't need to be encouraged to eat. Since his wedding he had put on almost twenty pounds; that is the reason he needed a new suit and shirt. He would never fit into his old ones.

The day was clear and cold, especially cold for the Willamette Valley at that time of the year. Snow might be a possibility for Christmas because the whole week was predicted to be below average temperature. While Katie went through her beauty regimen Jimmy spent the day cleaning, changing the oil and gassing up the Impala.

Jimmy bathed, shaved and dressed around five so he wouldn't be in Katie's way as her final assault on beauty took place. He heard the hair dryer going as he watched previews on television of the coming Sunday's Pro-Football games. The game of the week on TV tomorrow would be the Green Bay Packers at the LA Rams, it would start at one o'clock. *Good,* he thought to himself, *we should be back from Mass by then, because he really wanted to see this game.*

Just as the program ended he heard his wife say, "Jimmy can you zip me up?" He turned and before his eyes was standing the most beautiful woman on the planet. Her hair was perfection, the color of her dress set off her hair and eyes perfectly; he made a little gasp.

"Well I guess you answered my next question," Katie said with a smile.

"What was the question, darling?" Jimmy asked.

"Do I look good in this dress?" she laughed.

"Darling, you don't just look merely good, you look fabulous," he said in wonder. He only wished her dress didn't plunge so deeply and show so much of her cleavage, but he didn't say anything.

They were double dating with Dom and Becky but would meet them at the party. As they climbed the mountain toward the Inn Jimmy noticed just a few snowflakes floating past the windshield. They parked in a spot close to the stairs that led to the large porch that ran the length of the Inn. Jimmy ran around the car and opened Katie's door.

A cold blast of air entered the car and Katie, gasping, pulled her mink coat around her tightly, got out of the car and through chattering teeth said, "My, it is cold up here!" Jimmy held her arm as they climbed

261

the stairs and in a second they were in the warmth of the Inn. Jimmy checked their coats and they walked into the main dining room. The main dining room was huge; it would easily hold everyone at the party tonight. The decor was Western Rustic, meaning large logs finished but not covered made up the walls and the chandeliers were wagon wheels suspended from the ceiling with light bulbs that were supposed to look like candles. The room was decorated in red and silver bows and tinsel. Over the dance floor was strategically placed a very large spray of mistletoe. In the left-hand corner a small combo was playing a popular Christmas song, "Frosty the Snowman." As they entered the room the early comers turned to see who had entered. Jimmy saw a few of the wives' jaws drop, and a few eyebrows raised. As their husbands closely watched Katie walk into the room, these selfsame wives took their husbands arms and forcibly returned them to the conversations they were pursuing before Katie arrived. Coming dressed as she was she had made a few enemies; Jimmy noticed anger and jealousy in some of those eyes and faces.

Katie turned to Jimmy. "Let's get a table for four, umm how about over there by the fireplace."

"Let's get one closer to the window because that fire is kinda warm," he suggested.

"Ok, there is a good one, we can look out at the Christmas tree!" After they seated themselves Jimmy walked to the bar and ordered them drinks, a rose wine for Katie and bourbon on the rocks for himself. Then they sat and listened as the combo struck up "Silver Bells." As people arrived he noticed their eyes involuntarily moved to his lovely, if somewhat underdressed wife.

As he went to the bathroom he overheard just a snatch of a conversation between two wives. "Darn, I would kill for that dress!"

The other one said, "I could kill her. Now Sam will be looking at her and not me all night!"

When Jimmy returned from the bathroom Becky and Dom were just sitting down at the table. He noticed Dom looking closely at the cleavage. Then he saw Becky in her sparkling red dress; he couldn't take his eyes off her as he walked toward the table. The two most beautiful women in the room at the same table. The two couples sat and chatted before dinner, sipping at their drinks. The snow, coming down a little harder now, started to leave a trace on the deck. The four of them got up and walked to the door leading out to the deck.

Jimmy took off his suit coat and draped it around Katie's shoulders as they stepped out into the cold. The snowflakes were like granules of sugar, and they were dancing down from the night sky changing colors as they passed by the colored lights on the huge tree. In a few seconds Katie gave a shiver. "It is so lovely but I am freezing guys," with that they returned to the warmth of the lodge.

Dinner was served. Two entrees were allowed; the ladies had the salmon choice, the gentlemen the steak. After dinner was cleared couples started to drift to the dance floor and the two couples ordered a bottle of champagne and four glasses. After they each had a glass Jimmy took his wife out to the dance floor, Dom with Becky following.

Jimmy noticed as he danced with Katie that she seemed a touch nervous. "Are you ok, baby?" he asked.

"Yeah, why?"

"You seem a little tense," he returned.

"I am afraid my monthly friend is due, that is all," she whispered in his ear. "I put on a pad just in case."

"Poor sweetheart, you want to sit down?"

"No, no I am fine!"

After about an hour and another glass of champagne Jimmy casually looked over at Becky and noticed she winked at him. He leaned toward her. "You want to dance, Becky?" he asked her

"I do," she replied.

After they had left the table Katie slowly raised her eyes to Dom's face hoping he would ask her.

He smiled at her. "Well beautiful, shall we dance also?"

"I thought you would never ask me," she cooed. When they arrived at the dance floor Katie felt his strong arm encircle her waist and pull her toward his body; her heart raced and her whole being quivered.

"Gosh, Becky, you are gorgeous in that dress!"

"You look pretty good in that suit yourself, Tiger," she said smiling.

After that they didn't talk and Jimmy was looking out the window absently as they danced until he heard her say, "Boy they are in their own little world!"

"Who?" said Jimmy.

"Your wife and my fiancée," Becky said. "Look for yourself." They turned so Jimmy had a view of Dom and Katie, over Becky's shoulder.

The sight of Dom and Katie dancing instantly drove all other thoughts out of his head. Dom's right arm was around his wife's waist and was pulling her into contact with his body. Katie was leaning back slightly, her lips just inches from Dom's, the fingers of her left hand playing along the back of Dom's neck. Little smiles played over their lips and they were looking intensely into each other's eyes. Jimmy felt resentment filling his brain; he looked around and saw other couples looking at Dom and Katie then looking at him and then quickly looking away. Another couple dancing next to Dom and Katie said something to them; the couple was totally ignored.

Chinook:

From a table in another part of the room, small dark eyes stared with hate and loathing at Dom and Katie. She glanced at her husband and just as before he was looking at Katie with longing and jealousy. Her hatred burned ever deeper—this was the night she had hoped to lure back her husband, her one chance to rekindle the looks that he used to shower on her when they were first married. After four children her looks had gone south, her breasts sagged, their nipples dry, and around her hips and tummy were the ugly stretch marks. Oh they still had sex, but it was just sex, not love, not like it had been at first. Now he just rolled on her, he didn't caress her or kiss her. He satisfied himself without even considering her feelings.

He was just a fork lift driver, but since the union came in his wages had gone up to over half again what they were before. With this extra money she felt emboldened to buy a new dress. She also bought a Toni Permanent with a rinse to cover the gray hairs that were slowly replacing her normal jet-black hair color.

Her sister had given her the permanent, had said how pretty she looked.

The permanent, her sister said, "made her look ten years younger." How she wanted to believe that. Now that slut, that harlot had taken her last chance away. She would wait; someday maybe she could have her revenge.

Katie had an enemy; she was the enemy of a woman she didn't even know existed.

After that dance with Dom ended, Katie lost interest in the party; her mission accomplished, she looked at Jimmy and said, "I really don't feel good, can we go home?"

Jimmy glanced out of the windows as he went to get their coats. It probably was just as well, the snow was coming down harder now and he didn't want to slide off the road on this nasty night.

Halfway down the mountain he asked Katie what she and Dom had talked about.

"Nothing, just how nice a night it had been," she lied.

What she had really said was that Jimmy was leaving the morning after Christmas day and as she would be alone she would like him to come to dinner that afternoon. He had accepted.

When they arrived home that night Jimmy asked her for sex. "Yes," she said. "You better do it now because my friend feels like it will be here any day. This will be your last chance before Christmas." Her friend came the next day.

As was the custom Jimmy and Katie went to his parents on Christmas Eve. They spent the day and after dinner that night they exchanged gifts around the tree. Katie truly loved Julia, Jimmy's sister, and Julie, as everyone called her, loved Katie.

They both thought of themselves as sisters. Jimmy's mom knew that a special bond existed between the two girls and was very happy and pleased it did. Therefore Katie always bought Julie extra special presents, presents that Julie's parents could never afford. Julie adored Katie and adored everything Katie gave her. At about ten, Julie fell asleep against Katie's shoulder and Jimmy's parents were beginning to look very sleepy. Katie took Julie upstairs, helped her get ready for bed, tucked her in, kissed her and wished her a very merry Christmas.

Just after ten-thirty the young couple pulled up in front of Katie's parents' house where they would spend the night and Christmas day. The next morning they all attended Mass and then came back to her parents house for breakfast and the opening of presents. After breakfast Jimmy, John and Mike, Katie's younger brother home from University of Oregon for the holidays, watched football on TV. After dinner everyone turned in after watching an old Christmas movie. The weather that had turned cold before the Christmas party had stayed cold, though no snow was on the ground now there was a possibility of some the next day. Katie and Jimmy were sleeping in her old room and as they undressed for bed Jimmy put his arms around her, and quietly in her ear asked her for sex. She pushed him away quite sharply. "No," she whispered, "you know my friend is still here."

"Still?" whispered Jimmy.

"Yes," she whispered back. "Besides you know you get none when my parents and brother are just down the hall. I am not creeping to the bathroom and running a bath during the night."

"But I have a rubber, we can use that!"

She glared at him. "Not on me you won't. Jimmy, I am not a whore, you use them on whores, not on your wife. Where and why did you get that?"

"I got it at the drug store a couple of days ago just in case you said yes."

Katie gave him a black look, got into bed, turned her back to him

265

and went to sleep. Katie once again had lied to Jimmy. Her period had been over for two days but she had kept a pad on to discourage him from asking her for sex. When she awoke the next morning Jimmy had been gone for three hours.

At breakfast they had the weather report on the radio. The weatherman said snow was very likely in the foothills of the Cascades and probable for the valley.

April looked at her husband. "Darling, do you have to go up to the Franklin's farm?"

"Well, I may have to. Mrs. Franklin is due and you know she has them very quickly once they decide to come."

"I know you are worried, darling, but I have chains for my car and I will be ok; besides she may hold off for another day."

Katie looked at her mother. "I think I will go home."

April glanced at her daughter with alarm. "Oh Katie, don't you think you should stay, just one more night anyway?"

"No mother, I should go. I turned down the heat when we left and I am afraid the pipes might freeze. I think I'll go now."

Chinook:

Katie had just done something she had never done before in her life—she lied to her mother. She hadn't turned down the heat, the house would be fine. Katie had now lied to the people who trusted her the most—her husband, her best friend, her mother and her father. Her sins were piling up and her heart was starting to feel heavy, but not heavy enough to dissuade her from even greater sins.

Katie packed up and in fifteen minutes was on the road home. Everything was fine until she was approaching the Richardson Gap. She then noticed beyond the Gap what appeared to be a light fog. By the time she had passed through the Gap she ran into a wall of falling snow. Late last night a tongue of cold air had moved down from the mountains into the small valley of the Crabtree Creek, and had brought snow with it. Katie was terrified to drive in snow and almost turned around to go back to her parents' house. There was almost three inches accumulated on the road already, with the prospect of more to come. She slowed down to less than twenty miles per hour and remembered Jimmy said he had put on snow tires just in case she needed them. At the lowered speed her car handled just fine. She pulled into her garage with a sigh of relief and picking up her overnight bag went

266

to her back door. The door wouldn't budge; it was cold enough for the snow to freeze on the exposed door. She then tramped around the house to the front door that was protected by a porch and let herself in. The warmth of the house felt good and she gratefully took off her coat.

The first thing she did, after calling her mother, was go to her closet and reach into the very back and remove a box that was hidden under her shoes. She opened the box and pulled out the white silk negligee that she had bought at Pierre de Paris that day she was shopping with Becky. She held it up to her body, a small shiver ran down her spine. Carefully she shook it out and laid it on the bed. She put her hand into the box and extracted a bra and panties set she had bought on a whim one day. They both were very frilly. What had attracted her to them were the small yellow roses embroidered around the cups of the bra and the top of the panties. She laid these on the bed also. The last thing she removed from the box was another smaller box. In this box was a small rubber bag with a hose and plastic insert and a bottle of champagne scented douche. She wished she could be a virgin for Dom; she of course couldn't change the physical fact that she wasn't. However she could sweep away anything within her body that Jimmy might have left, and come to Dom as close to a virgin as she could be. Mostly she wanted to be as fresh as possible on this most important night in her life.

Then she went to her kitchen and started dinner.

Just after two o'clock she looked out the front window. The snow had been falling steadily since she had arrived home; it looked like it had added another inch or two on the ground. A raising fear in her heart had almost convinced her that Dom might not make it in this weather when she heard the growling of his pickup engine coming up the lane. He turned the last corner and now she could see his headlights through the thickening gloom of the afternoon.

As he pulled up to the garage she opened the window of the kitchen and said, "Dom come to the front door the back is frozen shut." She closed the window and she heard him stomping his shoes on the front porch as she opened the door.

"Oh gosh, I was so worried you wouldn't make it," she said to him.

"Wow, you know if I didn't have four wheel drive on my pickup I may not have made it. Man, it's really coming down." She took his coat. He looked so handsome with the snowflakes in his hair and a drip of melted snow slipping from the end of his nose. She wanted to jump into his arms right then; she wanted to feel his arms around her and feel his lips on her lips, but she knew if she did, she wouldn't be able to stop. She had planned this day too long to hurry it now. She brought Dom

267

into the kitchen, sat him at the table and made him a drink. Then she went about finishing and serving dinner. As she moved around the kitchen she kept up a rattle of self-conscious small talk. She could feel his eyes on her and so she accentuated all movements. She leaned over just a little more than she had to as she set the table, so he could look down her cleavage. When removing the roast from the oven she bent over at the waist so he could look at her legs; it was calculated but very stimulating. During the meal she continued to prattle on. She knew Dom found this amusing because he had a small smile that played at the corners of his mouth, but she just couldn't shut up for one minute. Just as she was removing the dinner dishes the phone rang.

The familiar voice on the line said, "Hi darling, it's me." In a gesture to Dom she held her finger across her lips. "Oh hi." She kept her voice light. "Are you in Phoenix?"

"Yes darling, I just arrived in my room. I'm at the Sands Motel, room 251 phone number CR9-1413."

She wrote it down on the pad by the phone. "How's the weather there?" she asked keeping her voice as neutral as she could belying her racing heart.

"Oh it is absolutely gorgeous, sweetheart, around eighty degrees, perfect blue sky. There is a pool here at the motel and as soon as I hang up I am going swimming."

"Oh you lucky dog," she said almost too lightly. "It is snowing cats and dogs here, probably six inches on the ground, and no sign of stopping!"

"Gosh, babe, I just talked to your mom and it had just started there; she said you had arrived home safely."

"Yeah, thank you for putting on those snow tires," she replied.

"Why did you leave your parents, sweetheart. I thought you would stay for a couple of days?"

"Well I thought I had turned down the heat and the pipes might freeze but as it turned out I didn't," Katie lied. "Well I am home now, how was your flight?" she said changing the subject.

"Fine, fine, I almost missed my connection in LA but I made it just in time. Gosh, darling, I wish you were with me," he said.

"I wish I was also," she winked at Dom. She was so glad she wasn't with Jimmy.

"Well I will just have to enjoy all this beautiful weather by myself."

"Ok dear, have a good swim. Will you be back by New Year's day?"

"I surely hope so. See you as soon as I can." He finished and hung up the phone.

Jimmy stood a few seconds looking at the phone. He had a vague premonition that Katie wasn't alone.

He shook his head. *That's stupid,* he thought and started to look for his swimming trunks in his suitcase.

Katie hung up the phone and leaned against the counter. "Was that the long distance driver?" Dom asked her.

"Was that who?" Katie asked.

"The long distance driver." Dom replied. "You see I am, and the other short haul drivers are called the short distance drivers and your husband is called the long distance driver."

Katie laughed out loud. The tension that had built up in her during the phone call released.

"Well that is what we will call him from now on—the long distance driver, good!"

Katie served dessert, so relieved she was almost light-headed. "I hope you like blackberry cream pie, it is my specialty." She put the dishes into her new dishwasher and taking Dom by the hand led him into the living room. She sat him down on the sofa and curled up into his lap; now she held up her lips to be kissed and he kissed her, and kissed her again.

Once again her heart was racing; he moved his tongue between her lips and into her mouth. He tasted of warm blackberry pie. He tickled and moved the tip of his tongue around the tip of her tongue. As he kissed her he moved his hand around to her breast; she turned so he could cup her breast in his hand. Deftly he moved his hand down her side and lifting the hem of her skirt moved his hand up the inside of her leg to where her nylon stockings ended, there he left it for a second on the soft bare skin of her thigh. She lifted her leg slightly allowing him access to cup her pussy with his hand.

When he touched her she gasped. "Darling, I have to go just for a few minutes."

"Why?" he asked.

"Darling, I want it to be perfect. I have special things to wear and I need to ready myself for you. I am not perfect now!"

"Baby, you look and feel perfect to me," he said kissing her again.

With her lips touching his lips she said, "I will need about half an hour. When I am ready for you to come to me I will call you!"

This had never happened to him before, he was kind of intrigued. "Are you sure? We could be loving right now."

"I am sure. The television is right there. Watch something, I won't be long." With that she slipped off the sofa and started for her bathroom.

He flipped on the set and turned to a college basketball game, but he never really watched it, his mind was someplace else.

Katie climbed into her bath. When she was done she went into her bedroom and put on her new frilly bra and panties and then her negligée.

She looked at herself in the mirror. She removed the bra and panties. "Ah that is better," she murmured to herself. She could just see the pink tips of her nipples through the folds of the silk. She brushed her hair until it shown gold. She turned off the main light and turned on a small lamp in the corner of the room. Then she walked to the door of her bedroom and said, "I am ready, darling." As she lay down on the bed and arranged her negligee around her she heard Dom turn off the TV.

Chinook:

Elizabeth York, nee Woodville, lay on her bed. She could hear the boots of the King, her new husband, walk down the hall. Slowly the door to their bed chamber opened and the King let himself in. He stood there for a second, his eyes getting used to the soft light that was coming from a fire that burned in the enormous hearth in the room. She heard him undress; first his boots fell with a thud onto the fragrant rushes that covered the stone floor of their chamber, then his tunic was cast aside.

He stood by the bed naked in the near dark looking down at the thrust of her pink nipples under the luminescent sheen of the silk. He climbed into their bed at her feet and kneeling took the hem of her negligee and lifted it, exposing her long legs and finally the soft golden mound of her secret place. Using his hands he spread her legs to allow himself access to her; he kissed the inside of her legs and then her golden mound as he lowered himself in preparation to enter her waiting body.

Elizabeth could feel his penis probing her, trying to find the opening of her secret place. She unconsciously spread her legs wider, then lifted her knees, still he probed. Then she lifted her bottom just a bit and she felt him enter her; she arched her back and waited for him to start. He withdrew slightly and then pushed himself back in again. In out, in out. Elizabeth picked up the rhythm. She was concentrating very hard to move in unison with her King.

At first it started like a pain in her chest. For just a second she was afraid that she was going to have a heart attack, then she found that the pain wasn't in her chest but radiating from that place where he coupled with her.

She discovered that it wasn't a pain but a good feeling, a very good feeling. She could feel her King thrusting in her at a more urgent pace.

And then in that place, in that moment, in that millisecond of time the Flame came to Katie, as it once had come to Elizabeth York. It ripped through her body filling her every cell, her every extremity with the fire of pleasure. Now she understood! She understood that when the Flame came to the heroines of Miss Pink's books this is what happened to them. She arched her back and dug her nails into her lover's back, she prayed that it would never end, but in a few seconds it started to subside. She started to relax but now that she had had the Flame this once, she could never go back to not having it.

Dom lay still on Katie, panting, letting his heart slow down to normal. He raised himself up on one elbow and smiled down at her. "Was that good for you, baby?"

"Oh darling, I didn't know it could be so good." She opened her eyes and looked up at him, moving her arms tightly around his back to as if to keep him there forever.

Well maybe old Jimmy wasn't giving his wife enough, he thought. *That was just fine because then she would be ready for him anytime.*

He kissed Katie on the tip of her nose and then on her lips. "Baby, I got to go to the bathroom to pee, and clean up." She slowly released him and he removed himself from her.

She watched him as he walked to the bathroom, listened as he peed, listened as he washed himself in the sink, and in a minute he was back in bed. She felt sleepy and relaxed. She moved to him, kissed the skin on his bare shoulder, cuddled her face into the crook of his neck and fell into a deep sleep.

The next morning she slowly began to awaken. It was like climbing up from a dark room; in fact she had been dreaming about a dark room. Jimmy and Dom were both in this dark room. Jimmy was trying to pull her back to him but she wanted to go to Dom. She opened her eyes—the light in the room seemed very bright and pearly, the result of the light of day reflecting off the snow. As her eyes cleared she saw a red dot before her eye; she pulled her head back slightly and when her vision cleared fully she saw it wasn't a red dot at all but she was looking at Dom's nipple. She smiled, stuck her tongue out and with the tip of her tongue tickled his nipple. He made a soft groan and rolled fully onto his back. She raised her head; Dom's chest was out of the covers his arms crooked above his head.

Settling herself on her right elbow she took the top of the covers with her left hand and started to pull down, revealing more of his body. At the spot where she expected to find his belly button she uncovered the tip of his penis; it was bright red. She hesitated for a second and then pulled the covers down to reveal his entire penis. It lay on his belly like a red headed spear. The head wasn't purple and covered with skin the way Jimmy's was. When she was in high school in her senior year there was a girl named Betty in her class for just a month.

One day after P. E. she was dressing and she heard Betty say to the other girls, "Men, they are all the same. Some are longer, some are shorter, but they are all the same!" Betty left soon after never to be seen again. Some of the girls said she was pregnant by an older man and he had married her. But Betty couldn't have been more wrong. Dom was nothing like Jimmy. She fought back the urge to touch his penis because she didn't want to awaken him. She pulled the covers down farther revealing his scrotum; at this point she stopped dead and stared. Below his penis lay a large sack of wrinkled skin covered with a fine fuzz of red hair.

Jimmy had a very small one. Jimmy had told her that when he was sick the doctors had told him his "balls," as Jimmy called them, were as big as oranges. After he got well they shriveled until there was nothing left. Katie dropped the edge of the covers and taking her left hand squeezed the sack and there were "balls" in there, they seemed almost as large as eggs.

Katie heard a gasp from Dom. "Be careful, honey, don't hurt the family jewels."

Katie jumped and looking sheepishly at Dom said, "I'm sorry, darling, I was checking you out. I didn't mean to hurt you!"

"Well now that you have checked me out let's check you out." He took hold of her negligee and with her help pulled it over her head. Once the negligee was off Katie lay back on the bed naked; a soft whistle escaped from Dom's lips. "Oh you are a pretty baby, you are!"

"Katie smiled shyly at him. "Do you think I am pretty, darling?"

"Umm," Dom moved his head toward her breasts, taking a pink nipple in his mouth. He started to gently suck it while moving the tip of his tongue around her nipple just as Gloria had once shown him. He heard Katie make a small "oh," sound. He glanced up at her face. Her eyes were closed and her lips partially open. After he was finished with her nipples he moved on to her; she parted her legs to receive him.

He entered her much easier now than he did last night. *Damn,* he thought, *she is so tight she feels like putting on a soft glove!*

After he entered her he lay still for a second. She said, "I'm sorry, darling, I wish I could be a virgin for you. I wish these had been my first times!"

He pushed himself up on his hands. "Am I bigger than your husband?"

"Oh yes," she said opening her eyes. "Much bigger!"

"Then you are a virgin, baby," and he started to move inside her.

When they were finished Dom visited the bathroom again and then started to dress. Katie went to the bathroom and then to the kitchen to make breakfast. When he had to leave Katie held him in her arms; opening her robe she took his hand and put it on her bare breast. "Can't you stay just a little longer?" she whispered in his ear.

"Baby, I would like to, but I got a haul to Coos Bay today and I am already going to be late!" He extracted himself from her arms and went out the rear door, which had now unfrozen. When he climbed into his truck he noted a warm wind was blowing and the snow was melting rapidly.

Katie, from her kitchen window, watched his truck go until it was out of sight. Then she went to bed, not even cleaning her kitchen first. She lay in her bed for over an hour, holding the pillow to her naked breasts, crying her eyes out. Finally she forced herself to get into a bath, and still crying washed herself quickly. Then she went back to bed again.

Chinook:

Why did Katie cry as if her heart would break, was it remorse? She had, after all, broken her wedding vows five years and four months after giving them so reverently to God, Jimmy and the world on her wedding day. Was it because she was now an adulteress and had broken one of the Ten Commandments, sins so vile, so vulgar that she thought she could never commit one? She didn't know, she knew she didn't feel like a sinner. She felt like god had given her Dom, and that Dom was hers and only hers; otherwise she wouldn't feel so good with him. So how could that be a sin? Katie was in a deep depression, maybe brought on by all the possibilities and choices her love affair had provided for her. Most of the possibilities and choices were bad for her and the environment of her life. So Katie found it easier to be in denial and easier to sink into depression. Maybe if she was miserable enough, cried enough, someone or thing would come to her rescue.

Five days later when Jimmy arrived home he had returned to find a different wife than when he had left. Her hair was oily and un-washed; it hung limply on her head. She had on no make-up at all, and she was dressed in old unwashed clothes with dirty slippers on her feet. The house hadn't been cleaned or aired out for a long time. Dirty dishes were piled in the sink.

Jimmy became very worried. "Baby, are you all right, are you sick?"

She looked at him with dull eyes. "No, I just feel down after Christmas I guess. The weather has been awful since you were gone. Well maybe I have a bit of a cold."

That night Jimmy had asked her for sex. She submitted as was her obligation but lay in the bed with her arms at her sides and her head turned away from Jimmy. Now Jimmy was really worried. She never was a passionate person but she always put her hands on his back and accepted his kisses while he made love to her. He had only kissed her cheek since he had arrived home.

"Honey, I think I should call in for a vacation day and take you to the doctor!"

"No, no Jimmy, I am fine. I just don't want to give you anything I might have. That is why I won't kiss you."

"Well sweetie, I am going back east and I won't be home for maybe three weeks, or more."

"That's all right, Jimmy, go. I will be alright, I am fine."

So Jimmy left early the next morning but he didn't feel good about it.

Two weeks after Jimmy had left someone did come to Katie's rescue, in the form of Ms. Pink's latest, and as it turned out, last and darkest book, *Flame Over Yellowstone.* Once she was finished with this tome, the old lady, now in her eighty-sixth year, put away her typewriter, took to her bed and was dead in three months.

Chinook:

Katie found out about the newest *Flame,* from her monthly edition of *Woman's World.* She quickly called the Downtown Bookstore in Salem, and explaining to them that she was too ill to come pick up a copy, had them send her one C.O.D. Three days later the book arrived and Katie settled in for a good read.

The book started in Chicago in 1921.

Jane Eleanor Kent, the heroine of the book, was nineteen, tall and slender with a boyish figure. She had a set of large soft brown eyes and

274

the top of her head was crowned by a tangle of unmanageable sandy hair. She was the female equivalent of her sire; had she been a son they would have called her "a chip off the old block." To say that Jane loved her father would have been an understatement; that she worshiped her father would be closer to the truth. Those feeling were returned by her Poppa, as she called him. She was his Princess; he could never deny her anything. Jane lived in a very large house among other very large houses overlooking Lake Michigan. Jane's mother was somewhat a stranger to her. She had been raised by a Hispanic nanny by the name of Emmanuelle. Just moments after Jane's birth Emmanuelle took the baby from the birthing nurse and had placed Jane directly to her breast. Jane's mother had always been considered small and delicate; her doctor had counseled her before her marriage about pregnancy. He taught her birth control but, to his chagrin, either she hadn't used it or it had failed. The doctor, an autocratic old so-and-so, who had been Jane's mother's doctor since her birth, had taken Jane by Cesarean section though there was no need for it. While in there he made sure Jane's mother would never have another child. In actuality Jane's mother, while small, was as strong as an ox and could have had six children without a problem. Jane's mother had never had strong maternal feelings, so she hadn't argued when her doctor, whom she trusted implicitly, informed her that she was not strong enough to suckle a baby. The doctor had arranged for Emmanuelle, who had lost an illegitimate stillborn child only one week prior, to be Jane's nanny, her maid and in effect her surrogate mother.

One evening Jane's father called her into his study. He sat her down beside him and taking her under his arm cleared his throat.

"Princess," he started, "hum well yes," he continued. Jane knew something momentous was coming; smiling she turned and kissed his cheek, "Yes, Poppa darling?"

"Hum, well you must continue with your education, yes, as you well know."

"Yes Poppa, but I hate to leave you and I shall be very sad."

When he heard his daughter say that he got a rather large lump in his throat and just a small tear in his eye.

"Yes, hum, well. Princess MSDS is not far so we will be able to see you some weekends. Of course we will send the car for you on all holidays. Also you will take Emmanuelle with you, and of course Jumper and young Gorge!"

The Michigan School of Deportment and Social Education for Young Ladies, known as MSDS, was an exclusive school dedicated to the further education of the daughters of the very rich. These were the young women who would run large homes with servants, gardeners, chauffeurs, and various staff. They needed to be able to move in high society with confidence and ease. They would be assets to husbands, families and their businesses. One day they would be called to feed, house and entertain presidents, royalty, senators and captains of industry. For three years they would be taught how to handle any social situation with calm bearing and aplomb. They would upon graduation know how to speak fluent French and read Latin, to have an in depth grasp of the arts of the Western world and a sense of fashion. It was mandatory they could ride a horse and play tennis. Sailing, golf, ballet dancing and swimming were also encouraged but not mandatory. Then, of course, the practical, knowledge of budgets and staff and menu control. Each girl had to have a maid to dress her and control her wardrobe, and her own horse and groom. At the end of these three years they were expected to marry and to produce children so the family dynasties could be carried on.

So it came to pass that in July, 1924, two weeks after she had graduated from school, Jane Eleanor Kent, whose family controlled cattle shipping, slaughterhouses and railroads, was formally engaged to Mr. Arthur Templar Levits whose family controlled banking, and vast holdings in real estate. The wedding was planned for the first weekend in June 1925; it would be a large and gala occasion.

Arthur was four years older than Jane. He had spent four years at Penn matriculating with a Bachelors in Business and than attended Harvard Law School, from which he had graduated the year before. Now that his education was over, and he had entered the family business, he was expected to marry. Arthur was a dutiful son, though he had never had a girlfriend, was never interested, never had the time; he accepted the choice of wife his parents chose for him. She was a pleasant looking girl, quiet and seemingly intelligent. She would do as he knew he had to marry, she was as good as any.

The wedding was a great social event; *The Tribune* covered it on the social pages like the sports pages would cover the Cubs or The University of Notre Dame football games. The honeymoon would be taken in New York, where they would spend two weeks. John Kent had given his daughter and new son-in-law his personal Pullman coach for the trip to New York. Emmanuelle would accompany the newlyweds as this was a working honeymoon. The coach was as plush as a palace, two bedrooms, a kitchen, where Emmanuelle would cook, a bathroom and a parlor. Arthur installed Jane in the larger bedroom and he took the smaller one.

A suite of rooms was taken in the Waldorf-Astoria Hotel in

Manhattan for the two weeks. The main room had two bedrooms off each side, Jane was in one, Arthur in the other. Emmanuelle would be in a small room off Jane's suite so as to be at her right hand. Arthur would spend some days with international bankers working out details of developments that the Levits were pursuing in Germany and England.

While Arthur was so detained Jane had appointments at the leading fabric, china, furniture and decorating shops, accompanied by the bankers' wives, seeking to furnish their new home that was being built on the shore of Lake Michigan, just a block from both sets of parents. After a week Emmanuelle was beginning to worry slightly, she was certain that Arthur and Jane had not consummated their marriage. She was sure they had not shared a bed or even seen each other naked, as she had undressed and dressed Jane everyday. But it was not her place to inquire, and she shrugged; after the honeymoon there would be plenty of time for them.

A very busy year went by the young couple had moved fully into their new home. Jane had hired servants and Emmanuelle had been promoted to head housekeeper, in charge of all staff. She also took care of Jane as before, but because her duties had grown so much she had appointed a young girl who had just graduated from the Chicago School of Domestic Staff. This young servant would see to Jane's immediate everyday needs and took her orders directly from Emmanuelle.

Jane had three "best friends," girls she had grown up and went to school with. They would meet for lunch at each other's houses or at the Club every Wednesday. Now all four were married. Mary and Deborah had married in the summer after graduating MSDS. Justine was the last to marry. having her nuptials only three months before.

Generally the four would talk just girl talk, or staff if one was having trouble with a domestic. But for some reason today the talk turned to sex. Justine had married a boy named Beau; he had been an all-American at Notre Dame. The girls were all slightly envious of Justine.

Deborah smiling coyly said, "Justine, you are so lucky. Beau is such a beautiful boy. I just swoon when I see his muscles." All the girls giggled and agreed. Yes, they all said Justine was lucky.

Deborah, with a small sly smile and a cocked eyebrow, casually said, "Is he as good in the bedroom as he is beautiful?"

All the girls gasped and Justine turned a deep pink. "Why Deborah, how you talk!"

"Come on, Justine, tell us, we are all bursting to know," Deborah said, her eyes intent on Justine's now scarlet face.

Justine could feel all their eyes on her. "I am so sore when we do . . . that, it is all I can do not to cry."

All the girls' mouths fell open.

"I asked Mother if Father had been this insistent with her when they were first married. She said that she was a little sore but that changed once she had given birth to Bertrand."

Justine's head was bowed and she was looking down at her hands; the other three exchanged startled glances.

"What about you girls?" Justine asked. "Do you have the same trouble with your husbands?"

Deborah was the first to answer. "No, no, Rob was quite randy but I never was sore at all. In fact, quite the opposite. Of course now that I am eight months pregnant we have stopped entirely."

All eyes turned to Mary. She blushed slightly. "No, I am the same as Deborah, though I have always found it to be rather a bore and messy. I am so glad that I am pregnant. Dan is being so thoughtful to me now."

Finally all the eyes turned to Jane, who blushed and looked down at her plate. Jane didn't know what to say, she didn't really know what they were talking about.

On the night before her wedding her mother had come into her bedroom and they had had a little talk.

"Jane darling, tomorrow night Arthur will want to do something to you; he will want to make love to you. You must submit and let him have his way! Darling, do you know what I am talking about?"

"Yes, Mother I think so," Jane had said.

She remembered her mother looking immensely relieved. "Well I wasn't sure. I knew nothing and was quite startled when your father . . . well, but you modern girls are so much better educated than we were. Only one more thing, darling, it may hurt a little at first but it goes away quickly."

But on her wedding night Arthur had not wanted to do anything to her; he held her hand and kissed her cheek, then they went to their separate bedrooms; that was it.

So Jane said, "Well it hurt a little at first, but it went away quickly and it is fine now."

All the girls were indeed envious of Jane; Arthur was neither a handsome nor a tall man. He was in fact not a half inch taller than Jane. He had a sharp face, a dark complexion and black, rather small, eyes. But he was very, very rich!

His family was certainly the richest in Chicago, probably in the country, and he was without doubt a true gentleman. He was gallant,

278

suave, sophisticated and honorable, and he treated Jane the same way her father treated her, like a royal princess; he denied her nothing.

Jane was content in her marriage. She was happy. She didn't love Arthur; the only man she would ever love was her father. But she respected Arthur and she felt he respected her; she had all the money anyone could ever want and in her house she was total queen. Arthur never questioned her taste or any decisions she had made as to the decoration, or operation of their home.

By Arthur and Jane's second anniversary all of Jane's friends were mothers. Jane showed no sign of pregnancy.

Jane's mother was worried; she had tried discreetly to probe Jane's love life, and the answers she received didn't quite click. By all outward indicators Jane and Arthur were quite happy yet the signs of young passionate love seemed to be absent in both their demeanors.

Finally Arthur and Jane were invited to the White House for a weekend as the guests of President Coolidge, as Arthur was a leading contributor to the Republican Party. While they were gone Jane's mother called on Emmanuelle.

When she left Emmanuelle she went straight to Arthur's mother and said to her quite frankly that if they had plans to be grandmothers the children should be sent off somewhere by themselves—that means no servants, no family and especially no business. So the mothers made plans to send the young couple to Yellowstone National Park for a couple of weeks for a proper second honeymoon. They both congratulated themselves and reassured each other that trekking in the wilderness was a very "in" thing right now, and where better then Yellowstone.

Katie turned to the title page. Yes it did say FLAME OVER YELLOWSTONE; she was beginning to wonder why it was titled that. Katie had been reading now for four straight hours; she needed to go to the bathroom very badly, also she was hungry. An hour later she was back on the sofa and picked up the story where she had left it.

Arthur and Jane were quite stunned when, after they had returned from Washington D.C. and were having both sets of parents over for a Sunday lunch, their mothers announced the planned vacation.

At first Arthur objected, very gently and respectively. "No, Mother, I can't leave just now I have . . ."

"Oh poo, Arthur," she cut him off, "your father and your staff can handle things for three weeks surely!"

Then Jane opined, "Mother, I cannot do without my girl. Who will take care of my toiletries, how will I dress for dinner?" Arthur and Jane

279

knew that to object was futile. Their eyes met and they mentally shrugged and it was decided.

They now had their own private Pullman car. Arthur used it for quick trips to New York, St. Louis and Philadelphia, and of course they had used it when they went to visit the President. So they connected it to a west bound train and in a few days disembarked in Livingston, Montana, storing their Pullman car on a siding until they returned. There they rented a car and chauffeur, actually a cowboy named Bud, who drove them through the most ruggedly beautiful country they had ever seen to the Old Faithful Inn in Yellowstone Park. When they were shown their room they noticed they had only one double bed. Arthur went to the front desk to ask for two single rooms, or failing that at least two beds in one room.

"I'm very sorry, sir," intoned the clerk at the desk, "but the request from the person who made the reservations specifically asked for one double bed and I am afraid we are totally filled. We don't even have a roll away bed to accommodate you!" The young couple unpacked for the first time in their lives without a servant to help. Then Arthur went for a walk while Jane had a nap. At the prearranged time of five o'clock Arthur knocked gently on the door of their room and Jane let him in. She had dressed for dinner, again for the first time in her life, by herself. She sat in a chair looking out at the Old Faithful geyser while Arthur dressed.

When they arrived at the dining room the headwaiter showed them to the table that would be theirs for the entire time they would be at the Inn. There were four chairs at the table and the headwaiter explained that another couple from San Francisco would be joining them. Arthur ordered a bottle of Champagne with which to celebrate the safe arrival at their destination. As the young couple sipped their champagne Jane noticed a couple of young men following the headwaiter toward their table. One was tall, as tall or taller than her father, with the same mass of unruly hair on his head, except this young man was not fair like her father but dark like Arthur—black hair, dark skin and dark wide-set eyes. The other young man was not so dark—had brown hair, ivory skin with a sweet feminine look about his face. This young man was shorter, maybe the height of Arthur. The two young men were seated, the tall one across from Jane and the short one across from Arthur. Arthur arose, shook both their hands and introduced Jane and himself. The taller man's name was Bret Hall and the shorter was Amos Hall; they were brothers. When Arthur took Amos's hand to shake it in greeting he felt something akin to a shock pass between them. Arthur had never seen another human as beautiful as Amos

Hall; his heart actually fluttered as he looked into the soft brown eyes with the little gold flecks dancing in them. Arthur had always had, even as a child, an interest in roses and so it seemed did Amos.

Arthur loved horses, had had a stable since young, he loved to ride. Amos, a city kid, knew nothing about horses, had never ridden in his life but he found the subject fascinating. Soon Arthur and Amos had forgotten about the other two. After they had ordered dinner Arthur felt something touch the instep of his shoe. Then that something moved slowly up his leg; he moved his leg closer to Amos. After they had finished eating Arthur turned toward Jane, but all the while kept his eyes on Amos.

"Dearest," he said to Jane, "maybe you and Bret would like to take a walk rather than be bored listening about horses?"

Bret smiled at her. "Yes, Mrs. Levits, we could walk the veranda. I heard someone say that bears sometimes walk past the veranda in the evening and maybe we could see one!"

Jane didn't really want to leave her husband with this strangely feminine boy. But Bret was nice and quite handsome and she did want to see a bear, so she consented.

Arthur tore his eyes from Amos and looking at Jane said, "When you get done with your walk, come back for coffee and cake."

When they reached the veranda Bret offered her his arm and shyly she took it; he seemed strong. She could feel his muscled arm through his dinner jacket. When they had reached the back side of the Inn Bret pulled up sharply, then Jane saw it, a movement like a hump of fir just below the railing of the veranda. Bret shepherded her to the railing and there was an enormous bear slowly ambling along.

"My god, it is a grizzly," he gasped. Jane felt a chill run up her spine and she instinctively moved closer to Bret. The massive bear meandered along not taking any notice of the two humans, and was soon lost to sight in the forest that ringed the back of the Inn.

Jane's racing heart started to slow when she realized she was under the protective arm of Bret. She stepped back. "I am sorry he gave me such a fright I . . ."

"Yes I know," said Bret. "That railing looked very thin for just a minute, not much protection for us."

They walked back to the table but it was empty. "Would you like some coffee and cake. I feel I need some to calm down," Bret said. So they had dessert and chatted. Bret finally glanced at his watch. "Oh goodness," he exclaimed, "it is ten o'clock already. I had better escort you back to your room." They said goodbye outside Jane's door and he walked away as she entered.

"Hum," she said to herself. "Arthur is not back yet. Good, it will allow me to get into my nightie and into bed before he arrives."

Bret walked to his room on the second floor. He tried to open the door but something was in the way; he started to push when his brother's voice came from beyond the door.

"Don't come in here Bret."

"Why not?" Bret asked with exasperation.

"Because I have a guest," the voice hissed again.

"Well where am I suppose to sleep?"

He heard another voice from within speak, then his brother said, "Arthur says go to his room they have a couch you can use."

Bret went back to Jane's door and knocked; the door started to crack open and Jane said, "Did you forget your key?" When she saw it wasn't Arthur she started to close the door and said in a fluster, "Mr. Hall, what are you doing here?"

"I'm sorry, Mrs. Levits, I was told by your husband that you have a couch that I could sleep on!"

The door swung open again. With an astonished look on her face Jane gasped. "Arthur said you could sleep here? Where is Arthur?"

"I am sorry, Mrs. Levits, he is with my brother in our room."

The door opened wider. "With your brother? I don't understand, did he say he would be along later?"

"No I am afraid not. I am sorry, I believe he plans to spend the night with my brother. May I come in?"

Jane just stood there so Bret walked in. "Mr. Hall, you can't be in here. I am not properly dressed to receive a person other than my husband!"

"But Jane, I mean Mrs. Levits, I have no other place to go, no other place to sleep tonight."

Jane's shoulders slumped and she sat down on the edge of her bed. "Mr. Hall, why is my husband with your brother?"

"I am sorry, Jane, but my brother is a homosexual. I guess your husband is one also!"

Jane's lips mouthed the word but no sound escaped.

"I am sorry, Jane, do you know what that means, homosexual?"

"No I am afraid I don't. What does it mean, Mr. Hall?"

"It means that the things husband and wife do together in their bed, make love I guess you would call it, two men or two women do. And the people who do that are called homosexuals."

Jane's head was reeling. She climbed into bed and covered herself up.

"Can I stay, Jane?"

"Yes, Mr. Hall, close the door and make yourself a bed on the sofa." Bret lay on the sofa looking up into the ceiling, cursing his miserable rotten brother; he tried to sleep but his eyes were wide open.

After a while Jane sat up in her bed. "Bret, would you like to come into bed with me?"

Quickly Bret undressed. Jane watched him undress and when he was naked he stood by the bed for a second. Jane had never seen a naked man before. He was very good looking, though not exactly how she had pictured a naked man would look. First of all his thing was huge. It stuck out. Would he actually place that in her body? Just for a second a flash of fear gripped her. If he did impale her with the thing, where would it go exactly? She had gleaned from some of the things her married friends had said that it went between your legs then into you. What if it didn't fit, what if it hurt?

He jumped into bed and moved over to Jane and pulled her gently down. Jane lay down rather awkwardly and Bret took her into his arms. Much to her surprise she felt very good in his arms; he started to kiss her lips and she thought that was very nice.

Ten minutes later Jane lay naked in Bret's arms. She was no longer a virgin, she was a woman. She had lied to her mother about knowing what would happen to her on her wedding night. When she thought of how uncomfortable her mother had been in trying to explain this she had to smile. Because of all the things her mother, or her married friends, could have told her about sex nothing would have convinced her that it would be like the experience she just went through.

She snuggled deeper into Bret's arms until she could feel the skin of his chest on her nipples, and then she fell into the deepest sleep of her life.

Arthur and Jane were both virgins when they arrived at Yellowstone. For the next thirteen days they were on their honeymoon, which they had never had together. The only difference is they had the honeymoon with people other than each other. The only times the two couples saw each other was at breakfast or dinner; those meetings were cordial but cool. Each day the two couples went trekking but in the opposite directions.

Ms. Pink explained in detail each sexual encounter as to both setting and other particulars. Suffice to say that at the end of the vacation they were all hopelessly in love with their partners.

Now Arthur and Jane recognized why the mothers had sent them off by themselves. Well, the mothers got what they wanted, because Arthur was extremely happy and Jane had become very pregnant. At the end of the vacation Bret offered to run away with Jane, but she refused;

her family would be crushed. So they promised to meet in Chicago whenever they could. Arthur and Amos didn't cry at parting because Amos was coming to Chicago. Arthur had promised him his own house and a living for life if he came to Chicago to live and be Arthur's lover.

Nine months later Jane produced two beautiful twin boys. They had dark hair and eyes like the Levits, and they were tall and had the facial features of the Kent family. They were the proud and adored heirs to both families' futures and fortunes.

As the two new grandmothers stood in the nursery their eyes met and they both gave a little smile—their plan had worked.

Arthur was true to his word. He bought Amos an apartment just off Michigan Boulevard and provided him with a very handsome income; they were secret lovers for fifty years until at the age of seventy-five Amos died.

Arthur was a wonderful father; he gave his sons every advantage, doted over them and loved them until his dying day. They in turn adored their father and after he had died missed him very much.

Jane never had any other children but her two boys; the doctor that had delivered Jane delivered her two boys, by Caesarian, though she could have delivered them naturally. No one ever knew of Bret or if she ever saw him again, but in her heart she loved him and dreamed of him all the rest of her life. Arthur and Jane were married for sixty years; in all those years Arthur and Jane never made love, never saw each other naked nor even slept in the same bed. Yet they lived a happy life and had a fulfilling marriage.

In their middle and later years they became the leaders of Chicago society. When Jane and Arthur had a party or a Charity Ball everyone who was anyone would be devastated if not invited.

And so the book ended and Katie went to bed but would rise in the morning with her life going in a new direction.

When Katie had finished her breakfast she looked around her home. It was filthy, the results of a month of depression, self-pity and inaction. As she was cleaning her brain never stopped working. First Dom; she had originally thought that she would only need the one night of sex with him, now she knew different. For a while she considered leaving Jimmy and running off with Dom. But that scenario, as she contemplated it, seemed silly. First of all Jimmy made so much more money than Dom did; in fact she was stunned how much money Jimmy was making since he had joined the union. His salary had doubled and now he would be making over one hundred thousand dollars a year. Katie had visions of buying houses in Low Sky, apartment buildings in Salem and maybe buying up neighboring farms to extend her land holdings. Besides Dom was from Florida; he had mentioned during dinner about going back there someday, after a few things had been worked out.

She couldn't do that. She could never leave her parents, she could never leave her sheltered life here to live in so foreign a place as Florida. Just the thought made her shiver. But she needed a plan to keep Dom here close to her forever. After awhile she hit on it, he would marry Becky and they would be lifelong secret lovers just like Arthur and Amos, the thought made her smile and tingle.

Jimmy, she had to stay married to him; first the scandal that would ensue if she left him, second the hurt she would cause her mother, Jimmy's mother and of course Julia, who worshiped Jimmy. But she couldn't sleep in the same bed with him ever again; the thought made her positively ill. After another hour of racking her brain, "his own bedroom and bathroom!"

*　　*　　*

Upstairs, the farmhouse had three bedrooms—two large ones and between the large ones a smaller room that would make a very fine bathroom. They called the large bedrooms the guestrooms and the small bedroom they used for storage. Jimmy never went upstairs unless he wanted his rifle, shotgun or some fishing equipment, which he kept there. She could have the storeroom converted into a bathroom and Jimmy wouldn't know until it was done. This was fine; she was making great progress toward the new life she had planned for Jimmy and herself.

As she was congratulating herself a small dark thought entered her mind. *If he couldn't make love to her would Jimmy find another woman and leave her? She could become the laughing stock of Low Sky, there could be nothing worse!* This would not be acceptable anyway—she didn't want Jimmy touching another woman, she didn't want him physically but she didn't want him having sex with some other woman! What was she going to do?

Then an idea came to her. *What if Jimmy had a male lover like Arthur had Amos,* she thought. *He would be outwardly the perfect husband like Arthur but he would have no reason to leave me,* she reasoned. She was unsure exactly what happened between male lovers. *I wonder how they have sex, if they do,* she thought. Ms. Pink hadn't really explained that!

She shrugged her shoulders. Well, that wasn't her problem. She decided Jimmy would have a male lover, what they did was up to them. A few days later Jimmy came home. When he walked into the house he could tell instantly that Katie was back to her old self. The house was immaculate and the smell of dinner on the stove made him reel with hunger. Katie treated him rather coolly though; when he asked her for sex she told him that she was in the middle of her period. They went to bed and she had on a thick flannel nightgown and lay stiffly on her side of the bed. He was only home for two days and had hoped that he would be able to make love to her. He was bitterly disappointed that he couldn't, but didn't say anything to Katie.

The morning he left she got up early to make him breakfast. "Jimmy," she said looking slyly at him. "I want you to read this book." She handed him *Flame Over Yellowstone*.

"I think this is the relationship that we should have, read it and see if you don't think so too!"

Jimmy read it, all the way to Texas. As he read it his heart grew heavy, a pang of fear and hurt settled into his stomach.

"Does she want me to be a queer," he asked himself, "a queer?" Jimmy had heard of a lot of marital problems; infidelity, loss of love, boredom, fighting over children, money, sex and, in extreme cases killing. If there was any problem ever between Man and Woman marriage seemed to bring it out. But he had never ever heard of a wife despising her husband so much that she wished him queer. He finally concluded that this was the way she was breaking to him the fact that she wanted a divorce. It was with a heavy heart that he completed this run through the southwestern states.

When Jimmy left to go to Texas Katie's period was over; in fact it had been over a couple of days before he had come home. She had marveled how easy it was to lie to Jimmy now. Since she had fallen in love with Dom he was the only thing that mattered in her life and to tell a lie to protect that love was, in her reasoning, justified.

The evening of the day Jimmy left, Katie called Dom.

Dom had just returned home from a trip to Medford; he was exhausted, he hadn't slept at all last night. For some reason his "Medford thing" had been extremely needy and she had kept him awake all night with lovemaking and talk, then more lovemaking. He had eaten dinner at the cafeteria in the cannery. When he reached home he sat down in his chair with a beer, turned on the TV news and promptly fell into a deep sleep. He was dreaming his mother was coming down the hall toward him with the front of her dress unbuttoned, but the dream was different this time. Somewhere there was a phone ringing, he expected his mother to answer it but she went toward her money jar.

With a start he woke up, it was his phone that was ringing. Groggily he pulled himself out of his chair, reached for the insistent phone and said "Hello!"

"Hi it's me," the voice said.

"Me, me, me . . . who, in the hell is me?" he wondered. But he just said "Oh hi!"

The voice went a note lower. "The long distance driver is gone and I am all alone. Want to come over?" the female voice said. Then he knew who the voice was.

"Oh baby, that sounds really good but I am exhausted. I just got back from a hard trip, and I have to leave tomorrow early." There was a second of silence, then he said, "How about Friday night, baby?"

There was another second of silence. "Hmm, that sounds nice, but I need you now. How about I come to your house, say in about an hour?"

"Baby, that sounds really fine. I'll leave the front door unlocked. Just come on in and if I am asleep I am sure you can find a way to wake me up, eh?"

There was a small breathy giggle over the line and a whispered "see you soon!"

Dom came back to the TV and turned it off. He got into the shower and then into his bed naked. The next thing he felt was Katie's warm naked breasts on his chest.

Katie woke up at 9 A.M. She had felt Dom leave around six but had not woken up. As consciousness slowly returned to Katie she groaned in pleasure and snuggled deeper under the covers of Dom's bed.

Katie got out of bed and looking at the clock saw it was almost 10 A.M. She stripped Dom's bed, washed his sheets and hung them to dry on a rack in the kitchen close to the stove that heated most of the house. Then she remade his bed with sheets she had found in a cupboard. That was about all she could do because the rest of his small house was immaculate. She made herself some toast and coffee for breakfast and then about 11:30 went out to her car and headed home. She glanced around as she walked to her car; she saw no one. There was not any reason to fear, no one knew her in Slayton so she didn't take any precautions. She was wrong!

Chinook:

She stood before the stove cooking lunch for her husband. The steam from the homemade soup she was making caused her forelock to curl and it lay now on her forehead irritating her. Absently she brushed

287

it up, but it returned almost instantly to the same spot. She would have pinned it up but she was deep in thought. She was thinking about the handsome man who had danced the lewd dance with the Blond Witch at the Christmas party. Just a week after the party she was standing in her parlor when she saw that man walk by. Quickly she went to the side window of her parlor to see where he went. By standing at the very far left of that window she followed him as he walked up a walk and entered the small house in the middle of the block, on the opposite side of the street.

Over the next few days she started to question her husband about the people at that table. He had told her that the men were drivers, the one with the blond wife was called Jimmy Burns. Every one at the cannery knew him, as he was the one that fought the union. "It really pisses me off," grumbled her husband, "he didn't want the union but he was the one that made out more than anyone else. I don't know the other guy's name but the dark haired babe in the red dress is a big shot in the office." He had spat out the words "big shot" like they tasted bad.

Finally she had had enough of the wayward forelock and turning her soup down to simmer started to walk to her bedroom for a bobby pin. On the way she detoured into her parlor, as was her fashion, to survey the neighborhood. She noticed a strange car parked in front of the little house the handsome man occupied. She moved to the far left-hand corner of the side window. Just at that second she saw the front door of the little house open. Who should walk out but the Blond Witch; her mouth opened with surprise and her eyes flashed with loathing. She watched as the Blond Whore walked to her car and drove away.

Her mind was in turmoil. "What do you think the Blond Whore was doing at that house at this time?" She didn't know but she would watch that house more and she would get to the root of it.

When Dom returned on Thursday he called Katie at home. "Hi baby, wanta do it again?" he purred. Within an hour she was at his house; this time he waited for her at the door and when she came in the house he swept her into his arms and kissed her repeatedly and passionately. An hour later they were laying in the bed entwined in each other's arms, satiated for the while. Dom was slowly teaching Katie some alternate, what he called, sex tricks. Katie had surprised herself; she would have never considered doing to Jimmy what she had done to Dom tonight. Yet she had enjoyed it and would do anything for him if he showed her what he wanted. So the affair was in full swing. Sometimes they met at Katie's farm, sometimes at Dom's little house during the week, because on the weekends Dom was with Becky.

Two weeks after the affair had commenced Jimmy came home from the Texas trip. Katie had dinner made for him and for the first part of the meal they ate in silence. Jimmy had a headache caused by the hurt in his heart and the lump of agony in his stomach.

Finally Katie looked at him and calmly said, "Did you read the book I asked you to?"

Jimmy kept his head down like he was eating. "Yes I did."

"Well," Katie said, "what do you think? You think we should live like that, like Jane and Arthur did?"

"No," Jimmy replied. "I want us to live like we do now!"

Katie glared at him but said nothing.

"Darling," Jimmy ventured, "do you want a divorce?"

"No," Katie hissed at him. "I don't want a divorce. Even if you want one I will not give you a divorce!"

A flood of relief spread throughout Jimmy's body. "You don't? I thought you did!"

As Katie looked at Jimmy a loathing of him filled her. She looked at his bowed head and meek demeanor and wanted to slap him. *How did she ever love this thing?* she wondered to herself.

Jimmy lifted his head and looked at her. "What about love, will we still make love?"

Katie almost laughed in his face. *Love,* she thought, *is that what it is, love?*

Dom had told her that sex without love was called fucking. "Fucking is something people do just for fun like on a date. Or maybe because they have to, like married people who don't love each other but still stay married, they fuck!" She considered it a rather horrible word, but it would suit for what she must do to keep Jimmy's paycheck and her respectability in society.

"Yes," she said to him. "You can still make love to me." That night Jimmy found what it would be like to make love to Katie for the rest of his life. She came to bed in her heavy flannel nightdress. She pulled the nightdress up to her crotch just far enough for Jimmy to enter her. She held the nightdress there with both hands wrapped in the loose cloth on each side, her head turned to the right, while Jimmy fucked her. She could handle this unpleasant chore if he didn't ask for anything else, or didn't try to kiss her lips. To Jimmy it was enough. He got to keep his Katie; in fact if it was possible he loved her even more.

The next time Jimmy came back home there was a letter waiting for him with no return address at the dispatch office. It was addressed Mr. Jimmy Burns c/o Slayton Canning Company, Slayton, Oregon.

It said, Dear Jimmy your wife has been seen coming out of a house on Second Street in Slayton, in the morning, A Friend. Jimmy read the note twice. What kind of sick head would send him this. They must have the wrong person—who knew Katie in Slayton anyway? He ripped it up and tossed it into the trash. When he got home, he was sitting at the dinner table and Katie was at the sink, with her back turned toward him, rinsing the dinner dishes.

"Honey," he inquired nonchalantly, "have you been in Slayton shopping lately?"

"No, I haven't been in Slayton for six months," she answered, keeping her face away from him so there was no problem of him seeing the smirk on her face.

Jimmy's triumph was sweet. He said to himself, "I knew it, somebody has got the wrong person!"

The next morning at the breakfast table Katie started to educate Jimmy about the way their marriage would be from now on.

"Jimmy," she started, "you know our marriage is not about love or sex, it is about family and economics. You make the money and I will invest it and we will have a very good life, but you must realize that I do not love you as much as you love me."

It was another blow to Jimmy's ego.

"Secondly is our families. I like your family and you like my family, and I know they like us. We will still see and do things with our families, there is no difference there, but I don't like sex! The sex we had last night is as much as you can expect from me, ok?" Katie held her breath while she waited for Jimmy's comment. After what seemed like an eternity, but in reality was only twenty seconds, Jimmy nodded his head yes.

The relief flooded through Katie, she had pulled it off. "I will keep up my end of the bargain, Jimmy. You will be well fed, have a clean house and a pretty wife, and someday maybe we will be very rich!"

Three months after the affair started Katie was lying in bed late one morning. She did not want to get up; the smell of Dom was still on the bed even though he had left three hours before. She held his pillow in her arms and buried her face into it taking a deep breath. Suddenly she felt a churning in her stomach, the bile rose into her throat and she sat up quickly, too quickly. She threw up in her bed. She groaned and jumping out of bed ran for the bathroom reaching the toilet just in time, she retched twice more. She felt really sick. She sat down beside the toilet holding onto the rim; slowly the feeling passed and she stood up gingerly and moved back to her bed. She stripped the wet sheets off the bed, pulling off the mattress cover at the same time. Thank heavens the mattress was not wet. Even though she was naked she took the whole lot of the sheets and cover out to the laundry room, put them into her washing machine and started to wash them. Then she went back to her bedroom and put clean sheets back on her bed; she climbed back under the clean covers and lay there rigid, her mind racing.

What have I eaten lately, she thought, a little shiver of fear ran through her body. *I hope I am not coming down with the flu, or have eaten some bad food?* She didn't throw up again and in about an hour she got up and ran her bath. Once in the bath the hot water soothed her and she felt a lot better. She thought herself very healthy and so she was. She had not even been sick since she was about ten years old.

Idly she thought about her period. Maybe that was the problem, she was generally like clockwork but she was late, it should have started last week. Also her nipples had been very sensitive this time, when Dom kissed and sucked them she cried out just a little. Dom had smiled at her. "Feel good baby," he had said.

A small random thought came into her mind; a chill went down her spine, putting both hands on her tummy below her navel.

No, she thought to herself, *no it can't be,* but all the signs were there. *But I can't have children,* she thought. *I mean almost six years with Jimmy and not even a miscarriage!*

She always took it for granted that she was the one who couldn't conceive; in fact before she had met Dom she was going to have her doctor examine her. After she had met Dom, though, the thought of a baby had left her head.

She would have to have it checked out though, just to make sure. "I am being silly, I am not going to have a baby!"

She needed to be anonymous, she couldn't have anyone she knew examine her so the next day she drove to Portland to the Oregon Women's Health Clinic; there she didn't need to give her name.

Chinook:

The OWHC, pronounced locally as ow-hic, was a state-funded clinic for poor women who didn't have either the funds or insurance to care for themselves or their children. They asked no questions but like the sign in the lobby said, "IF YOU CAN PAY PLEASE DO SO, that way we can better help our poorest patients!" Katie would pay but she would not give her name.

After the doctor examined her and she peed in a cup Katie was left alone in her room for about an hour. Her head was full of all kinds of scenarios.

"What if I am pregnant, what will I do, and why now, my life is finally perfect?"

The nurse came in. "Congratulations, you are pregnant, my dear," the older woman said. She noticed Katie's face drop and tears come into her eyes. "Is it a bad time to have a baby?" she asked.

Katie stared at the floor and nodded.

"My dear you are lucky," said the older woman, "you live in a very progressive state. Oregon has laws about reproduction that are different than other states. Would you like to see the doctor again?"

Katie nodded yes.

"Just lay back on the table, dear. Here let me cover you up, it is kind of cold in here at times." The nurse turned to go. "Relax, my dear, the doctor will see you again soon!"

Katie cried for a little while and then she dozed off awakening as she heard the door close. The doctor stood by her bed. He took her left hand in his and felt the pulse in her wrist.

"The nurse tells me that this is a bad time for you to bear a child." His voice was soothing. "We do have some options that can remedy this problem and if you wish I can tell you your options?"

Once again Katie nodded yes.

"As you are very newly pregnant the fetus is only a few cells and can easily be washed out of your womb. The procedure is somewhat uncomfortable but it is virtually painless. We can do this now but we have to have you sign a document that you believe you have been exposed to measles. This document is strictly confidential, it will never be made public to anyone, unless you and only you say."

Katie sniffed. "You say it won't hurt, doctor?"

"That is right. All you will feel is a slight discomfort because it is so early in your pregnancy. It is always important to choose an abortion early."

The word abortion smacked Katie in the pit of her stomach. "An abortion, she was going to have an abortion," her mind reeled. All her life the word abortion was an abomination. The Church said if you had an abortion it was murder and you would go to hell.

The doctor saw Katie's face go white, her lips trembling. "Darn," he mentally kicked himself. He shouldn't have said abortion. "Would you like some time to think about it?" he said to Katie.

She nodded yes.

After the doctor left Katie lay on the table. "I have got to get out of here," she said to herself. "I cannot have an abortion." She found her

292

clothes and dressed, she went out to the desk and paid her bill. She left a message for the doctor that she needed some time to think and went to her car. She sat in her car for awhile. Finally she looked in her purse for her keys; like always they were at the bottom.

As she scratched around in her purse a thought came to her. "Whose baby was she having, Dom's or Jimmy's?"

That thought stopped her. *My god,* she thought to herself, *I don't know whose baby is in my womb.* She stared out of her windshield trying to form a clear thought in her head. It was too much—this last added burden had done her in. What did the doctor say, "just a few cells, over with quickly, no pain?"

"Surely it would not be like aborting a real baby, it didn't even have a heart, or legs or anything."

In a few minutes she reopened her car door and stood up. She turned deliberately toward the Clinic and forced her feet to carry her down the sidewalk to the front door. She stood by the front door; she lifted her arm to open the door and it felt like she was lifting a thousand pounds. Her legs felt like lead weights as she dragged herself to the front desk. She looked at the receptionist. "Could you tell the doctor that I have decided to . . . to ah . . . to . . ."

The receptionist, having seen this many times, said gently, "Please take a seat, I'll call the doctor."

Katie sat staring straight ahead looking but not seeing. Soon she realized she was looking at the midsection of a uniform. With effort she raised her eyes to the face of a nurse, a younger nurse than she had before. It was a sweet face that shone like it had its own spotlight shining on it.

"Hello," a sweet voice came from the sweet face. "I am Nurse Jones. Would you like to come with me?"

Chinook:

Nancy Brown was born with a light emanating from her face. As a child she was invariably sweet, kind and charitable. Her large soft brown eyes emitted an innocent depth unlike anyone else. Her grandmother told her mother once, after spending a day babysitting the four-year-old Nancy, that the light of God shown from her face and her grandmother was right. Since she was old enough to comprehend God she had loved him.

Her Sunday school teachers were stunned at the intelligent questions she would ask, even at a young tender age. When most children had only gotten to the coloring of baby Jesus in the manger in their workbook, Nancy had already memorized many verses in the Bible. Nancy had always wanted to be a teacher. She said to her mother at the age of six, "Mommy when I grow up I want to be a teacher so I can teach children about Jesus!" Her Father, a Pastor at a Baptist Church, loved his only daughter very much and he always called her "my little teacher."

One night, in Nancy's eighteenth year, after arriving home from a prayer meeting, he came into her room to kiss her good night.

"How's my little teacher," he said as he kissed her on her forehead.

"Daddy," she said looking at him very gravely, "Daddy, I am going to be a nurse!"

Her father looked at her in surprise. "But Pumpkin, you have always said you were going to be a teacher and teach others about Jesus, why have you changed your mind?"

Nancy looked at her father. "Daddy, I didn't change my mind, God told me he wanted me to be a nurse. I don't know why but he did and so I shall be!" So at the age of twenty-five she was a registered nurse and working at a local hospital. One morning she got up and knew that today she would meet her future husband, because God had told her so during the night. All day long she had looked into the faces of every man she saw, but she didn't recognize anyone as her future husband. Finally she had finished her shift and left the hospital to walk back to her little apartment.

Bill Jones was a carpenter and for the last month he had been working on a new wing to the local hospital with his crew. It had been a bitch of a day; he had a raging headache. The night before he had been at a party where the pot and booze flowed. He woke up late this morning hung over; he felt someone beside him. Raising up on his elbow he looked into the face of a woman he had never seen before. He lifted up the sheets that were over her and gaped at her naked body. *Damn she is nice. I must have had a lot of fun last night. Too bad I can't remember it!* He quickly dressed and went to work. He was a little scared as he had been partying a lot lately, had been late for work many times and was in deep shit with his boss. Today he got lucky—his boss was on another job site.

The day hadn't gone well. He had made some major mistakes and had to rip out and start again on one wall he had been building. In the afternoon he had caught a glimpse of someone in white coming out of the hospital door. It was like a giant hand gripped him and turned his head in the direction of the person in white. There on the street, her mouth open in surprise, stood an angel in white staring into his face.

294

For some reason in that instant he knew that the angel standing there would be his wife. From that second on Bill gave up the party life. He would never again wake up next to a naked woman he didn't know and his lips would never taste booze or pot again. Five months later he would marry the angel; he had already been baptized and had become a Christian.

*   *   *

Now at the age of thirty-two there was no happier man on this earth than Bill Jones. He was a member in good standing and a Deacon of the East Portland Baptist Church. He had a pretty wife and three beautiful children, two boys and a girl. Just one thing clouded his mind and it had happened just this morning, Nancy had announced to him that she was quitting the hospital and joining the Oregon Woman's Health Clinic.

"But darling," he protested, "that is an abortion mill—surely you couldn't work there?"

Nancy smiled at her husband. "God told me last night that I was going to work there. I don't know why but he did!" So Nancy had been working there one year when Katie walked in.

Her Pastor at The South Baptist Church had talked to her and begged her to leave the job at OWHC, but she said, "I am sorry but God told me to work there!" The Pastor and the Deacons of the Church, one abstaining, had no choice; they told her to leave the Church until such time as she gave up that godless job. The other nurses and some of the doctors at the clinic had complained to the Board of the OWHC that almost every patient who wanted an abortion and was assigned to Nurse Jones decided against having that abortion. For some reason though the Board could not get enough votes to fire her even though most of the members wanted to.

Katie followed Nurse Jones to a small room in another part of the OWHC. The Nurse gave her a gown to wear and helped her undress and lay down on a table. All the while the nurse talked to her in a soothing voice, which at first Katie didn't listen to.

The nurse said, "We don't use names here so I call my patients either Miss or Missus. Could you tell me which one you are?"

Katie glanced at her. She felt like saying to her, "It is none of your business," but for some reason she wanted to cooperate with this woman so she said, "missus."

"So you're married. Did your husband ask you to have this abortion?"

Katie's backbone stiffened. *The cheek of this woman,* "No my husband doesn't know I am pregnant," Katie reluctantly said.

The big soft brown eyes turned on Katie and the face seemed to light up even more.

"Don't you think you should tell him, or are you afraid of him?"

"No I am not afraid of him, it . . . it . . . it might not be his baby," Katie whispered.

"Oh," the soft brown eyes melted into pools of sympathy. "The father is another man. Were you raped or did you give yourself to this man?"

"I gave myself willingly," Katie said now totally under the spell of that shining face and those brown eyes.

"Do you love this man?" said the nurse.

"Yes I do. I love him so. So much more than I ever loved my husband!"

"Is your husband a good man?"

"Yes," replied Katie, "he is a very good man."

"Does he support you properly, give you a good home?"

"Oh yes he supports me properly, he makes a lot of money and I can have anything I wish, but I don't love him."

"If you had this baby, would your husband accept it and bring it up well?"

"Yes, yes even though I don't love him he would be a good father."

The brown eyes moved closer to Katie's face. "Is the man who you love the same race as your husband?"

"Yes," said Katie.

"Then what is the reason you want to end your baby's life?"

"I don't want to end its life, it is just I am afraid that my husband would leave me alone with this child. That is not acceptable. You see I have lived in a small town all my life and . . ."

"Of course the humiliation, I understand," said the nurse.

"Also," Katie started to cry, "the man I love comes from Florida. He will want to go back there someday, I . . . I can't marry him, I . . . I . . . couldn't leave my home and my parents," sobbed Katie, "I couldn't go to a strange place. What if I didn't like it, what if no one there liked me, what if I died there?"

"How long has this man been your lover?"

"About three months," Katie wailed.

"And how long have you been married to your husband?"

"It will be six years in August," Katie sniffed, wiping her eyes with a tissue given to her by the nurse.

"How many times has the man from Florida made love to you?"

"I don't know," said Katie, though of course she did know and could remember every one. "Ten, fifteen times probably."

"Does your husband love you?"

"Yes he loves me very much, he tells me all the time!"

"Have you made love to your husband a lot?"

"Yes of course, hundreds of times," said Katie calming down now.

"Doesn't it make sense then that the baby in your womb is really your husband's baby? As your husband is a good man, provides wonderfully for you and loves you, don't you think he would stay married to you?"

"Yes, I guess you're right, he probably wouldn't leave me. He does love me and so do his parents and family, and my family loves him too!"

"Then there is no reason to end the life of your baby," said the nurse now pulling her brown eyes back from Katie's face.

"That is right," said Katie, "I don't need to lose this baby, really I have always wanted a baby anyway and my mother will be absolutely thrilled."

The nurse reached out and helped Katie sit up. She handed Katie her clothes and helped her dress, as Katie's hands were shaking.

When Katie was fully dressed Nurse Jones gave Katie a hug. "Enjoy your lovely baby. One more thing, if you stay with your husband you must never, and I mean never, even in jest or anger ever tell him this baby might not be his! Remember the God that made us all loves you, Jesus loves you, always turn to him when trouble enters your life."

Katie hugged Nurse Jones back and whispered, "thank you" in her ear. Relieved and smiling Katie left the hospital for her car.

As Nurse Jones started to pick up the room, she said a fervent prayer for the poor lady, and she prayed for herself thanking her Lord that he had chosen her to do his work.

A few minutes later the doctor entered and looking at Nurse Jones said, "Well, where's our patient?"

"Oh doctor, she decided she didn't want an abortion and she left." A small smile of triumph played on Nurse Jones' lips!

The doctor looked into those soft brown eyes in the light-filled face and said, "Of course she didn't," and turning on his heel left the room.

16

The next morning Katie called her father's office. When he answered his phone she said, "Father, will you be in the hospital for the next hour?"

"Yes, Princess, I hope to be in here all day. Is something wrong?"

"No, everything is fine. I just want to have a little talk with you."

"Come on then, I'll be waiting." Half an hour later Katie walked into the hospital and straight into her father's office.

He rose from behind his desk and came and gave her a kiss on the cheek. Holding a chair for her he said, "Well this is a pleasant surprise my dear. What brings you to see your old Dad."

Katie, still on a high from her experience the day before, bathed her father in a glorious smile. "Dearest Father, I have come to ask you a very personal question. Would you direct me to the best obstetrician that you know."

Her father's eyebrows shot up. "Oh Princess, are you going to have a baby?"

"I don't know, daddy dearest, all the signs are there but I need to see a doctor."

"Well," said her father, "I have worked with Dr. Ladner in Salem, he is a very good man. Shall I call him and make you an appointment?"

"Could you please, this afternoon if possible."

"Don't worry, Princess, he'll make room for my daughter!" After he had made his call to Ladner he took out his hankie and blew his nose, clearing his throat he said, "Ahem, at three o'clock ok, is that ok?"

Katie nodded in the affirmative and smiled again at her Father.

"Does anyone else know, Jimmy or your mother?"

"No, dearest, no one knows. I want to make sure before I get everyone excited."

"Well," he said looking at his wristwatch, "I think this calls for a little lunch. Will you join me at the Cafe, my dear?"

Of course Katie knew she was pregnant but she went through the ritual anyway. When Dr. Ladner confirmed that she was with child she acted surprised and joyful, wrote down all his advice in a notebook she had brought, and made an appointment for the next month. An hour after leaving Dr. Ladner's office she pulled up in front of her parents' home and knocked on the front door.

Her mother answered the door and seeing her daughter said, "Oh sweetie, what a surprise, is everything ok?"

"Yes, Mother, I was driving through from Salem and I haven't seen you for awhile and thought I'd drop in for a cup of tea."

They walked into the kitchen and April started water boiling. She picked up a cup and saucer and started toward the table. "So were you shopping in Salem?"

"Hmmm, no I went to see an obstetrician," her mother dropped the cup and saucer on the floor, her mouth opened. "Katie are you . . . ?"

"Yes, Mother, very!" In an instant her mother was in her arms, her shoulders shaking as she wept for joy.

"Does . . . does Jimmy know?"

"No, mother, you are the very first person I have told," Katie held her sobbing, laughing mother. "I am going to wait until Jimmy comes home this weekend, so I can tell him face to face."

Katie stayed at her parents' for dinner. When her father came home it was confirmed to him that she was pregnant.

April said to him, "Just a minute, you knew that Katie was going for a check-up and didn't tell me, oh John you are mean!"

John winked at his daughter. "I think you had better stay the night, sweetie. I believe I might be in the doghouse."

The next morning Katie called up the contractor who was going to put in her bathroom upstairs. He confirmed that he would start next week, on Wednesday. The day after Jimmy would leave on his next trip. Katie also called Jimmy's mother and asked her if they would mind if her and Jimmy came out to see them on Saturday. Then she poured herself a cup of coffee and sat down at her kitchen table to ponder how to tell her most important person that he was going to be a father.

Chinook:

Dominic Stanza had four children born out of wedlock, none of which he knew existed. One in Florida and three in California. His girlfriend in Coos Bay, Oregon had been pregnant but had miscarried early in her pregnancy and then, using her head, had started on the "pill." This was going to be different though, he would know about this child, because Katie was not going to just disappear out of his life like the four other women did. Katie was now very sure the baby she carried was Dom's. After the "almost abortion" incident she, much calmer now, had given it a lot of thought and the logic was evident. So Katie rehearsed very carefully how she was going to tell Jimmy. There would be no hugging, no kissing, just facts stated in a sure calm way.

Jimmy arrived home Friday night and after he had sat down to dinner Katie, standing at the sink, looked him full in the face and said, matter-of-factly, "You're going to be a father." Jimmy's first reaction was she was telling a joke.

So he looked at her and said, "Yeah right, me a daddy, ha, ha."

"No Jimmy, I am pregnant. I went to the doctor a couple of days ago because I have missed my period, and he confirmed I am pregnant with your child."

She watched the smug smile on his face melt and just for a moment she felt triumphant, superior and revengeful. Then she turned so he wouldn't see her gloat, and started to wash the pans in the sink that she had used to make his dinner.

She heard Jimmy ask in a stunned voice, "When did this happen?"

She shrugged her shoulders and without looking at him said, in a slightly irritated voice, "I don't know Jimmy, the last time or maybe the time before we had sex." It was like a fist had slammed into Jimmy's chest.

He couldn't breathe, he thought of the unsigned letter he had received at work. "Are you sure?"

She shook her head and fighting to keep her face calm turned to him. "Of course I am sure, do you think I would make this up? By the way, get used to it because tomorrow we are going to your parents to tell them!"

Jimmy went through the weekend in a daze. When they told his parents the next morning their farmhouse erupted into an outpouring of laughter, tears and joy.

Jimmy's dad slapped him on the back wringing his hand said, "Well son, you are going to make me a grandfather. I must admit I can't wait!"

Julie kept saying, "I am going to be an Auntie, I am going to be an Auntie," and prayerfully clasping her hands by her chin!

Katie basked in the attention because she loved Jimmy's family and wanted them to be happy. She felt now at this moment that this really was Jimmy's child. In the evening Jimmy and Katie went to her parents for dinner where the opposite was true with John and April making a fuss over the new father.

Chinook:

April noted that Jimmy didn't seem quite right. His smile, when there was one, was forced and he seemed very uncomfortable with the congratulations that were being heaped on his shoulders.

In an aside April said to her husband, "Dearest, do you think Jimmy is ok, he seems forced or something, not really happy?"

"Oh darling, he is just stunned. Gosh I remember when you told me you were pregnant with Katie I was almost comatose for a week after. All kinds of things go through a man's mind, darling. I mean, will I be a good father, what if I get in an accident and can't feed my family, it just never ends. He'll be fine once he gets his mind around it!" That relieved April a bit but she watched Jimmy closely and toward the end of the night after the children had left for home, she sat quietly contemplating this obvious, to her anyway, new problem.

You see April didn't tell Katie the truth on her wedding eve talk. She had said to Katie that the women of their family didn't have affairs, that other women may sleep with men other than their husbands but that they were loyal to their husbands for life. John had been missing in Burma for a year when his best friend from Hawaii stopped by for a few days on his way to the war in the Pacific.

Doctor Francis Douglas Lemon the third, beloved son of a grand old New England family, was the exact opposite of John. John was manly, large, dark hair on his chest and torso, with broad shoulders and muscled arms, Francis was short, the same height as April. He had cool blue eyes and blond hair; fine almost feminine features, an expressive mouth, with distinctly finely formed lips, which fascinated April. Francis told her how close he was to John. How for two years they had shared the same rooming house and had worked in the hospital operating room putting back together the shattered bodies of wounded men from the conflict in the Pacific. How he missed John and how he knew that he had been missing for a year. He explained to her and Ethel, over coffee, that he just had to stop by to meet them and to meet John's beloved little daughter, whom he talked about constantly. He also hoped to find out if they had any information on John dreading that he had been killed in action. When the ladies tearfully told him that they had no word he had held their hands to comfort them. He told them that he had four days to report so they begged him to stay with them as they had a bedroom open in their house and it would be so nice to have him stay, so stay he did. After dinner Ethel and little Katie went off to bed but April and Francis stayed up very late talking.

He told April how he was going to work in a hospital ship with the fifth fleet who at this moment were attacking the Japanese in the Marshall Islands. He told her that he had been home for almost a month on leave before leaving for his new assignment. How his mother had cried and how he had had this premonition as he hugged her that he would never do so again. After April went to bed she lay there for about half an hour trying to sleep but it was useless. Finally she got up and went to the room Francis was staying in. She entered the room and closed the door; she allowed her nightgown to drop to the floor and she climbed into his bed naked.

He reached out his hand to touch her. "Thank you, I had hoped you would come!" He ran his hand over her body, cupping her breasts. His finely formed lips found her nipples then her throat, her mouth. Slowly his hand caressed her body as his lips kissed her his tongue slipped between her teeth into her mouth. How differently he made love than John, who consumed her and entered her almost immediately. When Francis finally did enter her she was ready; she wrapped her legs and arms around him and pulled him into her. It was over quickly. He lay upon her panting, his lips searching and finding her lips in the dark. As they kissed he thanked her again, told her he loved her at first sight and held her until dawn when she went back to her bed. For the next two nights they went through the same scenario.

April didn't know that it was possible to love two men, yet she loved Francis as much as she would ever love John. When he left the morning of the fourth day she spent a few private minutes in his arms and she told him she loved him, she wept bitterly when he left. She didn't know if Ethel ever knew of her love affair with Francis, if she did she never mentioned it. April wondered if she had gotten pregnant by Francis. For a month she alternated between hope and dread. But when her period arrived four weeks later she was crushed and cried for a day.

On June 22, 1944 at 3 o'clock in the afternoon, the phone rang in the parlor of the boarding house. April was in the garden when Ethel called her in saying, "Dearest, Frances' mother is on the line from Vermont." April answered and her heart dropped when she heard a tearful woman's voice on the other end.

The voice said, "Mrs. Overmars, this is Veronica Lemon, Francis' mother. I know that Francis loved your husband very much and so I thought you like to know that two days ago he gave his life for his country."

*   *   *

Ishimori Shigimitsu was not a warlike man; in fact he was an avowed pacifist. He looked on with horror as his country devoured the countries on the Asian mainland and now the Philippines. But he did love and worship the Emperor, and didn't blame him for the carnage his country was inflicting on other less civilized men. He blamed the industrialists and the military commanders in their lust for power and riches. He was newly married and his wife had just presented him with a beautiful baby girl child. His heart burst with love and happiness when he sat with them in the evenings. But now his Emperor was calling him to come and give up this happy life for his country. For his honor and the honor of his family he could not refuse. So he left his home in his beloved city of Hiroshima knowing that his family would be safe and he went to war. He was chosen to be a fighter pilot. He loved to push his Zero into the clouds and see spread below him Japan, holy, sacred Japan. Finally he had the ultimate honor to be chosen to give his life to the Emperor. He was to become The Divine Wind, the Kamikaze.

On June 15, 1944 the enemy made the mistake of attacking the Mariana Islands, a direct threat to the homeland of the Japanese. On the morning of the 19th Ishimori and his best friend in the Kamikaze Mamoru were standing in formation when they were called to attention. The Commander of their wing strode to the front of the men and announced that the next morning they were going to apply the blow that would cripple the American fleet and drive them back to the Golden Gate. Ishimori and Mamoru bowed and congratulated each other that finally they would be privileged and honored to be able to give their unworthy lives to the Emperor and to Japan. They went off to write their final letters and to have their final meals.

The next morning they were sealed into their Fighters. Ishimori had a bandana wrapped around his head with the words, "I am ready to give my life to his Majesty the Emperor," with also the names of his wife and baby. They took off and flew for almost four hours; suddenly below them was the American fleet. One by one the Fighters of the Divine Wind peeled out of formation and headed for the ship they had picked to attack. Ishimori glanced over at Mamoru who waved goodbye and dove for the deck of a Destroyer below. Now it was Ishimori's turn. He followed Mamoru down, he saw Mamoru take a hit from the flack coming from the Destroyer and watched as his plane turned slowly to

303

the right and exploded harmlessly in the sea. It had been Ishimori's plan to follow Mamoru, but now he pulled up to look for a target he had a better chance to sink. There beyond the Destroyer lay a large ship with a big Red Cross painted on its side. Ishimori aimed the nose of his plane toward the big Red Cross, an easy target if he was hit. The flack got heavier, he felt his plane rock as he took a hit, but Ishimori was no longer in his plane. He was standing in his garden looking at the Cypress tree he had planted with his own hand. The chirping of a small bird in his Cypress tree mixed with a small giggle from behind him; he turned and there was his wife holding their baby girl. He smiled at his wife and reached out to touch her face.

Ishimori's plane, which was really a flying bomb, struck the Red Cross dead center and exploded in a million pieces. The Red Cross was painted on a large painted white square. The large white square was painted on a steel plate more than an inch thick that made up the side of the hospital ship.

Just beyond the painted Red Cross and white square and that steel plate was an operating room. In that operating room a young doctor was working on a wounded Marine. The name of that Doctor was Francis Douglas Lemon the 3rd.

John had gone to bed not long after the children had left, so April now had time to sit quietly in her parlor, on her large comfortable sofa, and contemplate her history. She had never thought of this before but, "what if John had been the one lost in the war and Francis had lived?"

She supposed, "I guess I would now be a doctor's wife in Vermont, instead of Oregon." When she spent those few precious minutes in Francis's arms just before he left for war, just after she had told him she loved him, he said, "and I love you my darling!" Then he looked rather guilty for after all this was the wife of his most cherished friend.

But he said, "Darling, if John doesn't make it and I do, I will be back. You'll never have to worry!"

April caught a tear on her sleeve that had wet her cheek as she had that thought. Even though she had known him less than four full days he was always in her heart, his memory tucked back in a secret corner. She had never regretted the three nights she had spent in his bed; in fact she was very glad. She had never had another man except John until Francis. She had always thought it would be the same. John would scoop her up into his arms and carry her to bed. He would quickly remove his clothes while she removed hers, a quick kiss and he would enter her, and would stay a long time. Francis would kiss her face, eyes, throat and her breasts; he would spend a long time kissing her nipples.

All the while he would caress her with his free hand especially between her legs. When he finally did enter her it was over in a minute or two.

Do I prefer one over the other? No, they were just different, she thought. *I but could have spent my life with Francis and I would have been happy and contented. The only difference would be Michael. He would be short and blond, with cool blue eyes instead of tall and dark.* She smiled to herself.

Now she brought her mind back into the present. "Katie, this was different, this was her daughter, her lovely shy daughter." She didn't like the way Jimmy was taking the news that Katie was pregnant. He was definitely holding something in. Jimmy was extroverted while Katie was introverted, but tonight there had been a role reversal. Katie was too ebullient, her eyes were too excited, her smile too bright, her manner too on edge. Jimmy on the other hand was too glum, too shy, his eyes too shifty, avoiding the face of the person talking to him.

Also why had Katie gotten pregnant now, hadn't they been married over five years? April knew that Katie had never tried to prevent getting pregnant. She had always wanted a child and had been sad when she had not conceived quickly.

"Well I hope I am wrong. I probably have acquired the mind of a wicked old woman." Shaking her sleepy head April went off to bed. She snuggled in close to her husband, felt comforted, and glad he had come home from the war alive.

Chinook:

The difference between April and Katie is that April loved both her men equally and would have been happy with either one. Katie loved only one, but was forced by circumstance to live with the one she despised.

Doc Baxter sat at his desk going through the paperwork of a case he had been called to by the local highway patrol. It concerned an old woman who had lived in the hills up a muddy road with about one hundred cats. Her home was an old shack with no plumbing, electricity or running water. Finally a relative had called the police and the police had brought the problem to Doc. The police and Doc had taken most of the day yesterday extracting the poor old thing from her situation. She was clean, highly sedated and resting in the hospital now. Doc still shivered remembering the smell, and the filth she lived in. What did the police Sergeant call her, "some dingy ol' bat?"

Just then his intercom button lit up. "Yes Mary?" he said.

"Doctor Baxter, Jimmy Burns is here to see you. Did he have an appointment that I didn't know of?"

"No Mary, but just send the dad to be in anyway." In two seconds Doc's door opened and in walked Jimmy.

"Well son, did you bring me my cigar? Congratulations to you and your lovely wife, the whole hospital is abuzz. I have never seen Doctor John so happy. Come, come, have a chair!"

Jimmy sat down heavily. Doc looked at him closely. "What's wrong, boy, you look a little peaked. You are supposed to look happy!"

Jimmy spoke without lifting his eyes. "Doc I, Doc I, I don't know how to say this but I have no one else to turn to."

"What's wrong, son, anything you say here will not leave this office."

"I know, Doc, I know. I consider you my friend and well the baby that Katie is carrying is not mine."

"Hey Jimmy, son! I know this can be a big shock to a fella sometimes, I had two kids myself, but Katie is a fine moral lady and by all indications she loves you." Jimmy didn't look Doc in the eye but hung his head. "And you, buddy, are a healthy young man in the prime of your life," Doc continued. "What would make you think like that?"

"Doc, did you ever hear that I was pretty sick in England?"

"Why yes, yes I did," said Doc.

"Well did you ever hear of the Congo plague? Well, that is what I had!"

"The Congo Plague?" Doc stared at him. "Yes, I have read about it. It was quite interesting, almost everyone exposed to the virus, they think it was a virus, I don't know if they ever isolated it, died."

"Except, Doc?"

"Except a butcher's wife in England and one American serviceman. My god, Jimmy, were you that young serviceman?"

Jimmy nodded his head in acknowledgement.

"I believe the young serviceman fully recovered except he was irreversibly sterile," Doc finished. Doc sat in his chair and stared dumbly at Jimmy. "But surely Katie knew this before you were married and would have taken precaution if she had an affair?"

"I never told her, Doc, she doesn't know. You are the only person in the world to know outside me and the U.S. Air Force."

"Good Lord, Jimmy, you married a woman and didn't tell her you were sterile?"

"I know, Doc, it seems awful but I just was too damn ashamed. You know I got it from a prostitute. She was the only woman that I ever had before I got married and I thought, well, I guess I just never thought."

Doc stared at Jimmy dumbfounded for a full minute finally rousing himself. "Come on, Jimmy, we can't talk about this here anymore. Let's go to my place!"

The two men walked in silence side by side the three blocks to Doc's house.

Once inside Doc pointed Jimmy to the couch in his parlor. "Sit down, Jimmy, do you want bourbon or scotch?"

"Uh, bourbon, Doc, Scotch tastes like medicine to me." Doc got out unopened bottles of Jack Daniel's and Johnny Walker Black Label and poured generous glasses. "You want ice or water or both?" Doc asked him.

"Just a little of both, Doc." Doc handed Jimmy his drink and sat in his old armchair just opposite Jimmy. They took slow sips of their drinks for a few minutes, the quiet settled around them.

Finally Jimmy spoke. "Why, why did she do it, Doc, why did she have to . . . this other guy?" he couldn't bring himself to say the word.

"Well son, there are a couple of theories out there dealing with the reasons women commit adultery. Actually commit adultery has fallen out of favor, not politically correct, have infidelities is the word most used now, it is less confrontational, less judgmental."

Jimmy looked at Doc like he was talking German. "What Doc?"

"Sorry son, I got a little too clinical there. Theory one says that because women are now liberated, that because they are no longer economically tied to one husband, per se, they feel free to have more and varied sex. That is because they were suppressed for so long by an unjust unequal society they have now broken free of the silly limitations that society imposed upon them. Theory two says women can't help it that they are driven by nature to find the best genes in the pool, so they have multiple sexual partners. I believe the latter theory. I believe that women have and will always seek to improve the offspring they bear. That nature forces them to do so."

"But Doc," Jimmy said, "I read a magazine just the other day that said only twenty percent of married women have sex outside of wedlock."

"Ah yes, probably a homemakers magazine," reasoned Doc. "They run these polls and the ordinary housewives lie to them. We, in the psychoanalyst business, know through psychoanalysis, that more like fifty or sixty percent of married women and forty to fifty percent of married men have infidelities."

"Really Doc?" Jimmy questioned.

"Well of course psychoanalysis is not a scientific model. After all, I am sure some people lie to their doctors. But we do have some hard scientific data that relates to this and that data is gathered by blood testing.

"You see, Jimmy, we have a measurement called the Single Family Unit; actually it has other names also but this will suffice. By Single Family Unit I mean a Unit of Family that contains 1 Father, 1 mother, and 2.7 children, and these 2.7 children are sired by the alpha male and bore by the alpha female. This is considered the standard family unit. Our hard data says that 1 out of every 5 children born to this Unit is not the offspring of the Alpha Male but of some other male not of the family unit."

Jimmy gasped. "You mean that if one guy and his wife have five kids one of them will be some other guy's kid?"

"Well it doesn't always follow individual families, some families have five children. All may well be the offspring of the alpha male. But some families may have one child, or two children that are not the biological offspring of the alpha male, do you see what I mean?"

Jimmy nodded his head. "Yeah, Doc, I think I understand, but damn it I gave my wife a very good life, she has everything she wants. I just don't understand why she had to have sex with Do . . . er with some other guy."

Doc glanced up into Jimmy's eyes, the hurt in them was real and deep. "You know, Doc, one night when we were just engaged I tried to make love to her. Huh, you know what she said, God wouldn't like it if we did it before we were married! I guess God doesn't care about adultery! Another thing she has been saying stuff," Jimmy fidgeted.

"Ah," said Doc. "Like what?"

"She has been saying that I am the biggest mistake she has ever made, and that if I never made love to her again it would be too soon! Also she wants me to be a queer!"

Doc sat upright. "Come again?"

"Yeah, she gave me a book to read about this man and woman who were married but he was a queer and never had sex with his wife, but they lived an ok life anyway."

"Well, Jimmy, that doesn't mean she wants you to be homosexual." Doc looked shocked.

"Well I told her last time I was home that some guy made a pass at me in a truck stop shower room, and she asked me if I had accepted.

"I said to her, hell no, I ain't no damn queer, and you know what she said to me?" Jimmy looked hard at Doc.

"No buddy, I can't begin to guess."

308

"She said, no such luck, no such luck," Jimmy picked up his whisky and in one gulp slugged it down. "I know, Doc, I wish I had told her that I was sterile. I know it is probably my fault also but that does not lessen the pain. In fact I didn't realize how much it can hurt. I feel like crawling into a hole and dying."

"Men have died and worms have eaten them but not for love," Doc quoted.

Jimmy looked up. "What did you say, Doc?"

"Oh nothing, Jimmy, I'm just being silly. I am sorry."

Jimmy looked down at his hands, clenched into fists in his lap. *Gosh, I wish I could understand just half of what Doc says,* he thought.

Doc got up and refreshed the drinks. Jimmy could feel the warmth from the bourbon spreading throughout his body and the pain subsided just a little.

He looked at Doc. "You know, Doc, I would have bet my life on Katie's, what did you call it, fidelity?" He giggled. "I'd be one dead son of a bitch now if someone had taken me up on that!"

Doc started to feel the booze also, and Doc had a secret that he had never shared with anyone. Now, the warmth of the alcohol and the feeling that Jimmy needed to know he was not alone brought Doc to his story.

"Yeah buddy," he said to Jimmy. "I know exactly what you are going through, and what you're feeling!"

"You do, Doc, how can you know?"

Chinook:

The pressure on Doc's psyche all these years to bare his soul to someone came bursting to the forefront, and he told Jimmy his most private secret.

"Jimmy, have you ever heard of someone whose name is Jock Kowaltski?"

Jimmy's brow furled in thought. "You mean Jock Kowaltski, the golden ghost? All-American halfback at the University of Michigan? The one who helped Green Bay and the Giants both win the NFL title, and now is the anchor on Monday Night Football?"

"Well I didn't know he had done all that," mused Doc. "I don't follow football that much, but I guess I know he is famous."

"Yeah, who hasn't heard of him, why?"

"Because," said Doc, "I raised his child."

"What, Doc, you raised his kid, but how?"

"Well I thought he was my son but I found out during my divorce that he wasn't my son at all, that in fact he was Jock's son."

"Let me start with my ex-wife. When I first met Jane I was stunned. I was just a hick from Iowa and Nebraska, I didn't know they made girls as beautiful as that. She was everything a boy could want. We were married just about a year when she got pregnant. I didn't care, it would be a struggle what with me still in grad school. But I loved her so much that I would have delivered pizzas. After the baby came it was fine. I was away a good bit of the time and when I was home I had to study, but she seemed happy and seemed to be coping.

"Then she got pregnant again and things started to go to hell, especially after Douglas was born. David was a stoic quiet baby but Douglas was always crying, fussing, needing constant care. It seemed Douglas took so much of her time she had very little left for me; we quarreled a lot. I was off for a conference in Philly and when I returned home in the evening she had gone back to Oregon. I guess in a way I didn't blame her, but damn I did miss her! After I finished my internship I headed out to Oregon. I got a position and we bought a house. She was already having an affair with her old boyfriend from high school, but I didn't find out about that for many years. Even though I may have suspected something was going on.

"The night Douglas graduated from high school she threw me out and her old boyfriend moved in my house. That part was the hardest. I still loved her deeply and to know this guy was in my bed and in my wife almost made me want to kill them both!

"Anyway the day of our divorce my lawyer and I arrived at the courthouse on time just to be told our court time had been set for two hours later than originally scheduled. We decided to stay rather then come back another day. I just wanted to get it over with. My lawyer went off to help another client. He found me an empty courtroom and I waited in there. After awhile I lay down on one of the benches and closed my eyes.

"In about half an hour or so I heard the door open and someone said, you can wait in here this room looks empty, and the door closed again. I heard some walking around and it definitely was someone in high heels, so I sat up and guess who it was? My darling loyal wife!

"When she saw me she started for the door then she stopped, turned, and looked daggers at me.

"It is no good, you know, we have come too far to return to where we were, she said to me.

"I thought her an arrogant bitch, but I played along. I said to her, are you sure, we could take up where we left off, I can forgive and forget. Actually I was trying to be sarcastic. I must not do sarcastic well because she smirked at me and said, we are well past reconciliation, Edward, we should have never been married in the first place. So I said, but Jane we had happy years, surely we could recapture that old magic if we just worked at it.

"She laughed at me, HA, HA. I was miserable from the first day I married you!

"Well what about our boys?

"Our boys, she flung back at me, they are my boys not yours, you are not their father!

"I tell you, Jimmy, when she said that I felt the knife go through my heart and hit my backbone.

"You see, Jimmy, when she was at Cornell she ran with four other girls; they called themselves La Group. All the girls were rich spoiled brats except Jane who was at Cornell on a scholarship because when she was in high school, she passed some tests.

"Her councilor, who knew the Registrar at Cornell, recommended her for placement at the University. Ivy League schools have very many rich alumni, they contribute vast amounts of money to scholarships for the intelligent deserving poor.

"La Gang, as I called them, consisted of Jennifer, aka Jenn-Jenn, whose father was some New York banker. Balinda, aka Boobie, father was a Chicago billionaire, and as the name implies she did have two very nice boobies. Teresa, aka Tessie, old Southern planter money, she is one of the most beautiful women to ever grace this earth.

"She married a guy name of Sailor, one of my best friends. And last but not least sweet little Margaret with the big brown eyes, aka sweet Margaret, old New England money.

"Boobie's last name was Kowaltski, her older brother was Jock and he was the one who impregnated my wife. Not only her but also Jenn-Jenn and Tessie.

"He also had sweet little Margaret, which I find almost impossible to believe, but didn't get her with child.

"It seems Boobie gave Jock to the La Gang members in lieu of presents on special occasions. Jane's special occasion was our first anniversary! Jane told me she confided to La Group that I was not very exciting in bed. So one night, just before our first anniversary, when I was gone somewhere, they invited Jane over to Boobie's house.

"They sent her into a bedroom and there lying naked on the bed with a pink bow tied to his cock was Jock. Jane told me that day was the first time she had ever been just fucked, and that in a way it was exciting because she doubted that Jock even knew her name. Needless to say she got pregnant with David.

"She also told me about Tessie. Her special occasion was her engagement to Sailor. La Group figured that because she was so infatuated with Sailor that she would never have sex with anyone besides her husband once she was married. Jane said that thank heavens Sailor looked quite similar to Jock, so he had never suspected Tailor wasn't his child, because Tessie would die without Sailor.

"I said to her, damn Jane if Tessie loved Sailor so much why did she go through with it? Experience, you stupid jerk, she told me, you men go visit whores, wine an' dine working class girls for experience, so why shouldn't we do the same? Besides Jock has such a great body!

"I said, you know I just saw Sailor at a conference on Psychiatry in Atlanta, he was bragging on Tailor. I guess he was an All-American at Harvard and now is at MIT, so now we know why he was an All-American! Jane looked at me and said, if you ever tell Sailor I will hunt you down and kill you, Edward, I swear.

"Ok Jane, I said, you had one fling, you got pregnant but surely Douglas is mine, he is so like me.

"Wrong again, she purred, his father is Welton I . . ."

"I screamed, you whore you fucked Welton, that loathsome bastard, Jane, he never washed his hair, he had dandruff, he was a fucking philosopher. You know how much I hated that smirking little prig!"

Doc's mouth formed a smile. "You know, Jimmy, just for a second I saw fear in Jane's eyes, her arrogance was gone and she was afraid of me. But I am afraid it was just for one second then the snarling bitch in her came back.

"You were gone all the time, and one night when I was nursing David there came a knock on the door. It was Welton. He had had a fight with sweet Margaret, she had locked him out for the night and he had nowhere to sleep. He was very interested in my nursing David, said he had never seen a baby suckle at the teat before, is the way he put it. So I let him watch, he had only an academic interest he said but I noticed he got a hard on. Well we only had one bed, besides I was very fed up with sweet Margaret for some reason I can't remember now, so I let him screw me. Actually he was very good at it, had a nice large cock and knew how to use it, lucky, lucky Margaret.

"You know, Jimmy, though it was hard to hear it at the time I am so glad she told me all she did. Because I could then make a complete break with her, I didn't love her anymore not in the slightest. So after the divorce I packed up my bag and never looking back, drove until I found Low Sky, and thank heavens for that."

Chinook:

Doc and Jimmy had a few more drinks and Jimmy passed out. Doc made him comfortable on the sofa and went to bed. When Doc woke up late in the morning Jimmy had already gone.

Katie looked up from making pancake batter when through the window of her kitchen she saw Jimmy drive in and park in front of the garage. In a few seconds he walked through the covered porch door into the kitchen. He had originally planned to just walk in, get some clean clothes for his trip and not stay for breakfast. However, the smell of bacon and pancakes cooking caused him to stop; he was terribly hungry.

Without looking at him Katie said, "You want breakfast?"

"Yeah thanks. Do you have some coffee made? I don't feel so good."

Katie pushed a plate of pancakes and bacon in front of him and brought him a cup of coffee. "Where have you been all night?"

Jimmy didn't answer her but tore into his breakfast. Finally satiated he addressed her, "I need to ask you some questions!"

Katie, who had studiously avoided his eyes since he had walked in the house, raised her eyes to his face with an unwavering steady gaze. "Ok, ask me what you want."

"Who made you pregnant?" was Jimmy's first question. She was ready.

"This is your baby, Jimmy, your child. I have told everyone that this is your baby, your parents, my parents, and soon everyone I meet will know that it's yours. You are going to be the father and you will always be the father of this baby. I will not leave you ever, if you want a divorce I will not give you one."

"Do you love me, Katie?"

Katie lowered her gaze just for a second in thought then met his eyes once again. "I like you enough to be married to you!" She continued, "Jimmy, we will make a good team, you make the money and I will invest it. We will be millionaires soon, we will have a good life and be rich. I will take care of you when you are home, you will have a clean respectable home and the best of food to eat."

"What about sex?" Jimmy asked.

Katie didn't hesitate. "We will go on like we are now. I can't give you more of my body than I am right now!"

313

"Well what about your breasts and nipples, you know how I like them."

"I am sorry I can't give you that anymore, but you can have regular sex, if you do not ask too much of me I will fulfill your needs."

Jimmy got up from the table and started down the hallway to their bedroom. As he left the kitchen she once again asked him, "Where were you last night?" He didn't answer.

Soon she heard the shower running and about an hour later Jimmy came out of the bedroom clean, shaved and with his travel bag packed.

"I will be back in about three weeks," he said and walked out the door. As she watched him drive down the lane she wondered to herself, *Had he spent the night with Becky?* She would soon find out!

Jimmy pulled up in front of Doc's little house and knocked. A very blurry-eyed and hungover Doc answered the door.

"Ah the young," Doc said when he saw Jimmy. "I may take a month to recover but you look like you never had a drop of demon rum touch your lips, come in."

Jimmy stepped inside. "Doc, I can't stay, I am going to work and as it is I will be late. I just need to ask you a very important question."

"Ok shoot, son," Doc mumbled.

"What I told you last night, Doc, will anyone ever know about that?"

"Jimmy," Doc came alive, "as a doctor, crap, better yet as a friend, no word of what we spoke of last night will ever leave this room, this I swear on my soul."

"Thanks Doc," Jimmy turned to go.

"Just one thing, Jimmy, will you stay with Katie?"

"Yes, Doc, Katie has informed me that this will always be my baby, so I am staying."

Doc reached out his hand and took Jimmy's hand in his with a firm grip. "I am proud of you, my boy, you did the right thing, thank you. A lot of people would have been heartbroken but for this courageous move." Jimmy smiled, turned and went to work.

Tuesday evening, the evening of the morning Jimmy left, Katie called Becky.

"Can I come over for about an hour. I want to tell you something."

"Sure sweetie," Becky said. "You want to come over for dinner? We are about to eat but could wait for you?"

"No dearest, I am not that hungry. See you in fifteen minutes."

Chinook:

When Katie arrived at Becky's she had an agenda on her mind. She would break the news of her pregnancy to Becky and see how she would react. She figured if Jimmy had spent the night with Becky he would have told her about the baby and she would act happy but not overly so. When Katie knocked at the door of Bessie's house she saw Becky get up from the table and hurry over to let her in.

"Come in quick," Becky said. "Tell us, we are on pins and needles. What is so important you had to come over to tell us?" The results of her news convinced her Becky was totally surprised. First Becky screamed, jumped into her arms then holding her at arm length said, "Oh, sweetie, how wonderful. Oh you have been waiting so long," then she started to cry and hugged Katie again.

"Now we will both be moms," she gushed, "and we can shop for baby stuff together and talk and lunch!"

"And I will need advice and will want to know what to expect," Katie said. They both looked at each other, screamed and hugged each other again.

When Katie left to return home she knew without a doubt that Jimmy had not spent the night with Becky. The plot thickened, "just where was he all night?" Would she ever find out?

17

The next morning, Wednesday morning, the contractor and his crew showed up to start to build Jimmy's new bathroom and bedroom. Katie left them to their work and drove to Albany where she selected a male Golden Collie puppy from a breeder. She brought the new puppy home and put it in a large box in the kitchen, there to wait for Jimmy. It was a sweet little thing, a ball of golden fluff with a small shiny black nose sticking out and bright gray eyes. In three weeks all would be ready for Jimmy when he came home.

Thursday evening at 6:00 she called Dom at his house. He didn't answer. She called again at 6:15, 6:30; finally at 6:45 he answered.

Dom answered, "Hello?"

"Hey, handsome, the long distance driver is gone, you lonely?"

"Hey beautiful, I am always lonely for you!"

"Can I bring some food, are you hungry baby?"

"I am hungry for you. I had a hamburger and a piece of blackberry pie at the cafeteria. Just bring that gorgeous body, that is all I need."

"I'll be there quickly," Katie whispered into the phone.

"I'll be in the shower, let yourself in," Dom finished.

Medford had been especially needy again, seems she was getting more needy all the time, and Dom was pooped. He stood in the shower a long while and let the hot water soak away his weariness. He shaved and just stepped out of his bathroom door when a naked Katie slipped into his arms. She had undressed in the parlor and was waiting outside the bathroom door.

"This is the way I like to find my woman," he whispered as he kissed her lips, "naked an' ready!" Their lovemaking was very hot that night, and when they finished he was bathed in sweat again.

She lay in his arms, her cheek pressed against his chest and her legs intertwined with his.

"Damn, baby it does get better every time, if that is possible."

"Darling, I have some news for you." He ran his fingers through her hair.

"Shoot," he said.

She pushed herself up on her elbow and looked him in the face. "I'm pregnant!"

A pang of emotion swept through him. "Does this mean you're going back to the long distance driver and leaving me?"

"No, silly, if anything I need you more now and want you more now than ever."

"But what about your husband's kid, surely you don't want to risk losing him?"

She leaned over and kissed the end of his nose and his mouth. "Darling, this is your baby. I am pregnant by you!"

"I think I am sterile. I don't think I can have children. How do you know it is not his baby?"

"Darling," she cooed at him, "I haven't allowed him to touch me," she lied. "Since long before we started making love. You are my only lover and the father of our child." Dom was starting to panic. He had never faced this situation before and Katie sensed it.

"Sweet darling, don't worry, you will not be involved in any way, and you will not have to worry, I will bear you a son but the rest is taken care of." Dom started to relax. "And thank you, darling, for our baby. I want him so badly and I love you so much!"

Three weeks later Jimmy came home. He noticed the box in the kitchen right away. "Hey, what do we have here?" he inquired.

"I got you a little something, as I have a little something coming I thought you should have one also! What are you going to call him?"

"I'll call him Laddie."

"Laddie?" Katie questioned. "Why Laddie, why not Rover or something?"

He glanced at her. "It is a name that someone used to call me, a long time ago."

"Really," said Katie, "who called you that, your mother?"

Jimmy didn't answer her. He picked up Laddie and scratched his ears. For a reward Laddie licked his face. From that instant there developed a lifelong love between the man and the dog. Katie then took Jimmy upstairs to show him his new bedroom and bathroom. She had taken all his stuff from their old bedroom and had placed it into his new rooms. Now there was no reason for Jimmy to come into their old bedroom. "Why did you do this?" Jimmy asked her.

"Don't you like it?" she countered.

"Yeah, it is fine, looks nice, but why?"

"Well I am going to be big and unpleasant soon, then I will be nursing and the baby will cry and I thought that you would be much happier up here, that is all!"

Jimmy shrugged. "Ok!" Later when he went up to bed he took Laddie's box with him. During the night Laddie whimpered and Jimmy rolled over in bed and put his hand in the box. Laddie curled up around his hand and they both fell into a deep sleep.

Chinook:

Now Jimmy had a reason to come home because he wouldn't have if just Katie had been there, and of course clever Katie had realized that fact.

When Jimmy left three days later Laddie set up such a whimpering and crying that Katie put Jimmy's dirty clothes into Laddie's box at night. The little puppy would settle under the clothes and calm right down.

So life went on. Katie slept with Dom when she could, she shopped with Becky for baby stuff, they would lunch and gossip, and do girl things. Each time Jimmy came home he noticed his wife getting thicker and thicker and Laddie was growing. They had had no sex since February.

When Jimmy came home in May he was very short with Katie. His temper was up and everything Katie said to him was answered gruffly or he ignored her completely. Katie couldn't have this, so that night after Jimmy went to bed she put on her long flannel nightdress, and her thick robe and went to Jimmy's room.

She knocked on the door. "Yeah," she heard Jimmy say, "what do you want?"

"Can I come in?" she said softly.

There was a short pause then Jimmy said, "Yeah."

She stepped inside his room. "Would you like to make love to me?"

Jimmy looked at her. "Sure," he said. Jimmy was much nicer to her after that, so she made a resolution that she had to come to Jimmy each time he came home even though his touch was distasteful to her.

Jimmy always seemed much better and much calmer after sex with her, and he had to be much better and much calmer especially around their parents. If this was to work all their loved ones could have no suspicions. Jimmy and Katie would have to portray themselves as a happy couple waiting for a blessed event.

318

                              *   *   *

The summer came and went and also the fall; suddenly it was November and Katie was ripe with child. She had moved into her parents'
house toward the end of October so as not to be by herself if something
happened. On the eighteenth of November she gave birth to a eight
pound baby boy. He had red hair and almond shaped eyes that were
such a light blue they were almost white. She called the baby John Norman after her father and Jimmy's father. Jimmy was in New Jersey
when John Norman Burns was born. He found out about the birth
when he called his parents; he tried to sound happy and enthusiastic.

After the baby was born Katie paid little attention to Jimmy. He
was around between driving assignments and went, with her insis-
tence though he would have rather not, to his and her parents with the
baby. He had never carried, held or touched the baby. When it was time
to feed him and they were at their house Katie went into her bedroom.
She had never nursed the baby in his presence.

Laddie was now almost fully grown; Jimmy, whenever he was
home spent most of his time with the dog. Jimmy would take his 30-30
rifle and they would walk up into the mountains. Up through the pasture, over the fence, through the woods and the clearing with the large
blackberry bushes, up the trail to his stump. There, seating himself
with Laddie stretched out beside him, he could look down on the farm
and for miles around. Also he could see the trail that led around the end
of the canyon into the woods opposite, the same trail that the bear
came up that first time he had discovered his stump. He always looked
for the bear but he never saw it again. Right below the stump was the
tall fir tree growing up from the side of the canyon. The tall tree being
there made him feel secure as he sat with his legs dangling over the
edge of the stump into space. Sometimes Jimmy would sit there for
hours with Laddie by his side, other times they would walk farther up
the trail to the top of the mountain.

Johnny was now three months old and Katie was starting to pine
for Dom.

"Johnny was after all his child, his son," she reasoned, "surely he
would want to meet his own son."

So one Thursday night she called him up. "Guess who," she gushed
into the phone.

"Oh let's see," Dom kidded her, "is this Patricia, or Tammy or wait,
Margaret?"

"Oh you beast," Katie retorted, "it just happens to be your woman
and, not least, the mother of your child!"

"And my lover baby too," he said.

"I miss you, darling, when will we see you?"

"Well," he said, "I have Monday off, how about then?"

"Oh yes we can spend the day together just the three of us, and I can cook for you. I bet you miss my cooking?"

"I miss your cooking that is for sure, but I miss some other things more," he whispered into the phone.

"There will be plenty of both big boy, what time will I see you?"

On Monday Dom arrived just before lunch and Katie was ready for him. He pulled into the open place in the garage and as he got out of his pickup Katie jumped into his arms. After kissing him she led him into the kitchen where lunch was almost ready. After she fed him he went into the parlor and stretching out on the sofa took a nap as she cleaned up in the kitchen.

He dreamt he was back in Florida, this time his mother was holding his sister and she was crying. A baby was crying but the sound was not coming from his sister; he awoke with a start, the baby was coming toward him in Katie's arms.

"Sit up darling," she told him, "and meet your son!" He sat up; he had held his sister before so he knew what to do and Katie placed the crying red-faced baby in his hands.

Dom looked up at her. "He is a noisy little sucker, ain't he?"

Katie smiled at them. "He is hungry, pretty much he sleeps or is hungry." When he spoke the baby hiccupped and opening his eyes looked at Dom very solemnly.

Slowly the baby's mouth spread into a toothless grin. "See, darling, he knows who his father is!"

"Could you just hold him for awhile, I have to finish up in the kitchen," she lied. Her kitchen was spotless but she wanted them to get acquainted. When Katie walked into the kitchen Dom looked down into the face of his son and it was like looking at a miniature version of himself. The eyes were like his and the hair was the same color as his when he was a boy. They both looked at each other in wonder for about five minutes then the baby started to cry again.

"What did I do, I didn't do anything to him," he glanced up to Katie as she walked into the room.

"He is just hungry, darling," Katie unbuttoned and removed her blouse. She took Johnny into her arms and sat next to Dom. She slipped her bra strap off her shoulder baring her left breast. Holding Johnny in her lap with her right hand under his head she cupped her breast with her left hand and inserted her nipple into Johnny's open mouth. The hungry baby eagerly clamped down on her nipple and she gave a gasp, and then snuggled under Dom's arm.

Dom looked at her. "Did he hurt you?"

"No, darling, it is just when he first chomps down on me and my milk starts to flow it always makes me gasp."

After the baby had been suckling for a minute Dom said to her, "How does that feel?"

She glanced up at him. "How does it feel or how do I feel?"

"Ok, how do you feel?"

"Like a cow," she answered.

"Like a cow?"

"Yes, darling, when I was pregnant with Johnny I used to walk up through the pasture and I'd see the young calves always demanding to be fed or ramming their noses in the cows udders. I wondered what it would be like to have an infant needing to be constantly fed, now I know."

Dom looked down at his son sucking heartily, his small hands almost gripping Katie's breast. "So you don't like it?"

"Oh no, darling I do like to nurse him. I feel like I am an important part of his life, that my milk is giving him strength and making him grow."

"Ok then how does it feel, you know physically?"

"Oh," Katie smiled at him, "it feels fine, but you know it is not like you. There is no tickling or kissing, this is work; I have milk and he is hungry."

"Ok, so he won't make you forget about me then?"

"Silly," she said, "of course not. However, there is one thing that is kind of irritating."

"Oh really, what is that?" said Dom.

"Well after he is full and I burp him he always wants me again. He clamps me until he falls asleep, and if I try to detach myself from him he has a screaming fit!"

"He does?" said Dom smiling.

"Yes, I have other things to do but he is insistent, actually he is not unlike his father in some things," Katie replied a bit testily.

Dom broke into laughter. "That's my boy. Only three months old and already knows about one of the finer things in life!" But this time Johnny didn't clamp her when he was full, he released her nipple. She gingerly removed her breast and handed him to Dom. She took a towel off the coffee table and putting it over Dom's shoulder showed him how to burp the baby. She went off to get a clean diaper and a wash rag.

She looked back at the two of them and saw Dom was talking to his son. *How sweet,* she thought.

Dom heard a little burp and lifting Johnny off his shoulder said to him, "Look son, I know this is your mother but she is my woman. Remember you are just here for the milk, I am here for the fun, got it?" Katie brought the diaper, changed Johnny and took him to his cradle.

She looked in on Dom. "I am going to take a bath, I'll be right back." Dom turned on the TV and in about forty-five minutes Katie walked up to him in a negligée.

She held out her hand to him and said, "I have taken care of the son now I am going to take care of the father." When Dom left Katie the next morning she was pregnant again.

Chinook:

Becky was not a happy lady. The normal troubles that she and Dom had been going through since the start had for the most part settled down. Their relationship had reached a lull. They were going through the motions, the fire if not out was definitely dampened, especially on Dom's part. For the last few months, especially after the Christmas season, which had been good, he had been almost pre-occupied. Normally Becky didn't see a lot of Dom during the week. Sometimes he stopped in at the office and they had lunch in the cafeteria, but mostly they saw each other only on the weekends. Every Friday night he would come after work and stay the weekend. Bessie watched Sonny if they wanted to go out, and if they did go out it was usually a burger and movie. The sex they shared was getting routine; it was fun and all but now they usually had it only on Saturday night, and Dom fell asleep as soon as it was over. While he used to spend time to make sure she fully enjoyed the act, now he seemed mechanical and preoccupied. They never talked of marriage; she had her engagement ring of course, but every time she broached the subject of setting a date he didn't want to talk about it. At times she panicked, thinking maybe there was someone else he was interested in. But he seemed so calm, really tired and he slept so much every weekend that she couldn't find justification to keep the panic feelings going.

Just lately, though, she had been having taboo thoughts; maybe she should get pregnant and then that might spur him into action and they could get married. She didn't want a big wedding, a Justice-of-the-Peace and a witness would do just fine. She just wanted, and she thought deserved, to get married so they could continue their lives in a normal fashion.

She really couldn't plan for their future until they made that step. What finally pushed her over the edge is when she found out in April that Katie was pregnant again. Her heart almost burst. So, silly girl, the first week in May, just after her period, she stopped taking her birth control pills. She missed her June period, she went to Doctor Overmars and he pronounced her well and truly pregnant. Now she did panic; for a month every possible scenario of an abandoned woman flooded her mind. She saw herself alone with two babies and no husband. Finally one Saturday night after some lackluster sex, before Dom fell asleep, she broke the news to him. He was already reeling from Katie's announcement that he was going to be a father again, now it was Becky. Becky was surprised though when he said causally, "oh," and turned over and fell asleep. She would let the fact that he would be a father sink in and the next weekend would sit him down and set a wedding date.

Dom thought that the baby Becky would have would be handled the same way Katie's baby was handled. He would be left out of the messy process and when Becky's baby was three months old he would start shacking up with her again. Imagine his shock when the next weekend Becky announced they should be married before September. He let her set a date and seemed to agree with her that the Labor Day weekend would be good. But in his mind he said, *No way would he marry this bitch. Life was way too short to be married to a freaky woman like Becky.* So he set himself a date to be on his way back to Florida the week before their wedding took place. He had told no one anything about his plans; he just wouldn't show up for work on Monday the week before Labor Day. He was paid on the twentieth of August, cashed his check and closed his account at the bank. All the money he had saved he had put into a cashier's check. He had one last night with Katie at her farm, and it was extremely good sex; she was the only thing he would miss when he left.

Wednesday morning he left Katie's house at 4 A.M. He parked his pickup in front of his house and walked the few blocks to the cannery. His truck was loaded and ready to go for Klamath Falls. At just before five o'clock he pulled out of the loading dock and headed west toward Jefferson where he would pick up the Interstate 5 freeway. The freeway was not finished past Albany as yet so he had to exit on Pacific Highway route 99. Route 99 was a four-lane highway through the southern edge of Albany. There were only three stoplights so it would-

323

n't take long to pass through this small farming town. As he approached the sixth street over pass he glanced at his watch, it said 5:47. He was making good time but his mind was on Becky not his driving.

"Damn her, he pretty much had his life set up for the immediate future, then she had to go and get pregnant and screw it up!"

He was driving in the outside lane; there was only one other car on the road this early morning, an older Dodge, it was in the inside lane. All of a sudden the car ahead of him shakily pulled right into the outside lane that he was in. In that instant he forgot about Becky. *Uh oh this guy looks drunk,* he thought to himself and he pulled into the middle lane just before he reached the 6th street overpass. Watching the weaving older Dodge he passed under the overpass. He had the sensation of his windshield exploding and then his world went dark.

Chinook:

The night of September 14, 1918, was a night of terror for Milos, Kara and Alexia Cacak. They huddled in their root cellar as the war raged over their heads. The allies, Britain, France, Greece, Serbia and Italy with 700,000 troops, were sweeping the German, Austrian and Bulgarian armies before them out of Serbia into Romania and Austria. The next morning the war had moved on but the small family waited until almost noon before Milos put his head out. The sight revealed to his simple peasant's eyes was of total devastation to their village.

"Oh, Kara, bring little Alexia and come see!" Their house was gone, a burnt-out husk. In the village, where they had both been born and raised, they could find no one; not family not friend nor foe, and they were alone. For two days they stayed; they had nowhere else to go, they knew no other place. But then one afternoon they heard the big guns once again and they were terrified. All night the war raged just over the hill and the next morning they packed some few pitiful clothing and food and left their village. Milos and Kara became refugees; they didn't know where to go so they headed west in the general direction of Dubrovnik. About ten miles west of their village, new country to them, they wandered onto the estate of a rich family. Stumbling out of the woods they were confronted by a huge house.

"Milos," said Kara staring in wonder, "we have come to the palace of the King surely, for there could be no larger or magnificent house in the entire world?"

Milos started for the house. "Come, Kara, my dear wife, maybe they can tell us of the war," but the large house was deserted. For two days they stayed at the house; the people must have left quickly for the house was unlocked and its contents unsecured. In the cellar they came across open trunks, in one there were golden vases and silver plates.

"Aiii Milos, I told you the King lived here, look gold!"

In another a bag of rich leather; when Milos opened it he found money, lots of money. Milos took the money out of the leather bag and put it in a plain old dirty sack. They left the house quickly and headed west again. They slept in the woods that night; they were terrified of wolves but none came. The next morning they started out again. That day they fell in with more peasants also heading for Dubrovnik. They left Dubrovnik on a boat headed for Naples, Italy because one of the men said there was no war in Naples. The money came in handy to buy their passage on the boat. They stayed in Naples for five years. Then one day while working at his job down at the harbor, Milos noticed a large ship loading cargo. On a pole by the big smokestack waved a flag, the flag was red, white and blue, with white stars on a blue square and red and white stripes. Milos had never seen such a flag before.

He asked Sergio his partner, "Sergio, what country has such a beautiful flag?"

"Ah, Milos, have you never went to school? Everyone knows that flag—it is the flag of America."

"What is this America, Sergio?"asked Milos.

"Ah Milos, it is a large country where there is gold in the streets and everyone is very rich!" That sounded very good to Milos. That night he went home and told Kara and Alexia about the rich country. The next day they gathered all their money, bought food and water and that night when no one was looking they stowed away on the big ship. One week later when the big ship was far out in the Atlantic Milos and Kara with little Alexia turned themselves in to the Captain. The Captain was a big hairy man; when he found out about Milos and his family he cursed in a great loud voice. Milos gave the Captain a big wad of money; the Captain shrugged said something to his first mate and Milos, Kara and little Alexia became part of the crew. They were on the ocean many days, they saw the Panama Canal and finally after almost a month left the ship. They departed at night when no one was looking, in a place the Captain called Portland, Oregon.

They learned quickly that there was no gold on the streets of America. Ten days later they turned up at the Strout Reality in Albany; the circumstances that led them to Albany are lost in the wind. Alexia had learned some English on the ship. One of the crewmen could speak Italian and English. He had told Milos that everyone in America spoke English. It was hard for Milos to learn but little Alexia picked up a surprising amount of the English words.

The salesman at Strout Reality, whose name was Eddie, found out by talking to little Alexia that her parents wanted to buy a farm. Eddie knew a lot about farms because he had grown up on a farm in the area. He was a very honest man, they liked him and trusted him so they let him count their money. Just west of Albany over the Calapooia River bridge ran a road called The Poor Farm Road. On that road a farm was for sale, ninety acres with a serviceable barn and a small house that needed some work but was solidly built. They paid cash for the farm with some money left over to live until they had their first crop to sell.

They planted strawberries. Eddie had mentioned this particular ground was not so good for strawberries but they didn't understand; all they understood was the word strawberries so they planted them. They tilled the land by hand until they could afford a tractor. Then they planted raspberries and an orchard with cherry trees. Soon everyone in Albany flocked to the farm for fruit and berries in season. The locals called them Pop and Mom Cacak. The Cacak fruit farm became famous.

In 1938, at the age of twenty-four, Alexia met a man and was married. His name was Robert Tins, or Big Bob as they called him around the railyard where he worked. Big Bob didn't have a family, he had been an orphan since before he could remember. He had been raised in an orphanage and once he had graduated from high school had gotten a job in the railroad switching yards at Albany.

They bought a small two-bedroom house across the Pacific Highway from the Railyards on Sixth Street. In 1940 Big Bob and Alexia had a baby girl; Alexia named her Louta, because she liked the way it sounded. In 1942 Big Bob went off to war; he kissed his wife and daughter and was never seen again. Robert Tins was lost in action in North Africa, his body never identified. Alexia went to work in the railroad office as a typist/clerk and raised her daughter alone, she never remarried.

Louta grew tall like her father. She was not a beautiful girl but she had a friendly personality. All the boys liked her because she had quite a large bustline; behind her back they called her "Lota Tits!" All the girls in her class disliked Louta because she flirted outrageously with the boys and the rumor went around that she let any boy who asked her "go all the way!" In her senior year one of those boys she "let go all the way" got her pregnant, but she graduated before anyone knew. She had her baby, a boy, and then Alexia got her a job part time at the railroad.

When Robert Tins the second was four someone retired at the railroad and Louta was hired full time. In 1948 the Pacific Highway was widened to four lanes and the Sixth Street overpass was built. When Louta got her full time job she bought a little one-bedroom house just south of the highway on Sixth Street for her and Robert.

Louta Tins was not a nice girl; she liked men and she liked sex. Her reputation was not good and wives didn't allow their husbands anywhere near Louta. So Louta frequented the Seventh Street bar just a block from her little house. Almost every Saturday night she would bring some man from the bar home for the night. Robert, now eight years old, slept in the same bed as his mother, so he had to leave when Louta brought home her "Saturday night man." They had a signal for Robert to clear out if Louta had a man; she would say out loud "come on in," and slam the front door. At that prompt Robert would jump up, grab his clothes, open the bedroom window and run over the Sixth Street overpass to his grandmother's house where he would spend the night in the second bedroom. So he wouldn't disturb his grandmother's sleep they kept the second bedroom window unlatched so he could just climb in the window and put himself to bed. Sometimes he would stop and watch the traffic swish under the overpass; he liked to do that. Toward the middle of the overpass were a couple of decorated columns with lamps at the top. Each column was square and they had decorative niches cut into them and he had found out a long time ago that he could fit into the niche and it was like a secret hiding place. Sometimes he would take a stick that he had hidden there, and pretend it was a gun and he would shoot at the cars like they did in the movies. Then one day as he was digging in his backyard he discovered a rock; it was almost as big as his head, round and smooth. He took the rock to the overpass and hid it behind a bush. Then, this Tuesday night, after his mom put him to bed he heard her leave. She had not brought a "Saturday night man" home on Saturday like she usually did. Robert was glad because he liked to snuggle up to his mom when he slept. She was warm and she always put her arm around him and he would cuddle into her soft breasts.

But because she had not brought home her man on Saturday night she was a bit grumpy and restless all weekend.

At 5:30 A.M. the door opened and his mom said loudly, "come on in." He jumped up quickly put on his pants and shirt and grabbed his jacket. Just before he jumped out the window he peeked into the living room and his mother was in the arms of a man and they were kissing. He ran to the overpass and got out his rock, he carried it to his secret hiding place and looked down at the highway. There was not one car coming at all, so he waited. He waited a long time, and then he saw a big truck and a car coming. He picked up his rock and got ready, he could hear the truck rumble and he saw it change lanes so it would come right under him. He counted to four and dropped the rock. Above the rumble of the truck he heard a "splute" sound. He looked down as the truck came out from under the overpass and he saw it turn to the right toward the car. The man in the car slammed on his brakes but it was too late—the cab of the truck hit the car and drove it through the guardrail. Quickly the trailer of the truck caught up with the cab and it began sliding lengthways down the highway. In slow motion it slammed over on its side, sparks flew out from under the trailer as it slid along the cement. Robert could see the wheels still turning, he could see the bottom of the truck. In what seemed forever the truck stopped sliding and the sparks stopped also. Robert ran quickly to his grandmother's house and climbed in the window; he lay in bed not sleeping. In a little while he heard sirens as police cars came, just like in the movies.

Becky was not having a good pregnancy this time; she was having terrible morning sickness and had been late to work numerous time lately. She was hoping it would clear up as the pregnancy moved along. It was a damn nuisance; she hated to throw up. She was also spotting; every night when she returned home her panties had spots of blood. She had taken to wearing pads. Dr. Overmars was not really happy about the blood, he said she should actually stay home and spend more time in bed.

Yeah right, I can do that alright, she had thought when he said it. *I am after all the bread winner for my family, me staying home is out of the question!* But to her it was worth it; finally she and Dom had a future together. In fact he had taken her pronouncement that they had to get married calmly, had agreed to the wedding date without any objections this time. Becky was a happy woman.

*　　*　　*

Becky arrived at her desk just after nine o'clock. She settled into her work when she heard someone outside the office yell and run by the screen door. She didn't take much notice; her assistant came into the office white-faced, her mouth open in horror. She was going to ask what was the matter when her phone rang. She picked up the phone, it was the dispatch office. They had just heard from the state Highway Patrol there had been a truck wreck and one of their drivers had died. She felt the blood drain from her face, she stood up from her desk, a black premonition sat on her shoulders.

She came from behind the desk and looked at her dumbstruck assistant, "Mary, what have you heard?"

The girl said, "It is Dominic, he is dead!" Becky felt the cold wind; it passed through her skin as it would through an open window touching her bones deep inside her flesh. She couldn't breathe. She felt the hot blood gush around her pad and run down the inside of her legs. She could feel her legs buckling; she could see Mary reach for her, hear her scream, the world went black.

Slowly consciousness returned to Becky. First it was a sensation of white, everything was white, then she felt a warm breeze on her cheek. She turned her head slightly and saw sunlight streaming through a window, the window was partially opened, that was the source of the warm breeze.

She heard a voice, "well my dear, you have awoken, good!" She felt a warm hand on her forehead, another picked up her wrist and felt her pulse. Then a sleeve was slipped around her left arm and someone pumped it up until it squeezed her arm tightly.

"Hmm, still a little low, you gave us a fright, my dear," the voice said. "You seem on the road to recovery now. Your doctor will be in, in just a second." She heard a "pad, pad" sound as the voice left the room. She must have dozed off for a second because she felt her left wrist being picked up again and Dr. Overmars smiling face appeared before hers.

"Good, you look much better than you did a couple of hours ago. I think you are responding well."

She tried to speak, her voice caught, she didn't seem to have the power to move her lips. She felt a prick in her arm and heard Dr. Overmars say, "Don't try to talk, Becky, just sleep, just sleep."

Late that same afternoon as Katie was feeding Johnny the phone rang—it was her father.

"Hi sweetheart, it's your Dad."

"Oh hi, Father, what's up?"

"I am afraid this is a sad call. Becky Anderson had a miscarriage this morning and is in Slayton hospital."

"Oh dear Lord, daddy, the poor thing, how is she?"

"Well it was touch and go for awhile this morning. I was afraid we might lose her as she was hemorrhaging, but she has turned the corner and without any more complications I think she will be fine."

"Thank heavens, daddy, do you know why?"

"Well it might have happened anyway, this has not been the best pregnancy for her, but I think what brought it on is that her fiancée was killed in an accident early this morning!"

The wind left Katie's lungs, her mind started spinning, her jaw locked closed.

"Sweetheart, sweetheart, are you ok?"

Unconsciously she started to rise from the sofa where she was nursing Johnny, her nipple popped from the baby's mouth and instantly he started to scream bloody murder. That snapped Katie back; deftly she slipped her nipple back into Johnny's screaming mouth and said, "What, daddy, what?"

"Huh, it sounds like my grandson is giving voice heartily, but I forgot you and Jimmy are close friends with Becky and her fiancée. All we know is that there was a wreck involving another vehicle this morning and he was killed instantly! Sorry to have been the bearer of bad news, sweetheart, but the reason I called was to ask if you could come visit Becky maybe in a couple of days to cheer her up. I believe it would raise her spirits and we need to do that, ok?"

Katie said "Yes, daddy," and hung up. He had left her bed just hours before, she could still smell him on her skin, how could it be possible that he was dead. There must be some mistake, he had left without her kissing him goodbye. She held Johnny closer, her tears started to fall down her cheeks dripping off her chin baptizing Johnny with her sorrow.

The next morning Jimmy made his obligatory call to the office before he left the load site in Kansas City. He asked, as always, if there were any other instructions, confirmed that his truck was properly loaded with the right goods and also to give his ETA back to the plant. After his report he was told of Dom's death; he acted shocked. In actual fact he felt nothing—no happiness, no sadness. But he quietly wondered, when told that the latest news from the police was that Dom had been murdered, whether some husband had done it.

That afternoon the radio-phone on the small island just off the west coast of southern Florida sprang to life. "Hello, hello, Stanza Fishing Camp, come in." Angela picked up the hand mike. "Stanza Camp here, go ahead."

"Angela, it's Molly. I have a call from the Oregon State Highway Patrol for you, hold on I'll connect you."

"Hello, may I speak to a Mr. or Mrs. Stanza please?" said a deep voice.

"Yes," said Angela, "this is Mrs. Stanza."

"Good day, Mrs. Stanza, do you have a son by the name of Dominic Mihaly Stanza?"

"Yes we do," answered Angela, "why?"

"Mrs. Stanza, I am sorry to inform you that at approximately 6:00 A.M. yesterday morning your son Dominic was killed in a car truck accident on Highway 99 in Albany, Oregon."

Angela dropped the mike.

"Mrs. Stanza, are you there? Hello operator, operator I believe we lost contact with the Stanza party!"

That night Angela lay in Rico's arms; he had blessedly fallen asleep, but to her sleep wouldn't come this night. She had called Rico off the boat and they had spent what seemed like hours calling and talking to various people in Oregon. The part that was hard to swallow was the fact that Dominic had been murdered by some little boy dropping a rock off an overpass.

Chinook:

As the long hours ticked away Angela revisited Dom's life in her mind. Until, for some reason, she started to reminisce about the only infidelity ever in her life. At about that time she had lost Dominic, in that it was never the same between them. It was like he stopped loving her; he was so loving and almost clingy before that moment, and after kept her at arm's length. She had thought about it many times and she finally came to the conclusion that he had grown up and it was just by coincidence at that time. She never regretted having sex with that large German, even though she knew she should. When she had confessed the priest just gave her a standard penance, and told her to reflect on her sin and to go and never do it again. She knew she had broken one of the Ten Commandments but if she never had been an adulteress she wouldn't have had her beautiful darling daughter. Though she loved her boys without condition her life would have been barren without her daughter. Something had always bothered her though about the time right after she left the German's bedroom and Dominic yelled that he was home with the shrimp. Then it dawned on her she had only heard one screen door slam.

"Oh Dear Lord," she put her hand to her mouth and bit it. If only one screen door slammed that meant Dominic was already on the porch between the screen doors. That meant he watched her leave the German's room; he knew what she had done!

331

By the third morning after Dom had died Katie was feeling much better. She had reflected long and hard on losing Dom and now in denial she saw a distinct advantage to his death. First she would never have to worry about him cheating on her or leaving her, sooner or later he just might have. Second Becky would now never find out about them, she always worried that one day he might have a slip of the tongue. Thirdly she had Johnny who was so like him that he really wasn't gone.

Then, of course, she was the only woman in the world to have had the privilege of bearing Dom's children. Secretly she had been not been terribly sad to hear Becky had had a miscarriage; she would not have liked being constantly reminded that Dom had sex with and impregnated Becky.

So this morning she had dressed in her newest maternity clothes, the pale yellow dress with the blue trim and the matching white accessories. She dressed Johnny in blue, a blue that perfectly matched her dresses' trim. She was sure seeing them both would brighten Becky's day and buck her up so she would be well sooner.

Chinook:

Becky was starting to feel a little better. When they had gotten her up yesterday morning for her first walk, she felt so weak and light-headed she fainted and they put her back to bed. The afternoon was somewhat better, but she still felt very nauseous. This morning she saw spots before her eyes and felt like she would throw up. Just after lunch Katie blew in looking like a pregnant daffodil; Johnny had to be left in the waiting room with a nurse. From then until she left it was an emotional roller coaster, she wept about Dom, and she pushed her swollen womb into Becky's view while babbling sorrowfully about Becky's miscarriage. Becky was too weak and tired to contribute much, and frankly wished Katie would leave.

Finally, leaving a shower of kisses on Becky's forehead, she left. Becky felt relief, but more depressed than she had before Katie's visit. She loved Katie, she was her best friend. Becky thought she would explode sometimes about Dom if she hadn't had Katie's ear to pour her troubles and frustrations into. But having Katie as a friend was not without cost, and Becky felt the cost now. She rang for the nurse and asked her if she could get a pill to sleep as her friend's visit had worn her out. The nurse took Becky's pulse and temperature gave her a pill and vowed to limit visits to family.

332

That night in bed Katie had a pity cry. She lay tangled in her covers with the pillow Dom had used in her arms and cried as if her heart would break.

"I'll never see him again, I'll never feel his skin against mine, I can never kiss him again, I'll never feel him love me again, my life is over," she wailed.

Two days later Jimmy returned home and she verbally attacked him with viciousness born by her frustrations and deep sorrow.

Jimmy casually asked her if he could visit her room that night.

The look she gave him scalded him. "Why?" she said. "You do nothing for me, if you never touched me again it would be too soon!"

Jimmy opened his mouth to point out he provided her with a pretty good life, when she rounded on him. "You are the biggest mistake I ever made," she said. "Don't you understand you make my skin crawl!"

Jimmy ran from the house, called Laddie and went up the mountain to his stump. There he looked down on his farm and misfortune.

For the first time since he had married he contemplated a divorce. But now that he was a Catholic he knew divorce was a sin, and if he wanted to keep on as a Catholic he would then never be able to re-marry.

Surely, he thought to himself, *if she feels this way about me she will divorce me, and I will not have to go through the hassle.* When he got home Katie was locked in her room with her baby. Jimmy went upstairs, packed his travel bag and left without speaking to her. He didn't return home until October and then only for an hour as he changed his clothing in his travel bag and had a shower. He noticed though that his room was cleaned and his clothing laundered, folded and put in his chest-of-drawers. He heard from his Dad, when he called home in November, that Katie had given birth to a little girl.

His dad told him that the baby was named April Julia Burns and they had been to see her. That his sister was over the moon that Katie had named the new baby after her. The baby was beautiful and was a dead ringer for her mother, except her eyes, which were like Johnny's. He didn't mention or ask Jimmy about his marriage problems with Katie; Jimmy was very grateful.

Jimmy came home on December 19th; he had the rest of the year off. When he walked into the kitchen, he said, "Katie, are you home?"

He heard a muffled yes; he walked over to Katie's bedroom door and knocked.

"I am in here feeding the baby, I'll be out in a while." In about a half hour Katie walked into the kitchen, leaned against the door jam, her arms crossed below her breasts, and glared at him.

"Look," he said, "I will be home until January the 2nd, ok! I know you don't want me around but as this is my house too there is no reason for me to stay in a motel that long. I won't bug you in any way, I'll stay out of your hair."

She just said, "fine," and turned and walked back into her bedroom.

The next morning when he came down Katie was in the kitchen making breakfast. "You want some?" she said not looking at him.

"Sure," he said glancing down at the new baby asleep in her bassinet. Johnny was sitting in his highchair playing with his food; he looked at Jimmy with large eyes and for a moment Jimmy thought he would burst into tears but he didn't. After breakfast as Katie was cleaning up the kitchen Jimmy walked down the lane to the main road and picked up the *Albany Democrat Herald* newspaper from its box. When he came back a cup of coffee was sitting on the kitchen table but Katie and the children were gone to her bedroom. At about 10:30 he went upstairs grabbed his 30-30 Winchester rifle, a box of shells and his backpack. He came back to the kitchen, made himself a couple of sandwiches and filled his thermos with what was left of the coffee in the pot on the stove. He put on his heavy hunting coat for the weather was cold with a touch of snow in the air, walked outside and whistled for Laddie. The dog came racing around the side of the house and seeing Jimmy with his rifle and backpack started to scamper around Jimmy with unbridled joy.

"Come old fellow," Jimmy scratched his ears, "let's go for a hike!" Wagging his tail Laddie led the way out through the corral to the upper pasture. When Jimmy was about half way up the pasture he heard a car pull into the lane; looking back he recognized Becky's car pulling up, but he didn't stop.

Becky got out of her car and knocked on the back porch door, no answer. She opened the porch door and then the kitchen door poked in her head and yelled, "yoo hoo, anyone home?"

Katie was sitting on the floor of her bedroom playing blocks with Johnny when she heard Becky's voice. "Oh that sounds like Auntie Becky," she said to Johnny, "let's go see."

Katie ran into the kitchen and into Becky's arms. "Oh, darling, how good it is to see you. It has been an age!"

"Oh, sweetie, I am so sorry I didn't get a chance to see you in the hospital when you had the baby," she said kissing Katie on the cheek.

"I was working long hours, Sonny had a cold and one thing or an-

334

other came up. But I couldn't stay away any longer," she smiled. "I met your mother on the street the other day and she said your little girl was so precious, so I just had to come see her and you, and of course my favorite boyfriend Johnny!" Saying that Becky stooped and scooped Johnny into her arms and planted a big kiss on his cheek.

Looking about Becky said, "Is Jimmy home?"

"Oh I think he went hunting just before you came."

The friends sat at the table and chatted over coffee then Katie made some lunch. After lunch the baby woke up and Katie brought her to the kitchen.

"Oh my God, what an angel, oh she is so sweet, Katie," Becky raved taking the baby into her arms. In a little while the hungry and wet baby started to fuss. "Oh I'll go change her if you want to clean the kitchen," Becky said to Katie. Becky took Johnny with her into the bedroom and talked to him while she changed April; she got a lump in her throat as she saw the naked baby before her. "Maybe she would be having a little girl if things would have been different." Taking a deep breath she finished diapering April and slipping on her little nightdress carried her back to the kitchen.

"Sweetie," Katie said, "I just need two more minutes, could you play with them in the parlor just until I finish?"

Becky took Johnny's hand and walked into the parlor, sitting on the sofa she picked up one of Johnny's small toy trucks and handed it to him. The hungry baby feeling Becky's breast pressing on her cheek turned her hungry mouth toward it.

Becky said, "Oh I am afraid there is nothing in there, my precious one, you will have to wait for your Momma." The struggling baby momentarily opened her eyes and a jolt of electricity shot through Becky. The eyes were almond shaped with pupils such a light blue they were almost white, Dominic's eyes.

She looked up. "Johnny darling, come to Auntie Becky." Johnny toddled over to her and looked up into her face. An arrow plunged through Becky's heart, she felt its path as it struck her backbone and she doubled over with the pain. "How could I have ever missed this?" She grabbed Johnny's small hand and almost dragging him into the kitchen confronted Katie.

Glaring at Katie she said, "These are Dom's children!" Katie's face went white. "You, you had sex with my man, how could you, you knew everything, I told you everything!" Now both babies were screaming in fear and agony. Becky released Johnny's hand and thrust April into Katie's arms.

"Don't you know anything about friendship, you knew the trouble

335

we were having and you used that knowledge to seduce him. Have you no conscience, no sense of loyalty, nothing, did you hate me so much?"

"Darling, I never hated you," Katie gasped, "believe me it is just I loved him so, I never meant or wanted to hurt you!"

"If we were married now would you still be fucking him and having his children?" Becky screamed at her.

"You are the lowest the most despicable . . . I . . ." Becky ran for the door.

Katie picked up Johnny and with both her children in her arms ran after Becky. "Darling, wait please, wait I want to explain!"

But Becky had already started her car and with gravel flying from under her burning tires was putting as much distance between her and that loathsome creature as she could.

Katie, bitter tears running down her cheeks, went back into her house. She went into the parlor and removing her breast from her bra guided her nipple into her hysterical baby's mouth. Next she pulled Johnny under her arm and cuddled him against her side, soon he calmed down and started sucking his thumb.

She had to think logically now the world that she knew and took comfort from was lying at her feet in shambles. Dom was dead, she had lost Becky's friendship, maybe forever, and she had totally alienated her husband. She calmed down and started to think how she could restore something and the only possibility was Jimmy. She was aware that Jimmy still loved her and wanted her even though she had had another man's children. Of course she had never admitted that they were not his children, he probably thought they were his children. Well she could get Jimmy back very easily and would start tonight. Of course she couldn't let him go too far. He had seemed happy with what she had been giving him since she had fallen in love with Dom. He would just have to realize she couldn't go any further than that.

When Becky reached the bottom of the lane she pulled onto the road without stopping to look. She turned so sharply to the right her car almost slid sideways into the ditch. She corrected and slowing down some drove on.

She didn't want to go back to Low Sky just yet. "Where can I go to think?" Then she saw the road, a track really, that turned north toward the hill that made the Richardson gap. She remembered that now far gone summer's night when she and Ralph had came up here. Ralph had brought a blanket and they had wrapped themselves up in it and had sat on a log overlooking the gap and the valley beyond all the way to Low Sky. They had made love twice that night; maybe that was the night she had become pregnant with Sonny. She turned right and drove to the end of the track. She parked her car, climbed through the fence and started up the muddy path that led to the top of the Gap. When she finally got there, she was puffing from the long climb 1,000 feet almost straight up. It was like she remembered it; the log to sit on was still there. She looked out over the valley and a sense of forlorn sadness settled over her.

How happy she had been that summer's night with Ralph and how miserable now. An icy cold wind blew up the face of the cliff. She shivered and pulled her heavy coat around her tightly. She moved to the very edge of the Gap and stood looking down at the roofs of the farm one thousand feet below her feet.

How easy it would be to end her worthless life. One little step and she could float down to that farm and the pain would be gone. Everything she touched, with the exception of Sonny, had turned out badly in her life. First her parents; how she had hurt them by getting pregnant out of wedlock, how her mother had suffered from the dirty tongues wagging away.

Jimmy, how her impatience had pushed the boy who loved her away and how she could have had him back and had destroyed that chance with her stupidity. She had pushed him on to Katie, and maybe she had destroyed his life also.

Then Ralph had died, her fault, then Dom died, again maybe her fault, and then the hurt that was buried deepest in her soul, the loss of her baby. The waves of guilt were crashing onto her like waves on a beach. She could just step, just one little step, and it would all go away. Just as she was about to step she felt a warm gust of wind wash over her face and just at that very instant strong arms encircled her waist and pulled her away from the edge of the Gap.

She fought the strong arms. "What, what," her mind screamed.

"Calm down, Becky dear, easy, easy," a familiar voice whispered in her ear.

She turned her head. "Doc, oh Doc is it you?"

"Yes my dear, it is me."

"Oh Doc I almost . . ."

"I know, my dear, thank god I followed you."

"Doc, how did you know I was here?"

"Well my dear, you almost crashed into me on the road down there when you left Jimmy's and Katie's place, you were all over the road and I thought I should follow.

"Becky, what would cause a young beautiful woman with everything to live for come to this forsaken place?"

"Doc, I had just found out that my best friend had an affair with my fiancée, she has given birth to two of his children."

"Ah yes, I know about that and somehow deep down I had guessed that you had found out."

"Did you know, Doc, do you think Jimmy knows?"

"Oh yes my dear, he knows."

"Also Doc, I have killed my two fiancée's and my baby, I have destroyed my mother's life, I just didn't want to live."

Doc glanced around and saw the log. Keeping a firm hold of Becky's arm he said, "Becky dear, let us go sit over on this log."

"First of all, your mother and father felt pain, every human being feels pain at sometime. Your parents were embarrassed and concerned for you not for themselves, their lives were not destroyed.

"Secondly you didn't kill or cause anyone to die, ok? Ralph fell asleep at the wheel, and your fiancée, what was his name, Dominic, was killed by a very disturbed young boy, who acted out in a way to draw the attention of his mother to himself! The last then was losing your baby. You know sweetheart that Dr. Overmars was afraid you might lose your baby anyway. You were having problems and he felt that the fetus wasn't doing well, I'm sorry."

Doc felt Becky tense and shiver so he quickly changed the subject. "Also Bessie and I need you and Sonny because I am going to be his Grandpa."

Becky murmured "his grandpa?" Then she turned and looked Doc fully in the face, "Doc, darling, are you and Bessie going to . . . ?"

"Be married," he finished for her. "Yes, sweetheart, we are. Didn't you see her engagement ring?"

"Oh, Doc, I feel so stupid. I have been so tied up in my own problems that I didn't even notice. Please forgive me.

"Oh Doc, don't you just love her, isn't she the most wonderful person in the world?"

"I do love her, sweetheart, I have never met a person with the capacity for warmth as she has.

"She is the polar opposite of my ex-wife. At first I had a lot of resentment about my wife but now I feel so sorry for her. She has not a clue about how the love of someone other than herself could be so sweet. I have come to the conclusion that everything happens for a reason. After my divorce I was destroyed, full of hate and loathing for everything, especially for myself. Then Bessie came into my life and I want to live and want you to live also, ok?"

Becky glanced down at her hands folded in her lap, "Ok Doc."

"Come on, sweetheart, let's get out of here." Doc steadied her as they rose from the log. When she stood up from the log Becky glanced over at the abyss that she had, just a few minutes ago, almost stepped into. A shiver went down her spine and she grasped Doc's arm a little tighter.

As they helped each other down the muddy trail Doc glanced at Becky's face and thought, *and all my East Coast colleagues think there is no god, what imbeciles they are!*

Ten minutes after reaching the cars Becky pulled up in her driveway. She got out of her car and started up the back porch steps. She glanced up into the kitchen and her heart froze—there at the table, with his back turned towards her, sat a man, who looked like Ralph. Shaking like a leaf she opened the kitchen door and the man turned and looked at her.

"Jack," she cried. "Jack, you are here," and she ran to his arms. She lifted her face to him and he kissed her lips. "Jack, you have been gone for so long." Next she went to Bessie. "Dearest, please forgive me, Doc told me of your engagement and I could not be happier." Then Doc walked in and after greeting Jack said, "Ladies, your men are starving." So the ladies, laughing, started dinner going. One and a half hours later, all stuffed with food, they sat sipping coffee.

"Mom, that was so great, I had almost forgotten what good food was like," said Jack giving a rather large burp.

When they finished their coffee Jack held out his hand to Becky. "Come on, baby, let's go for a walk."

"Oh Jack, I should help Bessie clean up."

Doc laughed. "Go for a walk. I'll help Bessie clean up. I need some domesticating anyway!"

The evening was warm and damp, a fine mist hung in the air like a gossamer curtain, brushing their cheeks. The smell of wet leaves and damp earth enticed their nostrils. Jack had put his arm around Becky's shoulders and held her slight frame close to his side.

"Baby, I would like to explain why I have been away for so long without a word to you."

"Oh Jack darling, you don't have to. You are here now."

"Maybe I don't have to but I want to. When I left you last time I was going with another woman, she was giving herself to me and being lonely I took it. When I got home I was going to break up with her because just in one week I had fallen in love with you and the thought of her no longer thrilled me.

"The background of this whole thing was my supposedly best friend in Seattle, a guy at Boeing I had met named Con. We used to hang around together after our shift at this one restaurant and bar called 'The Lazy Bee'. He was married to a really sweet woman and they had a couple of kids, nice family you know. They had invited me over to dinner a couple of times, and it was a great thing, I felt at home there. One day he said he knew this woman who was single and why didn't I take her out with him and his wife on a double date.

"I said sure, sounded ok. We went to this really nice restaurant down on the Seattle waterfront called the Polynesian. It was on this dock right next to the ferry landing and had good food. It was really neat watching the ferries coming in all lit up in the dark. I never saw anything like that before. After a very nice evening I took Con and his wife home and then took Laura, that was her name, Laura, home too. She invited me in for coffee and came on to me really strongly, I mean she was all over me. She said I was the kind of guy she had always wanted and a bunch of other stuff. The upshot was I slept with her that night, on the first date. That was another first for me, I was really flattered. So that went on for about a month. Then I came home here for Christmas and New Years.

"If you remember," he turned toward her, "I put you to bed New Year's Eve night?"

Becky smiled shyly. "Well I don't remember the putting to bed part, but I do remember waking up in my pajamas with nothing on under them."

"Well, baby, after seeing you, I wanted nothing to do with Laura anymore. I was determined to break off with her. So I called her and we met at the Lazy Bee for a beer, but before I could break it off she announced to me she was pregnant. I tell you I felt as low as any man could be but she was crying and said she was frightened so I told her I'd marry her. Well we married at a JP's the next week with Con and his wife as witnesses. We went along and she had the kid, we had this nice apartment in Renton. It wasn't too bad I guess but then the other shoe dropped."

Jack stopped talking and Becky stopped walking and looking at him said, "Go ahead, darling, what about the other shoe?"

He looked at her, his face twisted. "This is the hardest part. It wasn't my kid, she had lied to me, it was actually Con's kid. They had been having an affair for years and when she got pregnant, he looked around and chose me for the sucker of the day. The funny thing is they never stopped having sex, she was doing us both up until the kid was born and then started up again with him.

"You see, she would leave to go get her hair fixed and be gone a couple of hours or she would go shopping and be gone all afternoon. After

340

Timmy was born I would watch him because she needed time by herself she used to say. All that time she was fucking Con and I was stupid."

"How did you ever find out?" Becky asked him.

"Well on a Saturday about eight months after Timmy was born she left to do her thing and I was feeling like I had a touch of cabin fever 'cause it was a gorgeous day. So I put Timmy in his stroller and headed out for Lake Washington, which was about a mile away.

"We were walking through this neighborhood I had never been through before and as we passed by this apartment complex I saw our car parked in the parking lot. I go over to it and sure enough it is my car. Damn has it been stolen or what. So I hung around for a while but then I think hey maybe Laura has figured out her car has been stolen and is trying to call me at home. She usually went to this shopping center called South Center Mall. I had seen on television that they had been having a lot of cars stolen from the parking lot. They said on TV that the cops thought some professional gang was doing it. Anyway I go home but she doesn't call. I am getting worried so I call Con's house, his wife answers but she says that Con is not home, he had gone off to the store or something hours ago. So I just wait for Laura's call. I figure sooner or later she will find her car missing. Well damn about two hours later Laura shows up at home as if nothing has happened. I ask where she had been and she said shopping at South Center.

"Well I am just a simple small town boy not used to big city ways but I get suspicious. Anyway the next Saturday she goes off again so I set Timmy down for his nap and I get the girl next door to babysit. I walk to that apartment house and there is my car again, so this time I get in it with my key and drive it home. I sit by the window of our apartment all afternoon watching for Laura.

"In a while a taxi comes into our parking lot and Laura gets out and she starts walking toward our apartment. Then she sees our car and she stops dead. She looks up at our place and then back at the car. Then the darnedest thing happens—she shrugs and walks up to our apartment and comes in as if nothing has happened.

"She says to me, I guess you have found out about me and Con?"

"CON my supposedly buddy CON, you been screwing CON? I am screaming at her. She looked a little frightened but she didn't run. Yes, she said, we have been in love since high school.

"Well I said to her if you have been in love so long why did he marry Samantha, that is Con's wife name? Oh, she said just as calm as could be, he got her pregnant and he married her because of the child but he still loves me the best and I love him. So I called Samantha, she answered the phone and I say, hi this is Jack and your husband is screwing my wife!"

Jack stopped again. In a few seconds Becky said, "And, and?"

Jack voice became a whisper. "She knew, she had known since high school."

Becky looked at him. "Then what did you do?"

"I went to the bathroom and threw up. You know, baby, I never thought about who Timmy looked like. I knew he didn't look particularly look like me but not all boys look like their fathers, sometimes they look like their mother's side of the family. But as soon as I found out about the affair I looked at Timmy and he was the spitting image of Con! Why I didn't see that before, I don't know? Anyway I moved out, got a lawyer and sued Laura for divorce.

"One night after I sued for divorce the three of them came over to my new apartment and they begged me not to leave. I said to Con, will you and Laura stop sleeping together and Laura stood up and said no she would never stop but we four could go on like we had before.

"Laura said she liked me and didn't want a divorce, and other than sleeping with Con, she would make me a very good wife. I threw them out!

"We finally got a court date, and my lawyer called me in and said it didn't look good because the judge we got was something he called a feminist promoter, or something like that."

Becky looked at Jack. "What the heck is that?"

"Well I had never heard of that either but my lawyer said this judge is the kind that thinks women have been persecuted forever and he wants to make sure her and the baby will have all they need to live a very good life. Anyway he gave them my entire paycheck. When my lawyer said to him what I was supposed to live on the judge said he will have to get another job to support himself! Then my lawyer said that the baby wasn't even mine, that I had been tricked into thinking that it was my baby by Laura and the real father. He even had a blood test report that showed that it was impossible for Timmy to be mine."

"Really," Becky said. "How did he get that?"

"I have no idea, from our doctors, I guess. Well then the judge called both me and my lawyer to stand before the bench and he asked me some questions. He said, Mr. Skinner, did you have sexual relations with your wife before you were married. I said yes, sir. Then he said and Mr. Skinner did you know that she was pregnant before you married her, I said yes sir but . . .

"He said no buts, Mr. Skinner, did you know she was pregnant before you married her? I said yes sir. Then he raised his gavel and said I rule."

Becky wrinkled up her brow. "Is that all he said, I rule. What did he do next?"

Jack looked off into the night. "He died."

"He did what?" Becky gasped.

"He died, he had a bad heart. I guess his doctors said he should retire but he refused and he died right there."

"Oh my Lord," Becky put her hand over her mouth.

"I was looking at him and his eyes went dead, his mouth was open and his head dropped on the podium. It was creepy, I still have nightmares."

Becky took him in her arms. "Oh darling Jack, you poor thing!"

"Then it took a long time but finally we got another judge, a woman, and she said that if I pay five hundred dollars a month to Timmy until he is eighteen she would grant me a divorce. My lawyer told me to take that deal and I did. So Laura got everything, my car, our apartment, all our furniture and five hundred dollars a month for Timmy. I also had to pay for my lawyer and her lawyer, so it has taken me all this time to get that paid off, and get another car."

Jack was looking up into the bare limbs of the tree they were standing under. He heard Becky groan and felt her falling; he turned quickly to catch her but she hadn't fallen, she was kneeling at his feet.

"Oh darling Jack, marry me, please marry me. I will be the best wife you could ever have. I will have your children and nobody else's."

Jack reached down and lifted her up.

Smiling at her he said, "You have made this so much easier." Reaching into his pocket he removed a box and slipped a small diamond ring on her finger. He said, "Becky, will you be my wife?"

18

After Jimmy saw that it was Becky who drove up their lane he turned back toward the mountains. Laddie, who had used the time they were stopped to check the wind and a couple piles of cow dung with his nose, now bounded ahead of him. Toward the upper half of the pasture Jimmy noticed Laddie had stopped to check out something in the grass. He walked over to it and found it was a jagged piece of a tree trunk with a couple of branches attached.

How did that get out here, he wondered. He grabbed one of the limbs and drug the piece up to the fence and threw it over, out of the pasture. Then he turned toward the usual spot where he crossed the fence. Laddie was already there waiting for him. He laid his rifle over the fence, picked up Laddie and put him over then climbed over himself. He picked up his rifle and turned up the trail into the woods. Laddie had already disappeared into the trees. He caught up with Laddie and they both walked along together until they reached the clearing.

Before stepping out into the open Jimmy stopped in the trees and looked out over the clearing. A cold breeze blew along the open area and the snow that had fallen the night before still covered the grass. Out of the corner of his eye Jimmy thought he saw a movement. He looked toward the blackberry bushes that ringed the upper part of the clearing where the mountain started to climb steeply. Sure enough one of the bushes whipped back and forth and it wasn't caused by the wind. Jimmy stood stock still and soon he noticed something black move in the berry bushes. In a minute out ambled a black bear, a small one probably about two years old and three quarters grown.

Laddie had been standing at Jimmy's side looking up at him when a gust of the breeze blew at them. Suddenly Laddie growled and his hair stood up on his neck and back. Jimmy reached down to grab Laddie's collar to hold him, but Laddie bolted into the open and made a beeline for the bear.

The bear, who had been looking for what was left of the late season blackberries, didn't know he wasn't alone until Laddie cannonballed into him, sinking his teeth into his haunch.

344

It all happened so fast, Laddie driven by the instinct bred into him for centuries to protect his herd and the bear reacting to an unknown assailant instantly became a blur of noise and combat. The bear pinned Laddie with his paw and bending down clamped his mouth over Laddie's head and bit hard. Laddie screamed. Jimmy could hear the bones in Laddies head breaking. Pulling up his rifle he popped a shot at the bear. The bear dropped Laddie and letting his own roar-scream spun round and round and then loped up the old logging road out of sight. Levering another shell into his rifle's chamber Jimmy ran to Laddie.

Laddie lay on the ground, the blood dripping from his mouth, a cry coming from his throat ki- ki- ki- ki. Jimmy dropped down and gently lifting Laddie's head slipped it on his lap. Softly Laddie bit at his fingers then in a minute his body went into a series of convulsions and he died.

"Damn, Damn Laddie," Jimmy cried as he sat holding Laddie's mangled head for a few minutes.

Then, gently laying Laddie's mangled head down, grabbed his rifle and yelling you son' bitch ran up the old logging road after the bear.

Jimmy ran with his rifle cocked and ready to fire. When he reached a point on the road opposite of his stump he noticed some blood on the road. He stopped, and suddenly he smelled wet fir like a wet dog but mixed with earth.

The bear was there, standing just off the left of the road where some small saplings grew. They were almost nose to nose; the bear was stunned. Jimmy could see the trail of the bullet he had fired at the bear. It started at the bridge of his nose and ran toward his eye; Jimmy could see the bear's skull where the bullet had progressed. His left eye was gone; there was just a hole in his skull where the eye had been. The bear's powerful arms hung down by its side. Slowly, together, in a dance they shuffled round locked eye to eye until bear's back was to the down slope and Jimmy's stump. Jimmy's rifle was at his hip pointed slightly up just an inch from the bear's solar plexus. Just at that second Jimmy's finger found the trigger and he pulled it.

It was like a giant hand pushed the bear away from him. At the crack of the rifle the bear took one step back, lost his balance and fell. On the way down as the bullet ploughed through its chest it rolled up into a ball. The bear crashed through the small firs that had grown around Jimmy's stump, bounced like a ball over the stump and plunged over the edge into the canyon. In a second Jimmy heard a terrible sound halfway between a baby's cry and a howling wind.

Gingerly, still shaking, he made his way down to his stump and looked over the edge down toward his tree. Then he realized where that piece of trunk had come from that he had found in the pasture, blown almost one half mile. His tree had been hit by lightning and the top had been splintered making it like a needle.

The bear's carcass was impaled on the treetop, the needle protruding out through its stomach. It lay there, its paws open to the sky, its head back exposing the throat. The lighting after striking the top of the tree had run down the trunk in a spiral. Now the dark sinister blood of the bear ran down the spiral, changing the color of the wood to red. Jimmy sat on his stump, his legs dangling in air. He looked down on the farm and noticed Becky's car was gone.

The low point in Jimmy's life came now. Deep depression filled his being. How long did he sit there running his failed life through his mind while he watched the blood spiral ever down the tree? He levered another shell into the chamber of the rifle and slowly moved the end of the barrel up until it was pointing under his chin. His finger moved to the trigger and it started to tighten on it.

Just then the warm wind blew over his face, and a fog enveloped him. He could smell the coal smoke and in front of his eyes he saw a sign, "Crawford Street."

A voice said, "Don't be daft, Laddie, don't be daft." Kathleen stood before him holding a bundle of rags to her bosom. "Ya canna be doin what your thinken, Laddie, ya canna!"

"But, Kathleen, my life is such a waste. Almost everything I love has turned against me."

"Aye Laddie, ya hav had a wee bit o trouble tha is true, but everyone has trouble, Laddie, no mon is immune."

"But Kathleen, I can't even have my own children, another man has impregnated my wife."

"Aye Laddie, still part of tha is not true."

"What part is not true?"

"Weel, Laddie, ya do hav a son," with that she pulled the bundle of rags from her bosom. A pop sounded and the wail of a tiny baby filled the air. Kathleen turned the bundle of rags around and there was a small infant with Jimmy's face in miniature.

"Kathleen, how could you have been pregnant?"

"I doe no, Laddie, I didna no meself until I crossed over. We will be waitin' here for ya, Laddie, but ya canna do that daft thing or you won't be wi us, Laddie, do ya no understan?"

"Yes I understand, Kathleen," Jimmy answered lowering the rifle barrel. "Kathleen, where is your little black baby?"

"Ah Laddie, he is wi his Da, just like your wee bairn weel be wi you in God's time. Laddie, your wee wifie weel never love ya, but her wee bairns weel, you are their Da on earth. Go bac, Laddie, and raise up them bairns for they are innocent o their mather's sin. Raise them up proper, Laddie an ya will join us here."

With that Kathleen, the baby and the fog were gone and once again he was looking at the dead bear. Jimmy stood up on his stump. He levered all the shells that were still in his rifle out into the canyon. Then taking the rifle barrel in his hand he slowly started to spin on his stump. Faster and faster until he released the rifle. It arched out and down hitting the tree where it protruded out of the bear's belly. It dropped on to the bear's belly and stayed there.

Without a backward glance Jimmy left his stump forever. He walked down to the clearing and gathered Laddie's now stiffening body in his arms. Carrying his dog's body he walked down the trail over the fence and down through the pasture toward his farm, to his children.

Book Three

Epilogue

Chinook:

My people the Chinook, the Haida, the Tlingit and their countless family groups came into the Pacific Northwest during the Ice Age. They moved down the coast from the Alaskan land bridge in skin and then later Cedar log boats. They populated an ice-free land on the eastern edge of the great ocean. I took great care of my people sending them untold millions of salmon to every river and stream. The beaches were filled with shellfish, the woods with deer and elk. They thanked me by naming me the Sprit Chinook. They used my bounty but did not destroy it.

The years have passed, the West my people knew has changed. The West is now more like the East, the wilderness gone except where it is managed in National Parks and forests. Jimmy's generation was the last to be born in a West where a man could provide for his family with a gun and a fishing pole. The final downfall of the West was brought about by World War Two, and the shift to the West of large portions of the population of the United States. Of course the large cities of the West had for many years brought the seeds of destruction to the frontier from the eastern cities. Gold, timber, clean water, unsaved souls and open land nurtured Los Angeles, San Francisco, Portland and Seattle.

First came the explorers, the Spanish, the British, the Russians, then the fur trappers, the businessmen, the lawyers, the railroads and the labor unions. Each group brought something from the East: whether disease or exploitation or greed, each ingredient took something away from this paradise. Now the West is indistinguishable from the East, the open land filled, the water dirty with pollution, the wild animals driven back into small nooks of semi wilderness. Lastly the "cult of the victim" has sapped the strength and the fortitude of the western people. It is now considered a ridiculous idea that people take responsibility for their thoughts or actions. Someone else must be blamed for any wrong done to an individual whether imagined or real.

351

When Jimmy stood on his stump, twirled around and launched his rifle off the mountain toward the slain and impaled bear symbolically he signaled the end of the frontier. So it will be until men move off the earth and start to colonize the planets and moons of our solar system. Homo sapiens need frontiers for the frontier gives them a reason to exist. To fill the void with their kind, to live and be men.

2000 A.D.:

Joe and Barbara Wallis:

Joe never fully recovered from the beating the union thugs had given him. His strength never fully returned but he didn't hold a grudge. He always said that the beating "allowed me to do my labor of love, to work my farm." One fall evening in 1982 after dinner he said to Barbara, "Sweetheart, I feel tired tonight. I think I will turn in early." When Barbara came to bed a couple of hours later he was sleeping very peacefully and deeply. The next morning when she awoke she kissed his brow to awaken him and he was cold. They told her the repair of his aorta had given way and he passed in his sleep.

Joe had asked Jimmy about the opening of Dominic's job after he had been killed; he wanted it for his new son-in-law. Jimmy had gone to Jake Johnson and Jake hired the young man. After Joe's death the couple, now with two growing boys, sold their house in Slayton and moved to the farm. Barbara is now a robust ninety years old and still runs the farm with the help of her daughter and son-in-law.

John and April Overmars:

After Michael graduated from University of California Medical School, he did his residency at Saint Francis Aquinas Hospital in Denver, Colorado. He returned to Low Sky five years later and took over at the hospital. He married his old high school sweetheart whom had been widowed by a logging accident two years earlier. Doctor John Overmars then became semi-retired devoting more time to fishing and doing a bit of traveling with his wife April and spending winters in a warm climate with their close friends the Baxters. He died early in 2000 a few months before his eighty-seventh birthday. John had had cancer for over a year; only two people knew, himself and his son Mi-

352

chael, who was sworn to secrecy. Toward the end he had quite a lot of pain but Michael had put him on steadily stronger doses of morphine, and he could comfortably live with that. After John's death Michael, his wife and her daughter from her first marriage moved into the family home with April. April will live five more years and die at eighty-six years of age surrounded by her loving family.

Edward and Bessie Baxter:

One week after Jack Skinner had proposed marriage to Becky Anderson they were married by a Justice-of-the-Peace in a double wedding along with Edward Baxter and Bessie Skinner. The two couples eloped with Sonny and Becky's parents, who were the witnesses, to Portland. Low Sky only learned of the marriages the next day when the wedding party returned to town. Doc and Bessie are now both in their eighties and healthy. They live quietly in the same house in Low Sky. Right after they were married Doc took Bessie back to Nebraska to meet his family.

They all loved Bessie!

Doc's brother asked him, "Why in the name of reason didn't you marry a lady like Bessie in the first place instead of that hyper bitch?" Doc and Bessie wintered with John and April in Palm Springs for seven years; the two couples were almost inseparable. Doc reconciled with his sons from his previous marriage. The two boys now both married love to bring their families to Low Sky; they refer to it as Quaint-ville. Doc and Bessie also visit Seattle a lot visiting Jack and Becky their grandchildren and now their great grandchildren. They are very happy and love each other intensely.

Jack and Becky Skinner:

After their wedding Jack and Becky lived in Renton, Washington, where Jack worked on the 727 and 737 lines. Later the "Lazy B," as the employees called Boeing, transferred him to Everett and he joined the 747 team. They bought a house on a view lot over looking the Possession Sound and Whidbey Island. The house was located in a small town named Mukilteo, a five minute commute from the Boeing Everett plant.

Jack adopted Sonny. He is so like Jack in his movements, looks and personality that there are times Becky forgets that Ralph was his biological father. Becky produced one more son and two daughters for Jack. They always said they had the perfect family, two of each.

The boys went to Washington State University and the girls went to The University of Washington. Cougars and Huskies mix like water and oil so during football season the family was divided, maybe even at war, until the Apple Cup was over. After thirty-nine years with Boeing Jack took a company offered early retirement in November 1999. With the kids all out of college their home paid for and a good retirement check Jack and Becky bought a motor home. They spend a lot of time on the road, they even took Doc and Bessie on a couple of long trips into the Canadian Rockies. Oh yes, I almost forgot, they are proud grandparents now. Sonny and Sheila, his wife, have two little boys, and their oldest daughter is pregnant. Life is so good for the Skinner family.

A few years before he retired Jack happened to meet his ex-wife Laura one day as he was shopping at Everett Mall. She had borne Con two children, she still was sleeping with him and they still weren't married. She told Jack that Con had retired from Boeing and he was no longer supporting her because he couldn't afford to, otherwise things were exactly the same as they were more than twenty years before. She hinted to Jack that she would like to be his wife again, that she was very happy when they were married. Jack totally ignored that hint. When he returned home he told Becky about the encounter. They looked at each other, both gave a small involuntary shudder and fell into each other's arms.

Becky was the only one to speak, "My Lord, what a poor woman!"

Katie Burns (Overmars):

After Jimmy had returned from the mountains that evening, he seemed a changed man and Katie swore to herself that she would be a better, faithful, wife. After all she had her children now and it was time to focus on the wealth building future. She even returned to the church after a soul purging confession at Our Lady of the Valley Church in Lebanon where no one knew her. She kept up her weekly shopping trip to Salem, though she now went alone. She had two built-in babysitters in April and Jimmy's mom who both were available to take their adored grandchildren anytime. So each Thursday morning she would drop off the children at one or the other's and flee to Salem. She had taken to having lunch at the Entrée Cafeteria because it was a very lively scene and she loved people watching. She tried, she really tried to be a faithful wife and for two years she succeeded. She was getting restless though and she ached for Dom's kisses and his arms around her. He came to her in the night sometimes and she would feel a little better after that.

Then one lunchtime as she quietly ate her food at the Entrée she heard a familiar voice say, "Miss Overmars, is that you?" She looked up and there stood Thomas Daily, a salesman from Valley Distributing Company. When she worked at Thurston's Market he was the wholesale rep that she bought the majority of the grocery's inventory from. She had thought him extremely handsome all those years ago. He was tall, slender and dark haired with laughing blue eyes and a sweet smile.

She remembered she had wished that he was single, but he wasn't. In fact he was newly married then, and when he talked about his new wife his eyes would light up. Now his hair was receding slightly, and he had put on some weight especially around his middle. Also he now sported a mustache but the sweet smile he gave her was the same.

"May I join you, Miss Overmars," he beamed at her.

"Of course, Mr. Daily, please do," she smiled back at him.

"Oh, call me Tom. Mr. Daily sounds like my father."

"I shall, but you must call me Katie and I am no longer Miss Overmars, I am Mrs. Burns now!"

"Excuse me Mrs. Bu—, er, I mean Katie." They talked for over an hour, she told him about Jimmy and her children and he told her about his family. He had three children and his wife was eight months pregnant with their fourth. Katie noticed how his eyes didn't sparkle anymore when he mentioned his wife.

Finally he looked at his watch and said, "Oh I have got to go, I have a meeting with a customer! Do you come here often, Katie?" he asked her hopefully.

"Why yes, I do, Tom, every Thursday I come to Salem for shopping and lunch!"

"Could I meet you here next week?" he inquired.

"Yes I would love that," she retorted. When he rose to leave the table she felt his leg brush against hers, she pushed her leg firmly back against his so there would be no question.

His eyes lit up and he gave her a large sweet smile. "Until then," he said.

"Until then," she smiled back. For Katie the week took ages to pass, but finally she was seated in the Entrée again and he was across from her, they quickly ate saying almost nothing to each other apart from hello. After they had finished their food they rose from the table and left the Cafeteria together. Two blocks away was the City Motel; he had booked a room and had the key in his pocket. They entered the room and he took off his shoes, and unbuckled his belt removing his pants and underpants in one movement.

Katie slipped off her shoes and in one fluid movement stripped down her panty hose and panties. Quickly she hitched up her skirt and lying down on the bed lifted and spread her knees. In a second he was on her, fumbling with his fingers at her bottom. She reached around taking his penis in her hand and pulling him to her. She placed the head of his penis at the entrance to her vagina. He pushed, entered her and for two minutes they melded as one until he letting out a moan reached his climax. He lay on her panting, his cheek touching hers, his face buried in the pillow. With her right hand she stroked the back of his neck and played with the hair curling around his ear.

Slowly he raised himself up on his left elbow. "I am sorry, I am afraid I didn't wait for you, but I needed you so much." She putting her hand behind his head and pressing it down slightly lifted hers until their lips met.

She kissed him running her tongue between his lips into his mouth; in a minute she whispered, "You didn't have to wait for me because I didn't wait for you!" So started their long affair. He found that he fell very deeply in love with her and thought her the most beautiful woman he had ever seen. She never fell in love with him, so far she had only loved one man, her Dom, but she did enjoy sex with Tom. She was happy and fulfilled as a woman again, and counted the days between each of their trysts. Finally four years later almost to the week they had started their affair, it ended. One day she sat eating her lunch, he was a little late but it didn't worry her. All of a sudden he sat down opposite her his face white as a sheet.

"I am sorry, darling, but I am afraid my wife has found out about us and she said if I didn't call it off she was taking the children and I would never see them again! I am so sorry, my darling, I do love you and shall miss you very much, but I can't lose my children," with that he was gone.

Katie was stunned, she was humiliated, never had she been rejected before; she was the one to reject. So she sat there looking at her food but not eating, her mind churning over. Milt Bronsen, State Senator from Lake County, co-owner of Bronsen's Tire and Brake in Lake City sat across the aisle from Katie eating his lunch. He smiled to himself as he assessed the situation he had just witnessed. Every Thursday for the last six months he had sat in this exact location watching Katie and Tom. He had figured out quickly when Katie first came to his attention what was going on between them. Once he had even casually followed them right up to their City Motel room. Milt was not a neo-phyte in the adultery game, he had been in and out of many married and unmarried women's beds in his sixty years. His long-suffering wife knew about some of his affairs and guessed at many others.

Milt had slept with them all but he knew quality when he saw it and this little blond that he had been watching was the most perfect specimen of the sex that he had ever laid eyes on. Milt wanted her badly but he bided his time, figuring his time would come and it came just now.

Katie had the uncomfortable feeling that she was being stared at. Without moving her head she lifted her eyes slowly, and true to her in-stincts there was a large older man looking at her intently from a table across the aisle. She quietly assessed him, very large, even sitting down he looked twice the size of Tom. She also guessed that he was the age of her father; strangely that didn't put her off.

Tom was now totally gone from her mind, what should she do?

Once again she raised her eyes. Yes he definitely was staring at her. She felt her heart give a little flutter. She made her decision and raised her head casually, she let her eyes contact his.

That was all Milt needed. He grabbed his coffee cup and standing up to his full height moved over to Katie's table.

"Hello, little lady," he said in his big voice, "I see you are alone and wonder if I might join you?"

Internally Katie gasped. He was such a large man that just for a second she felt fear grip her heart. She controlled her fears, nodded and smiled at the big man and he sat down. Within minutes she knew that she had nothing to fear because though he was big he was a gentleman to the core. One hour later she lay in bed in one of the rooms of the City Motel, her legs wrapped, as far as they would go, around Milt's back as he slowly made love to her. He was not a beautiful man like Tom or Dom had been. Coarse hair matted his chest and stomach, his hands were large and rough-skinned, but he was extremely gentle and kind to her and skilled in what he was doing. Katie found herself enjoying her latest experience very much. When they were finished Katie was bathed in perspiration and breathing very deeply; it had been wonder-ful. Their affair lasted for seventeen years, as long as the worthy citi-zens of Lake County returned Milt to the State Senate. Milt never regretted waiting those six months for Katie. Though she was the same age as his youngest daughter she was a minx, and the most beautiful minx he had ever loved. And love her he did.

You may think that sex dominated Katie's life, you would be wrong. True, romantic sex was very important to her but it was only one aspect of her life. Married sex meant nothing to her, she reluctantly indulged Jimmy with basic missionary copulation to keep him around for her own reasons; no romance or love was involved. Firstly she loved her family and paradoxically Jimmy's family also. Her children meant the world to her, she could not ever contemplate the world without them. But equal to romantic sex, her family and children was her love of business. She had promised Jimmy if he stayed around she would make him a millionaire, and she was well on her way. Before she had met Milt she had already purchased two neighboring farms and the building that housed Thornton's Market. She was learning the financing business, she had a contractor she trusted and she had a farmer who would lease any land she purchased. But this was peanuts compared to the deals Milt would introduce her to.

After they made love she would curl up in Milt's arms; he would tenderly stroke her naked body with those large hams he called hands, and they would talk. When she told him about her dealings in property Milt couldn't believe his ears. Not only was she beautiful and a great lay she was also smart. Good ol' Milt thought he'd died and went to heaven. The next time they were together he gave her his first tip.

"My little girl, you listen to your Uncle Milt and you buy the twenty-five acres out on the old Portland highway by 75th Street and you sit on it."

The next morning Katie took her children to the other Grandma's and one hour later walked into the offices of Salem Metro Reality Company. She told the salesman that greeted her that she was interested in buying a parcel of land on the Old Portland Highway.

He took her out to see the land and when she asked him what amount of money the owner wanted gasped as he told her "thirty thousand dollars."

"Do you think he would except a lower bid?" Katie asked.

"I am afraid not, Mrs. Burns, last week one buyer offered him twenty-five thousand dollars and the owner turned him down flat!"

So Katie bit the bullet and made a full price offer and the land was hers. The next Thursday afternoon as Katie lay cuddled in Milt's strong protective arms she told him she had bought the land. "I am kind of scared, Milt, I have never spent that much money all at once in my life!"

Milt chuckled in her ear as he cupped one of her exquisite breasts in his right hand. "Don't you worry, my darling little girl, Uncle Milt will not let you lose any money on that purchase!"

Katie told him that the bank would only loan twenty thousand and she had to come up with ten thousand cash, "that emptied both my saving and checking accounts."

"You all right money-wise, my sweet little girl?" he said turning her to face him.

"Oh yes, my husband's paycheck will be in the bank this week so I will be fine!"

"If you have any trouble making that note each month you come to Uncle Milt, ok?"

"Ok Milt I will," she kissed the end of his nose and smiled.

"Now make love to me again, all this talk of money is making me horny!"

Five months two weeks later the Oregon State Department of Juvenile Corrections announced that a new Juvenile Offender Rehabilitation Center would be built out on the Old Portland Highway. That night as Katie watched the "News at Ten," she saw Milt being interviewed by the reporter.

"We have with us tonight State Senator Milt Bronsen. Tell me, Senator, do you think the State needs to spend over two million to build this center?"

Katie smiled as she saw Milt's face the camera with a serious look on his face. "Oh yes, this is a quality facility that is sorely needed to return these young offenders to society and prevent them from re-offending."

"I see," said the reporter, "but the system we have in place now seems to do an adequate job and is a lot less expensive!"

"I think you will find, sir, that the young offenders will also learn a needed work skill so that if they don't return to school they will be employable. Also, this new facility will add over two hundred high quality jobs to the Salem area!"

So Katie made back her thirty thousand plus another one hundred thousand.

The next time they were together Milt told her, "Sweet little girl, you put that money in the bank at interest, you never know when you will need it for another purchase!"

That other purchase came one year later.

After they had had sex one afternoon Milt said to Katie, "Darling little girl, there is a two hundred twenty acre farm for sale out east of Oregon City that is going to be re-zoned industrial soon.

"No one has that knowledge but you and I. Knowledge is power, little girl, never forget that! If you have knowledge that someone else doesn't have, you have an advantage over them! You take that money that we made one year ago and you go buy that farm."

359

And so Katie did. Eight months later that farm and the surrounding area were re-zoned industrial just like Milt said. It also happened that the land Katie owned was the largest unencumbered parcel in the area.

Eleven months after that a Korean company, EDO-micro, the largest maker of computer monitors and printers in the world announced that a factory would be built on that land and would, at full capacity, employ over ten thousand people. And to placate the local environmental organizations, also to facilitate a quick approval by the State, EDO-micro announced that all land not used by the factory would be restored to its natural state, and given to the people as a park. On that deal Katie made over one million dollars.

After that large "kill" as Milt put it they backed off on deals for awhile, but Katie invested for herself and bought an apartment house and so it went. Finally in 1997 the voters of Lake County decided to send a younger man to Salem and Milt lost his first ever election. Milt would still come to meet her every month or so.

As he put it, "My sweet little girl, you are in my skin as much as I am, every breath I take is for you and until you dispose of my old carcass I am going to hang around you!"

In November of 1998 just a week after spending two days with Milt in a hotel in Portland Katie was watching "The News at Ten."

The news anchor said, "In other news around the state, The News at Ten has just learned of the unexpected passing of ex-State Senator Milton Bronsen from Lake County by a heart attack this morning.

"Senator Bronsen, known affectionately as just plain Milt, spent twenty years in the State Legislature. During his tenure Oregon saw a much needed diversification in its economic base away from lumber and farming into computer manufacturing, tourism and other non-traditional business. The word from Salem is the Capital City is in shock and will officially mourn Milt's passing for one week.

"The Governor said today, a great Oregonian and American has passed from us today to a better place, he has ordered all state flags flown at half mast. Remembrances, the family requests that all donations be sent to the Juvenile Offenders Rehabilitation Center, which Senator Bronsen singlehandedly procured for the state. At the time of his death Senator Bronsen was seventy-nine."

Katie cried herself to sleep that night. For over one year Katie stopped going to the Entrée Cafeteria, the pain was too great. She found that she had loved Milt deeply, as deeply as Dom just differently.

Now she was fifty-eight; in a few months she was going to be fifty-nine but the fire of the passion of romance burned as deeply in her

360

soul as when she was a girl. So on Thursdays she returned to her table at the Cafeteria. The second week of her return the cafeteria was very crowded; she sat at her table eating her lunch and reading her magazine.

Suddenly a man's voice said, "Pardon me, may I join you, it seems all the tables are full." She looked up into the face of a tall slender, handsome, black man.

"W-why yes," Katie stammered.

He seated himself and smiled at her. "Let me introduce myself," he said holding out his hand. "My name is Doctor Cornelius Debeau."

"Cornelius," Katie answered.

"Er, it is an old family name," he said.

Chinook:

The wind and rain rattled against the carriage as it turned into the side road and pulled up in front of the door to the rented rooms at Christ Church College, Oxford. Lord Erasmus Debeau, fifth Earl of Croft-Crunnie, sat for a minute staring at the doorway to the rooms he himself had occupied almost thirty years before. He let his mind relax, he didn't relish the task he had to perform. Presently the door opened and out trundled the old house servant with an umbrella in his hand.

"Mi-lord, how good it is to see you again, if under these circumstances!"

A smile came to Lord Debeau's lips. "I say Rogers how jolly to see you again and looking as you always did." Then a dark shadow passed over his Lordship's brow. "Is the young scalawag within?"

"He is mi-lord, and with the young lady in question, I'm afraid." Reluctantly Lord Debeau stepped down on the pavement, brushing the umbrella aside and swinging his riding crop he mounted the stairs. Passing through the door he stopped for a second as he allowed the past to rush into his conscience. Shaking off the nostalgic feelings he walked across the reception hall and pushing open the door to his son's rented room paused for a second stunned by the smell. The reek of puke, sweat, opium and stale sex assaulted his nostrils; he plunged into the room letting fly with his riding crop. In a second the scream of a young woman rent the air and she ran from the room naked, in tears, holding her left buttock where a red and rising welt swelled. Rogers was there to greet her with a blanket, in which he wrapped her up and conveyed her quickly to his room.

When he returned all hell was breaking out in the room. "Damn ye

361

sir," a swish of the riding crop and a bawling out of a younger male voice. "Dress yourself, sir, and go to my carriage," once again the swish of the weapon and another cry. Lord Debeau stepped out of the room, his face florid, his body shaking with rage.

He looked at Rogers and shaking his head slumped against the wall of the reception hall. "How long have they been in there, Rogers?"

"About a week, mi-lord, this time, and this time they wouldn't heed me, and I was at wits end at what to do. They haven't eaten for at least two days, and I was sorely worried and prayed that you would come soon!"

"How did he come to this, Rogers, how did he come to this?"

Rogers looked at the floor and didn't say anything for a second, then he said, "Mi-lord, I am afraid the girl is pregnant!"

Lord Debeau swayed like someone had just struck him. "Is it Cornelius' child?"

"It is, mi-Lord! Mi-Lord she is not a bad girl, I know her family well, her father is a respectable tradesman in the town, and Maybelle is the youngest of twelve children, mi-Lord.

"Her father tried to lock her up but she escaped and came here; she loves the young master very deeply I am afraid, mi-Lord."

"And she carries my grandchild." Lord Debeau passed a weary hand across his brow.

"Rogers, I have a young groom who has just lost his wife in child-birth, a rum business that. On the upstart he now has a babe which is wet nursed to a young woman in the village what just lost her babe. But he needs a wife and I cannot abandon my grandchild. How old is this Maybelle?"

"Seventeen or eighteen I believe, mi-Lord."

"Good a ripe age to be a wife." Lord Debeau reached for his purse and handed Rogers four gold crowns. "Could you see to it, Rogers, buy her new clothes and arrange for her journey to Croft-Crunnie. Also could you speak to her parents and tell them the young man that is to be her husband is a fine upstanding man, he will not beat her and will be fair with her all her life?"

"Oh, mi-Lord, this is very generous and I will tell them, and thank you, mi-Lord."

A fortnight later as Lord Debeau sat in his study a timid knock came at the door. "Yes, come in," he said and in walked his disgraced son Cornelius.

Hanging his head he approached the desk. "Father, I have come to ask for my inheritance, I wish to seek my own path. I have humiliated the family, angered you and made my mother cry, it is too much and I must go to try and redeem myself."

Lord Debeau pushed himself back from his desk and studied his youngest son in silence. After awhile he asked, "And where will you go?"

"To America, sir, a boat sails in two weeks' time from Liverpool to Savannah in Georgia. I hope to be on it."

"It is true as my third son there are no prospects here except the army or the church, do you feel inclined for either of those? I could buy you an officer's rank if you so desire?"

"No father, I want to try my hand in the New World."

"Very well, sir, but you must convince your mother if she says no then I say no, yea than I say yea. Is that understood?"

"Yes father, I understand!"

On May the 18th, 1801 the ship holding young Cornelius Debeau sailed into Savannah harbor. In his chest was a letter of introduction to William Charters a distant cousin to the Debeau's. The Charters were planters and one of the leading families of The Sovereign State of Georgia.

As Cornelius cleared the dock he spied an old black man limping toward him. "Suh, pardon me suh, would yo be Massa Deb-bo?"

"Yes I am Debeau," Cornelius answered.

"Gud suh gud, if you-all would follow me suh, I'se to take you to Marra Mount." They loaded his trunk on to the top of a carriage. Cornelius was seated inside, and he was whisked away through Savannah out into the country on his way to Marry Mount, the plantation of his cousin. In about two hours after leaving the dock, the carriage turned off the main road onto a long curving lane bordered on each side by flowering Magnolia trees. When the carriage reached the end of the lane Cornelius observed a large white house. Across the front ran a large porch, the roof supported by six Grecian columns, on this porch stood at least ten black people, most dressed in homespun.

On the steps stood two black people, the man old, bent, white-haired and frail-looking. The other was a robust large woman, probably in her late thirties. Both were dressed in black with white lace at their throats, the large black woman had a bright red scarf tied around her head. The old man stepped forward as the carriage rolled to a stop; he reached up and opened the door. Cornelius stepped out.

The old man bowed. "Gud day suh, I is Benchly th' butler an' dis here is Mary, she be de head house woman." Benchly motioned to the group of black servants standing on the porch and from behind a pillar stepped one of the most powerful looking young men Cornelius had ever seen. He was over six feet tall, his stomach flat and rippling with muscles, his shoulders broad with powerful arms. As he moved out of the shadow of the porch into the strong midday Georgia sun his black skin shown like polished ebony. He clambered up the side of the carriage and with one powerful hand grabbed Cornelius' trunk and brought it down as if it were a feather.

Benchly bowed to Cornelius. "Henry will bring up yo trunk to yo room suh!" Cornelius followed Mary across the porch through the entry doors into the reception area. A vaulted ceiling two stories high soared above his head; in front of him a large staircase swept up in a circular motion to the rooms on the second floor. He was given a room at the front with a view out over the porch onto the fields beyond. After letting down the trunk Henry stopped for a second to stare at the new young Massa, until a clip behind his ear and a disapproving growl from Mary sent him scurrying out of the room and down the stairs.

Mary chuckled. "Henry is a gud boy, Massa, sometime' he just need a little minden' das all. Massa Henry will be yo boy, he will get yo horse and go wif you around, he be jus a bit lazy, Massa, so you just mind him a lil das all," with that she left the room. When she left black servants flooded the room bringing water, a big bowl to wash, towels and a chamber pot. As they finished they bowed to him and left without a word, the last one gently closing the door. Just as he was taking off his coat a timid knock came on the door.

"Come in," he said. Slowly the door opened and timidly a girl stepped into the room. Around her head was a yellow scarf, her dress looked like it was made from a sack. 'Cuse me, Massa, I done come to put yo things away."

Cornelius' head whirled before him stood the loveliest creature he had ever seen. Skin the color of milk in strong tea, eyes large, soft, imploring, brown. An open sweet face small in stature probably barely five foot tall. Sixteen he guessed but with such a voluptuous figure even the hanging flour sack couldn't hide the shape of her young body. He couldn't even speak, just nodding his head and unlocking his trunk. The lovely creature started unloading it, depositing his things in drawers and wardrobes.

He tried to think of something to say to her, finally blurting, "What's your name, girl?"

"Tilly, Massa, dat's whats they calls me, mos'ly Tilly com hyar, Tilly wher is you, mos'ly Massa," she said not looking up from her work.

He stuttered, "T-Tilly, that is a nice name. What is your last name?"

"I don rightly know, Massa, just Tilly, dat's what they calls me."

She was silent for a minute, than she looked up and smiled. "Mebby my las name is Libby cuse I is Miss Libby's slave. I has been given to Miss Libby dats fo sho."

The word slave slapped Cornelius in the face like a wet towel. Of course he knew that there were slaves in America, especially the South.

On his way out from Savannah in the carriage he had seen black people in the fields and herding cows but he didn't think about them being slaves.

Suddenly Tilly stood up. "I'se all done, Massa, I'll sen Henry up to get de trunk Massa." She curtsied and left the room.

In a few minutes there was a knock on the door and Cornelius said, "come in." In walked Mary with Henry in tow quickly. He picked up the trunk and with a quick curious glance at his new Massa fled the room before the furious stare of Mary.

"Massa, de fambly would like yo to res' fo' a bit and will receive you at seven Massa. Supper will be at eight Massa." She turned on her heel and left closing the door gently.

Cornelius undressed and lay on his bed for about an hour, but he didn't sleep. Instead he watched the curtains rustling gently as a slight cool breeze blew through the louvers that were set in the window. Even though it was quite hot outside he marveled how cool it was in the big house. He, of course, didn't think the house was that big it probably wasn't quite half the size of Croft-Crunnie. Which was the manor house the Debeau family had ruled from for over one hundred years. Also this house was made entirely from wood as far as he had seen. All the Manor houses in England were made of stone, mortar and brick, yet it was majestic in rather a colonial way he supposed. Finally he opened his window shutters and looked out over the plantation. As far as he could see the fields stretched over flat ground. A curious green plant had covered most of the fields that he had seen coming from Savannah. That same plant covered these fields, then it struck him that of course this plant must be cotton. He wondered if they also grew tobacco here. He was very interested in the tobacco industry, many men had made their fortunes in the raising and sale of that crop.

At 6:30 he dressed himself in eveningwear and presented himself at the bottom of the stairs at promptly seven o'clock. One of the servants showed him to the parlor, as the servant called it. There sat his cousin William Charters and his very lovely daughter, Miss Libby Anne Stewart Charters, a true southern princess.

William came forward to welcome him and after shaking his hand Cornelius presented him with his letter of introduction. The evening went well! He was thrilled to meet Miss Libby who seemed a lovely delicate flower. Gold hair piled up on her head with long curls in the latest fashion, lovely blue eyes with extra long lashes. Skin as smooth and as clear as the finest white china his mother served tea on. The way she cocked her head to one side or the other when he addressed her, a small smile flitting around the corners of her exquisite mouth enchanted him.

Her soft southern accent, the way she exchanged one vowel for others when she enunciated most words. The deep blue dress she was wearing. It set her coloring off perfectly and it hung off her white shoulders revealing just enough cleavage to tantalize him without being vulgar.

He didn't know it as yet but Miss Libby had set her cap for him the minute her eyes had fallen on him. He was hers, no other girl in two hundred miles would dare to tryst with him once they had discovered her wishes. The news of eligible new blood traveled fast through the gossip networks of the plantations. Miss Libby had sent out invitations for a gala four-day ball. She wanted all the girls to see and admire her new beau, and soon to be betrothed, catch. On Friday evening the carriages started to arrive and continued through the noon hour on Saturday, filled with every young unmarried daughter from all the great plantations for one hundred miles around Savannah. Many a mother had wetted her lips with the tip of her tongue to think her daughter might land the son of a real English Earl. They soon were disappointed when they found Miss Libby's hooks solidly planted into the young man.

Everything went as Miss Libby had intended, and one year later she was wed. For the honeymoon the young couple was dispatched to Europe, along with Tilly and Henry. They were to visit, for two years, Paris, London and of course Croft-Crunnie.

Cornelius's family found Libby beautiful, charming, pampered and a little too outspoken. The servants found her demanding, selfish, spoiled and snobbish. The servants and farmers found Tilly and Henry fascinating. They had never seen black people before, but acccepted them as equals. Cornelius and Libby shortened their stay a few months when word arrived that William Charter, Libby's father, had taken sick and might not last.

When they arrived home at Marry Mount William had "passed into the arms of the Lord two weeks before." A very distraught Libby declared a year of mourning.

Cornelius became the head of the plantation quickly acquiring the skills to run the large operation. After the prescribed year of mourning the gala balls returned, carriages filled with young people once again turned into the lane of Marry Mount. And for two years the young couple was the toast of Georgia. Then Libby's pregnancy curtailed the balls and the travels. Libby's baby was breach and died during its travel down the birth canal. Libby then hemorrhaged and within a few minutes after birth "followed her baby to heaven."

Cornelius lay that night in his bed stunned. The sounds of mourning filled the house; the singing, praying and wailing filled his ears and wracked his body with agony and guilt. Cornelius was an educated man and while he vaguely believed in God he did not believe in punishment for sins on the living. But now his agitated mind could think of no other reason for his wife and child's death but his coupling with Maybelle. When he had been home at Croft-Crunnie he had seen Maybelle with a small boy and infant girl many times, but he had never spoken to her. She was now the wife of the head of his father's stables; a young man his father thought highly of. His father had taken him aside when he and Libby had arrived at Croft-Crunnie and quietly told him that the infant girl was his child, but that he was not to approach them. He obeyed, but he still felt a quiet pride that he had fathered a child. Now that had all changed. He saw the error of his ways; he was humbled, brought low, filled with the feeling that he was a doomed sinner.

He was so deeply miserable he didn't hear the door to his room gently open, or the soft swish of homespun dropping to the floor. His first sensation that he was not alone was when he felt naked nipples brush his shoulder and heard a small voice in his ear.

"Massa, I's here fo you, jus like my Mama was here fo the Ol' Massa when de Lord took Miss Libby's Mammy, Miss Anne. And dats where I'se come from so Mary done tol me, cuse he was my Pappy, doe I neva said. Tilly is here to comfort you, Massa," she said while she slid her young body beneath his. And comfort him she did, for the rest of his life and she bore him seven children. He educated them himself teaching all his children to read, write and do math.

Cornelius died two years before the Civil War broke out. Quietly Tilly and her children ran Marry Mount until they lost it after the war. Cornelius' son Cornelius, along with Tilly and his siblings bought an old house in Savannah and they called it "Debeau College for the Education of Negro Children."

Now over one hundred thirty years later it is simply known as Debeau University, the most prestigious African-American University in the world. Generations of black Americans have earned degrees in medicine, law, physics, education and the liberal arts from Debeau

University including our Doctor Cornelius Debeau now seated across from Katie.

Cornelius had come to University of California at Berkeley to do his graduate work. His older brothers had taken over the family law firm in Atlanta so Cornelius had opted for a career in education. After graduation the young doctor started teaching in an impoverished school in Oakland, hoping to raise poor black kids out of the poverty they were born into. It was a noble thought but he soon found that he, an upper classman from the Deep South could not reach these kids on any level. In fact he was surprised the contempt they held him in, once overhearing them calling him a "fool and an Oreo." He quit teaching and joined the San Francisco public school district as an administrator. Then one evening at a party he met Miss Dorothy Marianne Drew Longwright, the beautiful pampered daughter of Hanson Longwright, a famous jurist and the richest African-American in all of California.

She was instantly taken with this tall handsome suave young man from the south with the famous last name. The morning after meeting him she stood in front of her mirror and tried out his name.

"Dorothy Marianne Drew Debeau, hmmm how about Dorothy Marianne Debeau, yes, I will have all my linen, my china, my silverware etc. marked with the initials DMD. Everyone will know instantly without asking who that stands for! It is settled, I will marry Mr. Debeau!"

After the wedding Cornelius quickly became the head of the San Francisco Public School System. He was in reality a figurehead. He did little actual work but his name coupled with that of his wife brought much prestige and money to San Francisco's public school system.

With the approach of his fiftieth birthday and twenty years of marriage to Dorothy, Cornelius' life began to pall. The constant fundraisers, parties, gala balls, weekends, dinners and even the golf outings hung around his neck like a heavy chain weighing him down. The beautiful young girl he had married when she was twenty-one had turned into a conniving, gossiping, backstabbing, social climbing; beauty-salon obsessed woman at forty-one.

They didn't have children, "no way will I ruin my figure for a bunch of rug rats," was the charming way Dots, as he called her, treated the subject of their procreation. By the way, she hated the name Dots, so he called her that every chance he got. Then one day out of sheer boredom he happen to pick up a magazine called *Education Today,* and there was an article called "Salem, Oregon a school system in Flux." The article mentioned the fact that this school district was having an influx of minority families and the old white establishment had no idea how to handle this new circumstance. They were looking for a black administrator to head their growing, changing, school system. Needless to say when the school board discovered that Doctor Cornelius Debeau, the head of the San Francisco Schools was interested in their position the vote was unanimous to offer him the job. Secretly Cornelius flew to Salem and quickly accepted their offer.

When he broke the news to Dorothy that they were moving to Salem, Oregon the worst two weeks in his life began. He thought he knew his Dots, but the depth to which her profanity and loathing sunk shocked him. Finally one day she came to his office to see him and she was a changed person, calm, measured and extremely elegant.

"Preston has asked me to marry him," she smiled at him sweetly. "I want a divorce."

"Preston, Preston . . . you mean Doctor Preston Walters."

"Yes," she smugly replied.

"But . . . but he is my best friend and he . . . he's white!"

"Cornelius, don't be a stupid redneck," she hurtled back at him, "don't you know that Preston and I have been lovers for eighteen of the twenty years we have been married?"

"Preston has been fucking you for eighteen years all the while playing golf with me, smoking my cigars and drinking my booze?"

Dorothy stood up, her voice spitting, "Cornelius, you are such a motherfucking neanderthal," so saying she turned on her heel and slamming the door to his office left his person forever.

He very much had enjoyed his ten years with the Salem School District; he actually was a vital cog in its mechanism not just a social, political head. The people up in Oregon valued his input. Not only did he run the Salem school system but he was also asked his opinions and directions for the Eugene and Portland districts. As these frontier backwaters grew and became more cosmopolitan many minorities began moving into the state looking for economic opportunity and a safe outdoor-oriented environment to raise their families. Traditionally Oregon had been populated by middle and working class white people. And having not a clue as how to accommodate their rising minority population drew on Doctor Debeau's expertise gladly.

He had never remarried; firstly sex was not a problem, he had had many bored plump housewives to choose from. Mostly they offered their services to him, freeing himself the task of having to choose.

And he found he actually preferred this plump mild-mannered housewife to the skinny, opinionated, hard princess he had been married to for so many years. They expected nothing, they had no cause to espouse and when the sex was over they went home to husbands, chil-

369

dren and hearthside. He had retired at sixty to a quiet life of books and a garden, still at leisure though to consult if needed. His access to the housewives was somewhat muted by his retirement and though he still had a Monday thing he felt he needed more. Now that "more" was seated directly across the lunch table from him and a very exquisite "more" it was too. Much to his delight this "more" was very amenable and he had filled his Thursday afternoons much more profitably than he could have ever dreamed.

Her life had changed it was true. Sam, though he was still a fork lift driver, was now considered a skilled laborer under union guidelines and his pay reflected that by lifting them from the working class to the middle class. Their children were gone, the last one graduating from Oregon State University the first one to do so in both their families. All their children were doing well. Especially their eldest son who had his own house building business and their middle daughter who had her own beauty salon in Sublimity just a few miles from Slayton. Once a month she would go to her daughter's shop and she would give her a cut, perm and facial for free. They still lived in the same house but their son had painted and modernized it and it was now the nicest house on their block. She had put on weight and her figure was now more rounded instead of painfully straight. She had bought new bras and clothes that fit her properly from J.C. Penney's. Then wonder of wonders she had turned one evening from her stove and had caught Sam looking at her bottom with lust in his eyes.

Her life had come full circle and it was good. Her sister had invited her to lunch in Salem one Thursday at this elegant restaurant called The Entrée. Her sister called it a cafeteria, you could choose whatever you wanted and the price was very low for the quality of food; she felt elated. As she ate her chicken pot pie she glanced up at a lady who was seating herself just across the aisle from her. She froze her lips over her fork filled with food, suspended halfway to her mouth. It had been twenty years since she had last seen her but she would have known her had it been a hundred; the Blond Witch! In a few minutes a tall black man seated himself at her table; she saw the Blond Witch's face form into a warm welcoming smile. After lunch her sister had to rush off but she stayed on the ruse that she wanted more coffee. She followed the couple through the residential streets of downtown Salem until they entered a small house.

She walked down the street past the house to see if she could see into a window; she couldn't but she had seen enough. Smirking she turned on her heel and returned to her car, when she reached home she wrote an anonymous letter to Jimmy.

"Dear Mr. Burns, On Thursday your wife was seen having lunch at the Entrée Cafeteria in Salem with a black man then sneaking with him to his house afterwards, A friend." She sent it to the cannery office.

Katie was enjoying her latest fling, in fact it had turned into more for her than just a fling. She was falling into love, not as deeply as she loved Dom but it was beginning to reach that level. Their sex was outstanding and this charming, debonair man was sweeping her off her feet. She had just one problem; she had a feeling that he was also occupied somewhere else. She could not accept this situation and she was trying to think of a way to channel all Cornelius' attention toward her one morning as she and Jimmy were eating breakfast.

That is why she was unprepared when Jimmy blurted out, "I am thinking about retiring next year!"

"Retiring, retiring?" She tried to bring her mind around to this new revelation.

"Impossible," she stammered in her brain, though the eyes that looked into Jimmy's face betrayed none of the conflict that raged behind her disinterested look.

"He will be around all the time, I can't have this, I have to spend more time with Cornelius, I, I . . ."

Calmly she said, "But ah, you are too young to retire, surely you would miss the road and visiting the many places you go to. You must have many friends out there that you would miss, ah what about that friend in Denver?"

Jimmy watched her eyes, they were constantly moving. Was it panic he saw in them?

So then the letter was right, she was screwing some black guy in Salem! Should he be mad, be humiliated, be jealous?

He thought to himself, *You know I just don't care!* He dropped the subject and he didn't tell her he had already made out the paperwork and the union had approved it. His retirement date was fixed on March 31st, 2000.

Jimmy Burns:

Jimmy had been dreading coming up to sixty years of age. He was healthy now; his last physical at the VA hospital in Portland had found no problems with his heart or any other organ. But that warning the Air Force doctor had given him so many years before, that problems might show up after his fiftieth birthday, haunted him. He had changed his life style over the last ten years, cutting out most red meat,

371

eating more salads and vegetables, laying off the white bread and pota-toes. Even though Katie hadn't noticed, he was down fifteen or more pounds from his former weight and he felt very good.

Still he didn't want to push his luck and had decided to retire at sixty, so he could enjoy whatever length of life God had allotted him. The union was very generous with the retirement he would receive. He would be able to live a very good life with the money he had saved, his union pension and benefits, such as free medical for life, and later so-cial security.

Some years ago the Slayton Canning Company had sold off their trucking division to a company called Western Valley Trucking Com-pany. While their main customer was still the cannery they also hauled for the Port of Portland and other customers. Five years before WVTC had taken a contract with the Phoenix Area Building Council. This was a group of home and commercial builders who had found that by get-ting a contract with lumber and plywood manufacturers in Oregon, and eliminating middlemen, they would save millions in building costs over the years.

Jimmy, as the leading seniority driver in the union, had his pick of routes and he had been delivering wood products from the plants in Or-egon to a central warehouse in Phoenix, Arizona. This was his only run and it kept him busy.

He had started taking his days off and vacations in the Phoenix area. He discovered golf, having never played the game before in his life he found that the challenge and frustrations of the game intrigued him. He started to look around for a house for himself and finally bought a home in Sun City, an older two-bedroom with a carport that the former occupants had fixed up very nicely. His next purchase was a street ready golf cart. He soon noticed that a lady lived next to him. He had never seen a husband so he figured she might be a widow. He had never spoken to her just a wave and a smile when he saw her on the way out. He thought her very pretty with an open bright face. Until one day when he was playing The Willows Creek course with an acquain-tance. The man who took their money asked them if they would mind playing with a single; they of course said they wouldn't.

Well it turned out the single was his neighbor lady.

As she drove her cart up to the 1st tee Jimmy walked up to her. "Well I guess as we're neighbors. We probably should meet. Hi my name is Jimmy Burns." She gave him a big smile.

"Hi, how nice to finally meet you, my name is Alice Marx."

Ten miles south of Lincoln, Nebraska just off Highway 33 runs a four-mile dirt lane locally known as the Hershberger Family Road. Written on the sides of the three mailboxes out at the highway is Route 1, 223, 224, and 225.

On this road are three large family farms. The first farm you come to is the Rothe farm, the next is the Hershberger farm and the last one at the end of the road is the Stutzman farm. The country is very flat and in the summer the crop grown is corn, corn as far as the eye can see.

In the month of June 1939 three young brides were brought to these farms and ten months later all three had babies.

Mrs. Rothe had a little girl, even as a baby everyone said she had a bright pretty open face, the Rothes called her Alice.

Mrs. Hershberger gave birth to a boy, he was big with wide shoulders and blond hair. The Hershbergers called him Royal.

Mrs. Stutzman gave birth to a little girl also. She was dark haired and had large dark brown eyes with long lashes; even as a baby everyone said she had bedroom eyes. The Stutzmans called her Mina.

The children grew tall and healthy. Both the girls loved Royal, though they never let anyone know. Both dreamed of marrying him after high school and moving into his parents' farmhouse as his bride.

One lovely spring Saturday in early April 1958 just two months before their graduation from high school, Mina called to her mother.

"Mom, I am going to take a walk down the lane."

"Ok, sweetheart, be home at four to start dinner." Mina knew that Royal's parents always went into town on Saturdays; she also knew Royal stayed home. She walked up to the Hershberger farmhouse and knocked on the back door.

Royal poked his head out. "Oh hi Mina, come on in," he said. Mina came in! She thought she knew what she wanted Royal to do to her. As she was growing up she always listened closely to the young brides and mothers when they talked about what their husbands did to them. Anyway she wanted Royal and she was willing to catch him anyway she could. A couple of hours later she had caught him. They were good kids; it was just two willing young people alone in a big house with all those bedrooms. Mina with those large limpid bedroom eyes gave Royal no chance, and nature took its course. Mina came back the next Saturday and the Saturday after that also.

She liked what Royal did to her, it made her love him all the more. On the fourth Saturday her period should have come, but it didn't.

Mina stood naked in front of the mirror on her chest-of-drawers, she touched her belly with the palm of her hand. "Was Royal's child in there?" She would give it one more week before she told Royal just to

373

make sure. On the fifth Saturday after she arrived at the Hershberger farmhouse she broke the news to Royal that she had missed her time of the month and she might be pregnant.

Royal took it like a man, kneeled down in front of her swore he would be a good father to their baby and husband to her. That was the easy part, telling her mother would be the hard part.

Her mother took it surprisingly well, mostly she cried, but she realized that she was not going to lose her darling daughter; she would be only one mile away at the next farm house. She told Mina that she would tell her father and told her not to worry. After the initial shock both of Mina's parents were not extremely unhappy about her pregnancy. They knew Royal and his parents almost all their lives and knew that Mina would have a good life as his wife. So a meeting with the Hershbergers was arranged and the wedding date was set for the first Sunday after graduation; these things couldn't be delayed.

When Alice heard the news it was like someone had hit her in her chest very hard with a large fist. She cried herself to sleep every night for a month. She moped around the house for a year, her parents worried silly over her odd behavior.

The hurt was close; Mina's wedding, Mina moving into the Hershberger house. Mina and Royal walking hand in hand down the lane on summer evenings. Mina's tummy swelling in the fall, the women fussing over her at the weekly quilting bee. Mina swollen up like a balloon at Church on Christmas Day. Finally in January Mina brought into the world a beautiful baby boy.

Alice had to get away and one day when she and her mother were in Lincoln she spied in the window of a shop this sign:

"Young Women learn to type, become a Secretary, learn Book Keeping, Apply now at the Lincoln School for Office Professionals!!"

"Mother, I want to be a bookkeeper or a secretary." Her father was dead against it.

"My daughter needs to be at home helping you, dearest," he ranted to his wife, but in the end he relented. He knew he had other daughters growing up that would help around the house. So off Alice went to live with her Aunt in Lincoln for a year while she studied for her future. At the end of the year the school posted job openings on a bulletin board in the school office annex. The Lincoln School for Office Professionals was highly regarded in the business community. The young women it graduated were extremely talented and ready to run an office.

Alice searched the bulletin board; she didn't want to stay in Lincoln, the hurt was still too fresh. Then she spied it, The Marx Manufacturing Company Omaha, Neb. needs a bookkeeping clerk and typist to start immediately. She went to the office, the school secretary called The Marx Manufacturing Company and they made an appointment to interview her the next day.

Alice talked her Aunt into taking her in to Omaha without telling her parents; she was hired! All hell broke out on the Rothe farm when it was discovered that Alice was going to live in Omaha. She had just as well told her parents she was moving to Sodom and Gomorrah. Finally after a day of tears, tempers and ultimatums her parents took her to see the Marx Manufacturing Company. When they found that their precious darling daughter would be properly housed and fed in a dormitory for young unmarried women situated on the factory grounds, they capitulated. For the first month Alice worked in the typing pool. Then, the company, recognizing her extensive training in bookkeeping, transferred her to Accounting. There, on her second day, a middle-aged man walked into the room with a pile of papers for the Chief Accountant. He was tall and slightly stooped, with thinning light brown hair, not an Adonis for a young girl to admire. Alice thought he had a very kind face. He stopped and stared at her for a full minute, Alice blushed and dropped her eyes to her work.

After he had left she whispered to the girl at the desk next to her, "Heather, who was that?"

"Oh," whispered Heather back, "that is the young Mister Marx, his father the old Mister Marx owns the factory!"

The Marx factory was one hundred years old. It was originally a bicycle factory started in 1859 by Absalon Marx. During the Civil War it grew to the approximately the size it was now by furnishing canteens, bayonets, wagon wheels and harness to the Union army.

Over the years they had made things for many different companies. Now their business was making hydraulic controlled ploughs and wheels for John Deere and Minneapolis Moline. They employed two hundred people; sons followed fathers for generations to work at The Marx Factory.

Henry Macmillan Marx, the young Mister Marx, would be the fifth Marx to head the family's business. Henry though forty-four, still lived at home. He was a shy retiring person who had never had a girlfriend either in high school or University. His parents fussed and worried that he would never marry and produce a future Marx to carry on the factory. But Henry had never met a girl that attracted him, until today. When he walked into the accounting office he saw a new face, a bright pretty face that jumped out at him from all the other faces there. He asked the Chief Accountant who she was; he wasn't really sure of her name but would call Mr. Marx as soon as he found out. One year later at the age of twenty-one Alice Rothe became Mrs. Henry Marx.

Henry's mother Evelyn instantly fell in love with the naive young girl from the farm. As soon as the wedding and honeymoon were consummated Evelyn began to school Alice in the arts, travel, golf, which all ladies played, and the running of a large house with servants. Eleven months later Alice became the mother of Ronald Rothe Marx, the heir to the Marx's future. Ronald was to be her only child.

In the early 1990's the factory had trouble securing new contracts, had trouble competing with China, Korea and Mexico. All current contracts had run their course by 1994. A dispirited Henry closed the factory forever. He gave much of his personal fortune to his loyal employees to assure an easier transition to their new jobs.

He sold the land to developers. In the *Omaha Daily Plainsman* an article appeared: "Site of old Marx factory to employ four hundred people, twice more than the old factory did. Developers today announced a big box shopping center to open; anchored on the west and east ends by Wal-Mart and Home Depot." What the article failed to mention was the ninety percent of the new jobs were going to be starting at minimum wage. Two thirds less per hour than the Marx Factory paid.

Ronald who was now married had not joined his father in the family business; he wanted to fly jets. So when he graduated from University he joined the U.S. Air Force and was stationed at Luke Air Base just outside Phoenix, Arizona. Ronald and his wife Pat had two children and Henry and Alice missed their grandchildren so they sold everything in Omaha and bought a house in Sun City.

They enjoyed living in the warmth of Arizona, "don't miss the snow, ice and cold wind," they used to say to anyone who would listen. They joined the Sun City Golf Club and they joined the Sun City Ramblers. This was a group of people who loved to travel in the summer when the Valley of the Sun became a blast furnace. Their life was good.

Then one morning in 2001 Alice had awoken to find her wonderful Henry dead in the bed beside her. Henry had died of a massive coronary in his sleep. He was eighty-five. Alice was sixty-one—she was an active person and kept her membership with the Golf and Ramblers Clubs. But she was also an old-fashioned girl, she felt funny and a fifth wheel being without her husband. Even though there were other widows who belonged to these clubs she personally didn't fit in as a single. The final blow came one day when she was talking and laughing with one of the husbands.

His wife scurried over and pushed herself between Alice and her husband, and pointedly taking him by the arm led him away.

Alice was humiliated and crushed. "Do I look like a woman on the prowl?" she wondered to herself. Anyway she dropped her membership to both those clubs. Then another blow, Ron was sent to Germany by the Air Force, his family went with him, and Alice was completely alone.

One day while she was meandering aimlessly down the Arrowhead Towne Center Mall she saw Mina coming toward her. Mina hadn't seen her yet so Alice stepped behind some potted plants so she could see and not be seen. How long had it been since she had seen Mina, thirty-five years? Mina had put on weight and her hair was silver but her eyes were the same. Those same dark limpid bedroom eyes that had trapped her Royal. The hurt hit her heart even after all these years, a knot pained in her stomach. She decided to step out and hail Mina but she saw Royal come out of a shop and walk to his wife. He was changed, still tall and strong looking and more handsome than ever, but thicker through his middle. The hair that showed around his baseball cap was white and when he took off his cap to mop his brow with the sleeve of his shirt he was bald down the center of his head. Alice watched as he reached out to gently touch his wife's arm with a smile filled with love. She knew then he was never hers, he was Mina's all along; then she knew that all those dreams she had had of him were for naught.

Those many times when Henry was making love to her, and she gritted her teeth and wished he were Royal were wrong; a disservice to her Henry. She shook her head and started to leave.

But her loneliness was greater than the temporary revulsion she felt for herself and she turned toward them, steeled herself and said in mock surprise, "Mina, Royal is that you?"

They had coffee and ice creams in the food court. Royal and Mina had been coming to Arizona for some time. Two years before they had purchased a winter home out in Sun City Grand and just loved it. Royal was retired now, except he ran the tractor in the summer for their son, and he ploughed in the fall before they returned to Arizona for the winter. They touched her deeply by being so kind when she told them Henry had passed suddenly the year before. They invited her to a barbecue and she went, but they had a circle of friends and she discovered they had so little in common. They had never been to Europe, art didn't interest them and once again she felt a fifth wheel. Then one day the house next to hers sold and soon a good looking man who seemed to be alone, moved in. He wasn't there much but when he saw her he smiled. She noticed he had a nice smile and sad eyes, she was drawn to him instantly.

377

When Jimmy walked down off the mountain that day with the body of Laddie in his arms he was a changed man as far as the children were concerned. He became their father, totally in every way just as a normal biological father would. The children loved him without question.

Even though Jimmy believed they looked not a bit like him he was stunned one day when his mother said, "Johnny is so like you, in his actions, the way he stands and moves, and in his face. His face especially; his chin, the way he holds it so reminds me of you at that age."

Jimmy started to return their love at that instant. The children knew that he was different; other children's dads were home all the time, their dad was gone most of the time, but when he was home he spent almost all of his time with them. Jimmy responded to their love and because Katie wanted nothing to do with him it was easy to be with them. He taught them how to fish, took them hiking in the woods, taught them to ride bikes, all the things dads teach their kids.

They were wise to the relationship between Katie and Jimmy.

One day when they were driving over to Grandpa and Grandma's farm Johnny asked him point blank, "Daddy, are you and Momma going to get a divorce some day?"

Jimmy almost drove off the road he was so surprised. "Well ahmm no, no I don't believe Catholics can get a divorce, Johnny," he stammered. They never asked him again!

Jimmy assumed that Katie had never told them the truth of their conception and he also figured that Dom's family never knew that they had grandchildren in Oregon. When they were ready to go to University he paid their tuition to the school of their choice. Both went to Portland State, a Catholic University in Portland.

Katie had made sure the children were brought up strictly Catholic; they never missed one holy day of obligation, Sunday Mass, First Communion, or Conformation. When they graduated April got a job being a lay teacher in a Catholic Grade School and John went for his Graduate degree in Sports Medicine at University of Oregon.

Now the children were settled, he could turn his mind to his own needs. Slowly he started to remove his possessions from the house in Oregon and transfer them to his new home in Sun City.

He might have told Katie he was leaving her but they never communicated; she obviously was occupied elsewhere probably with her new black lover in Salem. The only semblance of a marriage that they had was that she made meals for him when he was home. Finally a couple of days after his retirement was official he cleaned the room that he had slept in these many years when he was between loads.

He picked up the few clothes and personal items that were left in the house. He went down to the main floor where Katie was cleaning the front rooms.

Leaning on the door jam he looked at her back. "I'm going," he said. "Ok," she returned.

"The room is clean, my laundry is washed ready to go," he said.

"Ok," she returned without looking at him.

He was going to say see you in a couple of weeks like he had for so many years, but instead he turned on his heel. Walked down the hallway, through the kitchen, out the kitchen door, across the back porch, down the steps to his pickup.

Climbing into the cab he started the engine, put the transmission in gear and drove away forever.

It was a month before Katie found he had gone.

May 2004:

Katie and her two children were in the kitchen; the women were making lunch and Johnny was reading the *Sunday Albany Democrat Herald*. Katie always liked to have her children over for lunch on the big holidays.

But this year she had missed them because they had both been gone over Easter. However she had them now.

She causally remarked, "I wonder what your father is doing now?"

Absently April said, "Oh he is doing fine, Mom." April froze. What had she just said? She glanced quickly at Johnny who gave her a "shut up stupid look."

Katie said quite calmly, "Really, and how would you know how he feels, do you know where he is?"

April was stuck. "Yes, mother, Johnny and I spent a week with him over Easter."

"You spent a week with him. Where is he, I want to know?"

"I am sorry, mother," April said, "we won't tell you."

Katie turned on her daughter her face florid. "You won't tell me where my husband is, I demand you tell me."

April's eye's caught fire. "We won't tell you, mother, daddy is happy now and we don't want you to bother him again."

"I'll bother him if I want, you little smart mouth," Katie replied.

April, deadly calm, said, "For the first time in his life daddy is happy. If Johnny and I ever hear that you have contacted him you never will see us again!"

Katie alarmed now more than infuriated looked at Johnny and he nodded in agreement.

Summer 2004:

The Sun City Ramblers were doing a six-week trip to Europe this summer. They boarded the British Airways flight that went non-stop Phoenix Sky-Harbor to London, Gatwick. Eleven hours after boarding they were through customs and standing in a stupor waiting for the train to arrive from Victoria Station. Minutes later they were all aboard flashing through the English countryside toward London. After arriving at Victoria Station they boarded a bus to their hotel where, as the itinerary said, they had the rest of the day free to discover London on their own.

Jimmy and Alice had lunch at the hotel and went for a walk until 6 P.M. when they went to their room and fell into bed, not waking until the next morning at 4 A.M. London time. Starving they called the Concierge desk; a sleepy attendant mumbled that the kitchen would not open until 6 A.M. They showered in a rather small shower that had a gas heater on the water pipe above their head; it was either freezing or scalding hot. But they did fine. They looked out of their window and watched the small street below them slowly become light. At 6:20 A.M. there was a knock on the door and a porter was there with a pot of extremely strong but delicious tea, and a tray of welcome toast, butter and jam and soft-boiled eggs.

The first day was a welcoming tour of London, the second was a bus trip to Stratford–on-Avon. The third day was London on your own. A bunch of the "Girls" including Alice were planning a trip to Harrods and the Knightsbridge area of London for a day of shopping. The guys were going to see a soccer game between one of the London clubs called Arsenal and a Spanish team called Real-Madrid, a friendly they called it. Most of the guys thought that meant it was a pre-season game.

Jimmy opted out; instead he took the central line and went to Lancaster Gate tube station. Then he walked down Bayswater Road to see if he could find the Douglas house. He couldn't find it, everything seemed to have changed. There was a large hotel there set back from the road; maybe that was it.

He crossed Bayswater Road and went into Hyde Park via the Victoria Gate just as he had done those many years ago. Everything now but the street lamps had been changed. He walked toward the Serpentine and strolled along the lake until he came to a restaurant on its shore there; he stopped for tea. He sat watching the boats and water fowl paddle around the lake. Next he walked up to the street lamp that Kathleen had been standing under that pivotal night in his life; it was still in the exact location. Then he left the park and taking a left moved down Park Lane toward The Bayswater Road again. He crossed Bayswater Road via the pedestrian underpass and into the Edgware Road. There the scene changed from London to a street in Beirut, Amman or another Moslem city in Arabia.

*   *   *

A short fat woman came charging down the sidewalk scattering people. She was covered totally in black from the pavement to the top of her head, a black veil across her face with only her eyes showing. In the cafes that lined the road, dark, thin-faced men sat sipping coffee. He made no eye contact but moved on quickly, no one seemed to notice him but he felt uncomfortable. Further on he noticed an older building with an ornate front guarded by muscular young men who stood at the entrance. He wondered if it was a Mosque. He found Crawford Street and turning right into it found it occupied with Arab shops; the proprietors standing at the front door, their dark eyes following his progress.

Did they suspect he was an American, was that hate in their eyes? He thought he found Kathleen's building but he couldn't be sure.

He was very disappointed. He had hoped to feel Kathleen's presence, to feel her guide him. She was gone. He felt nothing. The area was no longer theirs, it belonged to a different people now. As he stood the voices of children speaking Arabic came through an open window startling him. He turned quickly and not wanting to return to the Edgware road walked north up to Marylebone Station, where he caught the tube back to his hotel.

Day 4 was a trip to Oxford. Alice wanted to see the world famous Bodleian Library and the Gothic spires. After lunch Jimmy took Alice on a flat-bottomed boat trip down the river; the locals called it a "punt."

Day 5 was their last day in London; after that they would all leave for Germany where Alice would leave the trip for a month catching up with them in Paris, while she visited her son, daughter-in-law and grandchildren.

The last outing was a trip to the Wallace Art Collection. Alice told Jimmy that it was the largest family collection in the world. Jimmy followed Alice around slightly bored while Alice explained various paintings to him. Finally in one of the back rooms Alice stopped to talk to another lady that was on the trip, so Jimmy moved ahead without her. He came upon a painting that caught his eye. It was set in a woodland; yellow streams of the sun came through the trees illuminating the scene. A young beautiful woman sat on a swing soaring up, her left leg pointing to the treetops causing the voluminous skirt of her pink dress to billow open. Below her was a garden statue, which stood on a pedestal and at the base of the pedestal lounged a young man looking up at the young woman, a lustful leer forming on his lips. At the back was an older gentleman who obviously was the person who was pushing the young woman on the swing.

Jimmy leaned forward and read the plaque on the wall next to the painting. It said "The Swing. Jean-Honore Fragonard, 1767."

Alice came up to him. "Do you like this painting, darling?" she said.

"Yes I guess," Jimmy said. "What does it mean?"

"Ah yes Monsieur Fragonard, you old rake you. Well darling, the scene was painted in the garden of a Chateau. Swings strung from trees were quite popular in eighteenth and nineteenth century country houses. You see them a lot in pictures from this period. The older gentleman you see in the background is probably the husband of the very pretty young lady on the swing. She is probably his second, or third wife, the others having died in childbirth. I guess she is his trophy wife. Well, darling, panties, as we know them, hadn't been invented yet; ladies in olden days didn't wear anything under their dresses.

"That young man hidden from the husband by those bushes there is probably her lover, or she is enticing him to be her lover by showing him her ahh assets." Alice smiled at Jimmy. "Ok darling?"

"Yeah," he mumbled as Alice moved on. Jimmy stared at the painting; the young woman on the swing looked a lot like Katie in her youth. Then it hit him, this was their life together. He was the old man swinging the beautiful young Katie and the young man lounging out of sight enjoying the view represented Katie's various lovers.

He ripped his eyes from the painting, hurried along to where Alice was standing, and took her hand in his.